THE COUSINS' TALE

THE COUSINS' TALE

Antonia Swinson

Hodder & Stoughton

First published in Great Britain in 1999
by Hodder and Stoughton
A division of Hodder Headline PLC

10 9 8 7 6 5 4 3 2 1

British Library Cataloguing in Publication Data
A CIP catalogue record for this title
is available from the British Library.

ISBN 0 340 71692 4

Typeset by Hewer Text Ltd, Edinburgh
Printed and bound in Great Britain by
Mackays of Chatham plc

Hodder and Stoughton
A division of Hodder Headline PLC
338 Euston Road
London NW1 3BH

For my husband Alan Reid.

Prologue

To Sarah Hunter, her cousin Bunny was always the big noisy one who led all their games until she wanted to take over as leader. Then they would roll around the garden lawn, their mothers shrieking and slapping the back of their legs with their copies of *Woman's Realm*, loudly complaining about the grass stains on their gingham skirts. 'You girls must think we're made of Omo!'

Sarah never had her nose out of a book, her mother would remark critically, as if her daughter were the local library's resident anteater. She had large, green eyes, and light brown hair which was long enough to be plaited very satisfactorily by the bored older girls who sat behind her in the music class. Bunny, on the other hand, was groovy! Far out! All the girls at school said so. *She* could do French skipping with a sherbet lemon in her mouth, while singing, 'My boyfriend's name is Fatty. He comes from Switzerlattie.' All at the same time without choking! Paul McCartney was her personal property, while Sarah quietly yearned for the darker attentions of George Harrison, and the moody lead singer in the Tremeloes. Sarah spent hours pasting pictures of them in her scrapbooks, while Bunny, eighteen months older, would spend hours in the downstairs toilet every Saturday morning reading *Bunty*. She taught herself to whistle at the age of nine. The theme tune of *Champion the Wonder Horse* was a favourite, though her Gran kept telling her it was unladylike.

Bunny had hopped out of her real name, Beverly Anne, by the age of four. By eight, she had collected fourteen Sindy dolls and three Tressy dolls. You could press a button in Tressy's tummy and her hair would come out of the top, ready to be butchered with the kitchen scissors. Whereas Sarah's endless crystal cats and dogs always seemed boring. 'Sarah they don't *do* anything!' Bunny would say.

'I know, but the light shines off them and I like to look at them.' Sarah would reply, half dreading her cousin's scorn.

They lived in Surrey. Once, when Sarah was seven, she heard a song, 'Surrey with the Fringe on Top'. She asked her mother how could a place have a fringe? She looked up Surrey in the family atlas and thought that the fringe must mean the Thames, bending round. 'How could a river be a fringe?' her mother had snapped at her. 'It's an American sort of carriage, Sarah, don't be so silly. Now, get the doilies out of the sideboard for your Auntie Marjorie.'

But Surrey really did have a fringe, because Sarah's mother, Doreen, and her sister, Marjorie, preferred everything in their houses to have either a doily underneath or a fringed cover on top. All the loo-roll holders were velvet with thick gold brocade, and the toilet seat covers were pale brown, matching the fringed bathroom mats. All the bedside tables had ruched tablecloths and there was even a telephone cover in the hall, in bright pink velvet with zigzag braid all round.

When they were ten, Bunny and Sarah decided to become detectives just like Enid Blyton's Famous Five and solve crimes and catch criminals. They bought a local paper and discovered that something called a rapist was on the loose. It was a man, because there was a funny drawing of what the police thought he might look like. Sarah guessed that he had killed someone with a rapier, so they looked it up in the dictionary and found out it was a sort of sword. How thrilling. The two cousins would be the Two Musketeers of Carshalton!

While their mothers were in the stinky hairdresser's achieving platinum and purple chestnut surprises under the dryer, Bunny and Sarah spent hours scouring the local parks armed with the long stick bits of their old hobby-horses, hunting for the rapierist. Until Bunny's father discovered the press cuttings pasted into Sarah's scrapbook on Bunny's bed one afternoon and suggested that hunting a rapist might not be such a good idea. Rapiers were sharp after all; you could cut your fingers. The man was probably really sorry he had been naughty and had taken the sword back to the museum.

So Bunny and Sarah promised they wouldn't try to catch him any more and went on to dream of catching jewel thieves instead. Sarah said she would ask for just one large diamond as a reward, whereas Bunny said she would want at least a quarter of the jewels as a reward or she'd keep the lot and not tell the police *at all.* How *naughty,* Sarah thought admiringly.

They would all go on holiday together each summer. Butlin's by the sea when they were very small and then, when their fathers went up a grade or two at the council, boarding houses at Clacton-on-Sea or even Eastbourne. The cousins would race each other along the sand. Sometimes Bunny would win, at other times Sarah squeaked ahead. The mothers would arrange themselves for public viewing in wide-skirted floral dresses and big straw hats, while the men grew red like lobsters, their fleshy torsos embarrassing their two daughters. In the evening the grown-ups would sit in the family room of the local hotel drinking Snowballs and eating pork scratchings, while Bunny and Sarah tried to win money at the fruit machines.

One day, when they were eleven, Bunny and Sarah were playing about in the hotel swimming pool. Some boys came up and started to splash them, daring them to swim in the deep end. Bunny could not resist a dare, but she was not a good swimmer and was soon out of her depth. She then seemed to change into another person. Sarah saw her face, like a fish her mouth opening and closing while her eyes bulged. There were no grown-ups around, and the boys had run off. Bunny, flailing her arms, hit out at Sarah, sending a huge wave across to the edge of the pool. She began to go under. Sarah opened her mouth to call for help, but only a squeaky little noise emerged. Nat King Cole was crooning very loudly on the record player down over at the bar. She remembered hearing the tune 'King of the Road' in snatches as, panic stricken, she repeatedly dived down to keep Bunny afloat. Instinctively she pushed her head into Bunny's stomach to force her into the shallow end of the pool. She'd seen pictures of life savers at Brownies, but Bunny, all arms like a huge desperate octopus, kept forcing her down to the blue tiles on the floor of the pool. It seemed an age, but Sarah finally forced her to the edge at the shallow end. Their heads ached. Exhausted, they clung together weeping. Neither talked of it afterwards. Bunny became less bossy and Sarah more assertive, and they saw each other every day. Later that night, sitting with the grown-ups, they learned from the embarrassingly over-friendly barman that to make the perfect Snowball you had to wash the glass with a dash of sherry *before* you added the advocaat. When they grew up Sarah and Bunny never drank Snowballs.

The next term there came the great divide, for Sarah, who had won a place at the Grammar School, found herself with a new Bible, a ridiculous flat school hat with ribbons trailing behind and a lot to live up to. Bunny however started at the local secondary modern where all the girls acquired white gloves and lifelong inferiority complexes. It was like an official branding on the forehead. Doreen and Marjorie argued bitterly about the Council's education policy, while Bunny and Sarah found it easier not to discuss school at all.

Bunny's period arrived one Saturday afternoon while they were both sitting in the lounge watching the Monkees. She was terribly shocked. Marjorie gave her an aspirin, a lecture and a belt to put round her middle to attach to something called an S.T. Bunny hated the pains every month, but quickly found out that The Curse, as her mother called it, was the perfect excuse for getting off school swimming. Bunny's Curses were discussed regularly by sympathetic teachers in the staff room and, judiciously managed, would usually last most of the term.

Sarah waited in dread for hers to arrive. Both started wearing Starter bras at the same time (to Bunny's chagrin) and they soon developed hairy armpits, new curves and inhibitions. Woolworth's cosmetics counter became a mecca. They bought bright blue eyeshadow and spent the rest of their pocket money on broken biscuits. Bunny grew like a weed. She had big bones, small breasts, topped six feet and one day sadly realised she would never look like a Sindy doll, much to Marjorie's despair.

Sarah, however, was in adolescence satisfactorily feminine, although she was to her mother's taste far too bookish. 'You'll never get a man if you're too clever. All this studying is giving you wrinkles and short sight. Men don't make passes at girls who wear glasses, you know.' Doreen would say this practically every day, while filing long, red, Shirley Bassey nails. Yet, even in her National Health specs, the boys loved pretty Sarah who, wary and unsure of how to handle their attention, studied all the time in the hope they might go away; whereas Bunny, who loved boys, was left alone, however short her skirts and perfect her vision and, as time went on, however generous her reputation.

It was round about March 1970 that it suddenly dawned on poor Marjorie and Doreen that, having missed out on the sixties, they were now supposed to embark on the seventies with two teenage daughters, while gravity reigned and their husbands' eyes wandered. That would have been fine if Marjorie and Doreen had had small egos, they would have just hunkered down and suffered, but theirs was a mousy little mother who never said boo, and had cleaned office blocks in south London for years in order for her daughters to go up in the world to the typing school. In consequence they were high-ego, big-haired 'girls' with an image problem.

Now unwilling to leave the centre-stage, they competed to look younger and be more exciting than the other, joining rival Weight Watchers, and trying to enlist their daughters in small venomous battles. For cousins, if nothing else, should be the unpaid secret agents of their parents' sibling rivalry. Bunny and Sarah remained good friends in spite of the daily barrage of the other's imperfections.

By the time Sarah went to university, her cousin had become like a comfortable coat. The sort you slip on when you are tired of dressing up. Almost all the sixth form were leaving home to try university towns in the north or to spend a year as an au pair. Bunny stayed at home with her parents. She was no longer groovy, for now prettier girls called the shots. She and Sarah would ring each other up from time to time, but each other's lives were now kept in touch by verbal bulletins issued by their mothers, carefully cut and tailored to advantage.

St Andrews is Scotland's oldest university, recognised by papal bull in 1413 and ever afterwards fiercely proud of its traditions and its place in the national pecking order. The town itself sits on the rocky Fife coast, surrounded by the world's most hallowed golfing turf and specialising in students, a mediaeval street plan and charming, white-haired ladies, who enjoyed hot buttered toast and learning about the Picts, once rulers over the kingdom of Fife.

Sarah steered a careful path between the Sloane Rangers and the Scots. Student patterns and dress codes were as confusing as everything else in the seventies, a time when dukes' daughters were up for grabs, Margaret Trudeau was still thought cool and a blonde grocer's daughter led Her Majesty's Government's Opposition.

Sarah bought contact lenses, which made her eyes even larger and greener, and grew her hair down to her waist, letting it flow behind her in the icy wind. She had never known such biting cold in all her life and now knew just what the Scots meant by the Soft South. The towered gothic buildings, the food, the accent, the way people wore their clothes, all hit her as forcefully as the gales which blew in off the sea. Sweetie shops, book shops, coffee shops, tea shops and second-hand shops seemed jammed together within three streets. Everyone knew everyone else, and soon Sarah knew exactly where everyone went at what time of day and even which table they would sit at. Her own survival from the cold came to depend on milky coffees and Forfar Bridies, thick meat with puff pastry in the union.

As a 'bejantine' or fresher, Sarah was assigned an Academic

Parent. Her new Mother, a fourth-year philosophy student who was keen to prove herself useful, provided tips such as which progressive doctor might be prevailed upon to prescribe the Pill and how to avoid those usual everlasting Don Juan academics, students and staff who live in every university and feed on the firm young flesh arriving each year. 'But remember, if you don't find a man by November you'll die of hypothermia!' Shocked of Carshalton! Sarah assumed she was joking for, schooled by Doreen about clean knickers and how to be a nice girl, Sarah was not, alas, too experienced in that department. By December Sarah believed her and now yearned not only for thick soup but also being swept up off her feet by a fourth year with an electric blanket and efficient central heating.

By year two, Sarah had hardened up and moved out of hall. She shared a house and three bars of a fire with two other girls from the south in North Castle Street, the end of which looked on to St Andrews Bay and the ruined castle walls. At night, she slept under nine blankets in thick jumpers. Through the rattling windows she would hear high heels clattering home from parties over the cobbles and the wind howling for hours before turning into the crueller roar of fighter aircraft from RAF Leuchars, strutting their stuff out over the sea and round the coast into the Firth of Forth.

Sarah chose to study art history with a casualness that no student would be guilty of nowadays. She loved to visit cool airy galleries, as an escape from home, for her mother's taste tended towards the market stall school of painting – dewy-eyed small children clutching puppies and Chinese girls weeping glycerine tears. Though as the years passed, through judicious reading of *Tatler* in the hairdresser's, Doreen had progressed to shiny reproductions of Van Gogh sunflowers and impossibly vivid Monet prints. She now thought her daughter's studies 'terribly U!'

And so Sarah found out all about European Art from 1800 to the Present Day, Post-war American painting & Art Theory and Art in Florence & Rome 1470–1700. In the process she grew up and developed into a charming, knowledgeable girl who stored her crystal cats and dogs in a shoebox under her bed, and the alphas for her essays in the very small box in her brain marked self-esteem.

How Doreen revelled in her academic success, and in St Andrews' ancient and upper-class reputation. Prince Charles hadn't found a bride yet and you never knew . . . The Royals really let their hair down in Scotland, she would say to Marjorie who, less enthusiastic, would agree to accompany her sister to what they termed the Frozen North.

Doreen and Marjorie both had hair which varied in colour depending on mood and budget, although their style remained frozen in the fifties. Each had a Hollywood pin-up in her mind. Doreen's heroine was Lauren Bacall, and she liked to comb her hair over one eye seductively, whereas Marjorie preferred the riper charms of Doris Day.

Every term they arrived wearing improbable tartans and exuberant lipstick, determined to see Scotland as that sunny, soft-focus place you see on the lid of your shortbread tin and not the hard-edged, chippy, generous country with a bloody history and a definite limit to how much it could stomach two not-meaning-to-be-patronising-but-succeeding Englishwomen. They raved about Sarah's red academic gown, which she wore on the students' weekly walk on Sundays along the pier that formed the breakwater to the small harbour, and from where they would take pictures noisily with small cameras. They spoke mistily of Dr Finlay, Moira Anderson, Kenneth McKellar and the White Heather Club, until Sarah was hopping with impatience for them to leave.

Bunny would come to stay too. On her first visit during Sarah's second term, she said she had never been so cold in all her life, why wasn't there a railway station in the town, and please could they turn the heating up? She was a vision of fussy nylon frills and seemed to Sarah and her friends to come from another planet. Still, as she was taller than the wiry east coast Scots, she proved useful for buying drinks in the Criterion, everyone's favourite pub in South Street.

Bunny had managed to obtain one A level in domestic

science and was now working as a hotel receptionist in Chobham. She said she thought students were living in cloud cuckoo land, but repeated herself a little too often to be convincing. It was only when they were on their own, sitting on Sarah's bed, gossiping and sharing pizza and cheap wine, that they could re-establish the friendship of their childhood.

So what makes a nice girl from Carshalton tick? Other students would describe Sarah as OK, one of the gang. Good fun. She lacked the urban, gritty street cred of the students from the North of England. Yet, though she came from the South-east, her accent and dress sense did not conform to the tribe of the public-school English pirates who swarmed into St Andrews, often eaten up with Oxbridge disappointment, and carving up the societies. Nor did she fit in with the Scots who, a year younger, seemed barely out of school, so Sarah kept her head down and worked.

She was turning into one of those girls who slog through university, doing undistinguished things perfectly happily when, at the end of the third year, to her astonishment, she fell in love. Which was a tad challenging as the man in question had been dead since 1938, but such is the power of love it turned her, to nobody's surprise but her own, into an academic.

Archie Milne Robertson was one of those Scotsmen who throughout history have taken on the world with their talent and charisma, but were probably hell to live with. He was a ceramicist, an artist-potter, who created dishes with attitude and decorated them with lustres which shone like mother-of-pearl or the most gorgeous sheen of precious metal, and cantered through Art Nouveau, the Arts and Crafts Movement and Modernism, all those useful labels on which art history students hang their studies. He didn't give a monkey's and just worked on, turning out one masterpiece after another.

Poor Sarah was hooked – always fatal for a nascent academic. Perhaps she had suffered from a deficit of peacocks in her life; her own father toiled at the Greater London Council in a Montague Burton suit, and her spotty, solitary brother was either train-spotting or poring over his stamp collection. Then, as she sat in the library watching the seagulls take off and land on the window-ledge, along comes Archie, the epitome of male glamour, leaping off the page in his loud embroidered waistcoats and precocious talent.

Looking back, she probably fell in love with the wrong man, but there you go. There was the tutor on the new ceramics course, a junior lecturer called Donald Gosford, who thought Sarah really special. He was a bouncy Glaswegian who had a bad habit, in the opinion of some of the older staff, of being rather too enthusiastic for true objectivity. Sarah thought he sounded just like Billy Connolly.

'Imagine,' he would say, standing in the middle of the lecture theatre, his arms held out, 'Here was Archie, born and brought up along the road in Kirkcaldy, one of eight, used to marching along to the local pottery with his piece for his lunch in his hand, and then he goes south and, before you know it, he is being trained in Vienna and discovered, hailed by the beau monde as the new Charlie Rennie Mackintosh of the clay. In 1911 it was all happening in Vienna, like London in the swinging sixties. Imagine young Archie let loose on all those creamy cakes and sexy Viennese women!'

The boys in the class were mostly asleep. 'Is his work worth anything now?' Sarah remembered a languid old Etonian called Jeremy, with an amuse-me-now air, asking, only to fall asleep again when told that though a giant of his art, Robertson's work fetched around £3,000. 'Is that all?'

'Not bad for a wee pot, when I've just paid £14 000 for a two-bedroom flat down the road,' Donald Gosford replied tartly.

Bunny would write to Sarah quite often in her lunch hour – big loopy writing on the hotel writing paper. Then, in Sarah's third year, Bunny gave up the hotel (and the sous-chef) as a bad job, and got a place in a London cookery school for a one-year course. Her letters, this time scrawled on the school's grease-proof paper, were full of stories about girls related to dukes, the terrors of classes in filleting fish and chicken and how she nearly cut off her arm with a Sabatier knife. She even sent a Swiss roll through the post. It arrived squashed and promising only to fall to pieces over Sarah's bedroom carpet.

In her fourth and final year, Sarah volunteered to organise a small exhibition of Robertson's work in the new arts centre next to the department. One autumn evening, lots of her class showed up for free wine. Her professor told her she might get a first if she worked and Donald said he'd back her for a PhD which, in the seventies, was a terribly nice way to spend your life.

Then came the last gallop to finals. Sarah, wrapped up in her own private bubble of books and notes, missed out on some of the most important political events of the decade. Scotland's Devolution referendum, such a disappointment for many, passed her unnoticed. Sheikh Yamani's sinister glamour travelled into the nation's consciousness, but not hers. There were petrol shortages, and the price went up to £1 a gallon, with each car in St Andrews rationed to £2 a visit. People found their legs and their taste for Arab jokes. Yer Mani or Yer Life screamed the tabloids. But Sarah had stopped reading newspapers. Her only contact with the outside world was weekly doses of *Tales of the Unexpected* and *Dallas*.

In May the 1979 General Election came and, with it, Margaret Thatcher. 'Vote Conservative! The vans patrolled the streets of St Andrews for weeks, most of it navy blue anyway, exhorting the faithful. Sarah heard them while she studied. Driving over the cobblestones outside her house, the electioneers' voices would jump, until they sounded like, 'Vo-Scon-Ive'. Which made about as much sense to Sarah.

The week before her finals started, Sarah noticed Margaret Thatcher on the cover of a glossy magazine on a newstand, and suddenly thought how odd it was having a woman prime minister, and then went home daydreaming of Robert de Niro in *The Deer Hunter*. The European elections in June were the same day as her architecture paper, so Europe had to get on without her.

'You are to stop writing now.' The voice of the invigilator echoed around the vast examination hall and hit Sarah as she sat dotting 'i's' and reading through her answers on European Art. When she put her pen down, she promised herself that she would *never, ever* do another exam as long as she lived and then let out the great breath of knowledge she had stored up for weeks.

Party time! The sea was blue; the shiny June light hit the cobbles outside; she could taste food and drink wine and look forward. This is the first day of the rest of your life, people said to each other. Funny how original it sounded then. Those post-finals summer days before the year disbanded were spent in bed or in the pub. Everyone was demob happy, desperate to enjoy themselves, have fun, make love, get drunk, go to bed late, sleep in.

Sarah was caught up in the euphoria. It was just as if the war had ended. For Sarah, anything was possible now. She felt fey, light-headed and so didn't read the signals. When you are in that sort of mood, anything can happen, and usually does. Bunny, who graduated from her own course, came up for the fun. When she stepped off the train at Leuchars, Sarah hardly recognised her. She was still six feet one and built like an oast house, but the nylon and polyester had disappeared. Bunny now wore pearl studs in her ears and a navy Alice band round her hair, which was cut into a bob and streaked blonde. She wore a burgundy cashmere jumper and a stripy cotton skirt, which whirled around in the wind of the station platform, and black pattern pumps. 'If they could see me now, cooking fancy food and drinking fancy wine,' Bunny bellowed and her Carshalton vowels ricocheted off the platform roof. Two young men in Husky waistcoats who had been looking at her approvingly looked confused and hurried off. Bunny had transformed herself into a Sloane. On the outside anyway. They linked arms and walked down to the bus singing the old theme tune to the Monkees. Here we come, look out world!

Years later in that early morning sleep just before waking, Sarah would go over that day. She would lie there thinking of Bunny, or the new Bunny's exuberance and seeming knowledge of the world as well as her own quiet certainties, so soon to disappear along with youth and her cousin's friendship. Precious losses. Then came that particular evening. The party, the large flat near the City Road, the bodies everywhere, sitting down, drinking, smoking and dancing on two inches of space. Ian Dury, furiously distorted and loud on the stereo was asking to be hit with someone's rhythm stick and the atmosphere was as high as you can get on cheap wine, cheap cider, cheap anything. 'Hit Me With Your Rhythm Stick!' People's faces were young, unlined and glistened in the heat, as they talked of getting married, having babies, buying flats, working for Morgan Grenfell, the Foreign Office, Marks & Spencer, bumming around, travelling to Afghanistan. Anything! She remembered Bunny shamelessly handing out business cards to the bright boys who were heading for the City, offering to cook them lunch.

The evening was hot and light until after eleven o'clock. Sarah remembered that the windows were open and how the laughter and noise must have spilled out on to the street, tinged with that desperate auld lang syne sentimentality as, post-finals, students clutched people whom they had passed by quite happily in the corridors for years as if they were precious, which they were, as fixed points in a fast dissolving universe. The junior lecturers, who were invited too, all got drunk along with the rest; all said that this year were the brightest lot ever. They always did.

Sarah remembered losing a contact lens in the dancing, and the other one had greased up. On her way into the bathroom she laughed about it to Bunny, who was now pissed on cheap white wine and propped up as insecurely as an overloaded Christmas tree. 'What have you got Hunter, six-six vision' Bunny's voice was swallowed up by the music.

Outside in the party, no one heard Sarah's desperate struggles in the bathroom. Coats and jumpers and even the odd baby's Moses basket had been flung into the bath in a pile, and it was into this friendly mess that she was forced down by a young man. No one heard her screams either, and she did scream at first, until his hand, which smelt of beer and smoke and urine, went over her mouth while his other hand ripped off her pants and forced her down. Shock and then the stupid, even greater, fear of spoiling other people's enjoyment of the party outside, kicked in. She lay there, every nerve repulsed and repulsing while her body was used by a stranger. The sickening jabs into her body seemed to last for hours. She remembered thinking how bloody unfair. How unfair. She had only slept with one boyfriend and was now being raped, whereas Bunny had slept with dozens. It didn't make any sense, except that he had obviously had too much to drink, and didn't like women.

For years afterwards she saw his face in her worst nightmares, just visible by the cheap strip lighting over the basin. Square jaw, a young, unapologetic, desperate, greedy face which sometimes seemed in dreams familiar, and therefore more frightening. Who was he? When would he stop! As she lay there, she knew quite consciously that a terrible damage was being done, even though he was not violent, except for thrusting into her, unwanted. He even kissed her roughly when it was all over, leaving her to grope blindly to find out where her pants had been thrown. She remembered feeling his sperm trickling down the inside of her legs like a last sick joke.

After he had gone, she had washed herself with a red towel and, looking at herself in the mirror, saw that she had not sprouted two horns, but looked merely startled and a bit pale, with lipstick smeared down one cheek. She remembered thinking what a joke feminism was, when men were so much stronger and could do anything they wanted. Then felt shame at her naïveté. And then a sudden hatred. Where had Bunny been when *she* had needed saving? Looking at Sarah's face that night, however, not even a painter could have told you that the chemistry of her life had changed for good.

For years, Sarah would imagine her mother's voice. Doreen, of course, would have said that it was such a very *silly* thing to let happen. 'Sarah you must have given him the come-on in some way, looked too sexy, wiggled your bum. Men don't just leap on top of you for nothing. I should know!'

Yet Doreen never knew; nor did anyone else. Certainly not

Bunny. Sarah never spoke of it. No one saw her leave the party, and the next day she caught an early train while her housemates and cousin were still asleep. She left a cheque to cover the last bit of the rent, but no note. She did not come back in July to collect her degree (first class with honours). Then the department received a letter thanking them for all they had done for her, but informing them that she had decided not to apply for a postgraduate place.

Donald Gosford, who had thought Sarah brilliant and beautiful in a Rossetti-ish sort of way, was gutted and rang her home in Surrey. A sharp, female London voice told him that Sarah was away at the local secretarial college. Her exhibition was dismantled, her dissertation put on file and the world went on. Whatever happened to Sarah Hunter?' people now working in banks, advertising agencies and galleries would say to each other at reunions in London or Edinburgh throughout the eighties, and even into the nineties. 'What happened to her? Do you know? We never heard.'

Carshalton, August 1979

A cork was pulled from a bottle. 'Do mind that Lambrusco, Ron,' said Marjorie to her husband. 'It's a bit early isn't it? What will Edward think? And mind, it will go right through my nice cloth, right through to the wood. You go through to the lounge Edward, there's a dear.'

Edward looked up. He had been flipping through her father's *Reader's Digest*. His refined, pleasant face was expressionless. Would he still want to marry her after this afternoon, Bunny wondered?

A sudden memory jabbed into her mind of a small blonde girl chopping parsley at the cookery school. Serena someone, engaged to a Scottish lord. To whom she had once said the dreaded word 'lounge'. The moment she had said it she had noted the small tight smile, the pearly teeth matching the fine pearl necklace. Afterwards, she had been treated with the pitying encouragement you might reserve for a young ambitious window cleaner. Rather than a girl who wanted to make her living as a cook. The L word joined all the invisible language which Bunny never used in her struggle to reinvent herself. Lounge, leeounge. Bunny shivered.

The doorbell tinkled. 'Come in, come in! Just as well we all live near what with expensive petrol no one can get to buy anyway!' Bunny could hear her mother's voice shrill in the hall, meeting those of her aunt and uncle and cousin. Marjorie and Doreen, Bunny knew, under the pretence of hanging up coats, would be mouthing silent messages about Edward in the hall, like a pair of Les Dawsons. '*Lovely. Public school. Hair thinning. Barrister's son!*'

'So! Here we are! Edward, this is my sister Doreen, her husband Ken, and Bunny's cousin Sarah and her brother Jonathan. Sarah's just finished university. This is Edward Halifax, Bunny's new fiancé.'

Auntie Doreen laughed, a silvery, tinkly laugh, her cerise pink lipstick very slightly askew, and said that Marjorie didn't have to say that he was new, it was not as if he were the latest in a long line! And then introduced Sarah once again, as her academic daughter. How stick-thin Sarah was! Bunny thought. Just a nose, under a tide of long hair in a black tunic. It had been weeks since she had woken up in that freezing god-forsaken St Andrews house to find Sarah had buggered off, without a word. She was still furious with her, and ignored Sarah's weak, watery smile. Stuck up cow. Well, she'd show all of them.

Over tea and Lambrusco, Marjorie and Doreen held court, as they always did, talking about their days when they were known as the Battersea Belles, both working in Arding & Hobbs, the big department store at Clapham Junction which was so grand! 'You have no idea of the money there was south of the river then you know, Edward. We were both secretaries there before we were married. Not shop girls. And London was so glamorous in the fifties and early sixties. Everyone dressed up! Not like now. That Lady Docker knew how to live!' Talk of titles led them to name drop shamelessly. The Queen Mother had visited St Andrews, but then in Bunny's class at cookery school, they had *four* girls with titles including, according to Edward, a *Law Lord's* daughter! Sarah pleated the table-cloth over and over, while Bunny quietly died a hundred times in her size 16 white blouse with its mother-of-pearl buttons.

It was Edward's watch she had noticed first that day at the bank, right in the middle of serving the Coronation Chicken. Obviously Cartier. How reassuringly it had flashed in the light of the boardroom chandelier. It had seemed worth all that slimming and reinvention when he had taken her to the races the following week. Epsom. She had won two races and he had told her that she would bring him luck. By now with an experienced outsider's eye, she could tell he had gone to the right school and knew exactly which were the right words to use. He didn't have a lounge in his smart, sparsely furnished mansion flat in Fulham. He was not clubbable like his peers and so, as he loved her cooking and her earthy views on sex and making money, Bunny had arranged their courtship unhindered by critical friends who might well have derided her.

On the dining-room table, beside her mother's marble cake and cucumber sandwiches, were the remains of a cocktail party Bunny had just done in Hammersmith the previous night. All of it was being gobbled off her mother's gold doilies so fast that no one would ever suspect the hours of work it represented. Tiny tartlets with salmon pâté squirted in; miniature Yorkshire puddings each with a strip of rare roast beef and a miniature dollop of horseradish sauce; tiny crêpes with strips of marinated duck, and prawns in garlic butter wrapped in mangetout.

'How much do you charge, Bunny, for stuff like this?' Her Uncle Ken looked speculatively at the prawns. 'What's this green stuff, then?'

'Mangetout, Uncle. I charge £6.50 a head, and everyone gets nine pieces.'

'It seems a hell of a lot. £6.50! I can see you're looking after Bunny's margins, Edward.' Her uncle picked the mangetout out of his teeth and put it on the side of his plate.

'Kenneth!' Doreen was outraged.

* * *

'Now where did you two lovebirds meet?' asked Auntie Doreen.

'Bunny was cooking lunch for our directors, I was there to make up the numbers and could not resist Bunny or her cooking.' Edward smiled at Bunny, who had never felt so grateful to anyone in her life. Though, God knew what he would see in her once her family had finished.

'Bunny, dear, let's have a gander at your ring.'

Bunny stretched out her hand to show her aunt the small ruby with a circle of diamonds. It was nice to be engaged and have a proper fiancé at only twenty-three, but she was conscious that the ring was dainty and her hand, although well shaped, was large. Being careful with money, Edward would not have splashed out much. She had wanted an emerald, but he had told her it could chip when she did the washing up. He seemed to know about these things.

'And what is the name of your company, Edward dear?' Doreen asked after checking the ring for flaws, and happily finding one. 'I hope you didn't do that Jeremy Thorpe case, did you? His *poor* wife.'

'I'm a commercial lawyer, Mrs Hunter, I work in the City.'

'Well I never!'

The two husbands, Uncle Ken and her own father, had finished their tea and were now standing looking out of the french windows at the crazy paving and the rain, their hands stuck in their pockets, jingling change. The material of their trousers stretched across their middle-aged bottoms. Edward didn't have a middle-aged bottom. He had a small bottom, a nice, bony, distinguished face. He played Wagner and Real Tennis, and knew just the right bit on the small of her back to stroke when they made love. He was also the first man she had ever known who was proving capable of keeping his eyes off her cousin. Although Sarah actually did look awful. She kept trying to sit close to her mother, who kept telling her to move her chair away and give her a bit of elbow room for goodness' sake. Perhaps all that studying stupid art books had sent her mental?

Then Marjorie, now on her third glass of Lambrusco,

commented how awful life was with *The Times* on strike. Bunny winced, knowing that her mother was trying to make Edward think she was an intellectual when everyone in the family knew it was Jean Rook before 11 a.m. or bust. But she was now in her stride.

'How's Sarah doing at the secretarial? A little different from your Scottish ivory tower, I should think,' she said, not very subtly paying Doreen back for the crack about Bunny's new fiancé. 'But then Bunny's always had a head for business. Her little cookery business is doing so well, she'll be needing a secretary herself soon! Watch out you men, we've got a woman Prime Minister in charge now! Ron, stop picking, here's another serviette, the duck's dribbling down your chin. Now, who's for more tea?'

'Try the Yorkshire pudding, darling,' Bunny said hastily to Edward. He smiled at her, helped himself, then passed it to Sarah sitting next to him. She shook her head and continued to pleat the tablecloth. Sarah would have to buck up if she was going to survive a job in an office, Bunny thought. What price that arty-farty university now? Anyway, from now on their worlds were going to be very different. Bunny's ring sparkled as she lifted up another plate and the jealousy and anger of her beautiful, clever cousin, hewn over time, at last began to shift.

Edinburgh [illegible]

[illegible]

What [illegible] is [illegible] [illegible]

[illegible] [illegible]

[illegible] [illegible] [illegible]

which we [illegible] [illegible]

[illegible]

[illegible] applied [illegible]

[illegible] and [illegible] to [illegible]

[illegible]

[illegible] in the [illegible]

[illegible]

[illegible] a glimpse of a [illegible]

Thus [illegible]

[illegible] even [illegible]

[illegible] in her [illegible]

[illegible]

CHAPTER ONE

Edinburgh, Sixteen Years Later

Why does life go in circles? How carefully we edit the past, remembering the best bits and repackaging the rest, as if all one's past choices made perfect sense in order to create a perfect c.v. for the present tense only to find that, like Winnie the Pooh on the hunt for heffalumps, we have been going round in circles after all. 'The future is just the past entered by another gate,' is a nice line from Pinero's Second Mrs Tanqueray, but not one which we want to hear most of the time.

Bang! The gavel came down and Sarah jumped. 'Sold to the gentleman on my right. Told you it wasn't going to be expensive,' the auctioneer bragged. A man standing near her in a black leather jacket, who had just paid £12,500 for a repossessed flat in Shawlands, south Glasgow, merely shrugged. Brief laughter rippled round the room. Sarah gripped her catalogue and waited for her turn. Fifteen lots to go.

'Lot 12, a four-bedroomed detached house in Ayr, ladies and gentlemen, right in the town centre. A lot of house for your money. I shall start the bidding at £30,000. £32,000, can I see? £32,000. £33,000, can I see? A hand on Sarah's right shot up. She had a glimpse of a turban, a heavy fountain pen hovered. Thank you sir, £34,000 can I see? Thank you madam, £35,000 can I see? Thank you, a new place, gentleman on my left.'

Sarah shifted in her seat, wishing she were taller, or was standing at the back. The auctioneer's hand was now flicking between the two rival bidders like an emperor, all-powerful,

powerful, adjudicating between two miscreant peasants. The house they had fought over had been someone's pride and joy and yet here it was, being knocked down for £39,000. By order of the mortgagees. Another repossession. Someone's loss. Someone else's bargain.

Outside the hot hotel conference room, Sarah could see Edinburgh's Pentland Hills, and birds circling. The Festival traffic glinted as it jostled down the road into the city. If only all those people knew that the best drama was here, comedy and tragedy, fast-paced, brittle, and right on cue at the crash of the gavel. Dreams lost and sold. Bang! The auctioneer's gavel crashed. Sold! £4,000 for a one-bedroom flat in Carnoustie.

The auction was played out in forty-one lots. Forty-one opportunities for the hungry-faced vultures in suits and ties and leather jackets, who all hovered at the back of the room, ignoring the auctioneer's regular entreaties to come forward and take a seat. For they preferred to watch narrow-eyed, talking urgently in whispers into mobile phones, avoiding each other's eyes. This was the real property market, unhinged from estate agents' hype. Bricks and mortar. Someone's daughter would be shedding tears for not reading the fine print at the bottom of the mortgage offer.

Up and down the aisles the girls from the auction company went, handing out forms for successful bidders to sign. 'Ten per cent deposit, please, and don't leave the room.' All smiles, as if they were working for a quiz show host. If the price is right, then rent out or sell on and double your money.

The TV lights made the room even hotter than it would have been with all these people. Property auctions seemed still to be news in Scotland and the cameras were there to record the show for the early evening news. Perhaps this was the reason for the men melting into the distance in the crowd at the back.

Surreptitiously, Sarah found her powder compact and quickly powdered her nose. A shiny nose, she had been brought up to believe, was almost as bad as not sitting with your legs closed tightly together. In the small mirror she could see that her fringe needed cutting and her eyes looked large and startled.

People still said she had a figure and legs to die for and wonderful hair, but it was odd that from thirty to thirty-five you could pass easily for twenty-five on a good day. But then between thirty-five and thirty-eight something happened, a sum of indefinable changes suddenly added up to make you look your age. Not that thirty-eight was old, exactly, but it was still a shock when inside your head you were still twenty-five and counting.

Bang! A feisty blonde in her early twenties smiled and put her arm down. Her partner grinned at her across the room. A six-bedroom house, in its own grounds, complete with granny flat, in Dunoon. Theirs for £50,000. Where was Dunoon?

Sarah marvelled at the girl's self-possession and thought of herself at her age, toiling up and down from Carshalton each day to the City, sandwich in her handbag, going nowhere fast and smiling sweetly. This girl was no prettier than she had been then but, from the toss of her head, it was clear who was in control. She was bidding, even when her man was here. Whereas the younger Sarah had so desperately needed love, and someone to come and fight off the baddies. She would have married the sweep if there had happened to have been one in Carshalton – any man who would treat her kindly. That she had found a handsome, well-connected banker to play Sir Galahad had always seemed a bit of a miracle.

Now here she was, Mrs Christopher Todd, patiently waiting in Jaeger to bid, never having bought even a chest of drawers at auction before. She preferred truffle-hunting ceramic goodies in junk shops and church fairs and, until today, had always left the paddle waving to Christopher – auction Action Man – who collected marine memorabilia as if it might run out. She thought of their house in London, filled with pictures of sailing ships and models of merchant ships, and *Titanic* flotsam, any suggestion of salt spray and the heaving seas carefully held in behind glass except for the row of female figureheads carved and painted for eighteenth-century male fantasies, but who now burst out all over the wall of the first-floor landing in 38DD magnificence.

'Can I see £18,000 for this charming, stone-built property on Loch Leven?' The auctioneer pronounced it to rhyme with heaven. 'You say, Leeven,' a Scots voice said behind her. 'English git,' the voice muttered. The auctioneer was a foreigner, but then so was she, back in Scotland after all these years.

She suddenly remembered how the sea in St Andrews had crashed on to the rocks and against the Castle ruins and how she had learned to say 'dreich' about the damp cold weather, how someone had a 'pawky sense of humour and how she was 'in a dwammy' if she absent-mindedly turned up for the wrong lecture. The gothic buildings had seemed at first as if they had been dropped in straight from a fairytale, which it had been for a while until she had found herself tossed back into the jowls of the 7.15 to Waterloo. Then one day she had met Christopher at the Edinburgh & Aberdeen Bank and he had brought a new sophistication into her life, a new way of looking at the world, dished up between courses at London's better restaurants which were known only to the City's upper middle classes.

Why could he not have been here today? 'Go up to 100K and that's it. If you get it, don't whoop, Sarah, not very *comme il faut*, darling.' 'Yes, Christopher,' she had said, fearing to let him down. What if she scratched her nose, and the auctioneer thought she was bidding? She had never been able to read signals, to her cost; this room with its secret signals and silent meanings was the very worst place to be.

A substantial detached property, built 1902, with Integral Annexe set in extensive grounds and enjoying views over the Firth of Forth and the Bass Rock.

GROUND FLOOR	*Entrance, Vestibule, Lounge, Sitting Room, Kitchen, Dining Room, Garden, Toilet, Rear Entrance.*
UPPER FLOOR	*Bedroom 1, Bedroom 2, Bedroom 3, Bedroom 4, en-suite bathroom and dressing room.*
SECOND FLOOR	*Bathroom, Bedroom 5, Bedroom 6.*

INTEGRAL ANNEXE	*Artist's studio.*
OUTSIDE	*Extensive gardens and grounds plus two outhouses.*

Freehold.

Then, on another sheet of paper were the guide prices. *Guide Price* £85/90,000.

'A lot of house for your money,' the auctioneer broke into her thoughts. This seemed to be one of his favourite phrases, and he obviously thought it would appeal to the Scots' liking for a bargain.

Sarah looked at the property details. Did the auctioneer even know who it had once belonged to? A Colossus of European design, Donald Gosford had said. Exotic shapes with their flaunting lustres, now forgotten. Their blues and greens, the colours of heaven. Sarah pulled her navy skirt over her knees and twisted her ankles, which were beginning to fall asleep.

The room was now even hotter. Plump-faced professionals in expensive suits, well-fleshed and satisfied, worked the room. They would be getting their fee whatever happened. By a pillar, one man stood out from the crowd. Detached and yet looking at every face. A big, powerfully built man with a high forehead and thick hair that fell over his face, wearing a thin jumper, not the usual suit and tie or leather jacket. Next to him stood a hard-eyed woman with a thin line of lipstick for a mouth, and rings which glistened greedily in the hotel lights.

In front of her, Sarah saw a mother and her two grown-up daughters suddenly arrive and sit down, breathless, just in time for their lot. They seemed real people looking for a bargain, rather than the bone-pickers who encircled them. One of the daughters, dark and capable, put up her arm to bid. This time it was a three-bedroom terraced villa in Catrine, Strathclyde, Sarah read. '£15,000 . . . £16,000 . . . £17,000 . . . make no mistake, it's in the market to be sold,' the auctioneer said with professional jocularity. Sarah saw the girl's hand go up and up and up and then falter. A quick conference with her mother, a sideways glance at her sister. A pause. Agony. In those lightning seconds Sarah felt their impotence. '£20,000, a new place, gentleman on my right.' The crisis passed and so did the house. Bang!

The three women sat for a moment, then got up. Sarah saw that the other daughter was pregnant. Their faces set in disappointment, somehow they squeezed their way out of the room and out of the market.

'Lot twenty-seven, Carnforth House, a substantial detached property built 1902 in the East Lothian town of Loanside, standing in approximately half an acre of gardens, formerly the property of Scottish ceramicist, Archie Milne Robertson.'

Sarah jumped. 'Are broken pots included?' a Glaswegian voice cut in with immaculate timing. Laughter. Sarah's heart was now banging as loudly as the gavel as she grabbed her catalogue and tried to remember Christopher's instructions. 'Don't go in straightaway, Wait till the bidding begins to slow then be aggressive, as if you are going to go up as far as it takes.'

The auctioneer leaned forward speculatively. 'I shall start the bidding at £70,000, ladies and gentlemen.' Sarah could see his tie, silver and grey like his own expensively streaked hair. 'I have £75,000, ladies and gentlemen, £75,000, any advance?' Sarah waited. 'A lot of house for your money.' The audience waited. A hand went up. '£78,000 on my left, thank you, sir. £80,000, £82,000, £84,000, £86,000, £90,000.'

Silence.

Like a crane, Sarah's arm went up. As one of the few women there, she could feel the glances. 'A new place, £95,000, thank you, madam.'

'£98,' said a voice somewhere to her left behind a pillar in the thick air. Again, her arm went up. £99,000.

'An exceptional property in a very charming village.' Momentarily the auctioneer forgot to be brusque and began to sell. '£100,000, thank you sir.'

Sarah forgot time, place, everything except the hunger to have that house. His house. A half-forgotten man whose work had made her once feel alive. Christopher's voice came back. 'Don't go above £100K. That's all we can rake together. Don't go mad, for God's sake.'

'£101, thank you, madam. £102,000, thank you, sir. £103,000 I have from the lady, thank you, madam. £104,000, with you, sir.'

'£105.' Her voice, a weak crackle of electricity, came out, hoarse and English, and aimed at the podium in front of her.

'£105,000 for the lady on my right. This house is sold today. £105,000. Any advance? I ask once. Twice.' He paused. Suspended between life and loss, Sarah forgot to breathe. Bang! 'To you, madam, at £105,000.'

Yes! A bolt of unstoppable triumph surged through her, the sort she had had when she had pushed out both babies onto the delivery table. She clenched her fists and let out a great breath. Archie's house. She had really got it! Then she looked around. No one met her eyes or looked in the least degree interested.

'Lot 28.' The auctioneer's voice droned on, as a girl in high heels and a tartan bow to her blouse came up with a form on a clipboard and asked for her cheque for the ten per cent deposit. What a lot £10,500 seems when you have not worked for years. Barely able to think, Sarah felt breathless as she seized the pen and tried to remember what her name was and where she lived. Her signature snaked drunkenly along the paper.

She handed back the forms, then she found herself gripped in a stare by the man with the floppy hair standing by the pillar. The thin-lipped woman was no longer near him, and he was standing there just looking at her. By order of the mortgagees. Was he one of the repossessed? Suddenly, Sarah had a memory of a fine vase, lit from behind, pink lustred and magnificent. Suddenly the man seemed to disappear. A hungry-looking young man with a mobile phone had taken his place.

Afterwards, Sarah rang Christopher's office from the hotel lobby, where his assistant received the news without comment. In the car park, the other bidders were sliding into black cars and disappearing up the approach road to the nearby motorway, while some stood in the sun, analysing the sale, clapping each other on the back and laughing.

She decided to drive to Loanside straightaway to see her new home, even if completion wouldn't be for a month. She had a clear view in her mind's eye what it would be like inside. Christopher had come back from the viewing mentioning that there were weird eyes carved into the wooden panelling and on the banisters. He had been rather put off by them, but she had known instantly that this was the fish, the Robertson motif; she had doodled it often enough. A signature.

Carnforth House had been a party house even if it had been over fifty years since Archie had lived in it. She had read about those parties, wild, masked parties, which had lit up the house and been seen for miles. The weaver's son from Kirkcaldy had captured the rich and the titled with his sharp Fife wit and good looks. The beaumonde had arrived in special trains up from London, sweeping into Loanside with their retinues. It had all happened in there. In mousey Sarah's house, who, had she been alive, would not have been given houseroom at the time.

Back then, her own family had been carpenters making household furniture in a small shop in Clapham Junction. What would they have known of studio ceramics? Archie had imported the first jazz band from New Orleans ever to play in Scotland. What must the guests, more used to reels than riffs, have made of that seductive music, luring them through the house and daring them to think differently? In this house, Archie had been celebrated in verse. Then had come the slow decline into debt, fuelled by drink and opium, and never being accepted by the public-school, Edinburgh arts establishment.

Berwick-on-Tweed A1. Sarah drove off the bypass and headed for Loanside. In the distance she could see hills. Berwick-on-Tweed. Exciting names for someone used to the Hogarth Roundabout, the M1/M25 interchange, and snarl-ups at Knightsbridge Corner and Hangar Lane. She put her foot down and moved out into the fast lane.

* * *

The event which led to the auction had occurred four months earlier on the night of a dinner party cooked by Sarah and orchestrated by Christopher in order to keep his London network sweet and fresh while he worked outside the City for the next couple of years.

It hadn't started well. 'God, I need a drink,' Christopher had snarled when he had come in from work, slamming his briefcase against the hall radiator box. His face was a livid red, not just the result of the cold walk from Turnham Green tube station, and he was in a foul mood, which the prospect of four courses for dinner did not improve.

Sarah suspected that this was due to Helen, wife number one, that painted maypole of costly wants and necessities, who had danced without pity through their married life. It usually was. She had seen the letter; it had lain on the doormat that morning like an Exocet missile.

Sarah had long ago decided that hers was a marriage of three, or rather five counting Fanny and Rupert, who came to stay every other weekend, and who cleared out her fridge and her purse, leaving her with nothing but guilt and a headache. She disliked the role of second wife and wicked stepmother into which she had been cast; the baddie whatever she did, her good intentions eroded by the poundings of a past she did not belong to. But then, as Doreen had often reminded her, if you take on a divorced man you had to take on all his past as well. Used goods.

Still, she had done her best. She kept their house in Chiswick's Bedford Park as well as she could, had produced two lovely children, though each pregnancy had been met by Christopher with 'Oh *God*, not *another* cost centre!' She had tried not to cost too much. Just as tonight she had not called in caterers, as Helen would have done, but had hit the cookery books to see what she could possibly cook for people who always ate out.

Sarah sat in front of the dressing-table, putting on her make-up and brushing her shoulder-length hair. The wide tapestry seat had room for two, and ten-year-old Liddy came and sat down next to her. Such a pretty, self-confident little girl. Sarah found herself praying that nothing would ever happen to her daughter that would change her, that their relationship would never dull into the stale politesse which she now endured with her own mother.

Next door, in his dressing room, she could hear Christopher snarling about like a caged animal, pulling out drawers, swearing, stomping, making a mess. Which she would have to clear up. Then the doorbell went and she shooed Liddy off to bed and went down to answer the door.

'How nice to see you,' she said to the couple on the steps. Who were they? Sebastian and Melissa? Lester and Penelope, or was Sebastian now married to Penelope? Christopher!

'I love your crab soufflé, Sarah darling! So high! Mine always sinks in the middle because Robert always has to open the cellar door to fetch the wine *just* as I am taking it out of the oven! Then we have the most *awful* row.'

The meal was nearly half-way through, and the woman on Christopher's right forked another mouthful into her red mouth. Her large, solitaire diamond ring flashed six carat magic in the candlelight, the successful result of much nagging and her husband's City bonus. Everyone laughed appreciatively, and the conversation tinkled on.

Schools, the merits principally of St Paul's or Westminster, the pros and cons of day schools, boarding schools; then came the rival charms of London's villages. Wandsworth had the low rates but then all those high rises were a pain. Blackheath was convenient for Dulwich College, but Hampstead was far too international. Property prices were also discussed in slightly muted tones for, though Hong Kong Chinese had been spotted in Chiswick, oh happy thought, prices were not yet rising high enough for satisfactory one-upmanship. Then came holidays. Sarah sat at the end of the table and listened, wondering where they would be going now Christopher was on secondment to the World Bank for the next year or so, and there would be no more annual bonuses.

The men on either side of her praised the food, and then turned away to discuss currency rates while the women talked of shoes and shopping.

'How many bedrooms do you have in this house?'

Sarah, crumbling her bread, had not noticed that the woman was talking to her.

'Six.'

'Six! Why, you will never have to move again until the smalls leave home. Lucky you.'

And then, Christopher stood up, smiled at her and raised his glass. 'To my wife.'

He had never done anything like it before. For a split second Sarah thought he meant Helen and almost looked around as if she had come in. Everyone else thought it was such a gallant gesture.

'Lovely man, Christopher,' they would say on their way home.

'Jolly nice to that little wife of his. What's her name?'

To Sarah, watching this tall figure saluting her from the other end of the table, this brought an unexpected rush of gratitude. Then the spirit of Helen, Lady Macbeth in Versace, seemed to drift behind him. Smiling.

Afterwards, she had thought he might make love to her. She put on her best satin nightdress and sat up in bed smiling, trying to look pretty like a little girl at a fairground. But Christopher just sat down and looked at her. 'You know, Sarah, we've got about enough gold cards to paper the downstairs loo.' Then calmly, as if he had been explaining to a room of City fund managers just what benefits a particular merger would bring to institutional shareholders, he laid out their financial position. Which, after a day of making crab mousse and gâteau nougatine, was no fun. He showed her a piece of paper. Mortgage £340,000 ('that includes three remortgages'), credit card debts £60,000, store cards (hers) £5,000.

The zeros danced around before her eyes unromantically in the dimmed bedroom light. He was saying it all had to go. The house, the children's private school fees, the people mover, the lot. Terrible fears of losing the familiar swept over her; the rules were changing beyond her control. And all this because Helen was insisting on the twins' living expenses for university for the next three years up front in order for the money to earn interest, even though she was now back in full-time work with her two children about to leave home. Payment in instalments did not apply. That night, Sarah lay awake all night looking at the pattern of light on the ceiling until the Piccadilly Line began to thunder past from Acton Town once more and the planes began to roar.

One of the men at the table that night later paid cash for the house and extra for some of the furniture. Christopher gritted his teeth and his entire collection of Montague Dawson yacht paintings were shipped off to Sotheby's where they sold well enough to pay off the credit cards. Friends told them of a house to rent in Ealing, and Sarah went into a purdah; no more dinner parties because she no longer had six bedrooms. She ferried her children to and from school each day, and for several weeks thought of nothing except what to cook for dinner, and how to keep two small egos and their fiddly small possessions in some sort of order.

Christopher, in between trips to Washington, did a good demolition job on their lives and their debts, and Helen was well satisfied with her cheque. Gradually, Sarah began to realise that leaving Chiswick was a new opportunity. She scoured parts of London she had never been to before: Surbiton, New Malden, and out along the M4 to Windsor for cheaper property near good schools. They had £100,000 for a house, but that was nothing, and Christopher was far too grand for a terraced house. Then she hit the phones, for the home counties and then even further afield. There was now no point in living in London anymore, or the South-east come to that. So in came details of properties in Northants, Lincs, Oxon, Beds, Bucks (with the grammar schools) and then for the unthinkable places. Doreen would ring most nights to commiserate on her misfortune and to say just how *brave* she was being.

Back home for three days of London meetings, Christopher

accepted Helen's invitation to supper and the three of them had sat on white wrought-iron chairs among the terracotta pots in her Kew garden drinking chardonnay and eating spaghetti carbonara and being terribly civilised. The twins, tall and self-possessed, ignored Sarah and slumped across the table, discussing their Cambridge future. 'Going where Mummy and Daddy went,' said Helen brightly. 'Where did you go, Sarah? I've forgotten.'

'St Andrews.'

'How sweet. Lovely place if you couldn't make Oxbridge. How exciting not to know where you are going to be living!'

Sarah had swallowed the pasta and everything else, only too pleased that from now on Christopher would be meeting them in London without her. There would be no more heckles from the baddies in that pantomime.

The next day the past came in by another gate when an auction catalogue for Scotland had thumped on to the mat. Its pages, mashed up in the fall, fell open at Carnforth House, just in case she had missed the cue. She stared at it, unable to believe that this was perhaps the start of an awfully big adventure. The name of Archie's house came back to her encrusted by time, as if it had been locked away underwater in a rusting filing cabinet. Christopher viewed it while on a trip to see his old bank in Edinburgh and had seen it as a reasonable investment; a large, cheap, family house for Sarah and the children while he travelled for the World Bank. Good state school nearby. He had been relieved that she wanted to bid for it.

Sarah found Loanside and the house, and parked. FOR SALE BY AUCTION. The sign had blown over to one side in the wind, and was now resting against the wrought-iron railings. She got out of the car, suddenly cold and ill-prepared for this brave, old sandstone house, which faced her squarely, its windows wrinkled by honeysuckle. She opened the gate and went down the overgrown front garden. The large picture windows were too high for her to look in, unless she scrabbled up some lower brickwork. She felt the rough texture of the brick, and automatically bent down to pick up a crisp packet which had blown in off the road.

It was odd being in this empty place, which had been so fiercely fought for in that conference room just an hour before. Outside on the street behind her, nothing stirred. Then a gull leered down towards her, and suddenly a fighter aircraft roared through the sky, taking her back to another time and place.

But only for a second. Present realities were stronger. She was the second wife, banished for cheapness, sidelined to Loanside, a suitable name for a family on the flee from west London's Bedford Park and loan madness: debts, credit cards, credit agreements, overdrafts, second and third remortgages, school fees, and alimony.

The front door of the house was black, eight feet high perhaps, and shut tight. Above, barely visible under the layers of paint which smothered it, Sarah could make out the faint outline of the fish, Robertson's small joke with the world. 'And *I've* caught you,' she said aloud. Then, suddenly shy, as if she were presuming too much on this first acquaintance, she turned and hurried down to the path back to the car to wait for the solicitor's clerk and the keys.

CHAPTER TWO

London – Four Weeks Later

Bunny Halifax was standing in the florist's waiting to be served. Around her in huge tubs and baskets were the expensive colours of autumn. Red amaryllis, and purply scabious, chrysanthemums and huge burnt red hydrangeas. Pepperberries, dahlias, and purply pink heathers. The smell was delicious. She looked out of the window. Outside in the King's Road the traffic nudged and nosed down to Sloane Square and women passed by with shiny bags from shiny shops. A taxi hooted. Smells of croissants and cappuccinos seemed by osmosis to seep from next door's brasserie to mix with the heady scents around her.

She was starving, and her feet were tired, and she wished this damn woman in front of her would hurry up and make up her mind. People should always buy signature flowers, it saved time, and everyone always knew exactly who they were from, and then you didn't have to think what to send.

A mirror ran along the wall floor to ceiling. It made the shop seem twice as big and Bunny looked as if she were emerging from a sea of blackberry leaves, rather like a twenties' birthday card, though they always had wispy women entwined. And she wasn't. Wispy. Instead, she was six foot-plus wearing heels, a Loden coat, Hermès scarf and a Dior bag. Come on, come *on*, you stupid woman. Hurry up! This was wasting time; she should have just got one of the girls to ring up from the office. Yet she loved any excuse to come into florists' shops, particularly the Chelsea variety. Perhaps she could buy this one when she retired, and sit all day among the roses, drinking next door's espresso and reading the paper. Flowers were Bunny's weakness. Cut, chic expensive flowers, not the sort you had to grub about in the soil for, getting dirty fingernails and a sore back.

'Could you add the peach roses? Ten please.' The woman had a monied, foreign accent. Yet more flowers were added to the exuberant pile on the counter. Bunny looked to see; there must be three hundred quids' worth of stock there. Next to her, the woman's child stood fidgeting on one patent leather shoe.

Scenes from her wedding day floated into Bunny's mind; her mother Marjorie, standing next to her outside the church in a hat covered with peach roses, which had apparently been bought to echo the peach roses in the bride's bouquet. The hat had been, of course, just the wrong shade of peach. Approaching orange, so that the pictures made her look as if she had high blood pressure or a drink problem. Until then, Bunny would not have known that there were different shades of peach, let alone shades which clashed. Another piece of dysfunction to add to the wedding horror story.

Her mother had rowed with the florist, the hat shop and, after the honeymoon, with Bunny. She would not be upstaged. And yet, 'My only daughter getting married', said in a dreamy voice, had been repeated, a weasel shibboleth, for three months prior to the so-called Big Day. It had ripped off stub after stub out of her father's chequebook, given them all sleepless nights for weeks; it had also succeeded in persuading Bunny to wear a dress decked out with Princess Diana frills which had made her look, she now realised, like a topheavy fairy on a Christmas tree.

The only two people who had got through the day with any sort of calm were Edward, who had looked as if he were wearing his own morning dress, which he was, as opposed to Moss Bros like her father, and cousin Sarah, who wafted about like Ophelia, and had been probably the only person whom peach satin suited.

Bunny shivered. She was going to give Hannah £5,000 to elope. Even now, seventeen years later, she could still see the them-and-us rows of people sitting on opposite sides of the aisle when she had arrived at the church with her father; the vicar asking everyone please to throw the confetti out in the road and *not* in the church grounds, and the godawful food at the hotel which had made her want to throw up.

Unlike other bad experiences, regrets about a wedding day never seem to smudge into forgetfulness. But then one never ever has again so many people working to their own egos and agenda, all conspiring to give you a really hell day.

'Can I help you, madam?' A second woman came out from the back.

'I would like to send fifty cream roses to Scotland please.' Bunny shoved her thoughts back to where they came from.

'Certainly, madam. Could you give me the address?'

'Scotland. Mrs Sarah Todd, Carnforth House, Loanside, East Lothian EH82 5RW. I'll scribble something to put with them if you give me a card.'

As the woman was writing down the order, Bunny found herself thinking what to put. It wasn't enough to send flowers with just 'Love, Bunny' to someone who seemed to have lost the plot. What could she write? Happy Moving-In Day. Think You're Mad! or Are You Freezing To Death? Wish You Were Here. Fancy moving out of London, and to Scotland too! Downshifting gone mad.

'That will be £142.40 please, madam. How will you pay?'

The small girl with the patent shoes was staring at Bunny with huge black eyes. She was obviously Lebanese, with that clear olive skin, and was wearing a stiff navy coat one knew had walked straight out of Harrods' childrenswear department. As Bunny fished out her credit card, she saw the little girl was smiling at her and pretending to stir something in a bowl. Someone enjoyed watching cooking on daytime TV, then.

Bunny left the shop and hailed a cab to take her back to the office. Weddings. Had she enjoyed anything at all about her own? Then she remembered that when she had thrown her bouquet, as the car left to take them off to the airport, Sarah, the family butterfingers, had missed as usual, while she had forgotten this was not a cricket ball and had thrown too hard. All those wilting peach roses had ended up draped over the neon sign outside the hotel. Then she had caught her mother's words as the window had slid up, 'Why does Bunny always have to be so *rough!* Even on her *wedding* day!' The words had just begun to sting and bring her down when a sudden knowledge had stopped the pain, dead. Not all flowers were delicate. From then on she was going to be a different person, from whom people would have to keep their distance or she would bloody well clobber them with a fish kettle!

What a revelation. It had almost been worth getting married for.

No one was at home when Bunny arrived for lunch. Hannah was still at the college and Edward had obviously been out since breakfast. The house was all hers. Well it *was* hers in fact; she was paying for it. The feeling that she had been successful enough to provide all this wealth for her family pleased her more than almost anything and was one of the reasons she drove herself so hard.

It was one of those stand-up-straight stucco London houses, the sort which look as if they are about to burst vertically out of their terraces; Victorian space rockets of career success. It was arranged on five floors with a basement kitchen and reception rooms on two floors which had views over Clapham Common and out over south London. Every square foot had been taken over by interior designers with big ideas and Bunny's money. Framing the picture windows, Jane Churchill brocade and damask had gone to town with Colefax and Fowler, with yards of cloth which billowed out over the floor in luxurious abandon. Marjorie on her first trip had gone on and on about waste and the Second World War and coupons, none of which Bunny had listened to. The wanton use of the fabric was what she liked after having been brought up with unlined curtains cropped off and hemmed at the window ledge. Bunny liked the idea of being wanton. She liked the word, whether applied to women or interior decoration. Though she had never been able to be. Wanton. You can't be if you are too tall, rather plain and not attractive enough to men. So she had made her house a costly wanton hussy instead.

In the hall, Venetian lanterns hung down, extravaganzas of wrought iron built for concussion. Along the wall there was an installation by one of Hackney's hottest artists. Millions of tiny bulbs illuminated photographs of dogs left in Battersea Dogs' Home. Bunny had always loved dogs. Her bearded collie had just died in the hands of London's most expensive vet, and Bunny still felt a huge relief if she came across dog hairs, as if he had not yet been vacuumed into extinction.

She went downstairs and hacked off some French bread and poured herself a glass of wine and then did what all career women always do when they are trying to relax and failing. She made a list.

Loanside

'Right, Mrs Todd. Here we go. Wot about this then?'

'Sitting room, please, in there. Just lean it against the wall if you wouldn't mind.'

Cockney accents in a Scots gothic setting.

For a woman, there are two definitive moments in moving house. Both of which unleash surges of triumph or timorousness or perhaps that pricking at the back of the eyes, pain for the loss of a precious home, or a marriage. The first is when the first object is pushed into the first cardboard box; its thud is the signal for a cold dismantling, striking the stage set against which you have lived. The second is when the removal men bring into the house the first object. Whatever was last shoved into the van before the back flap was knocked up is plonked down in the hall as if to say Finders Keepers. New territory to conquer with a new story to write. Scene Two. Act . . . how?

The first possession the men carried into Carnforth House was, of course, a big-breasted blonde with improbably protruding nipples which had been taken off the front of a merchant ship. Christopher had fallen in love with all seven feet of her at a house sale in Rye and could never part with her, however dire their finances. Her brassy wooden smile did not waver as she was manhandled down the hall. 'Don't get many of those to the pound mate, eh?' Sarah winced.

She stood in the bare hall stamping her feet in the cold, banging thick woollen gloves together to stop her hands losing all feeling. Upstairs, she could hear the children running about, pounding on the bare boards like cannonballs dropped from on high. Screams and shrieks. Bringing the cold, dead house back to life by force.

Slam! A door crashed. Automatically Sarah called out. 'Mind your fingers! Don't slam doors or there will be an accident.' A picture flashed into her brain, the auctioneer slamming down the gavel and then looking at her.

'Mum, Florence has escaped. We're looking for her. I think she's gone in the fireplace.' Her five-year-old son was hanging over the top floor banisters.

'Well, don't frighten her, Theo, it will all be new. Don't bang the doors. If any of you lose a finger, the nearest hospital is thirty miles away!' What would a canary make of this house? So austere, and Scottish.

She lifted up the hall phone. Brrrr. They were now at least connected to the outside world, and the gas and electricity had been switched on. Piles of redirected post and months of junk mail were piled up by the front door. She picked it all up and went downstairs into the kitchen which at least had a surface, a huge gnarled oak table, which stood perhaps fifteen feet long in the middle of the room.

Boxes and boxes of china and pots and pans were now being piled up by the men. The old Welsh dresser had already been pushed along one wall and was standing there, apparently crooked with surprise at no longer being in a snug London kitchen, but now in this cavernous basement where once cooks and maids had slaved. On it was a huge bouquet of cream roses. Sarah knew it was from her rich cousin before she ripped open the card. 'Hope you are happy in your new home. Think you are all mad. How will you survive without the *Evening Standard*? Love Bunny.'

'In 'ere, Sid, that's "kitchen" written on it, innit?'

'Leave it out, mate, I can read.'

'Mrs Todd?' A Scottish voice, female. Sarah turned to see a middle-aged woman in a thick red coat standing behind her. 'Mrs Paterson, madam, from the agency. I hope everything is all right?'

'Yes, thank you.' Sarah could see she was being examined. 'It must have been a big job cleaning a house which has been empty so long, Mrs Paterson.'

'It's a big old house certainly, but my girls did their best. All that wooden panelling.'

'I know. Perhaps Mr Milne Robertson didn't like wallpaper.'

'No, I never knew the last owners. Well, I hope you will be happy here. From down south are you?'

'Yes,' said Sarah. It felt like a confession.

'Oh, well. Loanside's just a tiny wee place really, lots of history but not much else. And the golf. But there are plenty of English folk here. The husbands work in Edinburgh, you see. Does yours?'

'No, not at the moment.'

'Well, the incomers usually settle. Now the girls will be here soon to help you unpack, Mrs Todd. If you need anything else, just ring me.'

Do the English settle here? Sarah showed the woman out. Settle like dust, or snow or sediment? Suddenly she was pressed against a wall as another ship's figurehead was carried through the hall.

'So, how's it all going?' It was a polite question. Christopher was always polite.

'Fine. The men are half-way through and are having their lunch now.'

'Well, don't let them slack. They're costing me a fortune.'

'What's the weather like out there?'

'Cold. Rainy as usual. Typical New York autumn.'

'New York. Aren't you in Bogotá?'

'Was. Left yesterday. The Colombians were their usual sunny selves, and it's nice to be here with decent plumbing. Had a great Japanese meal last night in the Upper East Side.'

'Oh good.' Standing on the first-floor landing Sarah could see from the front window two women, grey haired, with shopping bags, standing outside looking in at the activity. The children were now running round the garden and getting under the feet of the men who were bringing out yet more furniture from the van. What was the Scots for, 'There goes the neighbourhood,' she thought?

'So, house all right? Super to get it at such a price. Coping?'

'Yes thanks.'

What did he want her to say? Hours of work lay ahead of her, cleaning, unpacking, sorting, coping with the quarrelsome, insecure children. Sarah wanted to howl and run out of the house.

'Jolly good. It will make sense when I finish with the World Bank and get to HQ, you'll see. Must go, meeting starts in five minutes. Bye darling.'

Click. Off he went, Christopher with his stripey ties and his Japanese meals and his love of New York plumbing. Sarah couldn't see this making sense for him when he finally returned. She picked up a small box of children's books and went to the top of the house. He hadn't asked how the children were, she thought. Wasn't he just the twentieth-century Mrs Jellaby, helping the world and its kids, but forgetting his own?

When she reached the landing, she saw that the children had already written Liddy and Theo out in felt tip pen on pieces of paper and stuck them onto their respective doors. One good sign at least. She went into Liddy's bedroom, which looked out to the sea, and dropped the box of books onto the bare mattress. Florence the canary was now rustling, subdued in her cage, next to Liddy's violin.

The draught from the bare window took her by surprise. That would be bad for the bird. She shook the window to see if it could be forced up further, then found herself looking out, taken aback by the view. In London the eye is always brought up short by houses or railway lines or roads. Here her eyes were free to roam for miles into the distance. She could see the curve of the coast and the murderous waves pounding the rocks. And gulls, so many, wheeling over the ruined castle walls, circling to rest on the broken plaster of the Co-op building. She could imagine their eggs, not served suitably mashed with beluga on home-made croûtons, along with the London champagne chatter, but lying out there in the cold, unremarked upon.

Had Archie Milne Robertson ever prowled around upstairs and stolen into any of the maids' beds? Sarah shivered. He must have been hard to resist. There had been rumours at the time.

She suddenly remembered reading an old press cutting. Women with children had come forward after his death, only to find there was little to gain. The widow's family had stepped in to pay the debts, and, unappreciative of his work, had salvaged what was left of family respectability. What would it have been like working for the master in his heyday?

Sarah went out on to the landing and, walking down the stairs, her hands on the wooden banister, could feel a knobble on the wood every few stairs. She bent to look, and yes, there was the Robertson fish, small but drawing the attention of everyone who walked into the house. Interesting that he had continued this motif even up to the top of the house where the maids slept. As if to show all was his domain. Even in her thick coat, Sarah could still imagine the swish of the dresses his wife, Isobel, must have worn.

How would Isobel have run a house like this? She would have sorted everything out around her husband, running the house in a state of frozen and disapproving efficiency. You could tell that from the photographs, she seemed to stare, as if amazed at how a nice rector's daughter from Musselburgh had ended up with this exuberant, restless, classless genius with such big hands and appetites. Did they row? Sarah hoped so. Did they ever throw his pots at each other in fury? Or had their marriage been as polite as hers?

The wind was buffeting against the landing window. Down below in the garden, she saw her children talking to a man who did not look like one of the removal men. Was this some nosy neighbour coming to give them the once over, or the minister? He didn't look like one; he was throwing back his head laughing; her children were hopping round him, obviously enjoying themselves.

She hurried down the stairs into the garden where the wind blew icily straight off the sea.

'Mummy, Mummy, the man says there's an ark in the garden. Come and see.'

'How do you do, I'm Sarah Todd. Can I help you?'

'Zander Robertson. Good afternoon, I just came along to welcome you all to the house.'

'Thank you.' Sarah said. 'Zander?'

'Short for Alexander.'

'I see.'

Suddenly she recognised him. 'To the house? I *did* see you at the auction, didn't I?'

'Yes, I was there. And I thought you were very brave, bidding like that.'

She smiled up at the man, 'I was scared to death actually, I've never bid at an auction before.'

She noticed he moved and talked slowly, as if he was not used to company.

Sarah felt suddenly awkward. 'Was this yours? Your house?'

'Carnforth? No. It was my brother's. Rather, my late brother's. He'd taken out three mortgages on it and there was no way I could pay them off. It had to go.'

The man had very dark eyes. Almost black. A soft Edinburgh accent. Then she realised she was staring at him.

'Excuse me, but are you related? To Archie Milne Robertson?'

He smiled, 'Grandson. You've heard of him! Hardly anyone has. He's rather unfashionable these days. I was surprised the auctioneer knew. My brother and I were brought up here. Archie died long before I was born but, of course, I was brought up on stories. Family legends, you know.'

He was looking up at the house now, its sandstone caught in the light of sudden sun which had wrenched itself from behind the clouds. She could see now a wistfulness in his face.

'Mummy, Zander says there's an ark here in the garden.' Theo had run round some large object and was pulling the ivy off it. It looked like a tree trunk.

'What do you mean, an ark? Theo, what are you doing?'

'You know, Mummy, Noah's Ark, We did it at Sunday school.'

'Mrs Todd, what shall we do with this then?' Behind her, one of the men was carrying a statue of a cherubim, nicely mossed up, one of their lucky London purchases which was now to be plonked here in this wild garden, with its trees bent double by the force of the wind. How small and fussy it looked here. She was embarrassed that this Robertson man should see it.

'Would you put it just over there by the greenhouse? I'll have to decide later where to put it.'

The garden was large, nearly half an acre, and had evidently once been well tended. To the right-hand side there had been a kitchen garden, obviously a successful one looking at the old fruit trees. There were even the remains of a vine draped across the wall which sheltered the plants from the sea wind. In the rest of the garden there were roses, straggly now and unkempt, yew hedges, and huge bushes of rosemary and lavender. It was a beautiful garden, unapologetic for its disorder, assaulted by the salt wind which now made her eyes run and made her stagger as she tried to keep still.

She laughed. 'Is it always this windy?' she asked. He was looking at the iron object now being uncovered by the children.

'It's a windy place, but it can be calm, though of course we do get storms. But there is, they say, a microclimate which means we get more sun than other parts of Scotland. You'll get used to it.'

'I hope so.'

'Mummy, look!' Ivy was now strewn all over the long grass and they could all see what appeared to be exactly that, an ark, a small house on top of a boat made of sheet metal with slits for the windows. It was perhaps fifteen feet long. Theo looked and went inside first, screaming that he had found a bench, and a beetle, and it was all rotten.

'Why is it here?' Sarah asked. 'Who built it?'

'Grandpa Archie. He had an odd sense of humour,' the man said.

'Its a strange thing to put in the middle of the lawn.'

'Do you like it?' he asked her.

'Like perhaps isn't the word, but I can see it's a success with the kids.' Both children were now inside scrabbling about, she could hear their muffled voices.

'Mummy, I've found a giraffe, its body anyway.' Liddy emerged, her hair covered in moss, holding out a chunk of wood. The body and legs of a giraffe who had probably lost its mate as well as its head.

'Oh, thank you darling. Look, it's so cold I'm not staying out much longer. Are you all coming in, or will you stay out in the ark?'

'We want to stay here.'

She fingered the wood, now splintered and damp and, looking at it closely, she could still see the humour and care with which it had been made.

'Do you live here in Loanside, Mr Robertson?'

'Zander, please. I live in Edinburgh, but I have a small property here too, which I've just been visiting. Anyway, I must go. I hope you'll very happy here. Bye kids.' He shook her by the hand. His hand was cold and, looking down, she saw they were big hands with thick fingers, square ended, and she suddenly shivered. She walked down the path with him.

'This house, you know,' she found herself blurting out, 'it wasn't really a repossession, Mr Robertson, because, you see no one ever possesses a house. They're only ever on loan.'

'I know.' He said it simply and smiled down at her, as if really looking at her. She wasn't used to that anymore.

'I hope you will be very happy, you and your children. I hope you will enjoy it.'

'Thank you, I hope we are going to get along OK.'

'The locals will probably tease you and call you White Settlers, but don't worry.'

Looking up at him, she realised he was not as old as she had first thought, in his early forties perhaps – it was just that he had spent a lot of time in the wind.

'White Settlers?'

'Yes, I'm afraid it's the Loansiders' idea of a joke. But don't let it bother you. You'll enjoy it here. I can see some ladies waiting for you over there, inside. Goodbye.' He walked out through the side door. By the way he opened it, it was clear he was used to the house.

The feeling, the familiar feeling of falling into nothingness, started to grip her and yet, while buffeted by the unforgiving wind, she still forced herself to climb out of the abyss and back into the present before she fell too far. Behind her she could hear the whoops of the children, 'It's a wooden rabbit, give it to me. Theo, don't snatch!'

She walked towards the women, who were now looking at her curiously from out of the kitchen window.

Later that night, Sarah sat up in bed. She was cold and she could hear the wind thrashing against the window as if it wanted to break it. Her children were stretched out around her in the bed, draped across blankets and pillows. They had been much too excited to sleep, and too frightened to stay in their strange bedrooms because of the noise. The need for reassurance had overcome any adventurousness they displayed earlier, and Liddy had complained that the lighthouse beam kept travelling over the ceiling, waking her up.

An arm was sticking in her back. Sarah got up and, putting a shawl over her nightdress, went to look out of the window. The bedroom was large with two big picture windows which looked out over the garden and on to the sea. The lighthouse was to the left, and in darkness, yet on the count of three its beam crawled, sure enough, up the wall, over the ceiling, down the next wall and out again.

What a day! Her sense that moving here was going to be such an adventure had for the moment deserted her; she was now overwhelmed by the amount of change. Her possessions, which had been in storage for months, were back with her, now partly put away in drawers and partly boxed awaiting the men to come in to put up shelves, curtains and hooks.

All around, the house seemed to creak to the beat of the buffeting wind outside, mixing with the percussion sounds of the children's snuffles and snores. What did she feel? Very tired and disoriented, in a sort of limbo between a London future she once thought she had, and another still to be found, when there would be Loanside names and telephone numbers in her address book. The window was now shaking roughly in the gale. She groped across the room and picked up the tights she had worn during the day, now hanging half off the chair. Then a sharp pain seized her as she stubbed her toe on the chair. Then anger.

Blast Christopher. Why had they had to move? All this packaging surrounding her spoke of prosperity. All these boxes with expensive contents; all those pictures of bloody ships; all the demands of Christopher's past; they had cost them their home.

She started stuffing the tights into the gap in the window frame to stuff out the draughts. Suddenly she cut her finger on a sharp edge. She pulled it out and, switching on the lamp, looked at a piece of pottery, its surface, she could see in the moonlight, decorated with a silver lustre, smooth to the touch. She could see there were small dollops of the lustre on the edge. She peered closer to the window and, sure enough, right along the frame at the bottom, caught in the beam of the lighthouse she could make out bits of pottery, shoved in. Had Archie done this? Had he shoved in old pots to stop the noise? Had he paced the night disturbed by the wind and worried over debts, or had he been driven mad by the noise of the heaving sea outside? Had he thrown this in fury against the wall?

Gathering the fragments in her hand, Sarah held them, precious remnants of a past she could understand, that had once been, however briefly, a piece of her own. Looking to the blackness outside, she felt for the first time, for a very long time, just the tiniest bit alive. It was just a flicker, as momentary as the light which swept round the walls. But infinitely precious nonetheless.

'Mummy, I want a cuddle.' Theo was sitting up, blinking, his blond curls catching the beam as it swung once again across the room.

'I'm coming, darling. Mummy's here.' Sarah went back and got into the bed. Still clutching the pieces of broken pottery, and engulfed by her children, she was soon asleep.

CHAPTER THREE

London

It was just as well Bunny had been the star bowler in the Carshalton Ladies First XI. What a ridiculous thing for a nearly forty-year-old woman to be doing at 9.30 on a Wednesday morning! Bunny stood on the secluded graffiti-covered concrete railway bridge which overlooked the track of the London to Windsor line. She was throwing food rather effectively overarm, to her grateful assistant Lottie, who was shivering on her brick terrace twenty feet below. Lottie, even in this harsh October light, was looking pale and interesting, with the exception of dark roots, which at this angle, Bunny could see, were in desperate need of the attentions of a Mayfair salon.

Whack! A packet of muesli landed in a terracotta pot. Out! Come on, Bunny, you can do better than this. Bunny picked up the oranges. 'Lottie! Catch this without dropping it this time,' she hissed. They mustn't hear her from the next street. Lottie managed to catch both the oranges, and the goat's milk and the soda bread. Then Bunny stood on the bridge, wondering how on earth she was going to get back to her car without all the press recognising her. What a way to spend a morning! A familiar loud noise above her made her look up. Concorde was shearing through the air right above Chiswick on its way to Heathrow. Bunny could not help but admire its beauty while thinking, as she always did, how bloody noisy it was.

The day had started more than two hours earlier with a phone jangling next to her left ear. And Edward had plodded into her bedroom, as usual, with her freshly squeezed orange juice, as he liked to do each morning. He always left orange skins piled up high in his 'green' recycling bin for the compost before powering off to the corner shop in his gas-guzzler for the *Financial Times, Racing Post* and *Sporting Life*. Rather, as Bunny once observed, the way her father used to eat a slimmers' crispbread after a three-course meal to help him lose weight. Still, this morning, having been woken at 6 a.m. by a hysterical Lottie, she was more than usually glad of the orange juice.

'Bunny, darling, I'm cut off! I can't get out!'

'What do you mean, you can't get out? Lottie. Calm down. Is the front door stuck?'

'No! The press! They're crawling all over the street! I daren't think what's in the papers.' Bunny had sighed at the inevitable. 'Well, do you need food?'

'Yes, please, I'm starving. And milk.'

'Right. I'll come myself, I'll see you in an hour. Selina can cover at Warburg's this morning, and I'll get Melissa to start the canapés for the Lloyds do this evening. But really, Lottie, you can't go on like this. Can't you find a nice fund manager earning seven figures, and *stay* married?'

'I know, I know. My therapist says I have to stop repeating these negative patterns.'

'No, Lottie, it's too *early* for psychotherapy. I'll be over as soon as I can. *Don't* open the door and *don't* talk to the press. I'll ring Max for his advice. You don't need the money, so don't say one word.'

Oh what a beautiful morning! Ha, ha. Bunny dressed, plastered some make-up over the wrinkles, and went downstairs for her prunes and Greek yoghurt. Hannah, her sixteen-year-old daughter, was sitting, dressed in black, at the kitchen table eating cereal and reading a magazine.

'Give me a smile, darling, life's not that bad.'

'Oh no? I've had Juanita cleaning round me and singing "Climb Ev'ry Mountain" for the last half hour.'

'Think of me, then. I've just had Lottie on the phone squawking about the press at the door. Now would I please schlepp over to Chiswick with some food? As if I haven't got enough to do.'

'Serves her right, stupid cow.'

'Hannah!'

'Mum, she's a plonker! Why any of these men ever want her in the first place is a mystery to me. Anyway, I'm off. I'm staying over at Kate's house tonight, she's helping me with my project. Bye.'

'Right darling, enjoy, be good.' Bunny hoped she really would be staying with her friend, but what was she supposed to do about it? London children were aliens. Hannah kissed her mother perfunctorily, grabbed her bag and walked slowly out of the room. Already six foot one, she stooped, just as she herself had done, Bunny thought. If one more person told her Hannah could be a supermodel once her skin had cleared up, she'd spit.

Bunny went into the drawing room. Juanita, the Filipino housekeeper, was already hoovering and bullying the green scatter cushions, and piling up the magazines on the large coffee table. 'Morning, Mrs Bunny. What will Mr Edward like to eat tonight?'

'Just get in some smoked fish, will you, and some French bread? I'll probably have something left over to bring home from the school.'

'Yes, madam.'

It was impossible to tell what Juanita thought of them all, even after all the years she had been with them. Bunny secretly thought that she was probably quite rich, after years of squirrelling away her salary and living like one of the family. She had once caught her reading Edward's *Financial Times*, her eyes screwed up peering at the columns of the FTSE. It was the only time that Bunny had ever seen her embarrassed.

Bunny left the house, turned left and started to walk to the newsagent's on the Common. 'Morning Bunny darling.' Her neighbour, Sir Geoffrey Askew, boss of Channel 6, was getting into the back of his Daimler.

'Good morning, Geoffrey. Expect I'll see you at the IBA party next week.'

'It'll be a frightful crush, but hope to.' Sir Geoffrey eased himself into the back seat, and Bunny watched the car drive off; he'd already started spreading the FT before him by the time it turned the corner. I bet Juanita could give him a tip or two, she thought.

Just for the moment she allowed herself the luxury of looking at her house from the outside. The early morning sun, weak with pollution, was trying bravely nonetheless to shine feebly on the high, creamy stuccoed walls. She was pleased that the landscape people had planted tea roses. Jeremy's yew hedge looked a bit depressing in contrast. She remembered her father coming up last weekend and raving about his Busy Lizzies and his privet hedge. Bunny shivered. She'd come a long way.

At the newsagent's, it was worse than she thought: 'MINISTER CAUGHT WITH MYSTERY BLONDE', 'MINISTER FOUND IN SECRET LOVE NEST WITH BLONDE BOMBSHELL.' Sure enough, there was Lottie looking, well, just like Lottie, caught in the grainy photograph in an embrace with the handsome and semi-married junior minister and Member for Mossop and Bigneth Valley. Lottie was a clot! What a mess. It was only a matter of time before they connected Lottie with *The Bunny Cooks Company*. She'd once read somewhere that you never tasted the flavour of a decade until you were half-way through. Judging by today's helping, the nineties was a really unappetising stew of stress, money, sleaze and discontent.

Bunny went back to the house and started to raid the larder for some food to take over to her. As one might expect for a professional cook, there was hardly anything in the house; the whole household seemed to live on French bread and goat's cheese, but she found what she could and was soon driving west towards Lottie's house in Chiswick.

The Upper Richmond Road at 8 a.m. was nose to tail and, as usual, Bunny found herself wondering why, south of the river, people always drive like Neapolitan Mafiosi. *She* always did. At Putney High Street she waited, for ever, for the lights to change and rifled through her post on the passenger seat. Bank statements, yuck; council tax, hellish. A postcard showing improbable green hills peeked out, from poor old Sarah. On either side of her car, huge lorries throbbed, ready for the lights to change, and Bunny sat being squeezed and breathless reading the card which seemed to come from another world. 'Settling into Loanside, making friends with this rather extraordinary house. Children are finding their feet, I am learning to live without the *Evening Standard*. (And the traffic!) Thanks for the beautiful flowers. Love Sarah.'

The lights changed. Bunny's Mercedes smoothly outpaced the lorries and headed for Barnes. Odd thing to do, up sticks and move out of London like that. Wiltshire or Sussex she could understand; Edward and she had often talked about buying a cottage for weekends, but Scotland, and to the back of beyond, not even Edinburgh! It didn't make any sense, unless the serious Christopher was in deep doodoo on the money front, which she and Edward had often suspected. Though at least Christopher still worked for a living.

Bunny stopped, reluctantly, to let a woman pushing a toddler's buggy cross the road. Give me strength. Come on, come on, come on! She revved the engine and the woman turned and glared at her. Why did white Mercedes always make people glare? Finally the proverbial chicken crossed and Bunny roared off.

She had last seen the Todds all together at Christmas. Sarah had gone to town with the house; every piece of holly round Greater London must have been bought up. Stockings were hanging up at the fireplace, and Christopher, all charm and gold cufflinks, was standing warming his little behind and offering people large drinks, which then of course Sarah went to get. She'd become a doormat. She was always asking Christopher what he thought, and half the time the poor bastard didn't know if he was in Bogotá or Bayswater, working for the World Bank. Edward said that the bank must have farmed him out, while she rather thought he was after a gong, and a ticket to the Carlton Club. You never got the full story with someone like Christopher.

She had bumped into him one day at Sotheby's in the spring.

She had been looking at some pearls, and had come across Christopher on the same floor drooling over a model of a ship. 'Bunny, it's bone! Ninety-two guns, made by a prisoner of war. French, it says.' The guide price was £15,000–17,000, which to Bunny had seemed completely mad, but then Christopher had said he couldn't afford it. He was immaculately dressed as ever, but his face had seemed harassed, even a little haggard, over his Hermès tie. His eyes had an Oliver Twist wistful look, so she had suggested coffee to cheer him up.

They had found expensive cappuccinos round the corner and he had sat there stirring the foam and then had asked her if she had ever found Sarah hard to get through to. 'Sometimes it is as if she is in some glass tower, like that girl in the fairytale, you know, the one with the long hair.'

'Rapunzel.' Bunny had been rather pleased she had remembered. She had seen that Sondheim musical *Into The Woods* on Broadway in the late eighties, in which Rapunzel went mad and killed herself, but had not mentioned this to Christopher. Shades of an old loyalty to her cousin had made her say she didn't know why this was so. Though the fact that he and Edward had been to the same public school mill which specialised in grinding out emotionally damaged prime ministers and City chairmen (many now her clients) could not have helped. Still, her job that day had been to cheer him up in that hearty nanny-knows-best mode men like him were used to. 'Drink up, Christopher. She loves you; she is just rather a private person, academic, you know.' He had just nodded, looking down at his cup.

Not that you would think Sarah had got a first, or had an intellectual bone in her head. Her life was completely taken up with ferrying her children to their music classes and their dancing classes. Life was too short. Bunny herself had always employed expensive nannies who had nannied her, every bit as much as Hannah, criss-crossing London in the nanny-car with Hannah in the back in pursuit of their high-octane social life. While Bunny had got on with doing what she did best, making money. Thank God someone in the family still could.

Lottie's street was a few yards from the Thames, a cul-de-sac of chic and frightfully sought-after terraced houses which, though tiny, were so expensive that in any other part of Britain the price for one, even unmodernised, would have bought a four-or five-bedroom house.

Damn, Bunny had forgotten that it was a dead end. She parked at the top of the road, and decided to walk down with her scarf over her head, as if she were a Chiswick housewife. Could she go right up to the front door; would there be a back way?

She was so busy deciding what to do she didn't notice the legs of the *Daily Blare* hack sitting in the passenger seat of his car, shaving. A half-eaten bacon roll lay in his lap. 'Sorry love,' he called after her, but Bunny didn't stop. As she walked she was staring across the road. Oh dear, Lottie, for once, had not been exaggerating. All along the street, both sides, there were cars and press men gathered in groups, cameras slung over their shoulders, drinking coffee out of thermos flasks. Lottie's house at the end was now effectively cut off. The ruched drapes were drawn, and Lottie's milk lay uncollected on the doorstep. A man was peering in through the letter box, while another rang the bell. Stupid Lottie. Was any man worth it, let alone a politician? Bunny wondered whether perhaps Lottie had a much stronger libido than she. She had had a fair bit of nookie early on, but these days she preferred a nice baked goat's cheese to Edward getting excited. Anyway, his redundancy seemed to have knocked that for six.

Luckily, in spite of her height, no one glanced at her. Bunny looked so ordinary she was never usually bothered in the street, although with the right lighting and clothes she could look remarkably striking on television. Still, there was no way she could go up to the front door without being recognised by this lot.

She turned into the garden of the first house and pretended to ring the doorbell. She waited and, as no one came, turned and walked back up the street where she'd come. Of course, the bridge! She remembered she could get to the bridge which looked over Lottie's garden by the alleyway down in the next street. She found it without difficulty and, sure enough, once up the steps and onto the bridge, Lottie's garden lay below. The dozy press pack had not noticed that this was a way to track down their so-called blonde bombshell.

After Bunny had been throwing stones at her window for several minutes, Lottie suddenly appeared, waving. Bunny put her hand to her mouth, 'Sshh,' and then began to throw down provisions, feeling like a French resistance fighter. Or a total plonker.

Crash! Lottie failed to catch the tin of consommé and it crashed onto the brick terrace. Suddenly Bunny heard male voices tramping up the steps onto the bridge. They had discovered the back alley. She pointed frantically in their direction to Lottie, who, looking like a startled rabbit, gathered up what food she could and fled inside. Phewww . . . ! A goods train raced under Bunny's feet. She turned and ran across the bridge and down the steps to the other side. Behind her, she could hear shouts, and a 'Who's that?' 'Oi!' Then a click of a camera. But she didn't stop running. Although it had been years since she had run, let alone attempted it on high heels, Bunny legged it down the road and back to her car. Barely able to breathe, she somehow found the key and sank into the driver's seat. Never again.

Once upon a time Bunny had decided that the way to make money as a cook was to do as little cooking as possible.

This Damascene conversion to capitalism had occurred on her twenty-fifth birthday. That day had begun with Edward receiving a large annual bonus for never seeing his family, and the nanny handing in her notice because she couldn't bear the thought of potty-training Hannah, and she had also been offered a job with more money by Bunny's now ex-best friend.

Perfunctory cards and roses had been thrust at her by her departing husband as he rushed off to the office. 'Happy Birthday To My Big Girl,' he had written; and then her mother had rung up to say she had sent her a 'nice top' which would suit her, 'because you are so droopy, Bunny dear. You must get better bras and stand up straight.' Hannah's wails of, 'Mummy, Mummy,' had pursued her like demons on commission as she had gone to and from the kitchen loading up the car with all the ingredients for a three-course lunch for a unit trust company which specialised in low growth and the snottiest secretaries in the Square Mile. Then, when she had finally struggled through four miles of traffic hell into the City, the parking place she had been promised had not materialised and she had been given a ticket by a menopausal traffic warden.

The thunderbolt arrived when Bunny was just putting out the avocado and salmon salad on the plates which were perched on a photocopier. Next to her was a curtain, behind which was the Baby Belling on which she was attempting to heat up a casserole with some wild rice. It had only taken a plate wobbling and then slipping off the photocopier and into the wastepaper basket, to jam the angry machinery in Bunny's brain. A vengeful angel had crash landed on her shoulder, put electrodes down her ears and yelled, 'You don't have to do this if you don't want to, Sunbeam!' It had, in a way, completed the process begun on her wedding day. Bunny stopped being a cook in the City, had started thinking very big indeed, and now only picked up a kitchen knife for the largest of cash inducements.

A bank loan and a crash course in running a business had helped, as had the eighties boom in London when, if you could wash a lettuce leaf and open a bottle of Bollinger, you were laughing. *The Bunny Cooks Company* took off, a dynamic catering business run by a tall whirlwind in designer clothes now slimmed down to a size 14, who terrified the Sloaney girls who had once made mincemeat of her at cookery school. Then had come *The Bunny Cooks School*, and then the TV show and then the books. And money, lots of it, to buy flowers and throw parties.

But of course, life being a game of snakes, ladders and more snakes, it was when the business had really taken off that Edward, restructured out of a job post-Big Bang, had then decided that the rat race was not for him. He had not exactly admitted it outright. He had spent months looking at the appointments sections, but in fact he had had no intention of going back to work. He now spent his time listening to classical music, looking after his almost non-existent portfolio, betting on horses and being supported by Bunny, who now worked 100-hour weeks. Because she adored him and wanted him to be happy, she told her family and friends that Edward now worked from home for personal clients so, as far as the rest of the world knew, all was well in the state of Denmark.

Bunny was sitting in her office drinking strong black coffee and reading the newspaper. Both Lottie's ex-husbands, lovely men who had parted with thousands yet who still adored her, were now displayed like pinned Victorian butterflies in a double-page spread titled THE GIRL WHO RUINED FUN-LOVING MINISTER. Girl. Not perhaps an accurate description for Lottie who, at twenty-nine, was perhaps a tad past it. But there she was, grinning, coming out of Annabel's with the Hon. Lavinia; and there was the divine and beastly Gerald, ex-junior minister, who had quickly crawled back to his wife and his constituency chairman, though not necessarily in that order.

Then, inevitably, there was her name, Bunny Halifax – Britain's popular TV cook and employer of the scarlet Lottie. There was no quote from her, and at least they'd had the decency not to make one up. Lottie, too, had taken her advice and remained stumm. It was always better in scandals like this when everyone could afford not to take the nationals' thirty pieces of silver.

'I don't know why you employ someone like that,' Marjorie had come down the phone last night, repeating the sentiments six times under different guises.

The Bunny Cooks Company occupied a large unit in an industrial estate in Wandsworth. At the back of the office, the River Wandle oozed unconvincingly from Croydon and Merton on the way down to the Thames at the solid waste transfer station. It had never seemed a very satisfactory river. All around her on the walls were charts and lists. It was the only way Bunny could possibly keep her small but growing empire together. Phones rang constantly and nice smells from the kitchens reminded Bunny that it was 7.45 a.m. and she hadn't had breakfast.

Tap tap tap. Joanna, her secretary, was already at work next door doing an early shift, typing out the recipes for next year's *Bunny Cooks Summer Cookbook*, while the super-efficient Lucinda was planning recipes for the spring courses at *The Bunny Cooks School.* Bunny ran one-term courses for beginners, intermediate and advanced, evening classes, one week long and weekend classes. Dozens of nice young girls from the home counties paid through the nose for the privilege of being taught to cook by Bunny and her staff. They all seemed identical, although now there were increasing numbers of Americans, Arabs, diplomats' wives and Essex girls to leaven the loaf. Everyone wore sparkling white butchers' caps to hide their hair, chefs' trousers, overalls and the school's distinctive navy and white striped aprons. Bunny would float in twice through the course to teach a couple of show dishes, which they could then say that Bunny Halifax *herself* had taught them, while leaving Lucinda and her staff to do the rest. The added value was in Bunny's course notes, written in her own earthy prose with lots of shortcuts to culinary perfection.

'Bunny, your car is outside to take you to the studio, and there are two more photographers outside. Shall I get rid of them for you?' Joanna came in with a large clipboard.

'Thanks, and can you ask Frank to bring the car round to the back?'

'Absolutely.'

Bunny, still hungry, got up and folded away the paper. Eyes and teeth and on we go! What was she doing this morning? Roast capon with fruit stuffing. What on earth would Mrs Average sitting in Peterborough on a Tuesday morning make of that?

It is surely one of life's great mysteries, how we ever managed to get up in the morning before breakfast television.

* * *

'And now, *Bunny* is back to cook some more *impressive* dinner party fare!'

Jenna Grace rolled her eyes in delight and turned to Bunny. The camera shifted, and Bunny obediently smiled at it and then at Jenna, while thinking just what a patronising bitch she was.

'Cooking for a dinner party need not be hard work or a pain,' said Bunny brightly, trying to remember when she had last cooked a dinner party for anybody, and failing. 'One has to do just enough cooking to feel that it's *your* party, but you don't want to be all red nosed and exhausted when your guests arrive, do you, Jenna?'

'*No*,' said Jenna, who had now walked over and was standing, hovering, at the oven like a small boy waiting to lick out the cake mixture.

'So today,' continued Bunny, 'it's roast capon and fruit stuffing.'

'*Super*!' said Jenna.

'It's an all-American recipe,' said Bunny brightly, who had thought it up at four in the morning five days before and had faxed over the list of ingredients for the programme's home economist to sort out. 'And the beauty of it is that it is easy to prepare. You can do the stuffing the day before and stick it in the fridge.'

'So why a capon, Bunny?' said Jenna, who was now slightly green. Bunny suddenly remembered that she was a vegetarian, and rich chicken smells had been wafting all over the studio for the past two hours.

'Because it is a little more special than chicken and has a nice, rich, meaty flavour,' said Bunny mercilessly, who was now showing how you could chop apples extra fast without slicing off a nail. 'A seven pounder will feed six people generously, and there will be lots of bones left over for soup. Now, let's see what we need.'

She slowed down, obedient to the producer, knowing that the recipe was now being flashed up on the screen.

'Take one large cooking apple, cored, peeled and diced, one third of a cup of dried apricots, and then you need a firm ripe pear, medium onion, although this is optional, and one-third of a cup of seedless raisins. And what else—'

Thirty seconds later, she was shoving all the contents of the small glass bowls with the separate ingredients into a large mixing bowl. 'Make sure you always use two forks to bind the mixture together.'

'Now for the capon!' The uncooked capon was looking fleshy and depressed under the hot studio lights. Unappetising. Bunny grabbed it with a big smile and started sprinkling it with salt. 'You know, it is funny how words set off an association, isn't it Jenna?' Jenna looked nervous. Bunny loved winding her up. 'You know, I was brought up with a cousin. She was a bit younger than me. Our mothers were sisters, and I remember when I was fifteen they bought us identical red capes. My cousin Sarah wore hers, and being about five foot two, looked wonderful in it, just like Little Dorrit. I called her Cape On, but then of course I, being six foot two, looked—'

'Like *Big* Dorrit?' said Jenna sweetly.

'Well, either that or Batman on holiday. Anyway, not what Dickens had in mind,' said Bunny modestly. 'So I was Cape Off, and my mother went mad because the cape had cost her nearly twenty-five pounds.'

'A *lot of money* in *those* days,' said Jenna to labour the point.

'No, I was not flavour of the month. Unlike this.' Bunny was now putting stuffing into the bird, which slid everywhere. Some of the stuffing slipped off onto the spotless and gleaming marble top. Bunny always managed to leave pots and pans and mayhem at the end of her session. Not that she gave a damn. Washing up had never been in her business plan.

'The main thing about cooking for a dinner party is to have fun, enjoy yourself and don't worry about it,' said Bunny to camera as she skewered the neck cavity closed. 'The cooking itself is not that important. People will always remember if you are relaxed and the food is good. But if the food is marvellous and you are stressed with a bright red nose, they will only remember what a mess you looked and not the food at all. What I like to be is a pragmatic perfectionist, a P.P. Do what you can with the time available. Anyway, anyone who is given hot food these days is jolly lucky, particularly if it isn't out of Marks & Sparks. Oops, mustn't advertise.'

2.4 million women, sitting all over Britain, relaxed. Bunny was one of them. She understood them. She did simple food that didn't make them feel inferior because their kitchens hadn't been upgraded since the seventies.

Yet what no one had ever realised or suspected was that Bunny had never ever really liked cooking all that much. She'd only ever done it in the first place because she'd been bored being a hotel receptionist and Marjorie, sitting under the drier one day at the hairdresser's, had read the small ads at the back of *Harpers & Queen* and thought that a cookery course would do wonderful things for her daughter's social connections.

And so Bunny, with her large body and fussy clothes, had been frog-marched into a sea of petite Sloane Rangers with blue velvet headbands and pearly teeth and after months of hell, had emerged well roasted and neatly Cordon Bleued with a profession, Sloane Square vowels and a chip on each shoulder, the latter only now having been filled in with layers of compressed cheques.

Bunny pushed the stuffed capon to one side, deftly brought out the ready cooked one. 'Now, as the actress said to the bishop, here's one I made earlier.' Too late, Bunny remembered that Jenna's current husband was the son of the new archbishop, who had just made a much-reported crack to the Queen about the C of E planning to put more bums on seats than the RSC. Jenna's smile became even tighter. Bunny said quickly, 'So here we are. It should be cooked for three hours for a seven-pound bird and it should be all gold and juicy. I suggest you serve it with brown rice and steamed broccoli and, of course, don't forget to use the juices to make a nice gravy. It does look really yummy.'

Jenna did not wade in with a fork as she usually did if it was a pudding, but looked at the dead flesh and then at the studio clock. '*Thank you*, Bunny!' She turned to camera two. 'In a few moments we'll be talking to Dr Henry Winterfield about the slimmers' disease, *bulimia*! And now it's over to Jo in the news room.'

The red light on the camera went off.

'Do people really eat that muck?' Jenna always let her Liverpudlian vowel sounds out, as well as her stomach muscles, as soon as she was off-camera.

'Jenna, it's an OK recipe, but then you're a veggieburger so what can I tell you?' Bunny was wiping her hands and leaving the mess for someone else to clear up.

'Bye bye, Bunny,' said Jenna sweetly. 'I do hope your dear Lottie Lennard and the tabloids don't do to you what you've just done to that poor bird.'

Bunny could not be bothered to answer. With her own new show starting next month, she hoped she would soon need Jenna like a hole in the head. Lottie permitting. Jenna walked back to the studio settee and sat down, pulling her skirt over her plump knees. She smiled professionally at the bulimia expert, who was now nervously straightening his bow tie and pulling his jacket across his paunch. 'Twenty seconds,' said the floor manager. The bulimia expert looked as if he was about to be sick . . .

'I'm off. Bye all.' Bunny took off her signature blue-and-white apron, and walked off the set.

'The capon looked super, Bunny. Jenna's just grouchy because the ratings are down.' Claire, Bunny's home economist, met her in the corridor outside her dressing room. She was holding a list. 'Are you doing spinach crêpes tomorrow?'

'Yes, that'll be fine. Must go. Meeting my publisher for an early lunch at the Groucho Club.'

'OK, see you tomorrow, Bunny. By the way, what happened to that cousin, the one who wore the red cape?'

'She now has two children, lives in Scotland and is a much better cook than I am, only don't tell anyone. Byee.'

Bunny whizzed down the corridor and the studio car was soon taking her back to the West End. Onwards and upwards.

CHAPTER FOUR

Mexico

Christopher Todd was sitting in the mezzanine of the Mexico City Hilton drinking black coffee, and reading the *Wall Street Journal*.

Mexican coffee is always gritty and catches at the back of the throat before the caffeine roars up the bloodstream and into the brain. It is part of its lethal charm. Glancing up, he could see the cleaners sweeping the street outside. He put another spoonful of sugar into his coffee and sipped.

At forty-eight, Christopher Todd was the sort of man other men called 'a safe pair of hands'. This did not mean that he was particularly safe, but that he was able to keep his emotions locked away safely, and didn't rock the boat. His office politics had always been discreet, and his loyalty to his employers absolute; 'a good sort'. With other men he was able to make small talk and play a reasonable round of golf. He was also a decent man, not without kindliness or good humour, though economical with both. And his life, safe in non-leaking, non-conflicting compartments, worked smoothly to everyone's satisfaction, including his own.

'Another coffee, if you please.'

The waiter, American trained, came up with a coffee pot. 'Have a nice day.'

Christopher shrugged and put down his newspaper then, opening his briefcase, took out the briefing document on the Mexican economy.

After twenty-five years as a merchant banker working for that hallowed pillar of the Scottish financial establishment the Edinburgh and Aberdeen Bank, known universally as the E & A, Christopher had been granted, just six months before, what his director had called 'a new opportunity'.

It was never made clear what would have happened had he refused, but the hint of a gun to his head was taken. The 'new opportunity' was an eighteen-month renewable secondment with the Cross Sectoral Cooperation Department, which had recently been set up at the World Bank to promote and then coordinate projects undertaken by the private and public sectors in third world countries for urban regeneration.

Whatever his fears, Christopher had embraced this new job in the way only a man could who had two families, eight credit cards, a large overdraft and a £340,000 mortgage. To his surprise Washington agreed with him. He enjoyed working with such a wide range of nationalities and learned to savour Vietnamese cuisine in the small restaurants around his office. Yet, instead of a safe commute from Chiswick into the City each day, he would find himself flying to the sorts of places which required pin-cushions for arms, so many were the inoculations required, and dealing with so many warring egos and Machiavellian politicians that the City now seemed, looking back, quite a pleasant and simple place to work.

Then a chance encounter with an old school chum sitting in a departure lounge at Heathrow had made him think of those other changes. 'Lucky you, Todders! At least you don't have to live in London any more. Will you buy a house over the border, and schmooze your way into a job in Edinburgh at the E & A, when the World Bank's finished with you?' This had set him thinking. Old Roger had that pale, overweight look of a man not long for this world. About two months, it had transpired.

By which time Christopher had offloaded the mortgage, paid off most of the credit cards and the last of the London school fees and, renting a cardboard box in Ealing, was feeling solvent for the first time in years. Someone at a party at Cazenove's had mentioned property auctions, so he had got his secretary to ring around and, in the third auction catalogue that had arrived, he had seen the Loanside house. It didn't matter where Sarah and the kids were going to live if he was going to be abroad most of the year. And Helen and the twins were now happily provided for.

Liddy had whinged a bit about losing her friends, but Sarah didn't seem upset at leaving her beloved Chiswick. She had got the bit between her teeth and had been determined to get the house because it had belonged to that Robertson man she had learned about at university. Bully for her for bidding like that. He'd trusted her not to go overboard and bid too much. God, it was good to be free from debt. First time in years.

Christopher straightened his back. His new life certainly had its compensations, one of which would be coming down in the lift in a few moments.

He glanced at his papers. Mexico was proving to be the usual story. Huge disparities of wealth and poverty. Twelve dollar billionaires and sixteen per cent of the population living in slums. Most of the poor were Indians, forced into sprawling city slums and working along the border in the *maquilladoras*, cheap assembly plants which were massed along the Rio Grande. Hey-ho. In this job he had found that in almost every country it was the same story. The private sector and government machinery were controlled pretty much by the same families. How to get them together to think about social cohesion and urban renewal and economic regeneration and all that caring sharing nineties' one-world stuff was the challenge.

Still, it was a nice warm gravy train if one didn't think too much about the conditions outside the hotel or the conference room. Scotland, Sarah and the noisy kids wittering on about removal men and Florence the canary, who had apparently fallen off her perch after only three days north of Hadrian's Wall, all seemed thankfully a long way away. It must be bloody cold there in October.

A familiar tip-tap of high heels on the marble came towards him. A slim woman with a large red mouth and cheekbones which seemed to fly up to the ceiling came towards him. He couldn't help himself; he felt instantly excited. Her Chanel red nails clutched a slim leather briefcase and she wore a pale blue suit. Milanese couture, he supposed. He could smell her perfume from ten feet away. Christopher stood up.

'Good morning, Maria Antonietta, all ready to meet Mr Finance Minister?'

'Of course, Christopher. I was reading up on him after I went to bed. He is called Mr Privatisation here.'

'Contessa Maria Antonietta Guicciardini?' A bellboy came running up with a message, which she took and read briefly and then turned to Christopher, who was now gathering up his papers, and smiled at him. 'You're looking very English today, Christopher. In fact I've decided you are getting more English with every month that goes by. Is your wife as English as you?'

'Sarah? Reasonably so I would say.'

She laughed, and together they went through the marble lobby and out into the street. The stench of the city's pollution caught at their throats, like the hotel coffee, in spite of the chill in the autumn air. As their car glided towards them, a street child, aged perhaps seven or eight, came running up, begging for money. She had straggly black hair, and long thin legs which protruded from a cheap nylon skirt. The doorman shoved her away roughly and the girl fell onto the pavement. Her eyes met Christopher's, pleading for attention. He steeled himself and followed Antonietta into the car. One simply could not give to every beggar. But in those eyes, for an instant, he had seen his daughter, Liddy, and then, strangely, Sarah when they had first met. She had been a young girl then, well, in her mid-twenties, with long brown hair swept up and a sweet lost expression, pounding out reports in his department at the E & A. How amazed he had been when he found out she had actually got a degree, stupefied when he learned it was a first.

He leaned back a bit on the limo's cushions. Maria Antonietta smiled across at him. Then, very carefully, she picked a hair from his collar and, with a snap of her red nails, dispatched it to the taxi floor. It was a simple gesture which thrilled him right down to his black silk socks. Which showed, Christopher supposed, that there was still life in the old dog yet.

Loanside

Sarah pushed at the car door. It opened just a little way, and then slapped back shut. This was ridiculous.

'Mummy, I'm cold, I don't *want* to go out!' Theo shouted from behind her in the back seat, 'I don't *want* to.'

'Theo, we have to get you some shoes and the shop is just here. Be patient, be a good boy.' Sarah tried again. Risking a leg, she shoved the door away from her and put her feet on the pavement. Leaves, papers, soft drink cans and a plastic bag came sweeping down Loanside high street, tangling violently with the street lights and the litter bins. Wind. Her new enemy. Push hard! She tried again and got the door wide open and got out, just, her hair now streaming in front of her so that she could hardly see.

An old St Andrews scene snapped into her mind. She had been on her way to lectures and the wind had whipped out both contact lenses, leaving her blind and lost in the middle of South Street. A familiar shape, Donald Gosford, had come up and led her by the hand, blind, a bit like St Paul into Damascus, back to her flat for her glasses. She even remembered the replacement price for the lenses, £10 each, and having to cut down to one meal a day for a month to pay for them.

Now, keeping her eyes half closed, Sarah shoved the car door shut before the wind outflanked her further and pushed her over. In the bitter cold, her teeth chattered. Thank God Liddy had found a friend to go to. Now for Theo. With her back to the enemy she opened his door, undid his seatbelt and, in spite of his struggles, hauled him out in front of her, shielding him from the wind. 'I'm cold, I'm cold.' Theo's little face was a blue circle inside his new balaclava, his voice barely audible under the wind's savage whistle.

She slammed the door, locked it and, with Theo still sheltering in front of her, staggered to the shoe shop door. It was locked! Is it half-day closing? Dimly through her hair, she saw people inside. It was open, so why had they locked it? She banged on the door. A woman came and undid the top bolt, opened it and Sarah and Theo burst inside. Some of the shoes in the window flung themselves out onto the grey carpet in sympathy.

'It's an awful cold day.' The woman, who was wearing a tweed skirt, was a model of understatement. 'I have to keep the door locked on days like this because otherwise it keeps blowing open. Can I help at all?'

'We've come for some winter shoes, size ten, black if you've got them.' Sarah automatically bent down to pick up some of the shoes on the ground.

'Och, leave that Mrs Todd, I'll do it. Size ten, you say? Do sit down and I'll go and check. You sit over there, wee boy.'

Sarah turned to sit down and found herself being examined by several women who smiled shyly at her and particularly at Theo. Mrs Todd. They knew her name.

'You'll be finding this weather we're having hard after being down south. There's an awful cold wind today,' said one.

'Yes, there is,' Sarah said, 'but it's such a nice town we're delighted to be here.' She had been saying that for the last five days since their arrival: an apology to ward off the fatigue of coping on her own and, in a way, to placate the curious stares she had met in the post office, at the school gates and at the checkout of the small shop everyone called the supermarket. And then Sarah realised that the women were sitting at small tables drinking coffee.

This was something she had never encountered before she'd come here to Loanside. All the shops seemed to have several functions. The petrol station sold locally made cakes, and the gift shop cut glass. The newsagent's would get your heels done and your drycleaning taken care of, while the greengrocer sold local paintings. Now here in the shoe shop there was coffee and home-made shortbread to be had at two or three small tables. And here too, as with any other business in the town, there were piles of leaflets with events and new courses, advertising local theatre and tours of stately homes. It was a sort of new way of thinking about the world, and shops and shopping; it took some getting used to.

After the anonymity of London, it was also unnerving that in just five days everyone knew her name and where she lived. Carnforth House, which had just seemed a handy bargain to Christopher, was seen here as a trophy property, its auction and repossession a quiet disgrace, a symbol of the town's decline. It hadn't even been bought by a local.

Then, there was her voice. Christopher had the rich marble tones of the public schoolboy which had simply thrilled her mother when she brought him back home. Doreen, in uncomprehending wonder, had listened for hours as he had talked about life at school and the City. He had been head boy at St Anthony's when Bunny's Edward had been just an inky first year and Doreen, enthralled, had showed him off to all her friends like a prize parrot. But Sarah's own vowel sounds had always seemed ordinary until this week, when they had cut through every conversation like a cheese wire. Silly billy. She had emigrated and no one had told her.

Theo, newly equipped with shiny black shoes, stomped about the shop causing more smiles around the coffee cups. Yet, kind as they were, Sarah decided that she was not ready to join them.

'How much is that?'

'£29.99, Mrs Todd, thank you.'

'What a price for a wee boy's shoes! How do families manage?'

'It's a problem, Mary. Do you have a banker's card, Mrs Todd? Thank you.'

'You stay at Carnforth House? My mother used to tell me tales when Archie Milne Robertson himself was still living there in the 1920s.' The oldest of the women spoke up for the first time and looked straight at Sarah.

'Oh yes?'

'She used to work in the restaurant which was where the music centre is now. He would come in for his lunch sometimes when his wife was away. My mother used to complain he used to come in with his hands still covered with that clay stuff from the pottery. She would make him go and wash his hands or there would be no steak pie for him.'

The woman laughed. Sarah imagined the huge, flamboyant Archie being scolded and sent to the taps to wash his hands like a small boy. She picked up the plastic bag containing the shoes with some of the leaflets near the till and, taking Theo's hand, smiled to everyone to say goodbye. Outside, the thought that she hoped that she had made a good impression fled, half-complete, as the icy wind bit.

The shoes were a success, even if the wind was not, and Theo wore them to school next day without complaint. The phone was ringing as Sarah came back into the house. It was Bunny.

'Are my flowers still alive, Sarah? You must be freezing up there. We've had to turn the heating up in London, which is ridiculous as it's only October.'

'Has been. No, it's sunny today. Bunny, the flowers are beautiful, and thanks for sending them. Did you get my card?'

Sarah fingered the cream roses, which still bloomed expensively on the hall table. They represented something, she knew; all of Bunny's gestures were always for effect. But which, victory or dismissal?

'Yes. The least I could do for my cousin leaving civilisation. Listen, I'm ringing now because my spot is on in ten minutes, and I can't remember what we used to call your mother's jam roly-poly? You know, at Primary School?'

'Gold Star pudding, because she only made it if we both got over fifty gold stars by the end of term.'

'That's it. Couldn't remember. I knew we used to get it for some reason at the end of term. It was very good. I hope my girl's done it properly. Imagine if I undo the foil to find it's mushy – on live television.'

'Don't you cook it yourself?'

'Course not. I'm just showing you how to do it. I don't actually have to *do* it myself.'

'Oh, silly me.'

'So what are you doing today?'

'Clearing out yet more boxes; waiting in for the joiner and the plumber.'

'Poor you. I have a meeting with the producers for a new show, which is going to be filmed on location in different places doing different local foods. Sounds a nightmare of indigestion. The first is in Suffolk. And then I've got to get back to the office because eight Japanese are doing a one-day English cooking course. I'll do Yorkshire pudding with them and then we'll have lunch together. I'm also supposed to be opening a supermarket in Raynes Park at three p.m. Can't wait. And then I'm going to a party at the IBA tonight. It's difficult because I'm coping without my number two, you know Lottie, she's away.'

'I saw about her in the paper. Was it a problem, for you I mean?'

'No, not after the first couple of days because he resigned and no one spoke to the press so there was nothing for the door-steppers to do,' replied Bunny. 'Of course, the arrival of Madonna in London helped. All the doorsteppers decamped to the Lanesborough. Must go.'

To Sarah, Bunny's voice and life came down the line, crackling with such adrenalin. She knew that Bunny had given her a two-minute window, received the information she needed and was now impatient to ring off. What must it be like to run a business and go to parties in one's own right? And have money in one's own bank account and never to have to ask for it?

'Yes, you had better go, Bunny.'

'Yes. I'm in my dressing room at the moment. Jenna is interviewing some psychic who has just told her she'll be experiencing a change of life soon, which sounds promising. She's had a face like fizz since seven-thirty. Roly-poly pudding will possibly finish her off. Bye now.'

Greetings from another world where people sent fifty cream roses. Bunny had Made It. Yet, who had been the bright, clever one? Who had always got twice as many gold stars each term? And who had been the one with all that confidence and all the flair in spite of all the noise Bunny made? The Grammar School girl in the family. Sarah went downstairs into the huge, cold kitchen. With one eye on the small TV, she cleared up the breakfast dishes, fed the cat and washed the floor. Bunny appeared just as she was about to clear the gulls' mess outside on the kitchen windows. The sound was too low to hear, but Sarah could see that Bunny was turning in a bravura performance. She was mixing ingredients in a bowl, and laughing and talking to a well-known actress who was obviously a guest on the show.

'—in Scotland now. I hope she will be providing you with some good Scottish recipes for my new show. Have a turn, Laura.'

Sarah was horrified, 'Bunny, shut up!' she shouted at the set. The actress, Laura Marchant, stirred unenthusiastically and, of course, flour spilled onto her navy dress. She looked coldly at Bunny, but Sarah knew Bunny would just go on having fun and spilling flour and egg yolk everywhere, sweeping everyone along with her before depositing them, exhausted, into the 9.30 news break.

Sarah wiped all the kitchen surfaces, and dusted the dishes on the dresser. She heard Bunny talk of her childhood and this cousin in Scotland with false affection, clearly aimed, she supposed, at the middle-aged audience who would watch her show and buy her books. Bunny was so ruthless, she would cheerfully divulge safely forgotten memories on TV just for a punchline or to sell more books. Bunny had always been too big and loud, too overwhelming. And jealous. Once, playing hockey, Bunny had nearly killed her. 'Dribble the ball over to the bucket,' their teacher had said, and Bunny had practically flattened her in an effort to get there first.

Now who was scraping the sides of the bowl in the studio and laughing with household names, earning small fortunes from opening supermarkets? Who was scraping the muesli bowl at Loanside and wondering when the joiner would come? Who was now jealous of whom?

She put on her coat and, taking a mug of coffee and the post, went out into the garden now filled with autumn sunlight, and walked down to the bottom. She unlocked the back gate and then sat on the stone steps looking at the waves. Far out over the sea, a streak of pink light stretched, like a leg, across the sky. Cradling her coffee in her hand, she could smell the raw seaweed, and the salt air, and see in the distance dogs running over the sand and the stones. A paradise bounded only by familiar demon thoughts.

She pulled the post out of her pocket. There was a bill, a piece of junk mail and an envelope addressed to Mrs Sarah Todd. She opened it and pulled out an invitation. For her. To a private view of work by Zander Milne Robertson. He was an artist! Then she remembered those square-ended fingers. He had been surprised that anyone had ever heard of his grandfather. The private view was in two weeks' time, and he had thought of her. Houses are never possessed, only loaned, she had told him, and she remembered how he had looked down at her, smiling.

Suddenly she found her hands were shaking, though not from the cold, for the wind had fallen and the sun, though low, was warm on her face. She put the mug down. Hunched up on the steps, the new mistress of Carnforth House hugged herself and rocked to and fro, still shocked by her own stupidity and turning her hands over and over, as if moulding clay, over and over in grief.

CHAPTER FIVE

Rome

If this was supposed to be the age of information technology, could someone please tell him why the world was still so full of scrappy bits of paper? Christopher adjusted his earphones and looked around him, a bleary sea of documents and paper. The man on the podium, French, was whining on and on. The subject? The Synergy of Cross-Sectoral Cooperation. Whatever that meant. Everyone knew the French never cooperated with anyone if they could help it. All these bored, middle-aged people sitting around in a semicircle. Nearly all men, except the Russian tank and some dotty dottir from Iceland. Maria Antonietta had bunked off this one to go and see some cousin. In Italy she seemed more complicated and alluring than ever, as well as unattainable.

Christopher sat there trying not to yawn the sort of gorilla-like yawn which is unstoppable in mid-stretch. His life was now filled with good phrases and good works. Human development, environmentally sustainable development, and private sector development: the three legs of the World Bank stool, which anyway was not just one institution but made up of five institutions, all with competing empires and agendas. He had done his fair share of knocking heads together for the good of the midwives of Honduras and the literacy rates of Indonesia's Magetan, and would presumably therefore get his reward in heaven. But it was still odd, after a lifetime moving large amounts of money about, and making not a little himself, to have turned, albeit briefly, into a civil servant, a public administrator accountable to 180 member countries. His own small department, tucked away in a crevice, was not immune to the self-justifying bureaucratic volcanoes which went off at regular intervals throughout the organisation.

Long ago, when his mother had packed him off to boarding school, Christopher had discovered the usefulness of keeping his life in hermetically sealed compartments. This blazingly unoriginal discovery had come when he was eight, on a train going off, yet again, to boarding school after the Christmas term. The leaving would always take place at Paddington station, with hundreds of little boys being herded onto the train by tearful mothers, rarely fathers. It was always so embarrassing when one's mother blubbed, and he had begged his own not to embarrass him. He shouldn't have worried. His mother never did. She always pushed his case into the train and gave him a perfunctory kiss, then stood back on the platform, dutifully waiting for the train to pull out. In the winter, her breath streamed out in the cold air as she exhorted the other mothers to bear up. They were feeble creatures compared to his tall and dry-eyed mater. And then the train would move off and that would be that for three months, apart from a brief visit from his parents for a cream tea down in the town. Yet sometimes he had wished that she had shown she would miss him.

Once he had got into a state, and Motter, the Latin master, had grasped him by the collar and had shoved him to the end of the train, past all the other boys, sniggering and pretending not to snivel themselves, until at last they had reached the lavatory. All through the separate compartments down the long corridors. First class, full of businessmen with crisp white antimacassars and crisp white newspapers. Smoking compartments where they were smoking pipes and cigars. Ladies Only carriages, full of shopping bags spilling over into the corridor. And then third class, poorer people, some smoking smelly Woodbines which had made him cough. And then he had been pushed into the lavatory and told to pull himself together.

How cold his knees had been in his school shorts, there in

the icy, unheated lav. And trying to get the snot off his blazer sleeve and splash cold water on his face. And how he had been too short to reach the mirror, and how he had thought just how much he would be teased. Which he had been for days afterwards. After this, he had made jolly sure he never cried. Without being aware of what he was doing, he had ever afterwards kept everything separate for efficiency. Separate compartments with separate doors for going in and coming out. Earning a living, enjoying the money he made, Sarah and the kids, New York friends, London friends and, of course, a new compartment, shiny and exciting, Maria Antonietta. What a long train his life was becoming. Snig-snagging its way across the world. Choo-Choo! And in front, Thomas the Tank Engine the Really Useful Engine. There had never been a train in the books called Christopher, sadly.

Suddenly the man on the podium stepped down to thin applause, and the chairman stood up. '*Allora basta signori! Mangiamo la pasta!*' About time. And didn't *Signor* Fiori look just like the Fat Controller, so self-important and about to burst the buttons of his double-breasted suit? Christopher was pleased with himself. He'd have to share that one. He liked good nicknames. If kept in use, they could last a lifetime. There were so few things in life one could be passionate about. Safely.

London

For Bunny, these sort of 'dos' were the up-market nineties equivalent of a Tupperware party. All over Teresa's ornate drawing room, tables of expensive jewellery, dirt cheap Italian silk scarves, hand printed, Hungarian paperweights and the most chic little knick-knacks from Estonia were clustered temptingly near a small forest of shiny bags. Squeals of delight, as fake or genuine as the goods, were a prerequisite. And at regular intervals, as if by magic, more divine little finds would be produced from the nanny's room. More squeals, then yet more Guccied, siliconed and freshly rehormoned ladies rang at the doorbell. How they whooped for joy at seeing each other after so long . . . two days at least since the last dinner party. How they earnestly mwowwed into the perfumed air in order to save their own lipstick and each other's emotions. And how daintily they toyed with delicious morsels, knocked up by some sweet little (cheap) Filipino toiling in the bowels of the house.

'What absolutely super taste you have darling!' Everyone said the same to Teresa, who was looking as if she were the favourite girl in the class. Was this *clac* paid in paperweights, or was it simply the natural acclamation due for having carried off someone else's husband, who owned, practically, a whole merchant bank? Bunny could not decide; she just thought she probably would never know what it was to be so popular. Not with these women. She sat by the window, for once not the centre of attention, her own bag of shiny knick-knacks having earned her a seat, a Chippendale naturally, and from here she could sip her champagne and rest her red Blahnik shoes and the sore feet inside. As well as any stray raw nerves which might have been accidentally trodden on in the show. For, in spite of all her years of schmoozing and carousing with both rich acts and class acts, there was always the unspoken fear that the social denouement might begin when she least expected it. A silly fear really, for she had in fact long ago discovered that it was only beautiful women who had the whistle blown on them. Big ugly ones, however well dressed, weren't worth being jealous about.

Outside over Chelsea the early evening sky was glowing, dark and menacing, threatening rain just to show the poor sods beetling through the rush hour who was boss. Between the two blocks of mansion flats opposite, she could just make out in the distance the ridiculous bulk of Battersea power station, and low strings of lamps hanging along the Thames Embankment which always hinted at the endless possibilities of a capital.

Edward had once taken her to a corporate bash on a boat bobbing by the bank. It had seemed to her so glamorous and exciting, until she had sampled the sausage rolls and had ended up selling her services to the PA's secretary while everyone else from the firm had been dancing to Dire Straits. She had wanted to be introduced to people instead of just standing there, large and awkward, on the edge of groups, but Edward had been up on deck, knocking back the tequila. In the end, she had to half-carry him up the gangplank, a horrid end to an evening, and the feelings of anger and shame inside her had knotted themselves like a towrope. It had been the last party she had ever gone to as Edward's wife, as his guest. But the river, at least, still held its allure.

In front of her a bunch of expensively tailored behinds, Lottie's among them, were bent over boxes, quivering with aggression like eager players in a scrum. Perhaps thirty women in there, heads down, scoring for Christmas. It was a sort of ritual soothing of their extravagant consciences, so comforting that they were picking up bargains that would not have the Beauchamp Place mark-ups. Though Bunny put the odds at three to one that they would all end up forgetting who had been here, and giving each other the same thing for Christmas.

Automatically she did the costings of the canapés and the champagne. At least £6 per head if everyone had two glasses of this stuff. None of your sparkling méthode cheapoise in this bit of Chelsea. How could Teresa really make any money this evening? Then there was the cost of the air fares to Italy to scout round all these diddy little jewellery workshops, always described as tucked away in some exclusive Tuscan village. These twice-yearly jaunts were, she suspected, the excuse for getting away from the two late-life twins who now had a weekend as well as a weekday nanny. And then of course any profit would go into Teresa's bank account, and the cost of the food and travel would come off her husband's, who was so rich he didn't care as long as Teresa was off the booze and had something to talk about at dinner parties. It was all a game. Lucky Teresa, able to play at working just like Marie Antoinette, herding up society sheep at the Trianon.

But, of course, it was still the home-selling principle: hard sell to friends, usually ones with less money than you, who wanted to keep in with you. Her own mother, Marjorie, had taken home-selling deadly seriously, for years. Tupperware! All those little plastic bowls with their wonderful tight-fitting lids laid out all over the purple shagpile, and all the neighbours on their hands and knees making swooning noises. This had been a regular event when Bunny had been small. She would be told not to be clumsy but to pass around the fig rolls to the neighbours to jolly them along. Even then, young as she had been, she had been aware of the greedy glint in her mother's eyes, and seen the heavily ringed fingers counting up the cash at the end when the last woman had gone and the stock had been pushed in plastic bags under the stairs. After she had gone to high school, her mother had gone on to greater heights, becoming the most successful Avon Lady in Surrey. Ding dong! Marjorie calling with the new plum-coloured lip gloss.

When would Lottie finish piling up the silk scarves? Just like climbing Everest, she always bought this stuff because it was there. Who could compete with Lottie for flashing the cash for bargains? Or Lottie red in claw fighting in the china department on the last day of Harrods' sale. Bunny could still picture the young male assistant's face, pale with shock except for the livid marks of Lottie's fingernails. And when they had finally emerged on to Brompton Road, fighting for breath with the £29 tea set, she had announced that she hated Bavarian china. Who didn't? This was not the first occasion Bunny had been tempted to hurl Lottie under the wheels of a passing taxi. She was surely living on borrowed time!

'Pasta parcels are stale.' A thin woman, dangling a Dior bag the size of a postage stamp, came up to Bunny and sat down. Long red nails hovered, dissatisfied, over a small plate in her hand. The very serious flash of a square-cut emerald caught the light.

'Over a day old, I think. Have we met? I'm Bunny Halifax.'

'No we haven't, but I watch your show. Trust Teresa to give us yesterday's Save The Children Fund leftovers.'

'Oh, does she do that as well?'

'Save The Children? Probably not, poor little buggers. Personally I prefer the M.E. lot, they give such energetic parties. How are you? I'm Penelope Wincanton.'

Bony fingers were extended briefly. As in the race course, Bunny would have liked to have said, but didn't. For sadly you cannot buy insouciance in a shiny bag at a merchant banker's house or even on a good day at Harrods, however high your TV profile, or large your income. If you have a husband who gambles each afternoon away on horseflesh, the price is too high. So Bunny smiled her professional smile instead.

'My husband and yours were at St Anthony's together, did you know? My husband was lying in bed with toothache last week channel hopping and saw you with that terrible oiky Jenna Grace. And then he suddenly said, "Did you know that rabbit woman is married to old Yorkshire Pudding?" As in Halifax, you know. Why are men such babies? How is he? Johnny would love to know.'

And still smiling, as shinily as the bags spread all around her feet, Bunny said that Edward Was Fine. As one does, just before imbibing a large something of an alcoholic nature.

'You are sweet to let me stay the night Bunny. I'd never get up in time for a 6.30 a.m. dishing up otherwise. Aren't power breakfasts a simply horrifying idea?'

'Revolting, but molto high margin. So, how much did you spend, at Teresa's then, Lottie?'

'£353. And now all my Christmas buying is done, I can just relax and go to parties. What about you?'

'Do I have to answer that?'

'Yes, Bunny. You do.'

'£420. But in my defence can I say that I am going away for Christmas and I hate shopping?'

'Liar, you're worse than I am. Where are you going?'

'Frozen Scotland.'

'Bunny you'll die of the cold. You're mad.'

'I'm not. I need to get right away from the telephone. And my cousin Sarah, who is very nice and hugely unambitious, will make me feel successful, exciting and energetic. She always does. And her husband, while a prize striped-shirted bastard, actually manages to jolly Edward into some sort of normality. They'll be able to talk about the good old days they had at school and pretend to each other they enjoyed them. Anyway, Sarah actually likes cooking.'

'You mean she does it for *nothing*?'

'I rest my case. Now where are my keys?'

It is hard hobbling down a gravel path with lots of carrier bags on the outside and too much champagne within, but Lottie and Bunny were being heroic about it. The cab driver had clearly thought asking him to go south of the river as far as darkest Clapham Common was enough of a favour at 11 p.m. without helping them decant their possessions up the path to the front door. But at least it was a clear night, cold in a civilised London sort of way. For in the unlikely event that you are not mugged or knifed, in London there is always the added consolation that the Underground acts as a giant electric underblanket on the city's temperature.

Inside the hall all was as usual. The sort of Victorian meets art deco meets old class meets the Hamptons 'Look', which Bunny had put in at great expense last year, struck her as rather fine as they came though the door from the darkness outside. However, Bunny noticed it instantly, and knew it meant trouble. Sitting there like a large black Kafkaesque dung beetle was a motor bike crash helmet. Shiny and challenging, belonging to someone new, belonging to Hannah. From upstairs she could hear Brunhilde strutting her stuff from Edward's Wagner collection. He was still awake, then. And downstairs in the kitchen?

Some time afterwards, Lottie told Bunny it had taken her just one zygo-second to decide that the young man had the right name and would be a sensation. But then, Lottie always had gone for thin men with tight little bums and questionable morals. And on this evening, the net curtains of Bunny's childhood conditioning twitched as they always did when meeting any of her daughter's friends.

In the kitchen, all was white tiles and silence. Hannah, who was sitting with her legs resting on the kitchen table, did not look up from her *Evening Standard*.

'Hello, Hannah. Are you going to introduce us?' Bunny could feel her bright mummy's voice grating on her daughter's ear, but what the hell could she say?

'Mum, this is Studd. Studd, my mum and her sidekick Lottie.'

'Colleague, Hannah sweetie, colleague. How do you do?' And Lottie, the indefatigable Lottie, bore down on the young man, who was leaning over looking through Bunny's cookery book collection.

'Hiya.' Bunny groaned at his estuary vowel sounds.

'What did you buy at snotty Teresa's then, Mum? Has she had those brats put into care yet?'

'Hannah! She loves the boys. I just bought stuff for Christmas.'

'Cool.'

'Which reminds me, I meant to tell you, Sarah has invited us to go to Scotland for Christmas. What do you think?'

'No way.'

Bunny did not know how he did it. She saw Hannah look at this Studd boy's back and, although he did not turn round – he was far too much into the soufflés section of *Bunny Cooks Your Dinner!* – she could feel his very stillness was telling Hannah to refuse. Who was this whippet in a leather jacket?

'We're going out now.'

'Hannah, it's ten o'clock, you have college tomorrow.'

'Well, *you* have to work tomorrow and it hasn't stopped you getting pissed at snotty Teresa's, has it?'

'Don't keep calling her that. But really you can't go out. Studd I'm sorry but—'

'Night, Mum. We're just going clubbing for a bit. Don't wait up.'

'Hannah! Hannah!'

But she didn't want a row in front of the young man. She didn't want to lose any more face. And in pain she watched their feet going up the white wrought-iron spiral staircase, black leather boots on white, out of sight up the stairs into the hall.

'Should have asked them if they had their E in their pocket

and not to speak to any strangers.' Lottie had lit up a cigarette and was making herbal tea.

'But Lottie, she's only sixteen!'

'She's very nearly seventeen, Bunny, and a London seventeen at that. And you can't be superwoman and nursemaid at the same time. She can leave home now if she wants to. You shouldn't have sprung going to the frozen north on her like that. She couldn't afford to lose a fight with you in front of him. So he's won. For the moment. Give in gracefully.'

'No, I won't. Hannah! Come back!' Bunny was shouting. Then the front door slammed. 'Will she ride on his bike? Will he have a spare helmet? What am I supposed to do? You and I both have to be up at five to organise the Baring's do. And he has dirty fingernails! Why can't her bloody father ever do any parenting round here? Always those bloody racehorses.'

'Bunny, calm down. She's bigger than he is, don't worry. And she could go for someone much worse. I rather fancy younger men I've decided. Did you see his smile? He has great teeth. And he was obviously interested in your books. Anyway, you can't expect Edward to be a parent; he was sent away to school at the age of six and has closed down emotionally in consequence.'

'Oh, spare me the therapy session, Lottie.'

Lottie, ever the child psychologist for the very good reason she did not have any children of her own, whacked a consolatory dollop of brandy into Bunny's herbal tea, while down from the top floor Edward's Valkyries flew on gilded wings. Mockingly. Bit late in the day for the motherhood bit, isn't it *Liebling*?

Isle of Margarita, Venezuela

5.30 a.m. Christopher was lying in bed watching the dawn rushing up with Latin American impetuosity over the sea outside. Next to him, Maria Antonietta's breathing was in rhythm. Breathe in, sun comes up whoosh! Breathe out, a cloud passes by the sun. Breathe in, another dazzling glimpse of blue sea. Breathe out! . . . He felt hugely content. Replete. Nice word.

On the desk by the window his briefcase leered at a drunken angle. Inside was a secret which made Christopher feel far more guilty than his recent betrayal of his marriage vows. *Director World Bank Agency*, the ad in this month's *Economist*, now stuffed down to the bottom, had struck him like a thousand volts. *Remuneration US$*202647 (without dependents), $206201 (with dependents), rental subsidy, dependency allowance, education allowance for children, repatriation grant, employer's contribution to pension fund, 5 weeks' annual vacation, private medical insurance, return home flight every 2 years etc. The goodies in the package were every middle-aged man's Christmas wish list. And the letter to Santa Claus, alias Friedrich Gutmeyer Vice-President, would arrive with his newly minted c.v. in Washington in the morning.

'Dear Santa, please give me an international life, a healthy six-figure income and rid me of the feeling that I am a forty-eight-year-old E & A Bank has-been. Love Christopher. Aged forty-eight and a three-quarters. He laughed softly at his own joke, causing the woman to turn over, restlessly. Of course, Maria Antonietta could not possibly be told. No one must know.

He was not by nature the unfaithful type, not because he was especially virtuous, but because he was far too tired half the time. But here he was with the most gorgeous woman he had ever met, on a Caribbean island far from the crowded, frozen island in the North Sea where both his families past and present lived. Anyway, no one would get hurt. What man would not give his right arm for such a woman, curving like a Titian masterpiece over the white sheets?

He had experimented away at school, of course. Who hadn't? He had been infatuated with a prefect who was now on the threshold of Cabinet office, but he had never been deeply driven in that direction. On the other hand, women tended to make him nervous; it had taken him years to learn to flirt in the approved upper-class male avuncular manner. When, at twenty-seven, he did finally find himself married to Helen with his mother's full connivance, he had been devoted to her, out of sheer relief rather than anything else.

They had been married seven years, when she had casually suggested over cocktails one evening at the Dorchester that they should get a divorce. This had been his first inkling that their marriage was in difficulties. At first he had thought there was another man, which would have been painful but more understandable. But there wasn't, apparently. Then, for one sickening instant, he had thought it was a woman. Helen a lesbian! One read about it all the time, death to a fellow's *amour propre*. But no, that was not in Helen's emotion range either. Thank God.

Apparently she wanted another life entirely independent of his. The twins, now five, were at pre-prep school with their own lives largely mapped out by nanny and, as they all barely saw him except for occasional weekends, she could not really see why an amicable divorce would be a problem. Nothing need change except that it would free them up, as she put it, for new partners, fresh career opportunities, and children who would not see their parents beginning to row because they really had so very little in common. It could all be terribly civilised. She had been offered the editorship of *My Lady* magazine, which was just ripe for a relaunch as an upmarket glossy for the thinking thirty-five-plus woman. After years of marking time with two pre-school tinies, she was going for the burn. Margaret Thatcher had read for the Bar with twins, so why shouldn't she?

His mother, of course, when he had reported back, had given him hell.

'Go after her, Christopher; assert yourself for once in your life. Woo her back, for God's sake.' She had come down the phone at him in the same voice with which she had raged at him from the side of the rugger pitch. 'Tackle the man!' she would bellow at him on the rare occasion she came to see his team play. And so he had tackled Helen. Unsuccessfully. As had his mother. Ditto. And then the bank had sent him to Venezuela and a few months later, after signing a few forms, he too had been free, although at some cost. And a little bit of hurt too, underneath, though neither his mother nor his friends had ever understood why he had been so acquiescent. He hadn't liked to ask if he had bored her, or why she had not been able to love him. He hated scenes, as dear Helen knew.

Quite how he had managed to remarry someone else only a year after the divorce had come through was never quite explained to his or anyone's satisfaction, least of all to his mother, who had never given up hope that Helen would see sense given time. She had not approved of Sarah, who had always done her best, but had never quite measured up on the social breeding front. But something about needing to be needed, being looked up to as the all-providing male, had brought it all about. At a cost. Another large house in Bedford Park to fund, then somehow two more children with the Todd name and more school fees on top of the twins' whack. One Christmas term, when he had to sign over £20,000 in cheques, with considerable help from the bank manager, the need for an escape route had become obvious. Funny how life went in circles; now here he was back in heaven-scented Venezuela.

Silently, red nails, then long fingers, then a hand and then an arm slid like a snake around his neck. In its coil Christopher turned to nuzzle into the warm, demanding skin. Two half-thoughts, something about being hung for a sheep as a lamb and something silly and schoolboyish about on-the-job perks, rushed through his brain before he fell, helplessly, to paradise.

CHAPTER SIX

Loanside

She felt these days like a pioneer woman, one of the feisty ladies in need of face powder, who once hacked their way through the Wild West to California. Sarah had never felt so alone and so less married in her life. There were no signposts to follow, no one even to compete with. This hugely cold and fascinating house had far more history than was good for it; though she had never been the least bit psychic, she could feel the dramas imprinted on the walls. And, if it wasn't haunted by Archie strutting around with dried clay in his beard, then it should be, given the number of small Robertson bits left. How many clues wedged into forgotten corners had she uncovered in her role as skivvy-in-chief? How many strange carved cupboards had she tackled, all silted up with dust and forgotten rubbish?

Outside, the October gales smashed against the brickwork, and the tattered remnant of a clematis flailed around outside the window panes. It was dark, although it was only 11 a.m. The electric lights were switched on and so was the heating, which normally dutifully switched itself off as soon as the children left for school. And then, to fill the house with volume, there was the washing machine mashing its contents down in the kitchen, and radios loudly sprinkling unknown voices in every room. Even in the hall Theo's cassette recorder played Richmal Crompton's *Just William* tapes. And still she was as lonely as hell. And still she foraged in yet more dust and cobwebs. She began to feel sympathy for Violet Elizabeth Bott. 'I'll scrweem and scweem until I'm thick. And I can,' went the modulated voice on the tape. 'So can I,' said Sarah back. Then she pulled out a magazine. *Big Tits Monthly*. Great. Just what she needed.

The problem was she had no idea at all what they were all doing here, in this beautiful part of the world, filled with kindly caring people, to whom they obviously did not belong. Christopher, when he bothered to ring, spoke of a new contract with the World Bank. The whole idea of settling down at Edinburgh HQ to see out the years before retirement was obviously a deeply boring prospect, and one she could not discuss with him down the crackling lines. And the children, battling and feeling foreigners for the first time, would look at her, bewildered. And the wind would drive them into tears and recriminations. And then there were so many new signals to make and to understand. And all three of them kept making mistakes out of ignorance, and out of talking too much and trying to please too much.

Take wheelie bins. The children had never seen wheelie bins before now. They were green and neat and obedient, wheeled out onto the pavement each Wednesday for the wheeliemen. Then Calum and Ken, the wheelie bin men, would come and lift them into the council refuse truck and deposit them back lightly on the pavement. There was often a race to see who in the street was the tidiest and the first to wheel them back into their usual place. The Todds were always last.

Then there was the strange local habit of leaving babies outside shops while their mothers went in to shop. Used to London parental paranoia, this continued to strike Sarah as incredible. Then there were the small children, perhaps a four-year-old and a six-year-old, allowed to walk by themselves to school. All the children went to school on their own, and cheery lollipop ladies, swallowed up in yellow PVC, would manage a smile, even in force eight gales, and shepherd children across roads to school. All rather incredible to two chauffeured London princelings.

And then there were the huge numbers of active churches. Six for a population of six thousand people. And the manna from heaven richness of public spending in the libraries, schools and hospitals and GPs. All laid on and expected. Miraculous after years living through London's swingeing public spending cuts.

Then dress codes. Every time she was invited out she would turn up in the wrong outfit. At one coffee morning she arrived wearing a casual skirt and jumper, only to be greeted by crisply dressed ladies sporting jewellery and the latest in designer tweeds. The following evening she had gone to the village musical dressed up to the nines, to find everyone in old trousers and floppy jumpers.

And meals. She had forgotten this from her student days, that tea meant high tea, and supper meant cakes and a cup of tea at 8 p.m. Dinner would be eaten early in winter at about 5.30. Then the whole business of thank-you letters was a minefield. Being well-trained by Doreen, she had written thank-you letters for herself and for the children for every coffee morning or children's party they were invited to. Liddy's birthday party – five little girls to the cinema and a pizza afterwards – had gone well considering, and yet she never ever received thank-you letters back. She had been hugely offended until she realised that thank-you letters were just not part of the culture. You said thank you to someone's face and that was enough.

Where do you stay? This meant where do you live, without any implication of impermanence. 'I'll get you up the road' did not mean you would meet a person at the end of the road but that they would walk along with you. And although she was prepared, yet again, for being English and therefore an outsider, there were distinctions which had never been part of her student experience for there had been so many English students at St Andrews. Here there were the exuberant west coasters who had come in to work in the large engineering plant, and the canny east coast many-a-mickle brigade and native Loansiders. Two other camps were the commuters to Edinburgh, and those who worked locally, with two very different sets of aspirations.

The growing influx of English subdivided into proto-Scots (I'm a quarter Scots, Granny was born in Selkirk actually), and those honest to goodness English who never bought a Scottish newspaper on principle. Those from northern England were tolerated. They, too, had suffered at the hands of a distant Westminster. Worst of the lot, though, were the southern English who had moved up from London. They pushed up the property prices, drove too fast, demanded avocados and ciabatta in the local shops, and complained about the slowness of everything and wanted the FT delivered. Sarah would cringe at their forthright voices and had learned to scuttle about with her collar up. Yet they were often the friendliest to her, and they were arriving in increasing numbers as news of the good schools spread south of the border to burdened middle classes impoverished by school fees or lousy state schools. Carpet baggers.

Sarah had recognised all these distinctions in the first few weeks of being in Loanside and had catalogued them in her mind like a well-trained art historian finding a new pile of pictures. Zander Robertson had come round several times, knocking on the door usually when the children were back from school. He owned a couple of shop premises here in the High Street, apparently. He would listen to all her new impressions, usually leaning against the old dresser down in the kitchen, and then tease her, saying that she was making Loanside sound far more exciting than it actually was. Yet, she knew she was living through what a cursing Chinese would call interesting times. Discomforting when you were apparently a single parent with two of the most confused children in Britain and a father whose flightpath never included Scotland.

She did her best. Liddy was signed up for drama, ballet, violin and Brownies, while Theo went in for swimming and pottery. So her life was still a mass of small but nonetheless challenging logistical feats, ferrying them around to classes and being three places at once, just as she had in London although now this was done in a much smaller area. And then there was the local L.E.T.S., a local exchange currency scheme which enabled people to earn and spend Lollops, the local currency. One Lollop apparently equalled £1. She had thought it was a joke at first, and could hear inside her head what fun Christopher would have with such an off-the-wall, and what he would have described as a 'horribly downmarket', idea. So she hadn't told him when he had rung up sounding so pleased with himself from Venezuela.

L.E.T.S. was terribly clever. A would pay B to babysit, who would then spend their Lollops on C who provided garden maintenance. The directory offered Mexican cooking, computer tuition, even flying lessons (mega Lollops). Sarah was soon earning Lollops from home baking, and in turn bought computer tuition on her own new computer, and learned how to use the Internet, which was still terribly new and revolutionary to her as well as the rest of Loanside. She couldn't wait to e-mail Christopher! Her teacher, Eleanor Mackie, who ran the Loanside Museum with little support and absolutely no money, would come round to the house and afterwards share a bottle of wine while they planned imaginary exhibitions.

But she was also learning just how tired she had been in London. How exhausted the city had made her feel, although it had been years since she had had to earn a living. Now she could drive for miles through the Lammermuir Hills without ever meeting another car, and walking along the beach on the other side of the garden wall would refresh her soul in ways no Chiswick beautician could have managed. And strangely, in spite of feeling an intense loneliness, the decisions she now had to make alone were giving her a new courage. Many women of her age would be in a rut, doing the same things day after day, while she, for the first time in many years, was being forced to find answers. So she had gone ahead and invited Bunny and Edward and Hannah for Christmas. Bunny and she were no longer close, but they were still family. Not that Bunny would want to come, with all the exciting places she must be invited to. Still, she had been asked in spite of what Christopher would say. For the need for people to fill this old house drove her on.

One day, at the bottom of a cupboard, right at the back, she found another Robertson mould. This time for a long thin vase. So far she had found three, big yellowish white things wrapped up in cloth and shoved in the backs of cupboards. She took it upstairs to what had been Archie's studio. On the large table there were now several dozen fragments of green and gold lustred pottery, obviously from his later period, prised out from window frames and from behind radiators, plus the moulds and the broken and half-rotten wooden animals which the children had managed to bring in from the ark. Amazing that there was anything left at all in this climate.

On the table was also the card for that evening's private view. She could not imagine why Zander Robertson had invited her except out of politeness or pity. Odd name. And she hadn't a clue what to wear; she would get it wrong whatever she put on. The whole Robertson mythology bit was still too much. Sarah switched on the CD player in the corner; a loud blast of thoroughly English Elgar hit the wooden rafters and challenged the crying winds outside. Then she walked out of the room just before the door slammed itself behind her.

Edinburgh
'Where is Zander, the clever devil?'

'Hasn't Zander done *well*?'

It was as if she were an actress expecting to walk on to the set of *King Lear* only to find herself in a Noël Coward comedy instead. Everyone was smiling and joking and being so terribly witty. Some of the men were wearing tartan trousers and most had bow ties and were laughing loudly. Just one or two were looking at the sculptures and mixed media mobiles which sprang, as if from the shoulders of the guests, in sharp exciting shapes of wire, plaster and papier-mâché. Pushing through from the cold outside, Sarah entered the crowded gallery. Her feet were already tired walking the cobbles of Edinburgh's New Town. But all of New Edinburgh society was there judging by their loud voices and energetic insouciance. She didn't know a soul.

As well as people's backs, huge powerful shapes dominated her view. A glass of champagne was thrust into her hand by a young man who grinned at her, while a girl with a starched white blouse offered her a list of exhibits, politely pointing out which pieces were already sold.

In the crush at the end of the room, Sarah could make out

Zander's curly hair and hear his laugh. Unsure whether to go up to him or not, she suddenly heard, 'Good God! Sarah Hunter. *Good God!* We all thought you must have gone to work in the States!' One of the bow-tied moguls who had been holding court turned and was booming down at her. Several of the women looked at her, appraisingly. The man was vaguely familiar, and she realised that she had last seen him in a clinch with a second-year medic, snogging on the staircase. At a party. Long ago. She remembered how he had once asked Donald Gosford how much Archie's work would fetch. He was now in front of her, smiling expansively. People shifted to see who he was acknowledging in the New Town crowd. Jeremy? Jeremy something. Jeremy what? Help!

'Oh, hello Jeremy.' Her voice was steady enough.

'We always thought you would end up at M.O.M.A. in New York at the very least, or ploughing through the old fuddy duddies at the V & A. What happened to you? Johnny, let me introduce you to my fellow alumnus at St Andrews. Horribly bright as well as beautiful. Sarah Hunter, Charles Hollow. Charles is at the Royal Museum, while I toil with the Modern Art Gallery brigade, but you probably know that, don't you?'

It is always hell being discovered to be a nobody. It only takes two well-targeted questions and a five-second pause before you can see the interest dying out of people's eyes and the furtive glances over your shoulder as they hunt for better fish to fry. How she wished she had at least been Bunny, tall and imposing, even if she didn't know a Picasso from a Rembrandt. Bunny would have had the room roaring with laughter at the condition of the canapés if nothing else and then hurled pithy remarks at the art and drunk several glasses of plonk just for the hell of it. But Sarah felt herself turning into a frightened mouse, too hemmed in by big cats to scuttle into the nearest hole.

So she just stood there smiling weakly, absorbing this Jeremy's disappointment in her lost brilliant career. Lofthouse! His surname came back from the sludge just in time. She had blanked it out. She told him that she had bought the Robertson house, which she was doing up. She tried to make it sound exciting but she sounded, she knew, suburban and housewifely. Loanside, through Edinburgh New Town eyes, was clearly a dump at the end of a bad railway line.

'Sarah was so brilliant, you have no idea! She dug up all these old pots of Archie Milne Robertson, God knows where, and mounted an exhibition. All that, when she was doing her finals and getting a first. You had such huge energy and drive! I was always frightfully jealous.' Jeremy Lofthouse was merciless. 'You seemed to slope off after we all graduated. You never turned up to collect your degree, did you? We all thought you had lined up some cushy job on the quiet in some American university museum so we drowned our sorrows accordingly. Anyway, enough of ancient history, it's high time we had a retrospective of Robertson's work, I must say to Zander. He's the grandson you know. Wouldn't do Loanside any harm to have someone famous to celebrate. It's so terribly unprepossessing. That widget works, or whatever it is, doesn't help as you drive into the town, does it?

'A TV company has asked permission to film in the house, and I've found various bits and pieces.'

'Don't let them in! TV crews always take off the doors and wreck the joint.' Jeremy had now seen the producer of *ArtScene* arrive and he hurried off, trailing her lost past and brilliance behind him, and leaving her once more with just backs to look at. Turning blindly, she came up straight against a monstrous mobile, a huge black figure which dangled menacingly on fuse wire from the ceiling. The face leered down and smiled, the hunch of the shoulders as if from some nightmare, and the fingers swung in the breeze from the just-open door, large and prodding, just skimming over the guests' heads.

Then Zander was at her side, smiling, saying how glad he was that she had come. He took her elbow to guide her through the crowd. It should have been Christopher, but somehow she felt it never would be. 'What is that?' she asked, pointing at the figure now behind her. 'My brother. Now, let me introduce you to Hamish who runs the gallery.' She felt him standing over her protectively and felt, rather than watched, his smile. Someone wanted her here, then, after all. But then she remembered a piece of red graffiti on the loo at Loanside station. *What a stupid cow*, it said. The jagged image ripped this happy thought to ribbons. Served her right.

Suffolk

There are two sorts of TV chefs. First, and lower down on the media food chain, is the live TV chef or cook with the PSC or portable single camera, who flashes on and off daytime telly with great speed, cooking with their face to camera, hopefully catching just the right studio light. They also take part in sweatshop game shows in the afternoon, where they are employed to cook for the curious and the masochistic, tossing together miracles of gastronomy against the clock.

Then there are just the top half dozen who have evening time shows of their own. They are these days divided into the chefs, usually good-looking males, who have toiled up through the ranks of big hotels and top restaurants and who know both their oysters and their precious baby-boomer foodie audience. These are usually young men in a hurry with thick curly hair and street-cred vowel sounds, some of whom are dearly loved for roundly abusing the public. And then there is also the quieter, but no less effective, sisterhood of the women cooks, who having a less exclusive profile, connect with the deep insecurities of the average British housewife, often do the lower budget shows earlier on in the evening, when not doing celebrity demonstrations at the Ideal Home Exhibition or the Royal Highland Show.

Whatever the breed, the main thing for the TV personality cook with his or her own show is to have a gimmick. The young men go in for blow torches to caramelise the sugar on pert little crème brûlées glistening in their ramekins. The flames spurt across the studio, bringing applause from the hungry studio audience. Others cook at high speed – soufflés, fresh pasta, anything to keep the audience on the edge of their seat. Others prefer exotic locations, if there's the budget, while some prefer the more cerebral approach for the academic foodie who wants to know just the right temperature to roast a really good haunch of venison.

Bunny's TV career had started on the lower daytime rung of the ladder, but she had been thrilled to get it. It had all started one wet Thursday morning, through a lucky meeting at a City lunch she had been preparing with her girls. The chairman of the board of the new morning TV channel was looking for a TV cook and Bunny, in good form, had, as she usually did, seasoned the dishes with more humour than herbs. (She had actually left them behind by mistake.) But she had always found that if people were laughing they would say how yummy, whatever the quality of the food. So the chairman had bought both the food and Bunny and she had begun cooking each morning at 9.25 for five minutes. After eighteen months fencing with Jenna Grace she had acquired a following and, oh joy, a contract for *Bunny Cooks Big Time*, a ten-part evening show on location in various parts of rural England, which she was in the process of filming.

'Define *your* gimmick, Bunny' her agent had told her.

'I don't like cooking; I cheat wherever possible and I like a real kitchen around me. How can you believe in all those clinically minimalist surfaces all these people go in for?' Bunny had replied. And so she had signed both the TV deal and the accompanying book contract and spent her life planning what she should cook for her lazy and devoted fans.

She was, of course, very easy to underestimate, for Bunny *could* cook. But she was instinctive and usually thought recipes got in the way of the action – to the despair of both her home economist and producer. So her gimmick from the beginning was a set, messy verging on chaotic, although, in fact, fearfully expensive and consisting of only the best. Thus the knives were from Henkel and Sabatier and the dishes from Divertimenti in the Fulham Road.

And then there was the Bunny Halifax dress sense, if sense was what it was. Standing tall, she swept all before her – hors d'oeuvres, fish, meat puddings and canapés – all were whooshed together and came out looking delicious. She herself would whirlwind her way around the set wearing the most outrageous clothes. At six foot one and thirteen stone, it was a case of if you've got it, flaunt it. Cooking in hats with feathers, in incredible Peruvian tunics with wild parrots sewn on the shoulder, cooking in black leather and gold lamé trouser suits with fake fur sleeves. Other people would have looked grotesque, but Bunny always looked magnificent. Fuchsia with orange, and aquamarine with lime green. Colour would flood into the nation's sitting rooms. Her unique style became a source of celebration for much of the nation's gay community and was a constant source of angst and despair for her mother who, sitting in Surrey, bewailed just how much beige had always suited her daughter.

But then Bunny had never been a beige person and, with the lifestyle she and Edward and Hannah rapidly acquired, she could no longer afford to be. For if Bunny's stucco house off Clapham Common was not exactly like the witch's house in *Hansel and Gretel*, if the roof may not have been made of gingerbread or the windows of spun sugar, she never forgot that it was the whipping up of this media magic which continued to pay the six-figure mortgage every month.

So, on a wet end of October day, Bunny was filming in the kitchen of a Suffolk farmhouse, the sort with an Aga, lots of hanging overpriced pans and enough onion strings to make a Frenchman howl. All the property of a stockbroker's thrilled and neurotic wife, who was hovering outside in the hall.

What a nightmare! No one had told her before the shoot just what it took to make a show. Five hours for every dish! First there would be the wide shots, then the close-ups of her hands cooking the food in silence. Then she would have to do a second lot of close-ups, this time with identical voiced-over explanations which she had done on the wide shot, only by the time she got round to this she had forgotten what she had said.

And of course all this would have to be done in perfect continuity. Which meant Polaroids had to be taken every minute on the first wide shot. If the take started on a bright sunny day, and the Suffolk skies clouded over, continuity meant that bright lights had to be put up outside the house looking in, to give the viewer the impression that Bunny had whipped this little dish up in just fifteen minutes. It was now 3 p.m. and they had had four seasons' worth since they'd started filming at 9 a.m. The rain was also lashing against the windowpanes in stark contrast to the artificially sunny interior, to the sound man's irritation. If this combination of sun and rain had been real, Bunny would have expected one hell of a rainbow to come pouring in via the kitchen window. With hopefully lots of dosh at the end of it. Come back Jenna Grace all is forgiven. For an impatient person, there was a lot to be said for live TV done with a single portable camera and no retakes.

And oh, the quantities of everything needed for just one measly little dish! Today it was duck with cherries, so two dozen ducks had been bought in, with basins full of ready stoned cherries. All prepared to reach varying points of the cooking process. Sandra, the new home economist, was frighteningly efficient, and cleared up so fiercely it was making her nervous. God, she was so sick of fruit and poultry, why did every producer ask her to do it? Were they cloned? Bunny kept running her hands over her apron, which was dung coloured, having been dyed specially to match the fashionable dung-coloured walls. Every time she touched it, the girl with the Polaroid would groan just a split second before the director. 'Continuity love, continuity. Now eyes and teeth. Quiet everyone. Let's do the tight shot on the sauce. Don't bother to speak Bunny, darling, we'll do the spiel later. OK?'

'OK.' And then Bunny would grin to the camera and start again.

She always tried to talk to one person when she was cooking; it was a trick an elderly actress had taught her years ago. Today it was Sarah, because she was on her conscience. Three weeks had gone by and she still had not said whether or not they would be coming up for Christmas. Hannah was too bolshy and Edward was too pissed. And mean. 'I hope you can wangle the air fares Bunny, *I* can't pay.' She stopped herself from saying that he never did pay; it would be rather too disloyal. As she mixed the caster sugar, orange juice, port and cherries together in the saucepan, stirring it slowly, she thought of Hannah as she had been this morning. Moody and sepulchral in bold black eyeliner as usual, but this time not even bothering to be rude. It was as if her mother had not even been in the room.

After three weeks, Studd was a fixture, either keeping Hannah out late or else hanging about, constantly questioning her about cooking and how it was done.

Hannah still refused to leave him for Christmas. The most painful thing was that they were obviously sleeping together, in spite of all her many exhortations and cosy girltime sessions which had taken place from the age of twelve. All the things she had stressed about the importance of keeping herself for the person she married. Not that she had exactly, but it was good to aim for. But it was all a waste of time. And he was so thin and yobbish and *awful*, yet Hannah was crazy about him. It was all so inexplicable.

With half her mind wondering why the cherries were floating on the surface like eyeballs, the other discovered that she had turned into her mother. A mortifying revelation. Then the inevitable happened. The hot stoves and the hot arc lights did not help, and so Bunny felt the blush start somewhere down by her navel and spread like a bush fire right up to her highlights. Hopeless. Even this bloody sauce didn't seem to be mixing together properly. 'And cut! Make-up! Can we get Bunny a tad paler. She is rather sweating for Britain at the moment, and clashing with that super-duper frock and the cherries too.'

In the distance she could see Lottie smoking flirtatiously into the soundman's face while listening in to a mobile phone. 'Bunny, that was Hannah on the phone, She won't be back tonight. She and Studd are going to a gig. Hannah said you'd know which. Oh, and your cousin called, the Scotland one. And your literary agent rang. Your books are going out in Japanese. Mega yen ye ken!'

'Now gang, are we ready? Are we rolling? And . . . action.'

Bunny picked up the duck to do battle. Sod it. She chopped it into quarters and arranged the pieces. 'Now remember, spoon some of the sauce over the duck and arrange the cherries round the dish,' she said for the fifty-fifth time that day. Think of the money. Think of the money. Think of the money. Think of the money.

Loanside

What was it with her and committees? Back in London, if it hadn't been the committee of the mothers' Mafia in Chiswick, alias the Mother & Children's Club – that seething hotbed of intrigue and parentpolitik – it had been a case of Help the Aged or Christian Aid. Christopher had often, apparently jokingly, called it her philanthropy gene. But often it ended in disaster because he said she never grasped that there was always a hidden agenda and pecking order – until it was too late. She wouldn't last five minutes in a bank, he would say. 'You have to read signals like a recipe.' Sarah would listen to his criticism and carried on with her life, feeling that she was only tolerated for what she could produce for the cake stall.

Only she could have actually admitted at a Mother & Child coffee morning to having had both pethidine and an epidural for both her children. 'Such cowardice in one so young,' a BBC producer had remarked, while efficiently, and to universal admiration, feeding a large twin boy from each breast. Sarah's other observation, that she thought home births were seriously risky, caused her to be voted off the committee.

And then came the church jumble sale fiasco. She had told the local newspaper that designer gear from the richer parishioners would be on sale. Into the genteel confines of Bedford Park came busloads of mustachioed and female Eastern Europeans, obviously ex-roadbuilders from Ealing. Revolution in the vestry had ensued over the Armani and DKNY with Sarah, routed and helpless, watching as most of the designer jumble disappeared between the legs of the customers, unpaid for and off into bags. In the ensuing brawl the vicar had lost his toupee, and the churchwarden her sang-froid. Afterwards the parish church council voted for a series of fundraising raising cheese and wine parties specifically designed to keep the great unwashed, i.e. those not enjoying life in the local £500,000-plus housing bracket, firmly out of this most select of heaven's mansions.

So why was Sarah having a meeting of the local exchange trading group in her sitting room on this wild Thursday morning?

It hadn't taken her long living in Loanside to discover that, behind the camouflage of spotless curtains and freshly swept steps, there lurked real poverty, of a depth she had never seen in London, in spite of rich and poor living cheek by jowl.

The high street had given her the first clue. The boarded-up shops gaped like rotting teeth between thrift shops and charity shops precariously trading on short leases. The only decent restaurants seemed to be tax-efficient loss leaders which opened during the summer months for the tourists and for the rest of the year remained dark, like theatres without a play.

In the school, over fifty per cent of children were on free school dinners, and for Sarah, used to the diversity of incomes in London, this reliance on the public sector to provide employment, benefits and services, struck her as desperate. The big spenders in the town derived their incomes from Edinburgh's financial services industry, while others toiled in the engineering works, which dominated the town entrance with Victorian brutality. But neither group stopped to spend their money locally, preferring to speed up the A1 to the shopping malls on the outskirts of Edinburgh. There again, Loanside was anything but picture-postcard Scotland, however much the rest of East Lothian had cornered the market. She now saw her naïveté in thinking the house they had bought would be part of a Bedford Park-like prosperity. And how hard she would have to work to learn this new language.

On this particular morning, the Loanside L.E.T.S. Committee were meeting in her sitting room, cradling their coffee cups for warmth, in spite of the central heating. They talked earnestly about the forthcoming Local Exchange Food Fair which, it was hoped, would raise the scheme's profile, attract new members (hopefully those with useful skills like plumbing and DIY rather than the ubiquitous alternative therapists) and help people to trade in Lollops. Had Christopher been in the room there with them, Sarah thought, he would have been, as always, exquisitely polite and then, the moment that the last person had shut the gate, he would have started, 'Where on earth did you get these people Sarah? It's a talent.' Then there would have been a row.

But Christopher wasn't there, and the six people, a mixed group of men and women, obviously doubted he ever would be.

Mrs McAllen, the Chair, a retired bank manager's wife, had come through the door like a child in a department store Christmas grotto. 'My mother-in-law was saying she remembered when Archie Milne Robertson lived here, you know,' she announced, passing round the agenda.

'How many Lollops for this panelling then, Sarah?' Jimmy Ross, an artist, was looking round admiringly.

'Not for sale, I'm afraid,' Sarah said lightly.

'You're no fun.'

Eleanor, who was sitting there sharpening her pencil into a recycled brown envelope, told him not to be absurd.

'I see you've got Bunny Halifax's latest, Mrs Todd.' Morag Stonehouse, a single mother who worked as a school dinner lady, was looking through the piles of books on the large Mexican coffee table.

'Call me Sarah, please.'

'I've got three of hers. They're really good if you can't afford fancy food.' She read the inscription aloud. 'To cousin Sarah. Here's to your survival in the Frozen North. Recipe for lentil soup is on page thirty-five. Love Bunny.' She looked at Sarah. 'Are you her cousin then?'

The phone rang. Sarah went into the hall. 'Christopher here, Sarah, I'm coming back tomorrow for a week or so. Looking forward to seeing you all. I'm in Washington.'

'Good God, Christopher! It has been nearly nine weeks—' Before she could finish, a throaty laugh bubbled up like boiling chocolate in the background. Christopher was obviously smiling. 'So I'll see you four o'clock tomorrow afternoon. Hope Theo's managed to grow somewhat.'

'I'll meet you.'

He'd rung off.

As she went back into the sitting room, Morag was passionately explaining why the Loanside L.E.T.S. should not become just another club for middle-class do-gooders who could perfectly well afford to buy everything they needed in cash, but should be designed to attract the unemployed and those on low incomes to help themselves. Spending currency locally on goods and services they could not normally afford. Loansiders helping each other.

Fearful of saying the wrong thing, Sarah sat timidly on the corner of a settee. The laugh she had heard on the phone seemed to join other noises in her life which stayed with her always. Trembling, she reached out for a copy of the agenda. There was a scraping sound as branches from the elm tree in the front garden bent to scratch the window panes. Was it the spirit of Archie wanting ten Lollops for a pot perhaps? Or just asking who she thought she was kidding?

CHAPTER SEVEN

Loanside

It was so bloody cold. Unbelievably cold. He could not imagine how people round here stood it, not for one minute. Christopher was standing in Loanside high street waiting for a bus to fill up, move on and allow him to cross the high street down which, to his inexperienced senses, a force eight gale was blowing. Finally the bus moved off, full of old people juddering up to Edinburgh, and he made it across the road into the paper shop.

'*FT* please.'

The woman behind the counter looked at him curiously. 'I'm afraid the Laird has just taken the last copy. Would you take the *Telegraph*? There now, down below.'

Great. Why did the Laird need an *FT* on Saturday, for God's sake? Talk about bolting the stable door after the horse had fled. He was hardly going to read the How To Spend It pages, was he? Moodily Christopher bought himself a chocolate bar for consolation and a couple of papers, and then went out, bracing himself for the wind. He headed for the community centre, where some local good cause Sarah had wrapped herself up in was having a sale. Perhaps he could get a coffee.

Sarah had coped jolly well in the circumstances. The house was rather fine with nice gothic touches, and she had made it homely. The local people were really very pleasant and the children seemed settled; Theo's accent was becoming Scottish. Liddy had seemed taller and older and very much mummy's girl. But it was all rather noisy and overwhelming to come back to family life after so many weeks away. He supposed he had missed it.

In the community centre two causes were apparently competing for local support. The Save The Children Fund's second-hand sale was at full strength and, as the women looked very much like his friends' wives, Christopher went in. There were more Hermès scarves on the backs of the helpers than on the stalls, but only just, and a sea of wonderfully good-quality things swam before him including a naff, pink, plastic beach table with four chairs to match. 'That new accountant's wife put them in. So useful!' he heard someone exclaim doubtfully in an upper-class accent. He remembered his mother, who had been very hot on the local SCF, so Christopher waded in, wondering where on earth Sarah was. 'Hello, have you seen my wife, Sarah Todd?' But apparently no one knew her.

'Are you new?' A lady in a green Husky waistcoat handed him a large chocolate cake and waited for him to find some change in sterling.

'Todd, Christopher. How do you do? Just moved in, Carnforth House.'

'How lovely. I must meet your wife. Did you say she was manning a stall? Her name doesn't ring a bell.' Finally someone suggested he should try the room over the hall.

The Loanside L.E.T.S. Fair, the sign said outside the other room. Another world. Arty, crafty. Just the sort of thing he loathed. Fans and printed screens and pots and piles of defrosted home produce swamped the tables. Someone was giving tarot card readings. (The High Church Anglican in Christopher thoroughly distrusted such New Age excess.) Someone else was doing Shiatsu hand massage. He asked the price of a hand-knitted jumper and was told it was 80 Lollops. 80 what? Lollipops? Mystified, he turned to find Sarah manning a stall covered with children's clothes and lemon curd.

'Roll up, roll up, home-made lemon curd for only four Lollops a jar.' She was teasing him. Apparently. Theo was selling some children's books for what seemed like made-up children's cheques. All very odd.

'What are you doing, Sarah? And *what* exactly are Lollops?'

'It's an alternative currency with which local people can exchange goods and services.'

'But why not just use cash?'

'Because not everyone has enough cash, and it helps people to buy talents and goods which would normally not be sold in the marketplace. It also helps you ask for help from neighbours because you can offer Lollops.'

'It sounds very suspect to me. What does the taxman say about it?'

'There's a leaflet over there. There are thousands of L.E.T.S. schemes world-wide. I should think even the World Bank has come across them.'

Was she being sarcastic? Unlike her. 'I doubt it. So how many lollop things have you earned today?'

'Liddy, Daddy wants to know our balance.'

'Fifty-five this morning.'

'And what will you do with it? I didn't realise this was charity beginning at home.'

'I shall buy babysitting, upholster the dining room chairs and pay for Liddy's pottery classes with it. I have also bought some fragments of Robertson pots with different lustre examples.'

'Just fragments. They ought to be paying you! Still, anything that decreases my role as a walking chequebook has to be welcomed, I suppose. Are you going to be long?'

Suddenly a tall, thick-set sort of man came over and introduced himself, Sandy someone, whose brother had originally owned the house. Christopher didn't like the way he was smiling at Sarah as he bought six – excessive – jars of lemon curd. He didn't like the way Theo and Liddy ran up to say hello, and he didn't like the way everyone was looking at the man. He was really nothing remarkable: old corduroys and an Arran sweater which had obviously seen better days. Then a woman called Morag in a shell suit and a large mole on her chin with hairs sprouting out, came up and asked if he wanted to get his fortune told for five Lollops. Christopher fled.

* * *

'You seem to be very friendly with Sandy what's his name.'

'Zander? Short for Alexander.'

'I see. Short for Alexander.'

Christopher was sitting in bed reading *The Economist*, while Sarah was putting moisturiser on her skin. Her face, bare of make-up, gleamed messily in the side-table light.

'He's a friend. The kids like him and he has been a great help finding plumbers and people. It's not been easy, you know. Coming here. I don't think you have anything to complain about really, Christopher. Except the cold, which you actually do get used to after a while.'

'I'm sure.'

'I haven't told you, but I've invited Bunny, Edward and Hannah up for Christmas.'

'Did you have to?'

'Well, I don't even know if you're coming home for Christmas. You haven't said.'

'Certainly I'm going to try.'

'Surely the Third World gives time off for good behaviour.'

'Are the two hell grannies coming up too?'

'Yes.'

'Great. You can run north of the border but you cannot hide!'

'It seems to me you are doing quite enough running. When are you going to come home and stop doing this endless globetrotting, Christopher? It's rotten for the children.'

Her voice was on the edge of sharp and, although she had struck him as really quite pretty this morning at the fair, certainly much less stressed out, it was hard not to feel impatient with her. She had no . . . *élan*! That's what he know knew he liked in a woman. Even Helen was getting more as she got older.

'I don't know, Sarah. Just be a good girl and put up with it. Two families do not come cheap and things are much better now we're out of London, financially. Thank God.'

'Well, the supermarket bill has halved since we left Chiswick.'

'Oh goody.'

Out of good manners and because he had not seen her for two months, he made love to her, all the while, but trying not to, thinking of the sheets being curled round and round with Maria Antonietta in the middle. Still it was pleasant in the circumstances. The compartments in his mind remained intact and secure. Afterwards Sarah made no comment except to wish him goodnight.

Christopher lay in the dark, watching the beam of the lighthouse go round across the room, ceiling to floor, every thirty seconds. The wind coming in from the sea howled, and the draught from the big window was chilling him to buggery. He shivered down into the blankets and wondered when he would hear if he had got through to the second round of interviews for the director's job. Then Maria Antonietta's face appeared before him, red mouth parted, swallowing him up. Sarah had her back to him. Silent. He wouldn't have minded a cuddle. All of a sudden Christopher felt rather sorry for himself.

There were bits of pottery all over the table, and whole pots which Sarah had bought for cash or Lollops. Some of the bits were Archie's and others were examples of the local pottery, all chipped and bashed about, and worthless to anyone but her.

Sarah was sitting in the studio with Morag and Eleanor, drinking coffee. On the wall Sarah had put up a map of the Firth of Forth, which is where she was marking out where the old potteries had been along both sides of the coast.

'There were over thirty potteries in East Lothian at one time, and probably the same again in Fife. Archie left Scotland and went south in about 1902 to work at the Royal Lancaster Pottery for a man called William Burton, who was heavily into lustres. He produced a whole range just before the First World War. It was the sort of rich icing on the cake for the aspiring middle classes, one step up from your hand-painted porcelain.

'Have you ever done any teaching? It's fascinating,' asked Morag.

'I keep telling her she ought to give an evening class.

They're desperate for tutors.' Eleanor helped herself to another biscuit.

'No, I couldn't possibly. I studied all about Scottish ceramics at university, and coming back here seems to have unlocked the brown sludge in my brain, that's all. I actually know very little, and I couldn't throw a pot if you paid me.'

This was the first time Morag and Eleanor had come up here, not on L.E.T.S. business, and Sarah was anxious not to make any mistakes. Did she sound a know-all? They had both been so kind when her Loanside address book had just been full of white pages, turning up with shopping when she had had flu. And over the last few weeks they had become, with Zander, the key to understanding this place. 'My granny has some Wemyss ware, somewhere,' Morag said.

'I like Wemyss ware, it has the courage of its convictions, but there is a lot of snobbery about it. There was even when it began. And the trouble was that the Scots had such a weak domestic market they just couldn't compete with the international competition. So there was a real brain drain down south, which Archie was part of.' 'Typical Scottish story then,' said Eleanor.

'I suppose so. Though *he* did come back.'

Morag was sitting fingering the small pieces of fiery blue and silver, red and copper lustred work which Sarah had found in the houses of the older L.E.T.S. members and all over the house and garden. Old pots had been ground up in the flowerbeds, apparently for drainage, which was how she had got flu, spending two days in subzero temperatures out in the herbaceous borders panning for Archie.

'Sorry, am I lecturing?'

'No, it really is interesting. Where did you go to university?

'I read art history at St Andrews, a hundred years ago. Where did you go, Eleanor?'

'Aberdeen.'

'You're both so lucky,' Morag shrugged. 'I left school at sixteen and tried to do correspondence courses, but it was really hopeless. Couldn't concentrate with so much noise at home. I'd still like to.'

'You should.' Sarah hoped this wasn't patronising.

'I should, but it's laziness. You see, to me, Archie Milne Robertson is just a name. They called the new school extension after him when I was at primary school back in the sixties, but he was just another old Edwardian guy with a moustache who glared out of the old photographs in the school hall. Dead boring.'

'He wasn't the least bit dull. He had huge appetites, in every way, I gather.' Sarah started gathering up the pieces for labelling.

'Like his grandson.'

'What do you mean, Morag?'

'Well Zander's always been OK if a bit wild, when he was younger, a great man for the booze. But his brother David! Yeuch! We used to call him The Groper. He went off to Edinburgh to train to be an accountant. What a louse and he went bankrupt!'

'Poor man.'

'Yes, but talk about dysfunctional. The whole family have always lived on a knife edge, have for generations,' said Eleanor, 'because the Robertsons always married, or were attracted to, highly strung women. It was just a pattern.'

'Just as well Zander isn't married.'

'He was I think, Sarah, but it didn't last. He's been divorced for years. Eleanor sounded unimpressed.

'Anyway, Sarah, what did your husband think of the fair?'

'Oh, I think he quite enjoyed it, Morag. More coffee?'

'Not for me. Has he gone off again then?'

'Yes. United States and then Africa.'

'Is it hard for you doing without him? I mean, I've never had anyone except my Mum so I've no one to miss. Worse luck. How have you found it here?'

'Fine. But I've been lucky, meeting interesting people, like you for instance.'

'Crawler. Isn't she Eleanor? But then you're clever, Sarah. And attractive. You must make that big ugly cousin of yours sick.'

'Don't be daft. Have some more cake.'

'And you dress better. And you can cook better. Did I tell you I tried her recipe for carrot cake? Disaster!'

'Really! I can't imagine Bunny would make a mistake.'

'You're really too nice. I never thought I'd hear myself say that about the English! I know. Shut it, Morag!'

Sarah looked at her watch. 'Actually Morag, shall we go and pick up the kids?'

'I suppose so. I spend most of my bloody life at that school gate.'

It was already getting dark in the November twilight as they stepped over mounds of leaves which had blown themselves into a pile across the garden path. London, Surrey and Bunny seemed on another planet, and Christopher simply worlds away. Sarah thought of lentil soup and then of the dark and lonely night ahead. In Loanside, the past was just too close for comfort sometimes. She began to sing.

'Say, Sarah—'

'Yes, Morag.'

'If that's your idea of singing in tune, don't give up the day job.'

London

With just five and a half weeks to go, there was no escape. Harrods glistened all over with bright lights and goodwill and every supermarket melted into a sea of brandy butter, Christmas crackers and people; everyone spending as if money were about to be rationed. Fathers paid thousands for the latest plastic toy suitably hyped with character merchandising licenses, while children were revved up to shrieking point by schools and children's television. Yet all this expectation could never be fulfilled, however much debt you got into. How the hell is the average woman supposed to balance all that eating (and drinking) against the cold reality of the bathroom scales. £10 versus 10kgs. That'll do nicely. Sucker.

Bunny loathed it all. Christmas just meant for her uncomfortable memories of sweet sherry and fancy salty biscuits in small plastic bowls with flowers over them. Lots of false camaraderie with the neighbours and rows the second they had gone. Then everyone saying what a big girl she was getting. She had once read a brilliant sentence in a book at school. 'The bones of hospitality rattled' – EM Forster. Not that she had ever been able to feel hers. Bones. But the line had summed up her family Christmases exactly. But now, as Mrs Personality and for the good of her bank balance, she had to play up the charade along with everyone else in the media circus who prayed they would get their face on the front cover of *TV PAGES*.

Talking of which, this week the nice editor has wedged her weekly column between the horoscope and foreign cable channels. Bunny was giving *Ten Top Tips To Make Your Christmas Dinner Hassle Free*. (Bunny last cooked Christmas dinner ten years before, but her devoted fans were not to know that.) 'Do as much as you can beforehand. Christmas is for you to enjoy every bit as much as the rest of the family! Just think of a turkey like a large chicken with attitude.' She had dictated this in the bath one evening, having decided that Christmas was for women merely licensed slavery. What was Christmas supposed to be all about anyway? Even the first one couldn't have been much fun for the Virgin Mary in spite of all those choirs of angels singing her baby's praises. Being in labour on a load of straw with cows mooing around your head all night and no hope of an epidural. And Joseph hanging around being totally useless, and then inviting a whole load of smelly shepherds in when all Mary would have wanted was a cup of tea and a clean nightie. Bunny had decided the birth of Christ did not bear thinking about and pulled the plug out.

Christmas built up its own momentum, like a political campaign, in every area of her life. The school was raking in the shekels with the *Bunny Cooks Christmas Course* which, spread over five days, had been a huge hit with the wives of the Russian Mafiosi who drove in from Richmond each day in dazzling couture. How they lapped up all that Dickensian bullshit about mince pies and Christmas puddings. Though if Lucinda and her team could just get them to stop cooking without their diamond bracelets dipping into the mincemeat, that would be a start.

And then of course there was her evening telly *Bunny Cooks Big Time* starting off three weeks before Christmas. She had just given an interview with the showbiz editor of the *Daily Blare* who had raved at her new cerise dress. Had he been taking the St Michael? And then the Jenna Grace purgatory, which she still had to do three times a week until her contract came up for renewal in February, when hopefully her agent would screw more money out of them for fewer appearances.

And then the catering side. Lottie, thank God, had taken over all that and was pushing more canapés and sushi down City throats than ever this winter, so bubbly was the economy and accompanying bonuses. Bunny never inquired quite how Lottie made the late payers pay, but she always charmed the bastards somehow. And so it went on. And in between there were the after-dinner speeches – Bunny was on the books of an agency and it brought in £1,000 a time – though she would only do them within the M25 circle – and a bit of charity stuff for good PR. And the eighteen-hour days went on. Home was the place she came back to change and sleep. And so it went on. Have Yourself a Merry Little Christmas. Piss off.

Hannah had come down once or twice to the office. She was still refusing to come to Scotland for Christmas and so Bunny rang Sarah to say it was not going to be possible. Sarah had sounded really sorry, making Bunny feel more guilty of course. And then she had wittered on about cakes she was making – for free! And something about finding bits of pots behind radiators and earning lollipops instead of sterling. She had obviously flipped. And then her mother, Marjorie, had given her a hard time and offered to have the whole family down to sweet sherry land for Christmas Day. Hell in a doily. Aaagh! And then Edward had come into the kitchen one night and had said that they ought to go to Scotland and be together as a family because Sarah was obviously lonely, like he was all day. Her suggestion that if he had an office to go to, his life might be less centered on the afternoon racing had ended with him screaming abuse along the lines that she was never at home and was a lousy mother who didn't understand his daughter or him, etc.

Hannah turned up at the school just when Bunny had been spending a quality half hour with her diplomat wives teaching them how to do haggis crêpes with whisky sauce. She had chosen her moment to march in just when the haggis was spread out on the boards like brains. 'God, you're not going to give that to anyone are you?' had not gone down well with the Russians and Hannah had been marched away by Lottie.

'Where's that delicious Studd of yours, Hannah?'

'Down at the DSS.'

'How *enterprising* of him.'

Bunny had just noticed Hannah now had a snake tattooed down the back of one leg. She groaned. Then one of the wives, Ludmilla someone, had taken her haggis-smelly hand and said in broken English, 'Never mind Bunnushka, we are all mothers.' Which bit of homespun Cossack philosophy had solved absolutely nothing.

It was therefore in this mood of gentle despair and hyperactivity and after yet another sleepless night that Bunny turned up at Jenna Grace's studio one Thursday morning. As she sat in make-up watching the monitor, Bunny was surrounded by Christmas decorations and Christmas tinsel and Christmas placards proclaiming Merry Christmas. The two make-up 'girls' were talking merrily about Christmas presents they had bought at Hamleys just the day before. Mario, the resident keep-fit man, was asleep and looked shattered, his Latin lover act not in evidence. One of the girls was inventing cheekbones for Bunny. 'So what are you doing, Bunny love? For Christmas? Going anywhere exotic?'

'We're still making arrangements.'

'Well Christmas is for being with the family isn't it, more than anything? Especially people you haven't seen all year. I like a nice big family party myself.'

'Do you really?'

'Welcome back everyone. Coming up next we have Bunny taking all the hassle out of Christmas cooking and later on we have our resident counsellor, Jane, here to tackle some of your relationship problems. But now Mario is here to strut his Latin stuff! Viva Mario!'

The tango music started, and the lights and the tension shifted abruptly away from Jenna to the other side of the studio, where a galvanised Mario was attempting to smoulder like a poor woman's Marcello Mastroianni, while improving the nation's chubby thighs. Bunny, standing yards away in the studio kitchen, checked and rechecked the ingredients and the spoons. It was all so quick there was never a second to hunt for the right spoon or whisk, it had to be just there instantly in your hand. She always felt nervous, nerves never went away however often she went on live TV. 'Bunny you look *so* tired.' Serena, the home economist, was whispering something.

'What?'

'Tired. Bunny, you look exhausted.'

'Tell me about it.' The lights shifted, Mario had ended in the splits and, having urged the nation to Fighta the Flabba, Bunny's message was now to demonstrate how to pile on yet more. It was all ridiculous.

'Thanks, Mario. I don't think I'll be trying that *last* exercise!' dimpled Jenna. 'And now, as we all know, Christmas is coming fast, so here is Bunny back to show us just how *easy* it can all be! Now Bunny, what is it today?'

'Peanut pie, Jenna!' Bunny had learned to talk in exclamation marks on daytime TV and she knew exactly what Jenna would say next.

'Peanut pie? Now that doesn't sound very *Christmassy*, Bunny, and only last week we did the item on peanut allergy which can kill small children. Now tell us, why did you choose this?'

'Bitch,' thought Bunny, realising suddenly that she had forgotten last week's nut campaign. And wasn't the Christmas dish bit supposed to be for next week? Oh sod it, get out of this one Halifax.

'I am doing this particular dish, Jenna, because, though you're right some people *do* have allergies, lots of people *can* eat peanuts, so this dish is for them! You take three eggs, 75 g each of golden syrup and black treacle, and 100 g of sugar and peanut butter and half a teaspoon of vanilla essence and whip it all up in a bowl and, when it is smooth, add the peanuts!'

And, just as years ago the angel had crash landed on her shoulder as the food was tipped off the photocopier, so this time a strange and not very well brought up little voice in Bunny's head shouted, 'Christmas Stinks!'

'This is a dish for people like me, who are, frankly, fed up with Christmas already. It's a con. I feel got at every time I go out to the shops or turn on the TV. My family want me to go to Scotland, not to go to Scotland, to stay at home or go out to a restaurant. My teenage daughter will not join us for a family Christmas because she wants to be with her boyfriend who, quite honestly,' Bunny tipped the luscious muck into the hand-made pastry case and started aggressively forking it into submission, 'I find it difficult to get on with. All I ever get out of him is a grunt. So as far as I am concerned Christmas s—!'

'Now, *Bunny*!' Jenna leaped in like a rabbit, eyes out on stalks. 'This does look *delicious* and, of course, so many of us *feel* for you. Christmas *can* be a difficult time.' She paused. Obviously the producer was having a nervous breakdown into her earpiece, but Bunny didn't care. 'Now Bunny what *exactly* do you do now?' She looked doubtful as more filling was on Bunny's apron than in the dish.

'You whack it into the oven gas mark four for forty-five to sixty minutes. At least you don't have to stick holly and pour brandy over this pudding. Thank God.'

'Er yes, Bunny. As you say, it *is* important to make Christmas *original* and *unusual* isn't it? So here's the recipe!'

The recipe came on screen as Bunny's pre-recorded voice gave the instructions. The camera light went off.

'What the hell are you doing?' Jenna's voice, high at the best of times, was positive coloratura.

'Well, it's a farce. Christmas is sheer hell, so what's the point of playing happy families?' Bunny spat. The light on the camera turned to red. 'And here we are! Eat this up! A delicious peanut pie, with no *hint* of Father Christmas *anywhere* near, and you can whack on lots of whipped cream or crème fraîche and enjoy yourself before the guilt sets in. Which of course it invariably will, because guilt is what we mothers, poor sods, are supposed to live on throughout Christmas!' With that, Bunny took off her gloves, smiled to camera and, leaving a fuming Jenna, marched off the set.

In Clapham, Hannah, lying on the drawing-room floor with Studd watching her mother, was smiling and picking off the red leaves of a poinsettia.

Bunny only realised that she had touched one of the nation's rawest nerves later that morning when the producer rang to ask if she could come in the following morning to discuss tensions at Christmas and how to avoid them. 'No cooking, Bunny, just a spot of couch chat with Jenna. You see, the phone lines have been jammed with women agreeing with you!'

Then four newspapers, three tabloid and one broadsheet, rang for interviews/quotes/pictures. Bunny's press agent was at the dentist (typical), so Bunny gave them what they wanted. BUNNY'S XMAS HELL was not perhaps quite what the publicity team at her publisher were looking for, but in the following days it sold her books in thousands, overtaking even Delia Smith. Phone-ins were swamped by dozens of mothers pouring out their feelings of rage and frustration. Bunny received advice and sympathy from every columnist and agony aunt in the UK. 'None of my children are ever satisfied. I can never get it right!' wailed one poor mother from Wolverhampton in *The Times* letters page. Another suggested a new militant Mothers' Trade Union to bring back sanity into family life, 'assuming there is any left in this country'. Broadsheet columnists observed the phenomenon using words to the effect that Ms Halifax had lifted the lid on the Christmas stew into which everyone is hurled each year. Ban the turkey! One thought that Christmas ought to be for Christians only, and the rest of the nation should just be given two weeks to go abroad.

It was not what Bunny had expected. As a result of all this, Edward had an attack of the vapours which, thanks to the start of the national hunt season, sent him off to Ascot. Hannah was never at home anyway. Sarah did not ring and so Bunny assumed she had offended her mortally. Her mother, of course, rang every day to say that she had shamed the family and she had missed the rotary Christmas dinner in consequence. 'You never hear the *older* generation complaining about all those years' cooking. *We* just got on with it. And during the War *my* mo-*ther*—!'

In the end, help came in the unlikely person of a leading woman trades-unionist who spotted Bunny one day in the hospitality lounge at the BBC. 'Thank you for what you've done for working women, Bunny,' she said. 'I salute you!'

'Thanks, but I don't see what I've done other than given myself negative publicity, and my family an even bigger stick to beat me with.'

'Well, let me try and help you through this. What is your number one problem?'

'I haven't had time to do the Christmas therapy?'

'Very droll. Do you know what I do each week?'

'Talk about going on strike?'

'You *are* behind the times. No, I negotiate. You want to see more of your daughter don't you, and have a family Christmas in Scotland? So why not find out what you can do to make her boyfriend happy.'

'What can I possibly have or could do for him? Other than pay him to leave her alone?'

'Teach him to cook.'

'Teach him to cook! Studd in *my* school! Studd, learning to do crème brûlée with a ring in his nose, and no doubt every other part of his anatomy, unshaven, dirty hands, greasy hair, looking like The Fonz before his mid-life crisis.'

'Well, my daughter married a gynaecologist, so *you're* complaining.'

The fact that at that moment she was finally embarrassed by the whole world knowing her family's problems did not stop Bunny feeling more cheerful than she had for weeks. Up the Workers.

CHAPTER EIGHT

Copenhagen

Christopher caught sight of his reflection in the shop mirror and stopped to admire the Russian hat he had just bought. It made him feel like a Communist leader on a state visit. Topped him over six-three at least. It was all so pleasant here in the Strøget, it had to be one of his favourite shopping streets in Europe. No cars, clean pavements, everyone well mannered. No ghastly, whining beggars running around with their hands out. Exciting shops, manageably aesthetic eighteenth-century architecture and polite people. All the Viking genes must have been bred out of the Danes after years of reading Hans Christian Andersen.

Denmark was one of those converted countries it was so pleasant for the Cross-Sectoral Cooperation Department to preach to. Lots of state aid to the third world. Yet even here in this most egalitarian of countries, one per cent of the people controlled two-thirds of national assets. The Danes were rather pleasant, though with their tax burden one would not fancy living here.

Incongruously, down on the pavement a busker was strumming some flamenco tune, reminding Christopher of olives and red wine and sticky nights. Here, schnapps was the real problem. You had to catch your host's eye, then leap up with a toast. Skol! And then you had to nurse the hangover in the conference room the next day. Perfect technique for getting stuff easily voted through. Christopher grinned, thinking of everyone wincing at the feedback when the Djibouti delegate had banged the microphone. Deliberately, one imagined, just to make the point that he might be in dire need of yet more French aid, but being a good Moslem *he* hadn't indulged.

In his striking grey hat, he was feeling sanguine and successful in this crisp December air. He was now through to the second round of interviews for the director's job, which was looking increasingly attractive. Surely to God they would hold interviews before Christmas! Then there was the E & A Bank's New Year bash to get through. It would be good to remind them that he was not only alive and kicking, but now had a world-class network of contacts, while they were all sitting in Edinburgh pissing themselves with worry over Internet banking putting them out of a job before they could retire, if European Monetary Union and the Millennium bomb didn't do it first.

A small crowd had been gathering to look up at an ornate clock. There was a tinkle of bells, the clock began to strike twelve and then the gilt doors of the clock opened. Christopher stopped and looked upwards too. Small figures dutifully burst out of the aperture next to the clock face. First a dumpy woman in a pale blue headscarf followed by a man dressed in lederhosen who chased her round and round in through the doors and out. He had a wily grin and knobbly knees and this enthusiasm made Christopher smile. Then on cue another woman came out, black haired, this time with her hands on her hips, shaking her arm at the man. There was humour and purpose in the chase. Even from his view down in the street, Christopher could see the man's smile; he looked like Danny Kaye in the movie singing 'I'm Hans Christian Andersen' in a Hollywood accent.

Time for lunch. Smörgåsbord and Maria Antonietta. The 'Skol' without the schnapps. He was beginning to realise two things about her; that he never knew what she was thinking and that he never would get to know her any better. He didn't even know how old she was. There were no shared memories of television programmes, royal weddings or three-day weeks back in the seventies, which were such tell-tale signs of age with British women.

When he was away from her he only saw pieces of her in his

mind's eye; the brown skin, the lazy smile with the red lipstick which flitted to the corner of her mouth but never onto her teeth, unlike Sarah's mother who obviously thought sticky red molars were a fashion statement. Perhaps he didn't want to get to know Maria Antonietta. He had never once heard her mention the words children, petfood, curtain rails, three point plugs, mending the vacuum cleaner or that constant companion sentence which had run through both his marriages '—the washing machine is broken and will cost—'. The clock had stopped tinkling, the figures had disappeared and the carved gilt doors were now shut. The other people moved off, but Christopher remained looking up for some moments. Then he turned left and headed for the florist.

Loanside

The TV crew arrived at 9 a.m., just as Sarah was rushing back through the cold streets having taken the children to school. She had expected several large vans, miles of cable and catering vans on the street, but instead there were just four estate cars pulled up on the pavement. The crew were hanging around, their breath steaming; they were stamping their feet and banging leather-gloved hands together and looking out towards the sea with the 'God this is the back of beyond' expression Christopher had worn on his last visit. A cross between wonderment and a sneer.

They turned round as she opened the gate and introduced themselves. There was John, the cameraman, with his assistant Robin, who was also doing the lights. Then there was Freddie, the sound engineer, Rowena, the production assistant, suitably blonde with a clipboard, and Georgie the designer, who would be giving any rooms they would need a suitably art deco 'look'. Lachlan, the producer of *ArtScene*, was eating a sausage roll and made a great show of brushing the crumbs off his Arran sweater before shaking hands with her. She unlocked the door and let them in, asking if they would like tea, and where would they like to start filming first. 'Black coffee, if you please, and don't bother about us. Our production values are young, exciting, you know, plenty of moving camera work.'

'We'll mainly work outside in the garden near the ark and then upstairs in his studio and perhaps a little in the main drawing room with all that super panelling,' said Lachlan. 'Lennie Roscoff, the presenter – you've probably seen him on *Chimera* on BBC2 – well, he'll be arriving from Edinburgh in half an hour. He'll position the Archie Milne Robertson as Charles Rennie M mark two, artistic rebel, superstud, that sort of thing.' She nodded.

It was clear that they all thought she was a little housewife who knew nothing about ceramics or art in general and that their presence would light up her dull little life. The researcher had spent half a day in her house and had not wanted to know about her small finds. But then in reality wasn't she just a little housewife who knew just enough about ceramics to know she knew nothing at all? The more she learned, the more she realised just how much there was to learn. And why should she want to learn it? What was the point? 'Fill the kettle, Todd, and know your place.'

She had spent all week clearing and dusting and working to reduce the family muddle to reasonable proportions. A huge mixed bouquet lay on the kitchen table, unopened. An inexplicable present from Christopher. Very odd. Now she was in for a week with these people in her life, new names to remember, new stories to tell. Eleanor, however, had told her she was mad, and no amount of money was worth the hassle. She told dark tales of huge lumps of plaster being taken out of walls by film crews with no compensation. Her children, too, were against it, but only after she had written off to accept the company's request to film. Liddy said the children at school would bully them and say they were snobby. 'It's bad enough being English, Mum, without being any more different!' Guilt piled on guilt.

It was also so peculiar to witness a private obsession exposed to public view. She had been amazed that anyone would want to make a programme about Archie Milne Robertson. Whoever had heard of him, outside a very narrow academic or artistic group? But apparently the Arts Councils both sides of the border had declared this the Year of Ceramicists, and had provided suitable funding for independent film makers to record the work and lives of Britain's top ceramicists for the nation.

In terms of his love of shape and texture Robertson now was apparently seen as an inspiration for Lucy Rie although for years he had been derided for the gaudy colours of his lustres. Gypsy work, too dangerous for the upwardly mobile bourgeoisie who, having faced Armageddon on the battlefields, now wanted nice safe decorative work in their homes. He was just the sort of dangerous man when she was young she had dreamed of meeting one day. And just the sort of man Christopher would have despised as unsound.

In Loanside he had apparently gone out every day with his dog on the beach, a flower in his buttonhole. How those long curls must have been tossed back in the Loanside wind. There were still locals alive who had actually met him as children. One had had a granny called Big Betty, who ruled the station restaurant with a rod of iron. One day he had pushed away his soup, saying he preferred a steak. But she had ordered him to eat his soup or he would not get any pudding. And Archie, after staring at her for a full moment, had obediently fallen to his lentil broth.

He died conveniently in 1938, just in time before Nazism sent applied art into a coma, and for the Musselburgh family of his wife to step in, settle the debts and save the house for her and the children. Odd, the patterns of families. His grandson lost the house in the end, and his life, thanks to three mortgages, but no one had saved him.

'Mrs Todd?' The kettle was whistling and Sarah came back to the present to find a familiar, short stocky man with brown leather gloves and black eyebrows standing next to her.

'I'm sorry? Oh, hello, you must be Mr Roscoff?'

'Lennie, please. How do you do? Georgie is just setting up velvet and some dried flowers in the drawing room for the first shot, so we have a few minutes. Then I think they are going into the garden while it's still sunny, and then up into the studio. I think you are being very good letting us come here. I hope it's not too disruptive.'

'No. I like the company if I am honest.'

She took him upstairs and showed him the moulds and the bits of pottery and the one or two small Robertson ceramics she had managed to buy in the village and said how she had studied his work long ago.

'Pity, all this is not in the shooting script, but we really ought to use some of this. Have you ever spoken to camera?'

'Never. I'd be hopeless. You ought to speak to Zander Robertson, his grandson. He's coming round this afternoon, he is much more knowledgeable.'

'You know, you mustn't talk yourself down. I'll go and talk to Lachlan.'

'I'd rather you didn't.'

'You must have been planning for years to buy this house.'

'No, it came up at auction when we happened to be looking.'

'Obviously destiny then.'

At that moment a tremendous gust of wind thudded a tree against the window.

'God, don't you ever worry about the wind cracking the glass?'

'I do. I've spent a fortune on tree surgeons since we came. But there are just so many trees and the wind pushes the branches so far over to the house.'

Lennie Roscoff was fingering some of the red lustred pieces on the table.

'Do you know much of Robertson's private life?'

'No. I think Isobel his wife must have been rather long-suffering.'

'Very, I should say. I tend to think that Archie was rather in the Robert Burns mould. Enjoying life to the full. Have you ever thought that these are two sides of the Scottish character? Many a mickle makes a muckle is one side and you're a long time 'deid' on the other!'

'I suppose you must be right.'

'They say Archie fathered seven illegitimate children. It must have been hard being employed in this house if you were a young woman with a boss like him. Mrs Todd, are you OK?'

A shout came from downstairs. 'Lennie love, we're ready for the first take.'

'You go, I'll be fine.'

Sarah sat down suddenly on a chair and looked out to the distant sea. She drew up her knees to her chest and tears, coming quite gradually at first, then fell down her face. Large, ridiculous tears which are really not to be encouraged in grown-up women who pay bills, keep large houses and bring up small children. She was going to have to stop them some day.

London's West End

It was awfully hot in the book shop and Bunny didn't really know what she was doing sitting at a small table between Psychology and Politics, but there she was, squashed behind a small table with a large bunch of flowers in a vase which constantly threatened to fall over the polished wood. And she was there smiling, the sort of smiles when you can feel every muscle protesting at the effort. But it had to be done.

'Could you please put "To Dotty" in this one and "To Rose Happy Christmas" in this one and "To Betty and David Happy Cooking" in this one?' A plump woman with a large out of town hat thumped three copies of *Bunny Cooks Big Time* onto the polished table. The flowers nearly went over, but didn't.

'Thank you *so* much, I *do* hope you will enjoy the book.'

'Oh, they're not for me, I never read anything about cooking.' Still smiling, Bunny dutifully signed and, still smiling, wished the woman good afternoon. And still smiling, greeted the next customer who wanted her copy inscribed 'To Duckface Happy Holiday.' Which, still smiling, she did.

'Would you like a cup of coffee, Bunny? I'm sure they could organise one.' Nesta, the publicity girl from the publishers, was hovering like the flowers, expensively perfumed and top-heavy, while ushering the public into line. 'Would you like to meet Bunny Halifax?' she was saying constantly to the milling public.

'No, I want Dick Francis,' came back the answer. All very encouraging, she kept telling Bunny, the queue was stretching past New Age Therapies all the way round the corner to Ethics. And Bunny kept smiling.

She had already been there an hour when Hannah pushed her way through. 'Hi, Mum, Lottie said you'd be here. I've brought you some sherbet lemons.'

'Not at the moment, Hannah, thank you.' Bunny was still smiling. Only Hannah could think she could eat flaming great sweets in public. Must be deliberate.

'Oh, is *this* your daughter?' The green hat with a small person underneath wearing glinty determined eyes pounced, 'Well, you *have* given your mother a hard time. We all felt for her. My quilting group spent all morning talking about it. I hope you are going to have Christmas with her after all.'

'Well, you know what they say. A daughter's a daughter all your life, a son's a son until he's got a wife,' pronounced a circle of scarlet lipstick standing behind the green hat. For apparently no good reason.

Hannah twisted her nose ring and shrugged. 'That's sexist. Anyway, you must be pleased with this turn-out, Mum. Do you know?' She turned to the green hat. 'The first time she did a signing no one turned up except my friend's mother. It was *so* embarrassing, wasn't it, Mum?'

Bunny kept smiling. 'Where's your father?'

'God knows. He has obviously been back to the house, because there is a half-bottle of wine for the weekend. Is he the meanest man in Britain?'

'No, darling, he just doesn't like to spend what he hasn't got.'

'Huh.' Why was Hannah being (for her) so friendly and girlish? This couldn't just be because she had offered, like a mad fool, to commit culinary as well as commercial hara-kiri, and teach the dreaded Studd some dishes? Bunny shuddered inwardly and made a mental note to remind Lottie to provide him with plastic gloves. One look at his nails and the Russians would throw up.

'So what will you be doing for Christmas young lady?' The green hat was not going to give up. Bunny realised she had spelt Duckface with two Ks and did a fairy squiggle to hide it. Which made it look as if she had spelt Duckface with two Ks.

'Oh, we're off to Scotland. Mum, I rang Sarah. She's doing a telly documentary all about that potter person and sounds really quite normal. She seemed quite pleased. And Studd is starting this afternoon, isn't he? He's really looking forward to it. He's even gone out and bought a pinny!'

'Thank you so much, I hope you enjoy the book.' Bunny snapped the book shut and dismissed the green hat.

Next the red lipstick hove into view. 'To Chris and Steve.' She winked at Bunny. 'All my gay friends love you.' Bunny tried very hard to look thrilled, but she couldn't help her upbringing.

'Mum, you're a fag hag! Street cred at last!' Hannah, laughing, knocked the flowers all over the book. In the flurry of cloths and apologies and towels to wipe off Bunny and Red Lips' coat, and the long wait with added small talk while they found another copy of the book for her to sign, Bunny knew how her mother had felt when she had arrived home in hotpants one day and had pinched the vicar's bottom. She began to blush.

'I'd better go. Byee.' Hannah turned to leave, but was grabbed by the wrist by the publicity girl. 'There Hannah. Don't go. The *Evening Standard* photographer wants to take a picture. Now girls, eyes and teeth!'

Bunny and Hannah gave some eyes and teeth. 'HAPPY BUNNIES. TV COOK REUNITED WITH DAUGHTER.' Thankfully it was a black-and-white picture, which did not bring out Bunny's scarlet face and Hannah's carrion crow lipstick.

And this was the first item Christopher saw as he settled back in the cab at Heathrow which was taking him to Kew for a quick dinner with Helen and the twins before his connecting flight to Luxembourg. Bunny's red mouth had that O of surprise and her eyes looked like those of a well-known mad duchess, while Hannah had an earring through her nose. He was less thrilled when he read they were spending Christmas with family in Scotland.

* * *

Loanside

Liddy was sitting on the kitchen table swinging her legs. They seemed to be longer here in Scotland than they ever were in London. Her brown hair, too, had grown out long and knotty and free; it was, Sarah thought, as if she had been able to expand now that she was away from the cramped city. Chiswick was always described as the height of residential chic and yet, for space, children had to dice with death across roads, or walk with their elbows tucked in for fear of banging into other people. Here the eye had room to roam over long distances and children could scour the beach for hundreds of yards without interruption.

'So Hannah's said they're coming after all.'

'Who's Hannah?' Zander was sitting by the dresser with a cup of coffee, thumbing through *Bunny Cooks Big Time*, while Theo's railway track ranged over the kitchen floor between his feet and away to the back door.

'Our cousin. She's Bunny's daughter and she's really cool. They're coming for Christmas.'

'Hannah said that. They *are* coming. I'm amazed. I'll have to ring Bunny. What made Hannah change her mind?'

'Didn't you know, Sarah, your cousin and her daughter have been all over the papers this week? They've kissed and made up apparently.'

'Wicked!'

'Be quiet, Liddy. Why? I haven't even looked at a paper with all those television people crawling about.'

'Well, Bunny and Hannah are not the only TV stars. Mummy did a whole piece to camera all about your grandfather!'

'Did you really? Liddy are you your mum's new agent? Huh, they didn't ask *me*.'

'No she isn't and it was terrifying and I doubt I made any sense at all. Why didn't you turn up, Zander? I told them you would be coming and that you knew far more than I did.'

'I doubt that. Did you know your mother, Liddy, knows far more about one Archibald Milne Robertson, potter extraordinaire, than anyone else I have ever met? Though I'm afraid she sees him through rather rose-tinted spectacles.'

'She can't see a thing without her lenses. Anyway, I didn't think Mum knew much about anything outside homey stuff.'

He pondered this. 'I think perhaps, Sarah, you need a little repositioning in the marketplace.'

'What on earth does that mean?'

He was smiling at her. He was always smiling when he looked at her. Was it a nervous habit?

'Don't forget I was in advertising in my misspent youth, before I saw the light and downshifted into artistic penury. You see, Liddy, market brands are positioned to represent certain values. You think of your Mummy just as a mummy. Full stop. Whereas in fact she is much more than that. I am beginning to discover that she is not only great to look at but brainy and intuitive with a capacity for high-energy lateral thinking. She also hides her light under a bushel to the extent that I suspect she is in fact Scottish, because that's something we do really well.'

'Ooh! Wait till I tell Dad you think Mum's lovely to look at.'

'Don't be silly, Liddy, he's joking.'

'No I'm not. I'm an artist. I know all about female loveliness, and your father would no doubt have the good sense to agree with me.'

'Daddy doesn't talk about things like that. But wait till I tell him what you said.'

Liddy leaped off the table, content to have weeks of ammunition for teasing her mother. 'Mum when is Daddy coming back?'

'Not before Christmas, I don't think. Theo, that's my ankle, put the signal box somewhere else!'

'Sorry.'

'Why does he *never* come home? It's like he's dead and I don't have a father. Where is he now?'

'Bolivia. He rang last night. He's staying in the capital La Paz. Why don't you take Theo and look it up on the map? Perhaps he'll bring you back some stamps.'

There was quite a long silence after the children had run out of the room.

'So, more coffee?' Sarah bent to clear up Theo's engines, which had crashed into a pile by the wastepaper bin. 'Have you decided what you are doing for Christmas?'

'Going up to Aberdeen to stay with some farming friends.'

'I see. Pity, I would have liked you to have met Bunny.'

'It's an odd situation, isn't it? Christopher being away all the time.'

'Well, one gets used to it. He's always travelled away for his work. Lots of navy wives have to cope in the same way.'

'But why should you *want* to?'

It was one of those questions which need space to answer because one had to try several answers on for size and filter out the honest ones.

'Marriage is about getting by with half a loaf, you know. Full crusty loaves are only for characters in novels, or cookery books of course.'

'Seems a strange diet to me. Still, your cousin certainly seems to be earning the whole loaf.' Zander pointed to the picture of Bunny surrounded by cobs and French sticks in the chapter titled *The Bread of Life!*

'Yes, as a child she always wanted the latest Sindy doll or the most expensive doll's house. Whereas I preferred to imagine that I was running a zoo or directing a circus or a ballet. Poor Bunny, at school the kids called her the Incredible Hulk.'

'What did they call you?'

'Brainiac. Incredible as it may seem.'

'I don't think it's incredible Sarah.'

'Oh God,' Sarah thought. 'Why is he smiling at me, and why are men from another planet?'

London

He came into her office without knocking. He was wearing a leather jacket, a red scarf and impossibly tight jeans. Even from where she was sitting, Bunny could see that his legs went on forever into the tight black leather boots. Then she noticed that he had not shaved, his hand carrying his motor bike helmet was dirty and he had a long scratch down one cheek.

'Hi, Mrs. H. Are you going to do me now then?'

'Er, yes. Good afternoon Studd. You're on time. Hang your jacket and the helmet thingy on the hook. Joanna will tell you where to wash your hands and where the aprons are kept.' Bunny got up, hesitating whether or not to shake his hand, and then decided not to. He wasn't paying after all, whereas she was, with the most precious commodity – her time. 'She'll also get you a chef's hat to keep your hair out of the food, though you're not a chef yet, of course.'

'Not yet Mrs H. Give us time.'

He went out and Bunny could hear that the class next door with the Russians and the Sloane down from Marlborough had suddenly gone quiet. What they must think, Bunny couldn't bear to imagine. Perhaps she could pass him off as her bit of pre-Christmas voluntary work. Cookery classes in return for Hannah suffering a family Christmas and knuckling down to her A levels seemed a high price. That union woman, Brenda something, had made it seem so reasonable, but then she didn't have to teach the little oik.

Groaning, Bunny suddenly felt cheated. What an easy ride she had given her mother in spite of all the dumping and criticism. She had found a charming ex-public schoolboy with impeccable manners and gold cufflinks. The fact he had turned out to be a charming dead loss when it came to earning money was neither here nor there. He had been a catch when it had counted. It had taken her years to admit to herself that Edward was a failure, it seemed disloyal, but it was comforting when she finally did. It made life a bit easier to bear and gave a certain nobility to keeping the marriage going when all around were losing theirs. She would earn enough for both of them.

The school was bright and airy, with two interconnecting classrooms which had large windows with red blinds, and rows of cookers and chopping boards. Ranged high up the walls there were cupboards and shelves with scales and measuring jugs and cake tins and pans and colanders. There were also posters with metric and imperial measures. Secretly, Bunny had never come to grips with metric. 250 g didn't mean much to her, even though these days one had to pretend it did. Which meant she had to be more careful than ever not to rush or cheat.

At one end of the largest classroom a group of six women were clustered, heads bent making béchamel sauce. Lucinda, the fiery brunette who now ran the school, was half encouraging and half bullying the group of exuberantly made-up Russians. Why did they always arrive wearing very large gold earrings and the brightest of red lipsticks? Only Sabrina, the Wiltshire stockbroker's wife, stood pale and ethereal wearing her pearls outside her white overall. And she was looking at Studd with a most curious expression. Bunny couldn't bear it. What must she think?

'Now the first thing we start off with is to introduce you to the kitchen. Then we are going to talk about the different types of pastry – filo pastry, puff pastry, pâté sucrée, almond pastry, hot water crust pastry, choux pastry and short crust pastry, which we are going to make this morning. Just ignore the other students.'

'Doesn't sound very exciting.'

'Studd, you have to start at the beginning. If you can make good short crust pastry, then you can make all sorts of dishes.'

'But can't you just buy it at Sainsburys?'

'Look,' (you ungrateful little sod) Bunny thought, but steeled herself not to sink to his gutter level. 'You have to start at the bottom,' (you are the bottom) 'then work up to more complicated things.'

'Can Hannah do it, then, this short crust stuff?'

Bunny didn't like to admit that she had been too busy to teach Hannah even to boil an egg. 'I'm sure she can. Now then, what do we need?'

In a way, it was like teaching a not very bright child. Patience was not her strong point, his vocabulary was limited and he obviously had never even seen a garlic crusher in his own home. Yet in his own way Studd was quick witted. He had big, capable hands in spite of being so frighteningly thin. And he did listen to what she said, even to the extent of going into the fridge to cool his hands down before kneading the pastry. The trouble was he had no charm or small talk, no social graces; flippancy seemed to take the place of humour, however much he obviously wanted to learn. He told her he and his mum lived in a council flat near World's End. She was an office cleaner, and he was redoing his GCSEs so that he could do a course at the college. What was it Hannah called it in the shop? Street cred. He had gallons and gallons of it. Or rather litres.

It was like talking to someone from another planet who spoke not just another language but had another mode of communication. Bunny felt as old as the hills and like her mother, who went mad if she ever heard someone say con-tr*ov*ersy on Radio 2. What Sarah, floating lonely as a cloud through life, would make of it, if Liddy ever brought back a Scottish Studd? She'd probably have the vapours.

But Bunny battled through, with that bright professional smile she normally reserved for income-generating activities. She gave him the line about good cooks always washing up, which she never did but there you go, and repeated half fat to flour like a talisman, and when he was finishing off, she went into the office to pay the bills, leaving him with the tea cloth in his hand. Had she enjoyed it? Was she in love with her VAT inspector!

What does Hannah see in him? Bunny had thought this fifty times in the half-hour lesson. If she was honest, Bunny had always preferred the Duke of Windsor type, foppish and fussy in stripey shirts, the sort of man who had as little libido as her and didn't make a fuss. Sex was one of those things which, like most of the food one had to eat, was supposed to be marvellous but usually was not half as good as it was cracked up to be. Better to put one's energies into making money and saving up for a Dream. In Bunny's case this was a small and perfectly formed apartment in Monte Carlo, just near the Hermitage Hotel and a short walk from the Place du Casino where she could sit and watch the super-rich glide by while eating calorific gâteaux aux chocolat. Without giving a damn. Bunny could just see it in her mind's eye. It would have an English window-box full of lavender and geraniums and a palm tree outside. And staff: a motherly Frenchwoman who would call Bunny madame at all times and, unlike Juanita, would *not* read the FTSE 100 Index when she supposed to be cleaning,

When Studd's peach pie emerged from the oven after forty-five minutes at gas mark 7 it looked lopsided but, in his eyes at least, was a culinary triumph. The Russians, who were by now well and truly béchameled, crowded around admiringly to look at the wonky strips of pastry for which Lucinda would have given them hell had they produced them. Studd looked terribly pleased with himself, and cracked a few one-liners which, even though they didn't understand, sent the women into more exclamations. His pasty face lit up and he began to show off. Bunny began urgently to need a drink.

'When can I come back then, Mrs H.?'

How long could she bear to be called Mrs H? 'Wednesday five p.m.'

'Great.' Studd wrapped up the pie. 'See you.'

Then he was gone. Great. Don't say thank you, then, you ungrateful little oik, she thought.

'*Who* was that?'

Sabrina's cut-glass vowel sounds broke through the growly chatter of the Russians. Bunny was about to say that he was just someone she was teaching for free, before adding something about working with young people to cut juvenile delinquency etc. etc, when she saw that the woman's eyes were shining; the human iceberg was positively glowing. 'What a charming young man!'

'Sexy young man. And we like! Good taste. Lucky Mrs Bunny!' On cue this came from a Russian, the one naturally with the biggest gold earrings and the most generous red mouth. Bunny had scuttled back into the safety of her office before the laughter subsided.

CHAPTER NINE

Most people will have heard of Charles Rennie Mackintosh for British architectural and interior design, but not many people will know that another ground breaking giant of European design in the twentieth century was a Scot who lived right here in Loanside.

Archie Milne Robertson was born in Kirkcaldy in 1884 the eldest of a family of eight. The Robertsons had been prosperous weavers for generations, but the arrival of the big industrial looms made them paupers with no welfare state to bail them out. At the age of twelve Archie became an apprentice at the Methven Linktown Pottery in the town, one among dozens of small potteries dotted along both sides of the Firth of Forth employed in turning out creamware and earthenware.

Sarah sat in front of her brand-new computer, squinting at the screen. Eleanor, her mentor now turned tormentor at the museum had inveigled her into writing this for the *East Lothian County* magazine. It was years since she had written a line and it was taking her hours. She had spent the morning going through her old university notes but the trouble was they seemed to have been written by someone else entirely, someone hugely bright. Whereas her own brain seemed to have furred up like a cheap kettle.

At the time, Archie must have been glad to eat, but must have seen life stretching ahead working as a potter churning out pots to support his family. However, in 1902 he finally escaped south to work for William Burton who ran Pilkington's Royal Lancastrian Pottery in Clifton outside Manchester at the sum of 2s 6d a week. He joined a brilliant team which in 1906 brought out a range of lustres, colours which shone like precious metal, which proved a hit with the aspiring middle classes. These lustres were a pigment of metal mixed with acid which were painted on glazed pottery which would then be fired in the kiln while the oxygen was burned off by adding broom or willow branches. This reducing atmosphere broke down the compounds of silver, copper and gold and if the firing was successful there would then be left an iridescent layer on the glaze. Platinum was now used for the first time, and reds, golds, silvers and greens became available in industrial ceramics. Archie quickly established himself as one of their chief potter-artists whose designs are much sought after, and by 1910 his pay had increased to a princely £1. 15s a week.

Perhaps she should describe him? His face seemed to have been with her for so long it seemed odd that no one knew what he looked like. It was hard to convey in this video age just what charisma Archie must have had. People who had met him had never forgotten his conversation or the powerful gaze of his eyes, rather like a Robert Burns or a Rasputin, or perhaps a cross between the two.

Archie had glamour. Over six feet three inches tall with thick wavy brown hair, he had a lifelong fondness for yellow waist-coats, tartan trews and kid gloves. In Fife and Manchester he must have cut a dashing figure, and later would enthrall society ladies in the elegant strassen of Vienna and later in the drawing rooms of Chelsea and the Edinburgh New Town.

For in 1911, Burton sent him to Vienna to study under the great Michael Powolny, later to teach Lucy Rie. At that time, the city was a melting pot of ideas and talents which helped drag the arts and crafts movement into the age of modernism. He was called 'der schöttische VarietéKeramiker', *the Scottish music hall ceramicist, perhaps because of his sense of humour and extravagant and colourful dress sense.*

By the time Archie returned home, he had changed from a rough and ready artist-potter to studio ceramicist and sophisticated man of the world. However the First World War arrived and Archie was posted first to the Manchester Regiment and then to the 5th battalion of the 1st Staffordshire, ironically the Potters Battalion which drew workers and pottery owners' sons from all over the Stoke-on-Trent area and brought Archie into contact with industrial potters from Burton's fiercest rivals such as Wedgwood. The battalion suffered heavy casualties between Arras and Loos. Archie survived, although a stray shell exploding near him caused deafness in his left ear for the rest of his life. Each week bits of metal would come out of his head, usually when he washed his hair. But not always. Sometimes the pieces would fall into the slip and would then fuse together with the clay in the kiln. He called these ruined pieces 'the Kaiser's Revenge'.

Sarah looked at the clock. Her feet were numb and the heating had gone off. What would it have been like to live with a man like Archie? Would she have combed the metal out of his hair each morning?

Poor William Burton did not in fact get his money's worth from Archie's expensive Viennese training. In 1920 he returned to Scotland to set up as a studio potter in Carnforth House in Dunbar Road here in Loanside. Two years later, at the age of thirty-eight he married Isobel Ritchie, a Church of Scotland minister's daughter from Musselburgh. They had two children, one son Donald and a daughter who died in infancy. Archie was apparently a devoted and energetic father.

Draw a veil, a thick one, over the illegitimate children. Hagiographies were the order of the day for these readers.

From this time until his death in 1938, Archie was at his most prolific and brilliant. He perfected a red lustre which he called his

Red Poppy Lustre, named in honour of his fallen comrades. This had a richness and fire not seen since the days of Georgio Andreoli, the great Italian master of lustreware in the Renaissance. Yet Archie's lustres in fact looked back to tenth-century pre-Islamic Egypt for inspiration; he called himself an alchemist. For it was in trying to turn base metal into gold that the ancient alchemists stumbled on the secret of lustre. They did not waste this knowledge, for if they could not procure the real thing, then the lustreware provided their Fatimid masters with the illusion that they, like Midas, could eat off real gold!

Ahead of his time, Archie was often derided for his lustreware which, however popular in industrial production, was thought vulgar and flashy and was not accepted widely in studio ceramics until the 1960s. He taught at the Edinburgh College of Art and was active in promoting studio ceramics to a wider public. In 1921 he helped found the Red Rose Guild in Manchester, a trade body for studio ceramicists and also became a leading figure in the Arts and Crafts Exhibition Society in London. All this led to much train travel – one of Archie's favourite pastimes – when naturally he would travel first-class.

And what of debts and drunkenness and losing his house and the minister's family actually selling off his muffle kiln? Keep stumm, Sarah told herself. Everyone in East Lothian was related to everyone else. Unspoken alliances forged through centuries of intermarriage remained traps for the unwary foreigner.

Unfortunately, the recipes for Archie's lustres have been lost, increasingly a cause for sadness among British potters, for whom his Red Poppy lustreware remains unequalled. At a recent sale in New York his work achieved a record $10,000 – believed to be one of the highest prices ever achieved for a single piece by a twentieth-century non-American ceramicist. A true Scot, proud of his working class Fife heritage, Archie took on Europe's finest artistic talents. His work endures in museums and private collections. He was a Scots' colossus.

Sarah was exhausted. She printed off the article and stood in the studio reading it through. She remembered another small article she had written years ago for the *Ceramic Review*. Everyone had told her that this would be the first step to curatorial greatness. Donald Gosford had toasted her to the skies.

She ran off another copy and addressed brown envelopes to Eleanor and the magazine editor. She thought of Zander and one image slid over another; she saw how like Archie he was, although if possible even taller and more muscular than his grandfather. He was in Leith and she was here in Carnforth House. And it was cold and dark with hours before sleep came. The Leith Police Dismisseth Us. Her grandmother used to make her say it every day for good diction. As a little girl she remembered thinking who were the Leith police, and where on earth was Leith? Now she knew.

Leith

This was an area to rush through with your head down. The road he lived in was a mixture of poverty and fashion. Boarded-up shops stood next to bistros and shops selling alternative remedies. People hurried by with hunched shoulders.

'Hello Sarah! Come in. Hello kids! So how many Lollops do I owe you?' Zander was standing holding open the huge metal door as Sarah and the children puffed up the four floors to the top of the warehouse.

'You must be fit here Zander. What do you mean, Lollops?'

'For the article. Come on break it to me gently how many Lollops do I owe you?'

'You're not even a member of the L.E.T.S., more fool you.'

'Oh well, how many L.E.T.S. members have you got now? Five? Seven?'

'Ninety-two, actually.' Liddy finally got to the top of the landing, only to sit with a bump on the stone flags. 'And we now have earned one hundred and forty Lollops and Mummy had a massage yesterday and I'm getting riding lessons.'

'And I'm getting my face painted on Christmas Eve,' Theo announced, red in the face from the climb.

'Liddy, give Zander that holly. Don't make a mess either of you, this is Zander's studio, where he works. Be careful and *don't* touch anything.'

'Wow!'

Liddy and Theo crashed into the studio only to stop and stare up at the huge suspended figures towering above them made of papier-mâché and metal. Behind them all along the window sill, Sarah could see dozens of glass jars filled with small change. They flashed in the light of the rush hour cars which snaked down the road below and in an apparent reflection of a fainter snake which wriggled along the opposite shore in Fife. Nearby, over in the deserted docks, just one harsh floodlight shone eerily into a blank yard.

'Happy Christmas,' said Liddy. 'So you really are an artist person. We've brought you shortbread we made ourselves in the kitchen, and Theo's got some decorations. Made of loo rolls.'

'A cornucopia, Liddy! Now look, My Christmas tree's a bachelor tree. It's lolling over there fairly undecorated as you can see, all waiting and ready for a bit of care and attention. Your presents are there, too.'

'You shouldn't have bought presents for us, Zander.'

'Sarah, I wanted to. Anyway, I'm off the day after tomorrow till after New Year. Also, by the tree there's a Jiffy bag of stuff from my childhood, pictures taken in the house. I should put them into a nice wee album, but I know I'll never do it. I don't like to label the past like that. Good excuse for laziness.'

'You prefer the impermanent. Like that figure over there.'

'That one? That's for the Scottish Dependable Life's HQ, may I say! Is the Clydebank ready?'

'I hope they're paying you well. Far from looking dependable, he looks as if he's about to lose his neck.'

'I haven't finished hanging him properly. Then he will be Mr Dependable himself. He's supposed to represent the seven ages of man in each of which, presumably, Scottish Dependable Life is able to help by flogging him yet more financial products.'

'Do they yet know their supplier is so cynical? I see that mobile of your brother is back. Didn't it sell?'

'No, but it wasn't really for sale.'

'Anyway Zander, here's your present.'

'Can I eat it?'

'Of course.'

She hoped she sounded bright and Christmassy rather than bone-weary as she was. Days planning for six guests – Marjorie, her parents, Bunny, Hannah and Edward, Jonathan having decided in typical brotherly fashion to stay with a friend in Ireland. What a business Christmas was. Making beds, cooking and freezing vast quantities, all of which involved vast numbers of ingredients and consequent fierce battling through the trenches at Tescos. Christmas meant keeping up the Santa Claus act for days and days; an Advent calendar on legs. The seventh guest, Christopher, might or possibly might not get around to carving the goose on Christmas Day itself. (For years he had told her turkeys were 'not the thing'.) He had phoned from Azerbaijan to say he would if he could. But if not, he'd be back on Boxing Day. And not to forget the Bank's New Year Ball. For which he hoped she had acquired some sort of dress.

She said she had. And she didn't protest this time at *his* total lack of dependability. Merely commented that it would be nice to see him. And she had then thanked him for the second lot of flowers, red this time, which had arrived earlier in the day from an Edinburgh florist. Eleanor had been sitting in the kitchen when they arrived and had given her a funny look. She had never married, so perhaps didn't approve of such extravagant gestures. She must think it odd a husband not knowing whether he'd be home for Christmas Day or not. Don't make a fuss, Sarah, and it will be all right. It was her mother's constant refrain, be it for cut knees or schoolgirl tantrums. Later on she had been programmed to use the formula for more serious indignities. And in not making a fuss, Sarah had neatly cut Sarah out of the equation altogether.

'A penny for them.' Zander was holding out a glass.

She shrugged and took it.

'Cheers. Happy Christmas, my dear Sarah, to your first Christmas at Carnforth.'

'I can't believe that we have been here three months!'

'By the way, about your article. Did you know that the Potteries kept the 1st Staffordshire officers' mess supplied with free dinner and tea services right up until the seventies?'

'Clever! But I don't suppose the officers would have had much use for Archie's dishes, would they?'

'No. His designs were rather impractical, particularly latterly. Though I suppose the Red Poppy lustre would have been appropriate.'

'Poor old Archie. What a past he had.'

'Well you can't escape it Sarah, God knows I've tried. David's and mine were fixed before we were even born. So you just have to enjoy the present. Cheers.'

'Look, Mummy, you and Zander are standing under the mistletoe.' Liddy was nothing if not observant. Like the various figures in the room, it swung from the beams suspended from fuse wire.

So naturally he bent down and kissed her. Instantly she could smell his hair, a particular smell, what was it? It was a chaste in-front-of-les-enfants kiss, performed in a brotherly Christmas spirit. Yet a syringe full of neat adrenalin suddenly shot right through every vein down to the soles of her size five feet. Pow! In front of her, Mr Dependable, destined for the solid Scottish Dependable Life HQ, hovered gently on its metal springs swinging in the air from the draughty window as if to say, quite politely, could he be next in line and would she like some free financial advice? Under no obligation, you understand. There would naturally be a fourteen-day cooling off period.

'Mummy! Yeuch! You and Zander are *kissing*!' Theo squawked. Who said children lack comic timing?

London Heathrow

They'd made it. Through December right up to Christmas Eve. It had cost her thousands, but in the end what the hell. It was a question of survival and keeping one's sanity. Every year, Bunny always vowed to do all her Christmas shopping in the July sales and keep a sense of proportion. But by 12 December she was always forced to ring ShopAholics & Co – that small Battersea-based saviour for all London's high-powered media women – to finish off the shopping for her. It always cost hundreds but it was worth every shiny Bond Street carrier bagful they delivered, all beautifully wrapped American-style. Their calligrapher would even whack your signature on the present tags too! Lottie always vowed that she would leave Bunny one day and work for ShopAholics. 'Imagine, shopping all day long and spending other people's money!' To which Bunny would reply that Lottie always went shopping on other people's money anyway, but then Lottie's attitude to her ex-husbands had always been the healthy 'what's yours is mine, what's mine is mine' variety, and so was impervious to such barbs.

And so Christmas came round every year with the tax bills just a wink away and Bunny's overdraft on the verge of a nervous breakdown. (Why did clients always take months to cough up? What about *her* cash flow?) Happy Christmas! Yuletide Greetings! Tell me about it. 'Why is it that the letters DR on the bank statement always get darker, the more money you're in hock for?' Bunny had once asked a glamorous Warburg's wife at a drinks do, who told her that was why she never opened bank statements on principle. DR stood for Deep Rinkles. The lady, it should be said, was wife number three and the result of much silicone and very little Essex education, but Bunny had decided that if you could afford to, it would be very good sense just to ignore bank statements completely.

So they had arrived, somehow, at Heathrow for the Edinburgh shuttle. The cases, five, all regulation Louis Vuitton, were queuing up with Hannah (sulky/sultry), Edward (buried in the *Sporting Life*) and Bunny who had caught the trick of the famous of looking vaguely into the mid-distance, while wondering desperately where the VIP lounge was and did she qualify? This did not protect her from a large family of large-bosomed grannies from somewhere ghastly, dark and northern, stepping over her cases to give her a merry Christmas hug, and calling her 'chuck'.

'Here's your boarding card. Thank you.' The stewardess with a charm-bypass gave them to Bunny. She should have had a cartoon bubble coming out of her head with 'sod off' written in large letters.

'Mum, is there time to look at the shops?' Hannah asked.

'Not really, darling. We have to get through security, and there's already a queue.' Hannah merely hunched her shoulders and looked mutinous. So they queued, in the heat and the chaos of parcels and people. Edward was talking about the racing he would go to in Musselburgh. He had actually bought himself a new shirt and tie and was looking urbane and well kept, which he certainly was. A quarter husband but better than nothing. Always beautifully mannered when he wasn't half cut. Not like Sarah's perfect, successful husband, not as good looking or as intelligent, but there you go. All part of the mystery ties which bind us.

And then she saw him. With a start, Bunny recognised who it was even before she saw his face, by the back of his head and the tilt of his neck. Christopher was standing just ten yards away talking to a woman. His face was animated, tender, his head back, roaring with laughter. She was slightly taller, in fur, full length and black, with a red hat and lipstick to match. She was almost as tall as Bunny, but beautiful of course, exotic and slim. Naturally, just the sort of exciting foreign mistress a man like Christopher *would* have. Silly Bunny for not guessing sooner. And silly Sarah for allowing herself to be shipped out of London so conveniently.

A further announcement that the plane was about to board pushed the queue forward into the arms of the security men. Of course, the fur coated woman might not be his mistress, might just be a friend. A colleague. Why should she think that there was anything in it at all? Was it just her nasty suspicious mind jumping to conclusions after too many of Lottie's escapades in the tabloids. Or perhaps that was why she could spot a mistress at twenty paces. Was it the got-him (!) body language that was so obvious once one knew the signs? And the kept-woman fur? When Bunny turned again, she had gone.

'My wife loves your show, Mrs H.' Studd! It could have been Studd talking, but it was the cheery security man, who was checking Edward over with long bold sweeps. The conveyor belt for the hand luggage to be checked had been decked on either side with tinsel, and there was a holiday mood beneath the chaos. Bunny smiled automatically. But something was shifting in the fixed-point certainties in her life and the effect left a bitter taste in her mouth. A cocktail of told-you-sos, triumph and pity which no amount of reindeers and tinsel fake snow could distract her from, mixed with half-buried loyalties. She and Sarah had not been bosom buddies for years, yet even so it was rotten. Could Sarah already know? Then Bunny realised that it was the first time she had ever seen Christopher really smile, with his eyes. It was a shock to discover that he could. Champagne. In the circumstances, it was the only reasonable solution.

Christopher sat towards the back of the plane. An absurd number of children and lax mothers were disturbing the calm of what was usually a civilised businessmen's flight. He wondered whether Maria Antonietta's Milan flight would be quieter.

He opened up his *Wall Street Journal* and glanced vaguely over the share prices. Perhaps he would soon have more reason to look up the Dow Jones Index. The director's job was his. He had been told, unofficially. So things would have to change. Sarah had to be told about Maria Antonietta after Christmas, no point upsetting her with all her family around. No point, either, in not admitting that he had failed once again to make his marriage work. No getting away from that. Sarah had worked jolly hard at everything, but he had never felt he had really known what she had been thinking. Only when she had been collecting those damn pots had her face really lit up. Still, God willing, there would be a civilised separation. Nice and friendly and hopefully not too costly, unlike with Helen. Sarah had always been perfectly nice to him and the children were sweet.

But the time had come to be honest. It was kinder. Anyway, one didn't like to be underhand about these things.

He had already spoken to his divorce lawyer, a veteran of his mauling by Helen, who had praised him for moving Sarah out of town. 'London divorces are frightfully costly, well done. I'll put you in touch with one of my Scottish lawyer buddies. Shouldn't cost much, even with those ghastly Child Support people. No school fees, you said? Nice bracing Scottish state school will save a packet.'

After all of which, life would be Washington, a Foggy Bottom apartment with Maria Antonietta, convenient for the shops and the office and the Kennedy Center. Plus stimulating White House company and a salary package to write poems about. The children could come over in the summer; they could stay in the Hamptons; Liddy could ride. A large body brushed past him and he suddenly was aware of Bunny bending over him. God, she didn't get any better looking. And she looked like she was wearing a sort of orange lace doily. Thoroughly in character.

'Christopher, happy Christmas darling!'

'Bunny, how lovely to see you.' He leaped up, ever the gallant brother-in-law. Lord! Had she seen Maria Antonietta? 'I didn't realise you would be on this plane. Are you with Edward?'

'And Hannah, yes. Christopher, this is going to be a real Scottish family Christmas, how clever of you and Sarah to fix it, it's even got Edward smiling!'

A real Scottish family Christmas. He smiled, letting her pass by to the lavatory cubicles beyond, then stood for a moment looking over the other passengers' shoulders out of the plane's windows to the mustering clouds, before slowly taking his seat. He found himself wriggling, uncomfortable. Like a fish on a hook.

Loanside

It was dark and raining fast, but even as the rain fell, the wind pushed her along the pavement, then tried to snatch the carrier bag out of her hand. But she hung on to it so fiercely that out of spite it whirled her round and round rather like a small man throwing the hammer at a Highland games. The carton of milk smashed against the wall, but still Sarah would not give up. Her eyes were streaming in the wind and her hair whipped across her face until she could not see, yet she could hear the sea pounding its wrath onto the rocks nearby. Fighting on, she staggered down the road away from the high street lights and up to Carnforth House.

It was all lit up in the darkness, a party house. The trees in the front garden were bent double with curiosity at the alluring fire burning in the giant grate, visible here even from the street. The Christmas tree gleamed with its Chelsea-white lights, and she could make out huge shadows from the figures standing by the fireplace, Edward and Christopher, making manly conversation while her mother and Bunny's made competitive small talk amid the chaos of the children's new toys. No curtain had been drawn because she had not drawn them, and so the house lit up the dark wet street with an ersatz Christmas cheer as if to say, 'Look at me. Push your nose against the glass and eat your heart out!'

Sarah pushed the gate, its metal creak answered by the trunk of the cherry tree as it bent again, insistent in the wind, right up against the drawing-room glass. Archie would have felt at home standing where she was, drinking in the larger than life exuberance of this house, putting on a show. A work of art in its own way. Except, of course, the lights would have been from gentler candles or gaslights. Electric light would have come later when middle age disillusion as well as debt had banished the parties from his life. How she wished she had been at one of them. She reached the front door, after fishing for her keys in her pocket with stiff cold fingers, opened the door and was swallowed up by the life and needs inside.

It was all very strange. After months on her own with the children in this unfamiliar town, here they all were suddenly transported from another world as if by magic. Her mother and her father and her aunt, and Bunny and Hannah and Edward and even Christopher, had all come zooming back into her life, full of Christmas excess and requiring meals three times a day, with menu variations to take account of incipient angina, obesity and vegetarianism. After endless trips to the supermarket, each time pushing a trolley piled so high she could have run over several children and small grannies without noticing, Sarah had finished shopping and was on the point of collapse on Christmas Eve. Except then she couldn't because, of course, there were planes to meet and over-excited children to placate and miracles of cuisine to create, for a TV supercook for a cousin, a perpetually dissatisfied mother and a husband who was like a polite stranger, used to eating in the world's best restaurants. But it helped in a way because as she had to work from morning till night, she was too busy to think of Zander, who was now far away and whose physical presence made her feel not the usual dead boring Sarah, but someone who had glamour and brains. If she could just bottle it! But now the show must go on. Christmas with towering egos to please, while trying to see that her own children were happy, always happy. As a child Sarah had dreaded those broken expectations and the stiff social gatherings.

'Can I help?' they all asked. 'Can I help you?' 'Do let me help.' This was said on average five or even ten times a day as a sort of talisman protecting them from actually having to get up and do anything. For, of course, no one actually wanted to help, nor did they. That was not in the script. They were all on holiday. Sarah didn't work, after all. She had nothing else to do.

Christopher reminded her every day that they were *her* family. His own were elsewhere, for Helen and the twins were staying with friends in Wiltshire and his mother had decamped as usual to the Australian summer. He would open the wine, looking frightfully distinguished, and then wander around with a corkscrew oozing *bonhomie* and saying it was the least he would do. Which it was. He would also carve the meat, mean little slices which took so long to produce that the meal was always stone cold by the time everyone was served. Sarah would beg him to let her do it downstairs with the electric knife and he would look aghast, just as he did when he had caught her putting out fish knives one day for some dinner guests.

Families have pecking orders. Sarah had always wondered who established them. Why was one positioned in them in a particular way, and what secret, invisible alchemy made the order shift and then ossify for years, while the person at the bottom or at the top had to live their life in two realities, their own and that of the family? She had grown up, as much as Doreen would let her, reasonably near the top. She was the pretty one, the clever one, the one who would get there one day, wherever 'there' was. Then there had been a change of role, and she had been cast as the neurotic one who had problems of an unspecified nature. Even after she made a good marriage to a high-earning City man, who could read right through the *Financial Times* as if it had been written specially for him, after she had produced two beautiful, clever children and had entertained and had lived in one of the smartest parts of London, still the position had remained. Fixed in Surrey superglue.

Why? Bunny had been the also-ran, but this holiday, with her new peak-time show finally breaking through to the big time, she was far higher up the family pecking order. She was the rich one, the famous one, though Sarah could not feel jealous or envious of her success. In fact, she admired Bunny for having done so brilliantly. Yet the thought was there that she somehow had slipped several degrees down some invisible ladder. She was here to serve. Marjorie and Doreen grew more indomitable as they grew older; they spoke over what she said, except when she told them about Loanside L.E.T.S.; how they howled with laughter! Only her children put her top of the tree, first to see their stockings and sample their fun. But for how much longer?

Hogmanay had arrived. Tonight she would cook pheasant, served with mangoes. Everyone said that they could quite happily live on bread and cheese with something to bring the New Year in, but when she said that would be wonderful, their faces fell. 'Bread and cheese! Rather a depressing way to bring in the New Year Sarah! Any more sherry?' Doreen was surrounded by all the TV guides and, being at the top of the family pecking order, had hold of the TV remote control panel.

'Now, before The Hogmanay Show it's either the *King & I* or *Genevieve*.'

'Again!' There was a groan which dissolved into the rival attractions of Yul Brynner and Kenneth More, while Sarah went downstairs like a tweenie maid to start the supper. The light was off in the kitchen and, as she fumbled for the switch, she could see the white snake of the lighthouse beam sliding across the ceiling and the walls and the floor before disappearing. She just stood for a moment, letting its slow methodical creep come round and then darkness, and then around, then darkness, while outside in the blackness, the wind whirled. 'Sarah, are you down here? I'm opening the Chardonnay for this evening. Do we have any more pudding wine?' The light clicked on behind her. Christopher was standing there, looking annoyed. 'What on earth are you doing here standing in the dark? I thought there had been a fuse for a moment.'

'I was just watching the beam.'

'Why? You've been here too long without a break. I think you ought to have a weekend in London. I'm sure Helen would be happy to have you.'

'I would hardly go to her, now would I?'

'She's *very* fond of you. Now your mother wants more disgusting sweet sherry. I am sure she must be the only person on the planet who still drinks it, and your Auntie Marjorie wants *yet* another martini. Your father is asleep in the dining room, Hannah is upstairs with the children, teaching them God knows what! Edward and I are going up to the studio to talk like adults. Though I wonder what he does with his life these days.'

'Don't touch the lustre pieces.'

'Those bits of old pottery? I nearly cleared them out. No I won't, though I think that room really ought to be a study with curtains.'

'Would you like me to make it into a study for you, Christopher, for when you come back permanently?'

'I'll just take this bottle upstairs. God, Christmas is hard work.'

He was off. She looked at the bunch of mistletoe lying on the sideboard. Perhaps he needed the mistletoe treatment?

'I do think this house has potential, Christopher, there is so much you could do with it, you could knock through and have a nice Edwardian-style conservatory.'

'We have already spent enough, Doreen, actually.' Later that evening, when everyone had eaten and nibbled and drunk enough to make them want to not move even the smallest muscle, they were all sitting in the drawing room looking into the fire. The television had even been pushed into the corner until midnight. Hannah was lying on the floor by the fire, her legs cased in tights, spread right across the blaze. Theo was sitting on her stomach, already in his pyjamas, but having wheedled his way into staying up.

'Maybe I could film one of the programmes in my series from here?'

'I don't think so, Bunny. Sarah would not thank you. She had a TV crew clambering all over the place doing a programme about that potter who used to live here.' Christopher's tone was disapproving.

'Archie Milne Robertson. Did I tell you, Mum, that I did a piece talking to the presenter about him?'

'No, darling. I would have thought it was rather a long time ago when you were into all that sort of thing. Funny how everyone thought you were going to be the V & A's great white hope. I always said that they didn't know you like we did.' Doreen sipped her wine cautiously, while her red nails glided over the box of chocolates spread on a nearby table, ready to pounce for the butterscotch.

'I dug out all my old notes, and it comes back.'

'Hannah, your aunt was fearfully intellectual and the time I visited her in St Andrews she never stopped working and producing essays with big words like modernism and post-modernism.'

'Better than fricassee and marinate, Bunny.'

'Not if you're hungry they're not. Hannah, they had, I don't know if they still have, the weirdest traditions. They wore cloaks on Sundays, and then processed through the streets, of which there are only three at a rough count. No train station and lots of wind. I can't imagine how the students didn't go loopy. Except that most of them were in-bred Sloanes, and pretty loopy to start with.'

'They were not, Bunny! Anyway, the dressing up was part of student tradition.'

'Oh I know, Sarah, *I* wouldn't understand. Do you know, Hannah, in your aunt's day students used to get plastered all the time. They weren't all short back and sides and doing MBAs like they are now.'

'Studd isn't.'

'Hannah dear, he's getting to be quite a decent cook, but he's hardly university material, is he?'

'Don't be snotty, Mother. So, Auntie, what was he like then, this Archie bloke who had this house?'

'Oh well, he lived here for sixteen years and did all this carved panelling. He married and had a son and created the most remarkable pots. What I would give just to own one.'

'Can't you afford to buy her one, Christopher, with all your World Bank dosh?' Bunny sat nursing her whisky, 'You must have saved a fortune selling up in Bedford Park.'

'Well, it would depend how much they went for at auction. There is no way I would pay the mark-up at a gallery.'

'Not all lustreware is expensive. A Gordon Forsyth bowl for example, went for just £1000 at Christie's a few weeks ago.'

'I don't know how you possibly know that, Sarah.'

'Lachlan Brodie, the producer of the programme, told me.'

'Do I hear a so-there in the ether? Seems an absurd amount for a china dish.'

'Funny to think that there was another family here for years before us. Sitting here getting overweight and sloshed just like we are, well, as *you* all are.' Hannah sat up and reached for the peanuts.

'Speak for yourself, Hannah! Seriously, though, I don't think you ever *own* a house, not totally. You are only ever lent a house to live in.'

'Usually, Sarah, because it effectively belongs to banks.' Christopher laughed at his own bitter joke.

'No, I meant in a spiritual sense.' Sarah was insistent.

'Oh in a *spiritual* sense, I see. You would never think you were a banker's wife.'

'What were they like? The Robertsons?'

'I've got pictures of Archie and his wife upstairs in the studio, Hannah, but there are some pictures of Archie's grandchildren near you, over there on the piano. The grandson Zander is a friend.'

'He kissed Mummy under the mistletoe,' Liddy cut in.

'Lucky Mummy,' said Christopher. Sarah wondered why she had never realised before just how ridiculously abusive people can be while being apparently, on the surface, so terribly terribly amusing.

Isn't it odd the power of pictures. How you can recognise the familiar and the almost long forgotten. Theo could see the ark, and two small boys, obviously Zander and David, in the cut-down adult clothes children wore in the fifties and early sixties. And the very old lady sitting grumpily in the corner was obviously Isobel with a lorgnette, looking on perhaps disapproving at their boisterousness. The pictures spilled out all over the floor. Sarah wished she hadn't started; she knew Christopher in this mood would make some crack about bankrupt artists and repossessions which, in the panelled drawing room, bought and paid for with so much raw talent, would have seemed a betrayal.

Christopher, Edward and Bunny, she could see, were just looking at them for clues, small signals which could be understood and decoded to show the Robertson's exact social position.

'What did the father of these boys do?'

'Archile's son? He was Iain Milne Robertson. He worked for one of the Edinburgh banks I gather,' Sarah said.

'Looks like a bank clerk.'

'No I gather he was quite high up.'

'Senior, Sarah, not high up,' he corrected her.

Soon everyone got bored. It is very boring looking at photographs of people one has never met, and so they were quickly handed back. Doreen remarked that in America people's possessions are auctioned off on the pavement. She had seen a documentary about it.

Then Sarah saw the face.

It was a shame. If only she had just bunched them up and pushed them back into the Jiffy bag, then she would have just seen David and Zander as small boys with their parents. Harmless. But there was the face, contorted while lifting a log in the garden. The same face she had seen hanging from Zander's studio ceiling. The same face which had been up close to hers long ago. She turned the photograph over. '*David in the garden*' someone had scrawled in pencil.

'Relax, don't scream. Don't be a stupid bitch. God you're no fun! What's the matter with you?' She flinched. The voice hurled itself with such force into her head she was surprised everyone else did not hear it. Now she was holding the picture so tightly she could no longer feel the paper. Had she made a mistake? It might not have been him. She looked at it again. She knew. It was him. What a stupid stupid *stupid* bitch.

She could hear exclamations as she rushed out of the room. 'Is Sarah all right?' 'Was it the pheasant? Oh dear, we've all had it.' 'Did she undercook it? She usually does. What a way to bring in the New Year.' She ran up the stairs and wrenched open the heavy carved door, and fell onto the cold tiled floor. She vomited, again and then again. There were sounds of screaming in her ears, and a sobbing fury. She had bought his house. *His* house! She felt a huge, raging sense of loss, and a complete loneliness. Then Liddy's hand was rubbing her back, crying out, 'Are you all right Mummy, are you all right?' before she passed out.

CHAPTER TEN

London

Lottie was in the shower, so at first didn't hear the phone. On the radio Gloria Gaynor was singing about how she would survive, which was turned up very loud. Lottie always enjoyed the chorus, testament to the seventies when she had been both extremely young and cellulite free. It was only after several wails about how she would survive somehow or other with all her life to live, that she heard the phone from the bedroom emitting an expensive purring sort of wail. 'Bunny, is that you?' It was obviously a payphone. Lottie could see water coursing down onto the cream carpet under her bathrobe. Chudder chudder, a train on its way to Windsor, chundered past followed by slower, filthy goods trucks.

'Lottie, it's Bunny. I seem to have found the only place in the UK where my mobile phone does not work.'

Bunny's voice sounded reedy and distant, as if ringing from some far away country where years ago you had to book your calls in the middle of the night. Lottie shifted one perfect, well-shaved leg, admiring the French polish on her toenails.

'Happy New Year, Bunny darling.'

'Don't! I have my daughter and husband eating themselves to death, my mother and aunt have been introduced to the delights of the WorldWide Web this holiday and they are now busy planning a Surrey pensioners' Website. And my cousin fainted while being sick last night before midnight and now is in bed looking all whey-faced and interesting. Either she discovered that her husband is having an affair – I saw him with his fur-coated cliché of a mistress at the airport – or she is pregnant. My brother-in-law Christopher is, naturally, horrified at the prospect of entertaining her family single-handed and is wandering around not able to find anything to eat. Because, of course, he's hardly ever here and doesn't know where anything is. So I have just sneaked out for an omelette pan. Somebody's got to feed the mob and Sarah is down to three knives, not a Sabatier in sight and the oldest set of pans you ever saw.'

'Horrors! What's it like? Scotland?'

'Cold! Come back Beauchamp Place. The people are kindness itself, but the cold, and wind! I feel a hundred and can't stop eating lentil soup. I'm putting on pounds. And to make things worse my books are remaindered in the local shop! Anyway, I've only got a pound, so I'm just ringing to ask what's happening, if anything.'

'London's dead at the moment. I don't know why I never go away at this time of year. Three bookings came in the day after Boxing Day for spring parties, someone wants a quote for a wedding in Herefordshire, and your agent rang and wants to fix up lunch with a new editor.'

'Another one! That's the fifth.'

'Anyway, you'll have to ring her. Oh, and forty Soroptimists from Dublin want to do a one-week course in the spring sometime, so I sent off a brochure.'

'What do chiropodists want to cook for?'

'I've no idea. I can't stand these women-only things.'

'No comment. Could you book just one last lesson for Studd – I think six lessons are more than enough doing the sainted mother bit, and get him to sort out the recipe index if he's bored. I feel Hannah *must* believe I've done my bit. Might buy her a car next year. That would take her mind off him.'

'Bunny, your daughter is only as crazy about him as every other woman under forty.'

'But why? What is so special about an oiky little boy with too much grease on his hair? Lottie, stop acting as if you're sixteen.'

'Well if you can't see why, Bunny, then there is no hope for you.'

'Don't seduce him, that's all I ask. Still got twenty pence left. What are you doing today?'

'Going to church.'

'Church! I thought you were a designer Buddhist, or was that last month? Oh Lord.'

'What, Bunny, you can't be that anti-church?'

'I've just noticed Christopher is hovering outside this kiosk looking furtive. He obviously has *not* twigged that I'm inside.'

'Oh, Bunny. How could he?'

'Exactly. Men *are* predictable bastards.'

'Your poor cousin. Well, you're lucky anyway, Edward isn't a bastard.'

'No he's a love most of the time, if achingly predictable. OK, here are the beeps.'

The line went dead.

'Poor Sarah,' said Lottie, who just for once was feeling on the side of the angels.

Loanside

If she closed one eye, she could see the lighthouse sitting high up on the rock, its tall white tower barely distinguishable from the white winter sky. If she closed the other eye she could make out the Bass Rock towering and glowering out to sea amongst the seabirds. It was a beautiful view she hardly ever had the leisure to see; she was never in bed in the daytime. Then a long, slow, red tanker glided between the two on its way to Leith, slow and yet it passed both points surprisingly quickly and was soon out of sight. In London she had become used to the regular flights to Heathrow passing overhead, noisily carrying passengers in from Australia and the USA. Yet here, with the same regularity, there would be boats coming in from Africa and the Azores, filled with cargo bound for the docks. What would it be? Bananas? Rice? Copper? Should she hate this house now? She couldn't decide. There was a sort of black, leaden, crow-like weight sitting on her head.

There was a cartoon figure when she was a child who had been made to wear a pointy white cap with a D on it. A dunce's cap for a dunce. Perhaps it would be easier on the pain if she wore one, to label her stupidity. Everything was changed, all the furniture in her head had shifted, until she no longer recognised the rooms her spirit lived in all these years. The rape. David Milne Robertson. There! She'd said them both. It was like a huge snake bite, or an abscess, its poison seeping into everything she did, even if she did not know it at the time. And she had let it, of course, because it's hard work being a victim, and of course everyone agreed Sarah did love hard work. But how did you stop the poison of some old semi-forgotten mistake seeping and staining the fabric of your life in a way you could not, ever, wash out? They had yet to invent the soap powder.

She remembered the first time she saw Christopher at the E&A Bank. She had been working in Corporate Finance, wearing a new navy woollen suit, with her hair looped up in a chignon. And he had walked past her desk, a stripey-shirted God in a Savile Row suit. He had invited her out for cold white wine at the wine bar over the road. In his coolness and politesse she had recognised such a comfortable haven from the lashings of her own spirit. He had liked the fact that she had not leaped into bed with him, her fear matching his *froideur* exactly. He had also liked the fact she had the collector's bug; they had tramped around junk shops and auction rooms like a pair of pirates with a treasure map. With marriage, the poison had been halted because she had been given so much to do. But what a joke. All the time, the snake in her past was just waiting in the wings, for the cue to slide back centre-stage. And so she had gone and bid for Carnforth House. Lovely biting black comedy. She could just howl.

No doubt Archie, had he been alive, would have told his grandson to sow his wild oats. Had Archie ever pushed some girl on to a carpet? Only later, as he had worked his wheel, persuading himself that she had been asking for it? Women have always been programmed to be polite, to smile sweetly and not make a fuss until the damage had been done. How many backstreet abortions had he paid for? Everyone knew of the seven illegitimate children, but how many more poor little bastards had he fathered, who had spent their lives running around East Lothian, not adding up? Sarah suddenly wished she could be like Bunny, rich in her own right, with her own bank account, her own stocks and shares, successful and invited to things. But then, if any man laid a finger on Bunny, she would kick his head in.

Overhead there were thuds and footsteps crashing as the children played, and she could hear voices in the garden, her mother's mostly, pointing out various plants to Marjorie. 'They're euphorbias, supposed to thrive in this salty air, though these obviously have without Sarah's help.'

The door opened and Christopher came in, carrying a tray. A cup of tea and an omelette presented à la Bunny with circles of radicchio and sculpted carrots and tiny roasted potatoes.

'Right. Here we are. Bunny has been, as they say, at it!' Christopher put it on the bed and leaned over to plump up her cushions. He was wearing a yellow cashmere sweater she had never seen before and wore aftershave, discreet and unEnglish.

'You smell nice.'

'So, how are you?' He sat on the bed, his arms folded. What a distinguished figure he must cut in his other life.

'I'm fine darling, thank you. I'll be up soon.'

'Don't rush. You still look pale. Your mother thinks you might be, well . . . Shall I get a kit from the chemist?'

'Do you think I'm pregnant? Hardly! We've not exactly been swinging from the lampshades lately.' She hoped she sounded light-hearted.

'No.'

'Christopher, I'm not.'

'Good. I just thought you might be.'

He sat staring out to sea. He didn't say Zander's name, but with that instinct of someone who has probably been married far too long, Sarah could read him like Marjorie's *Reader's Digest.*

'And I haven't been swinging from the lampshades with anyone else, I assure you. I'm just a bit run down.'

'I quite understand.'

'So when do we have quality time then, Christopher, you and me?'

She took his hands and noticed they were smooth and manicured, the thumbnail a perfect arc.

'Well of course there's the ball tomorrow night. If you'll be up to it.'

'I meant besides that.'

'Oh Sarah.' He stood up. She expected him to bend over her and kiss her on the forehead, but he didn't. He looked down in a good-natured, vague sort of way and walked out of the room. 'Get some rest now. I'll try and keep the children quiet.' The door closed with a click of dismissal.

It was the wreath on the door which reminded Morag yet again that Sarah was different, well, from almost anyone she had ever met. None of the usual tinsel and bells, but dark pine with crimson velvet ribbons intertwined with dried cones and odd bits she didn't recognise. It was also the solidity and wealth of the house, from its wrought iron gate to the expensive pots in the front path. No plastic hardware store jobbies here. But then Sarah was the first rich English woman who had bothered to get to know her. The rest were so noisy, arriving with loud voices, driving too fast. So bloody over-confident, as if they owned the place, when it wasn't even their own country. 'Don't get started Morag,' she said to herself. Come on, Sarah. Would she never answer the door!

Morag tried the bellpull again, and stamped her feet on the frosty ground. A tall man opened it. 'Hello, Christopher, remember me from the L.E.T.S. fair? I'm Morag. Is Sarah about at all?'

He looked as if he had a bad smell under his nose, Morag thought, as she was shown into the sitting room where an old woman was sitting on the couch with Liddy. Even upside down, she could see they were wedding photographs. How like her mother Liddy was getting. Same thick hair and expressive face. Just a quick thought dropped its cargo on its way before she stepped forward to say hello. The husband's got a nice tight bum. But why on earth did Sarah ever come to marry a cold, upper-class fish like that?

'Hello, dear.' The woman had immensely bouffant light brown hair and red lipstick and looked apparently very pleased to see her. 'Now! I think the cleaning stuff has all been taken down to the broom cupboards in the kitchen. This room needs a good going over and the kitchen floor should be scrubbed, really. Those fancy French tiles really do trap the dirt, I find. Nothing like a nice bit of lino. Though we've all done our best, of course. We'll be down to paper plates soon!'

'Gran!' This is Morag, Mum's friend!' Liddy's face was scarlet. There was a short silence.

'Oh, silly Gran, I thought your father said the agency was sending someone round.'

'Hello. I'm Morag. I'm a skivvy in other people's houses but not this one, thank God. I wouldn't fancy doing all that wooden panelling. No skiving off with a wee bottle of Mr Clean-it with all that, eh?'

The woman just gave a tight smile, without showing any of her teeth. She had Sarah's large green eyes, but that was about all. Her lips were red and fleshy and her nails were red claws.

'Mummy's in bed. We think she's got a bug.'

'Liddy and I are just looking at Mummy and Daddy's wedding pictures, aren't we? Look at all those nice silver horseshoes we had on everybody's plate. And there's your granddad in his Moss Bros looking ever so smart, don't you think, talking to Lady Morton, your daddy's godmother. It was a lovely function room. What do you think of my hat? Sixteen green silk roses on it! Don't hover, dear, do sit down.'

'Thanks.' Morag sat down. 'Is Mrs Halifax here?'

'No, Bunny and Edward have popped up to Edinburgh to look at the shops. Should think there'll be lots of fans buying her book with their Christmas vouchers. We all fly back tomorrow, so it is a last chance. I went up yesterday and got this lovely cardigan from Jenners. You Scots are so polite; the assistants couldn't do enough!'

Morag was glad she had the *Bunny Cooks Big Time* safely tucked up in a plastic bag. Odd you tended to lump all the south-east English into one rather snobby bag, but Sarah's mum had a different English accent from Christopher's, and she had a horrible charm bracelet which dangled and flashed in the Christmas lights.

'Where do you stay in England?'

'Surrey, dear, south-west of London. Do you know it?'

'No. That's the sort of place you hear of on the news. Where pops stars live. I've actually never even been to London.'

'Never!' Liddy looked up, utterly shocked. 'Not once. I can't imagine anyone grown up never having been to London in their whole lives!'

'Well, not everyone can afford it you know, Liddy. But then, London isn't what it once was. It was such fun in the fifties and sixties. You could dress up and have a nice day out, lunch at Swan & Edgar and take in a show. Now you're filthy in five minutes and find you spend a fortune on nothing at all. You can have a whole carriage on the underground and hardly see a white face. It's very sad.'

Morag smiled politely and there was silence. She admired the Christmas tree decorations – white and gold to match the lights – and the way the Christmas cards had been looped up on velvet ribbons; really big cards they were too, on stiff card. Some with foreign languages on the front. But there was a post-Christmassy depressing feeling in the room. In spite of the fire, it was cold. She then thought of her own wee crowded flat down on the Scheme, and tried very hard for at least thirty seconds not to feel envy. Here, everything was straight out of a magazine. Just the way the cushions had ruched contrasting pinks. Another way of living altogether.

'Sarah says you can go up,' Christopher called through the doorway. 'I'm pleased you've come because Sarah is clearly not well and we have to go out this evening. I'm sure you will buck her up. May I take your coat? How many Lollops do I get for making the coffee?' There was five seconds' worth of smile as she took off her scarf and bonnet. What a smile! It hit her like a great whoosh of Hollywood sunlight. A very good reason for Sarah to marry him, if it wasn't so carefully rationed. Now she wished she hadn't worn her plastic mac.

'Christopher, will you give me a kiss?' Later that afternoon, Sarah was drying her hair at her dressing table and looking out to sea as Christopher came in with the coffee. Her face was as white as the sky, but at least she was alive. Just. Christopher placed the cup and saucer on the glass top. Doulton china. No mugs for Christopher when he was home. He lightly kissed her head, as one might kiss a niece one hadn't seen for six months. 'I mean a proper kiss.'

'All right, a proper kiss.' This time he brushed her lips and looked at the carpet, like a dutiful husband who thought his wife needed a bath.

'Thanks a lot.' Sarah switched the hairdryer back on.

'You're most velcome, *Fräulein*.' Christopher put on his stock German accent. Still, Morag would be back soon, and then mousey wife number one would show him! She brushed her hair fiercely. The worm would turn if it could, just for once, find the courage to stop being a worm.

One of the most exciting discoveries Sarah had made about Loanside was that it had secret treasures and a thick layer of sophistication, which lay hidden behind the novelty shops and the Everything Under A Pound signs, often lurking behind very ordinary-looking front doors. She would never have known it but for the L.E.T.S. scheme and it had made all the difference some days when the culture had seemed too different.

This secret treasure was not to be found in the county set who lived outside the town behind high walls, whose divorces made headlines in the better tabloids, though not in the respectful local rags, and who tended only to mingle with the *hoi polloi* at the off-licence. Nor among the Edinburgh professionals, who travelled from Loanside up to the financial services companies in Edinburgh cocooned in fast company cars, who never guessed just how much they were despised by the native Loansiders. These people never shopped in Loanside, unless they had run out of milk, and then complained loudly when yet another local shop went out of business. Between these two groups, Loanside was burdened under a pall of prosperous apathy which even the ever-generous public services could not replace.

No, this treasure was found in another group, uniquely Scottish, the returned Scots who had made the big time down south and had come back to raise their kids. Thus, the local restaurant was owned by a chef who had been trained at Le Manoir aux Quat' Saisons, one of Bunny's favourite Michelin munchers, and the hairdresser had trained at Vidal Sassoon. The chiropodist's wife had been Jean Muir's chief cutter for years, and the beautician who worked from home had been in the make-up team at the BBC.

These people were a priceless resource who, now back on their own patch, kept their heads down. 'I kent yer faither', or you're no better than you ought to be, being the curse of the Scottish psyche. But Sarah had winkled them out, even though in London she had rarely visited the establishments where they had worked. Here in Loanside, their conversation was full of names which had once dropped out of her *Evening Standard* every night, reminding her of that old world she had once lived in, though to such little effect.

Tonight she was going to need some of these special people and Morag had gone away promising to organise it. Bliss. Someone else to do the organising for her, for once.

'Sarah, you look awful! What's happened?' Morag had said when she had come in earlier, like a gym mistress whose favourite pupil was stuck on a rope. And so she had told her she'd had a shock, something in her past that had come back to haunt her. She couldn't go into details, but it had knocked her for six. And Morag had agreed it was awful when the past came back to haunt you. 'Like whenever I see Kirsty's bastard father hanging round the Co-op with his shirt hanging out and his fag dripping off. Waster!'

'Well, I have to leave to go to the Edinburgh & Aberdeen

Bank Ball in less than three hours, and the dress I was going to wear looks awful on me, because I feel lousy.'

'And you do look like shite, Sarah, actually. Heroin chic Cinderella. What's the time now? Half past four. See me? I'm your fairy godmother. Just you wait.'

How Morag ever got all these special people to turn out the afternoon of New Year's Eve when they had families to be with, Sarah never knew, but perhaps the Cinderella line worked, in spite of the handsome prince who stomped in and out looking for cufflinks and his shaving foam. But there they were, Kerry to sort out her hair, and Eilidh who was laying out tubes of foundations and eyeshadow ready to pounce once she had chosen what to wear. Which dress? Morag's mum, Jackie, was laying all the dresses on the bed for Sarah to choose. Ten of them, all sparkling with possibilities and more or less *décolletée*. Jackie worked at the local dress agency and had the keys over Christmas because the owner was away in the Bahamas. So all the stock, size 12, designer stuff brought in from Edinburgh, was lying there on the double bed.

'I hope these are in your colour range, Sarah.' Jackie gave a Catherine Walker silk gown a twitch.

'I don't know what my colour range is, Jackie. As long as it's not black.'

'Mummy, can I come in?' Sarah could hear Liddy's voice outside the door, higher than ever with excitement. 'All right, just for a minute, but we're busy darling.'

Morag opened the door and in came Bunny with a tray of glasses filled with champagne. 'Fooled you! Doesn't Liddy sound just like I did at her age? Chip off the old chopping block. Here we are. Hello, I'm Bunny Halifax. Can I join you? Nice little Catherine Walker there Sarah, and, good God, a Lindka Cierach! You jammy dodger. She dresses all the best duchesses you know, Kent and Westminster for starters! Sarah you *shall* go to the ball. Hi, girls, I'm Bunny Halifax. And you're the Loanside fairy godmother brigade I imagine.'

Whether it was because Bunny was over six feet tall or whether it was because these days her personality was used to projecting itself to millions, somehow Bunny whacked a spell over the room which magicked Morag's mum, a chatty, motherly whirlwind half a minute earlier, into a wee wifie hovering and tongue-tied. Morag metamorphosed into a clumsy, moon-faced teenager and Kerry, a tall striking girl who had cut the hair of some of London's most famous heads, was once again the salon junior. And Sarah, minus fairy coach, was back to being the younger cousin in the family pantomime.

Bunny was smiling at her from the other side of the bed, a glass of champagne in one hand and the other hand on her hip, ready for action. She now painted her nails scarlet, Sarah noticed for the first time. She had always bitten them when they were children, but now they were long and predatory. You had to admire her.

'Good God! You've *still* got them. I haven't got a single thing from my childhood, everything got pulverised.' Bunny was looking at Sarah's crystal dogs and cats on the dressing table, which sparkled in the bedroom light and every sixty seconds flashed as the beam from the lighthouse winged around the room. 'I used to tease you so much about them. I thought they were completely useless, but here they are after all this years, while all my dolls were dismembered years ago. I was heavily into big-breasted fashion dolls, I'm afraid girls. With the benefit of hindsight and articles by psychotherapists in glossy mags, I now know of course these had a very detrimental effect on my body image, whereas playing with transparent dogs and cats would have been much healthier unless I had snapped a leg off, cut myself and bled to death of course.' Bunny's laughter mingled with others', as infectious as the bubbles on the champagne now rising in long straight lines up their glasses. It was so long since Sarah had thought about their childhood with Bunny and the unexpected sweetness of it swept over her. They were having a party.

Suddenly the door banged and Bunny disappeared. 'Where's she gone, Jackie?'

'She's had an idea I think, hen. What a whirlwind! You're not at all alike are you? Now which one are you going to wear?'

Heavy steps running upstairs and Bunny burst in with an armfuls of goodies. 'Right! Black satin evening shawl Edward bought me at Harrods' sale. Monty Don bracelet to die for, emerald necklace Edward bought me at Christie's, well, he put his hand up and I threatened to bite his armpit if he didn't keep it up! Finally an evening bag bought on the Via Condotti, which cost about ten million lira, possibly the price of a three-bedroom terrace job in Romford but then my maths when it comes to lira is not great!'

'Bunny, thanks!'

'Don't be wet, Sarah. Now get a grip. You've got to stun that husband of yours, so he can't take his eyes off you. *Make* him realise just how lucky he is. Husbands take you for granted if you let them. Look, I'll lend you whichever you like or the lot. Make a decision, let's get weaving!'

There was a bitterness and an understanding in Bunny's tone which Sarah had never heard before. She watched her cousin lay the booty on the bed; an unlooked-for ally. Perhaps the black abyss, into which she had threatened to fall into all these years, had a bottom after all. She had reached it last night when she had held that photograph in her hand. She now knew the man's identity and knew, too, that he was dead. So even as she still trembled with the shock, there was a strength coming from knowing she had survived whatever the cost. She was alive and living in the man's house and being made beautiful for a ball while he was dead, an accountant who didn't add up. And she wouldn't think any more about what his grandfather would have said if he had known. Archie was nothing to do with it.

They had finished! And if, as Morag said, when you are thirty-eight it takes two hours and four people to wave a magic wand, rather than two seconds and a pumpkin, then at least the magic had worked. Sarah knew it had by the way Christopher blinked as he stood on the landing letting her pass. He always did this when he was impressed and couldn't think of anything suitably urbane. Bunny was right. She could look stunning! Who'd have thought it?

Kerry and Eilidh thought she could give Jerry Hall a run for her money, while Morag's mum said she looked like Charlotte Rampling or Liz Hurley. 'She looks fuck all like Liz Hurley to me,' said Morag and they all fell about, the champagne having worked its own magic by then.

'Mummy, you look beautiful.' Liddy's real voice this time came up the stairs like sweet perfume as Sarah walked down. Down below, sleepy Theo lay in Edward's arms and Eilidh and Kerry and Morag and Jackie stood behind the family in the hall, beaming proprietorially. They had gone for the dark pink Lindka Cierach in the end because it brought out the green of her eyes and set off her fair skin. It had a full skirt and a nipped-in waist with a beautifully beaded silk jacket over a tight ruched bodice. It was meant for someone with curves, and the courage to enjoy them. 'Ladylike, sex-kitten,' Eilidh had said, as she put the sixtieth layer of lipstick on with a brush and pressed it off. 'Perfect for an Edinburgh wankers ball,' Morag had added, now on her third glass. Sarah's hair was swept up excitingly and subtly streaked with temporary sparkles. She wore Bunny's emerald necklace, which did wonders for a girl's *décolletage*!

Down the stairs she went, to her family who were all waiting to see her off. Of course, just because you are paranoid does not mean that your family are not out to get you. Sarah suddenly thought of Batman and Robin walking into The Penguin's lair.

POW!

'Well, you look a lot better now than you did last night. I went round the loo with a nice strong bleach, by the way.' But her mother's opening broadside simply pinged off her skin. Feeble.

ZAMMM!

'Oh, Doreen, look. Shame that you've got so round shouldered Sarah, but you do look a bit like Audrey Hepburn in *My Fair Lady*, you know, in the scene when she floats down the stairs and Rex Harrison finally offers her his arm and she goes off to the ambassador's ball.'

SPLAT!

'Although at the time Audrey Hepburn was not in her late

thirties with two children.' Easy-peasy, Auntie, Sarah thought, you can do better than that.

'You look great, Sarah.' Bunny was standing there proudly with another full glass in her hand. 'Knock 'em dead.'

Sarah kissed her on the cheek.

'You are pretty, Mummy.' Liddy's voice was suitably awed, while Theo wondered if he could have some of the sparkly stuff on *his* hair.

'I preferred Audrey Hepburn in *Breakfast at Tiffany's* myself, with that long cigarette holder.' Doreen picked some imaginary dandruff and stray hairs off Sarah's beaded shoulder. She'd always done that on the pretext of wanting her to look perfect, but in fact Sarah now recognised it was just to bring her down to size.

'And *Gigi*.'

'That wasn't Audrey Hepburn, it was that French girl, you know, used to be married to Peter Hall.'

'I thought she was married to somebody Swiss?'

'No, Marjorie, you're thinking of Petunia Clark.'

'You mean Petula, Auntie Doreen.'

'I know what I mean, Bunny. Anyway, Peter Hall isn't Swiss.'

'I never said he was!'

Sarah and Christopher left them in the hall and hurried out to the car. 'You look very nice,' Christopher said. 'I like the frock. Is it new? You don't normally wear that colour.'

There were times when he was almost human. 'I'm glad you like it. You look pretty dishy yourself, Mr Todd.'

He smiled and they drove down through the High Street with the Christmas lights dancing in the wind above them. Happy New Year Me, she thought.

Edinburgh

It is not easy being a minnow in a world of chomping cuttlefish, but the Edinburgh & Aberdeen Bank did its best, or rather the Gordon family did, and was still doing, its level best. For after 300 years of being a big fish in the Scottish financial pond, it wasn't going to let nasty Dutch-owned conglomerates snip its fins or its profits. Its venture capital arm stretched into the most inventive and promising of new industries from Singapore to Seattle and it was enmeshed into profitable alliances throughout the world. The headquarters were in Edinburgh, but of course most of the real money-making went on 400 miles south, in the Square Mile, just off Charterhouse Street, in the building that the third Robert Gordon had the presence of mind to buy freehold for almost nothing in the 1904 recession.

Though their public relations material was of a masterly blandness, the E & A Bank was buccaneering in a discreet and thoroughly piratical Scottish fashion. It would whisper in Japanese behind the tartan curtain in the boardroom and fund huge nation-changing projects, which then spawned coups and countercoups, behind the screen of an old world integrity and a Sir Walter Scott grandeur. It ducked and dived on phone lines to the world's markets from early morning till late at night, while all the time pictures of that ultimate bad boy on the take, Bonnie Prince Charlie, gazed down, admiringly.

The partners, nearly all related to the Gordon family by birth or marriage, were discreet products of Eton or, failing that, Fettes or Glenalmond. They bred suitably from within the clan, and lived impeccably and invisibly in discreet houses in the New Town and in more exuberant Georgian architecture in the Borders. They entertained lavishly, but you would not have found them in any gossip column. The children were sent off to Harvard to do MBAs if they were boys and to Sotheby's in New York if they were girls. Some married titles and old English Money, others into New England real estate. One or two had even got into the richer than rich old German princely houses, whose wealth seeped into every bank in Luxembourg. Others ran stud farms or boarding schools or breweries. But family allegiances were maintained with a dedication that would make the Cosa Nostra seem casual. It was all about money. It always had been. And the keeping of it for the greater glory of the Gordons. *Ad infinitum et in aeternum.* Amen.

It had taken Christopher a ridiculously long time to work out that he was in fact just a well-paid drone. About twenty years, in fact. Which for someone of his intelligence, education and drive was rather a pathetic discovery to make so late. Enough to bring on a mid-life crisis, which it normally did for senior management when they went to university reunions to find that really stupid people they had once studied with were now managing partners in City institutions. The consequence was that there were a lot of redundant E & A senior managers nursing sore egos and large malts in the home counties or the Edinburgh suburbs. A partnership in the E & A for non-Gordons was possible, just like finding a pink pearl on Euston Road was possible. Currently the two non-Gordon partners who did all the graft wore their status like a medal and, even though the stress was fast killing them, aped the *grand seigneur* manner of their masters.

But Christopher, lucky man, had been given a golden parachute. Being away from the Bank for these past few months had taken away the scales from his eyes, firmly placed there by the Gordons when he had joined them straight from Cambridge. It had taken World Bank fresh air to see clearly that the family style inclusiveness of the E & A culture, which for years had cocooned and satisfied him, was in fact exploitative paternalism of the most Victorian variety. It kept the natives working all the hours God sent, while the Gordons bought themselves racehorses and non-executive directorships of opera companies and New York auctioneers.

Maria Antonietta's warm body had changed all that. In Washington the elite was at least one of equals. No more working for the company store for him. Director of the Cross-Sectoral Cooperation Department. The Gordons could put that in their sporrans with knobs on. For a pillar of the establishment, Christopher had in his own very quiet way become quite a little American revolutionary. It gave him the beginning of an erection just thinking about it.

Of course, no one would have guessed what Christopher was thinking when he walked into Stuarton House with Sarah that evening. 'Christopher, my man, welcome back!' The Chairman, Lord Gordon, was standing to greet guests in the hallway in full dress kilt with a ram's head, naturally, for a sporran. He was a big man, nearly six foot five, and pumped Christopher's hand for several minutes. 'Our prodigal son back from the World Bank! Good evening, my dear,' he was saying to Sarah. She looked OK this evening, Christopher thought, though she could have done without the sparkly bits in her hair.

After the welcome, they sipped the champagne cocktails and went to look at the dinner seating plan. Christopher was a good kremlinologist, which you had to be if you're to survive in the E & A for five minutes. World Bank *realpolitik* was just soft bagels in comparison. And so Christopher, with a casual air, studied the table plan. Would he be in frozen hell next to the kitchens with the corporate walking wounded, or would he be in the main body of the kirk? Where was he? Todd, Todd, token English bod. Yes! Good God, the *Chairman's* table! Why? Vital to work this out before they sat down to inevitable haggis and neaps for hors d'oeuvres. Who else would be on it? The sultan's representative, the US ambassador, that man who owns all those cable TV stations, Mirv Spirios arbitrageur extraordinary, and a billionaire with interests from diamonds to microchips. And himself worth about twopence halfpenny with a wife who tended to witter on for hours about bits of pots she had found stuck behind radiators. What a swell party this was going to be! *Why* was he on that table? Still thinking furiously, he took Sarah's arm and, smiling at her, passed through the main vestibule into the drawing room beyond.

Stuarton House was one of those Georgian piles of elegance on the outskirts of Edinburgh which survived on lots of public money, and the penchant of the financial establishment to give big parties. It was classic stucco with Scottish touches, large stag heads protruding out of walls at irregular intervals and lots of tartan curtaining draped around in the latest approved corporate fashion. It was the view from the window looking down over the city lights which was always a feature, although this evening there was such a dense haar you might have been cut off on some wild headland somewhere.

The annual Hogmanay ball which, for some inexplicable

reason, was always held on the first of January, was the E & A's little number which it threw each year to win new friends, keep old ones sweet and generally put on the Ritz in order to herald in a new profitmaking, Gordons-glorifying twelve months. Christopher and Sarah were used to the old routine, the champagne cocktails and the chit-chatter with the fund managers and the brokers and the usual City big boys who flew up from London, invariably nursing hangovers. There were diplomats from the EC and Tiger economies, also one or two financial journalists from the *FT* and the Scottish press who had been invited to be kept well buttered-up, provided they didn't eat peas off their knives. And in the corner there was the obligatory violin quartet composed of penniless blonde music students from the Royal College, all looking about twelve years of age, once again playing the 'Skye Boat Song' with an air of resignation.

Promptly at nine, the first of the five courses would be served with military precision, during which you were supposed to charm customers without peeing into bottles underneath the table or groping their wives! Then would come the speeches from the Chairman and the Chief Exec, each with the E & A corporate message for Edinburgh and the Square Mile. Finally, when all you wanted to do was go to bed, there followed the lethal fascism of the Scottish country dancing; high-flying careers had been wrecked in the eightsome reel. One senior manager, who had accidentally stripped the willow the wrong way, had ended up flogging traded options on the Tel Aviv stock exchange.

In London, every Tuesday night for years, Christopher had had to frog-march Helen and then Sarah to a church hall in South Kensington to learn the steps. There, he would meet other frightened bastards working for Scottish life offices and financial institutions, all doing the same. The class spawned a masonry of non-Scottish management and their wives, all having to swallow enforced Scottish culture to pay the mortgage. Most of this tartan rubbish, as everyone knew, Sir Walter Scott had made up on the hoof a century or so ago, but you didn't dare ever to insinuate that it was less ancient than Robert the Bruce or else. (Cribbing up some Scots history and learning to turn your mouth down at the mention of Culloden were other necessary moves if you wanted a decent bonus.) It was all part of learning the corporate steps for survival. Christopher and Sarah could now reel quite respectably and quote Burns and the date of the battle of Stirling Bridge with the best.

'Hello, Christopher! How are you Todders? Brown-nosing the Chairman again I see! Hope it doesn't give you indigestion.' The usual faces, not seen for months, turned to greet him. With care, Christopher locked the compartment in his brain marked New Life and, click, Maria Antonietta and his new title, Director of the Department for Cross Sectoral Cooperation, were forgotten, as well as that rough draft of his resignation letter to Robert Gordon already lying dormant in an anonymous-looking file in the memory of his laptop. All vanished. He was back as an E & A one-of-the-boys boy. At first, they sniffed round him like dogs wondering whether to welcome in a returning member of the pack. Ever charming when it mattered, Christopher exuded the right corporate smell and soon found himself in one of those tight little knots of men, while Sarah took herself off to the tombola or the ladies, or whatever other wives did.

'. . . we live in interesting times, but E & A are confident that we can enjoy them and, as importantly, make money out of them with our friends. Thank you for listening so patiently, I give you the coming year and City fortunes!' The Chairman raised his glass and a growl of assent from the fund managers and the hedge betters and the financiers filled the huge dining room. The growl then changed to a low hum of chatter. Christopher looked around and smiled. It was all going on smooth rails as usual, and Sarah was doing her stuff. When on form, she had always been very good at this sort of thing because she was a good listener. Trouble nowadays was that you could find yourself sitting next to someone's wife, who could turn out to be a brain surgeon and would then pour details of her latest operations into your ears and put you off the pud. American women, too, would chew your balls off just to take their mind off eating the food. Christopher shivered.

With the pudding, whisky cranachan naturally with small slabs of Christmas pudding decorated with kiwi fruit, out came an army of men in rather ill-fitting dinner jackets to do table magic. This was new. And after all those speeches twenty-two minutes thirty-three seconds of them, it made a pleasant change. Cards were plucked out of ears and silk scarves from ladies' handbags. All was childish wonderment from men who could bankrupt countries and create markets out of dust. It broke the monotony. Quite an agreeable evening.

Then he heard it. The full, throaty laugh floated like a cloud of smoke from a Havana cigar right over the table. It spread through the cracks in the door of that compartment labelled Christopher's New Life and, when it came again, it raised the hair on the back of his neck and made his whole body rigid. Marie Antonietta was here! Here! Where was she? He hadn't known she was coming! His head jerked round to see where she was, and when he turned back his eye fell upon Sarah, who seemed a figure moving in slow motion, her face half smiling at the magician, her hands raised in the air like a child about to receive a present. Poor girl hadn't a clue.

Then the laughter came again. The wife of the US ambassador was talking to him, but he could barely hear her. 'And so where do you stay when you are in Washington?' he thought she said. He opened his mouth to say Foggy Bottom, then found he could not speak; his mouth just opened and shut like a frog.

'My, those Italians know how to enjoy themselves! I saw her only last week, at the Palace, that Donatella, such fire.' The ambassador's wife suddenly laughed, a dry restrained American laugh this time, though it had all the confidence of a really expensive facelift.

Slowly, Christopher turned around and a woman, slightly older than Maria Antonietta, was showing off to the guests at her table a silk scarf a magician had just given her. 'Who is she?' he managed to say.

'Oh, Donatella's married to the Consul here in Edinburgh.

They haven't been here long, but she's such fun. From one of those old Milanese banking families who bankrolled the Borgias, you know.'

That was all right, then. Italians often did look and sound alike. What a fool he was. Christopher relaxed and talked about Foggy Bottom and its delights with determination, until the master of ceremonies announced that coffee would be served and dancing would begin in fifteen minutes in the ballroom. He smiled across the table at Sarah and she returned his smile uncertainly. But the US ambassador's wife hadn't finished. No sirree. 'Say, you might have met Donatella's little sister? I've just remembered she's at the World Bank right now.' Bang! Her words exploded into the air, and on cue the musical laughter came again, and this time shot across the table like a billiard ball.

Then the train compartments in Christopher started shunting together in a way the Fat Controller would have thoroughly disapproved of. The ambassador's wife, who loved to 'connect' people, invited Donatella over to meet Sarah, told her that Sarah's husband was working with her little sister. Fancy! And Donatella, full of carefully calculated charm – for the Italians are the most unsentimental race in the world – told them that, naturally, her sister had told her all about Christopher and his masterful banging together of heads all over the third world. She looked at him with that insouciance he had always found so exciting. She did not have Maria's style, but suddenly he had an unbearable longing for Maria's face and body, which felt disloyal with Sarah standing there. She looked beautiful this evening, if rather pale. Oh God, he would have to tell her soon, once the written confirmation of the director's job came through.

Sarah said she was going to the powder room before the dancing started and floated off with the ambassador's wife.

'I like her dress, Christopher. I recognise it.' Donatella was gazing up at him, smiling.

'Do you? It's new, I gather.'

'My Lindka Cierach. It looks so different on her, but she has the English fairy princess beauty. Actually I recognised it.

Darling Lindka always puts extra tiny pleats in for me at the waist. Now her new clothes are ready for me, so, naturally I sent it to Second-hand Rose in Stockbridge last week.' She laughed and patted his lapel with a friendly air, just before her knife really went in. 'Oh, you Scotsmen are always so mean to their wives, but my sister tells me *not* with your mistresses!'

He was about to explain that he had been born in Wiltshire, actually, which meant he was . . . but still laughing, she had already walked away. It took a full minute for the Borgia poison to seep into the bloodstream; his wife was wearing his mistress's sister's cast-off, and the sister knew it. And she knew he and Maria Antonietta were lovers, and she was here in the middle of the E & A Ball! God help him. God help him.

Then the figure of his mother, ever present when he had nightmares, strode into his mind's eye. 'Christopher, pull yourself together!' But Christopher could only stand there clutching the back of the gilt-painted chair, suddenly alone in his Savile Row dinner jacket, drowning in muck and bullets.

'Lord Gordon, may I join you?' Sarah asked.

It was nearly midnight, but noises of the dancing, with obligatory and patriotic 'yeechs!' shouted by the dancers as they changed partners, carried into the still quiet dining room. Just a few waiters were on hand to serve coffee and liqueurs but they had little to do but gossip. Most of the other diners had wandered off to look at the pictures, to try their luck at the tombola or network fiercely at the three bars. But the Chairman, Lord Gordon himself, was sitting beneath the portrait of one of the Stuarts, smoking a cigar. The fact that he was alone could perhaps be explained because he was the outgoing chairman, his power was on the wane, and so the sycophants worked their seam elsewhere. Yet even this small sentence was a brave move, given that she was not a partner's wife but merely the wife of a senior manager, one seconded overseas at that. But when you are an older Cinderella and feel reduced to rags and foolishness by life's vicissitudes, you cease to be awed by princes, whatever their age or hue. Besides, her feet ached and she needed to sit down.

'Please do, my dear. It's a crush in the dancing isn't it? You won't mind my cigar,' and he made a leaning forward gesture which was a consolation prize for not leaping up to see her into her chair. Shyly she looked around and, for the first time, had an opportunity to take in the beauty of the vast room with its high ceilings, where overweight painted cherubim swooped with abandon around improbable ladies with long hair and startled expressions.

'They're the Muses, goddesses of the arts. So they tell me. They all look like Ophelia in varying stages of mental ill health to me!' The Chairman smacked off nearly an inch of cigar ash into a heavy silver ashtray. 'Perhaps they have neglected to apply for an Arts Council grant, which accounts for their sour expressions, or perhaps the artist hadn't been paid!' he added. Sarah laughed. And this led to a conversation, a real one, not the usual corporate small talk. Of course, his third question was where did her children go to school. With people of this type it always was the third question, and the fact she said the local state school made him silent, either from pity or approbation. But, ice broken, she went on, telling him about buying the house and studying history of art at St Andrews and the bits of pot and Archie Milne Robertson and life in Loanside. Somehow talking in such positive terms cleaned the wound which had been opened up two days before. Her past was not all bad if she tried to make it sound good to other people.

'Aye, Loanside's a sorry for itself dump now isn't it?' he observed, when she had finished. 'I was born and spent the first eight years of my life there, did you know that? I even remember I met Archie Milne Robertson as a wee child. I was frightened of him then. He had a great black dog which roamed the beach after him. 'Get *down*, sir,' he would cry when it raced up to other dogs and to other people. He towered above me and terrified the local boys. Yet sometimes he was friendly and would take us to his studio, maybe at Christmas, and give us apples with cinnamon in, although I don't think his wife ever approved of anyone crossing the threshold and certainly not in muddy boots.' Lord Gordon drew powerfully on the cigar and its smoke spread its pall all round them. 'I don't think he would think much of the town nowadays, do you my dear? In those days, Loanside was still smart with lots of visitors. I would caddy for the golfers for a shilling. Then bring the money back to my mother and she would write it down in a large book. I would have to account for every halfpenny I spent at the end of the month. Good discipline for a banker.'

'I should think so! But you know, it's a shame Loanside is now so down at heel. It could be marvellous; there are still some wonderful buildings. I've got to know the curator of the local museum and I gather even ten years ago Loanside still had quite a large fishing fleet and the other industries based on that, like net making and fish processing. Plus the golf and tourism. There's nothing much left now except small shops and people who commute.'

'Ah, but my dear, good business is all about seeing potential. And I'm afraid the good folk of Loanside prefer to moan and blame the local council. And the English. They always did.'

Which was how, on her third cup of coffee Sarah had the bright idea of using Archie Milne Robertson to promote tourism in Loanside. 'If Ayr can have its Burns country logo, why not Loanside? Archie Milne Robertson Lived Here.' Then she told him about the TV programme, her own article for the local magazine and the record prices he now fetched at auctions in New York and London, then she fished a small fragment of Red Poppy lustre out of her handbag. She said she kept it there for luck and he laughed and held it up and admired its texture.

The music had changed to a more sedate reel and a bunch of red-faced wives came out, heading for the cool of the powder room. In their flight they looked at Sarah curiously, as if one of the hens had got out, but did not smile. They had important repairs to make.

'So you keep busy with your Robertson pots while your husband flies the globe?' And she told him that she, too, was an economist of a sort with the L.E.T.S. Which made him laugh, a rich cigar smoker's throaty laugh, although he proved knowledgeable. He asked her if she knew that the Chairman of the World Bank had said in a recent speech that the L.E.T.S. were the future for the financial system for local communities, as trading blocks grew larger.

'You must tell that husband of yours. Knowing him, I imagine he's had his money's worth of teasing. So in the future tell him, you will spend your Euros when you visit Europe, and your Lollops to do your local shopping. Did you know the Mancunians call their currency Bobbins?'

'No I didn't, but there are Groats in Stirling and Tweedlets in Berwickshire, and Kelvins in Glasgow!'

'Good names, but you know eventually you'll need us bankers to exchange Lollops for Bobbins. The Gordon L.E.T.S. Bank, where first-class computers whir away. Can you see the headlines, my dear? Bobbins Slump! New Tiger Economy In Lollops!'

Sarah could see Christopher in the distance, emerging out of the dancing with the Italian consul's wife, laughing and looking around for her. She turned back to the old man, who seemed to be looking at her with a kind of eagle attention.

'I tell you what, my dear, if you can find some way of putting together a package to promote Loanside through Archie Milne Robertson, I would put it to the Bank that we should sponsor it. They're putting me out to grass soon to run the Community Fund. Nice and cosy for an old man. The bank must watch its back these days in Scotland with devolution in the wings. Helping local regeneration might fit the brief well. And I'd like to see Loanside prosper. Wherever I am in the world, I think of those rocks outside the harbour there and the light dancing on them. The vivid colours. Nowhere like them. Which is why the Scots always come back home, however far they roam. Like elephants to their graveyard.'

'There you are, darling!' Christopher broke the silence which had fallen between them. He was obviously extremely surprised to find Sarah *tête-à-tête* with the Chairman.

'There you are darling. Good evening again, sir. I hope my wife has not been taking up your time.'

'No she has been entertaining me and giving me the benefit of her charm and her beauty. You should value what you have there, man.'

The Chairman got up heavily and thwacked a friendly, if senior, arm on Christopher's shoulder. 'Oh I do, sir, I assure you.' Easily came the charming reply.

Sarah bent down to pick up her bag, all fairydust disappeared. But the smoke of the Chairman's cigar still lingered round her protectively, as she took Christopher's arm and walked out of the party.

The A1 was deserted as they crossed through the black countryside. Sarah was pretending to be asleep because she had no strength left for conversation, but Christopher hummed a little under his breath and drove with the relaxed air of a man who had done his duty. They passed by Haddington, a glare of red and blue Christmas lights still flashing desperately from a garage forecourt.

'So, did you enjoy yourself?' he asked.

'Yes, thank you.'

'Good. You certainly made a hit with old Gordon. Which will help.'

'Help what?'

'Well smoothing the wheels. All helps.'

'Does it?'

A car suddenly came at them its full lights on, only dimming them as it neared the car. 'Wretched people. Antisocial.' Christopher always said this.

The silence was like a rolled-up blanket stuffed between them and Sarah had no idea how she could unroll it. There were too many bits hurting. It was as if she had been a pot, which though cracked from top to bottom had held together and served a useful purpose until that photograph of the man had laughed at her, mocking her for having had the presumption to build a life. She had been, of course, only an earthenware pot, homely and serviceable, nothing to get excited about. Until tonight, when with cracks glued together she had been fired with gold and coral pink and decked out as something special.

Now she lay in pieces, every piece a voice calling out different words. And she had no idea how she would ever find the strength or the energy to put the pieces back together.

'Why did you not tell me that the dress you're wearing was second-hand? It belonged to Donatella, the Italian consul's wife, did you know? Embarrassing, to put it mildly.'

'Oh dear. I didn't tell you because I had nothing else to wear. The black one made me look ill.'

'Well it did not look good, you going around wearing second-hand clothes. My God, if that got out!'

'Well, it couldn't be worse than you having an affair.' There was a long silence.

'Sarah, you're not making much sense.'

'It was that laugh. I've heard it behind our conversations when you ring up. Venezuela, Washington, Mexico. I admire that sort of throaty Italian laugh. I thought you were going to shoot up to the ceiling when I heard it again tonight. When that American woman told me that there was a little sister at the World Bank, two and two made seven quite easily.'

They were now past East Linton, heading for Loanside.

'Don't lie to me, Christopher, please. I'm not stupid.'

'No you're not. Sarah, I'm sorry. I intended to tell you after your family left, but the fact is,' he sighed. 'Well, oh, God it's hard to put it into words. The thing is, I *have* met someone else. I'm sorry. And I want a divorce.' Christopher stretched his arms against the steering wheel, but continued to stare straight ahead at the black road.

'I see.'

'Yes I know it's bit of a devil. Look, I am sorry to hurt you, Sarah. It is one of those things, I certainly didn't plan it. It was nothing you did or didn't do, except perhaps I have always found you hard to get through to sometimes. Not that I am Mr Emotional exactly. We can sort everything out in the next few months, and I shall make sure you and Liddy and Theo are well provided for. I'll be working full time in Washington, and will get an apartment there, with with Maria Antonietta.'

There! He had said it! And the third partner in their marriage skipped out of the silence to sit on the dashboard, like Tinkerbell, hands on hips in mockery.

Sarah fell silent. The bitterness, she could almost taste it. And the silent rage and the sense of waste. Yet hardly any of this was directed at the man beside her. Another man had done this. How can you keep a husband when you are empty inside yourself?

She was still silent as the car pulled up outside Carnforth House. Then when they went inside, she wished him goodnight and hurried upstairs. He came up the stairs behind her. 'Sarah. Are you all right? I'll sleep on the settee downstairs tonight.' In the half darkness of the landing he stood, still handsome, even though lines now came down by the sides of his mouth and she saw his hair was slightly thinning around his forehead. Quite gently, she said she was. Tears were threatening to slide down her face, but she still kissed him on the cheek, in farewell.

CHAPTER ELEVEN

Wandsworth

Bunny was back! Big time! So of course both the school and the catering business were instantly in fifth gear with the engine whining. On Monday the Intensive Beginners Course began – three months in the inferno for the unsuspecting who had never realised that making apple tarts, Normandy chicken and crème anglaise could be so complicated or so satisfying. Tuesday saw the Intermediates hit the kitchens, but their smugness at being now one level up swiftly disappeared as Lucinda set a faster pace. This was a purgatory of soufflés, flambés, exotic fish, French pastries and gâteaux with bursts of Thai and Californian. They made convincing hot cross buns, and pheasant flamed with whisky and, this being purgatory, they very soon knew just enough to realise how very little they really knew. This piece of self-knowledge was clearly evident in the humility of those saintly souls who, on Wednesday, began the Advanced Course. This was a paradise of chaudfroids, aspics, consommés, canapés, croissants and spun sugar where you finally understood the mysteries of sushi and vegetarianism. You could worship head chefs from top restaurants who arrived to perform their particular brand of culinary miracles and sing paeans of praise at 5 a.m. in Billingsgate and Smithfield.

Already, desperate enquiries about next year's courses were flooding in from anxious parents in Gloucs and Wilts, so Saint Bunny decided to raise the fees to £4,000 a term.

So much for the school. On the catering side business, the fax machine went demented as large bookings arrived in the wake of City big boys nursing hangovers and two-comma bonuses. Smells fought as the girls battled to meet the deadlines. Chocolate and grand marnier bavarois clashed with trout en papillote and guinea fowl. All Bunny wanted was cheese on toast and *peace*! But it was soon clear they needed more support staff so the 'right sort' of catering agencies were trawled. All the pros were off cooking in ski chalets and house parties, so now Bunny had to spend hours testing and interviewing legions of battle-scarred ladies with grand surnames and pearl studs in their ears which had not protected them from hard times in the divorce courts or Lloyds. It could be a bit embarrassing and those who had put her below the salt in her student days at cookery school and at dinner parties years ago, or whose husbands had badmouthed Edward post-Big Bang, were rejected only after the *most* careful reflection on their qualifications and abilities. Those lucky enough to be accepted were then shaken stirred and chopped into small pieces by Bunny, Lottie and Lucinda until they emerged, battered and set in the *Bunny Cooks* mould.

'Come on, Mum, can't you just draw it?' Hannah, who had barely been at home for days, was hovering at the door of Bunny's office, making demands. It was obvious to anyone else that Bunny had ten mega-important things to do in the next fifteen minutes, with a class due to arrive, a telephone interview to give to a Sunday newspaper (the man said he would ring back in five minutes) and ten faxed bookings waiting for answers.

A perfect mother would have dropped everything and said, 'Of course, darling, how many colours would you like me to use to illustrate the exact structure of my business for your A level project?' but Bunny, secure in the knowledge that she was probably the worst mother on God's earth, snapped back. 'Hannah, get out of the office and ask someone else. How the hell do I know how to draw the structure of my organisation? Make it up!'

Hannah sulked and uncurled out of the doorway. 'All the other parents are doing their company structures.'

'Well, bully for them,' Bunny snapped. 'The men will get

their secretaries to do it, I'm sure. And the mothers will either do the same or, if they have time, will be earning tuppence halfpenny distressing wooden coffee tables and half their friends. And *don't* bother Lucinda or Lottie or they'll blow up, we're really busy this afternoon, Hannah!' No answer. Business studies for A level, whatever next?

With impeccable timing, Bunny's mother rang. Marjorie, who not having feasted quite heavily enough on both Bunny's and Sarah's deficiencies over Christmas time, had just rung up for a little chat. And being a young-at-heart sixty-nine-year-old with a will of flint, she managed a nice cosy chat, in spite of Bunny telling her firmly that she had to get off the line 'NOW, Mother,' because Rome was burning. This chat included references to Hannah's round shoulders which would stop her getting a husband, Bunny's growing weight problem, Edward's cheating at Monopoly on Boxing Day, and Sarah's general patheticness in the face of living in such a cold and inhospitable place. 'Really, I don't know what Christopher—!'

Bunny shoved the receiver on the top of her in-tray and went to ask Lucinda about menus for tomorrow's Advanced Cookery Class – half some village or other in darkest Wiltshire had signed up – then she went back and managed a 'Yes, Mother,' before putting the receiver down again and pulling out a fax which was winding its way out of the machine with infuriating slowness. This was from her agent to inform her that she had made the top ten in the hardback non-fiction list for the fourth week running and wasn't she clever and she could probably get that Monte Carlo flat very soon.

Monte Carlo was too close. 'Anyway—' Marjorie's voice floated up from Surrey mentioning something about Doreen's dreadful new hair colour and how those children of Sarah and Christopher never stopped eating sweets and never went to bed and how different children were brought up nowadays—'

'Mother, I have to go, I'm sorry. The *Sunday Express* said they would ring up at five.'

'Oh well, if it's like that I won't take up any more of your valuable time.' Her mother's miffed tones were always judged to perfection. 'Anyway *I'm* busy too, you know, I'm off with the girls to a Shirley Bassey concert tonight in Croydon. Now *there's* someone in public life on the wrong side of forty who has kept her figure.'

'Yes, Mother,' said Bunny, feeling the old feeling of being about six years of age whenever she was near her mother. No wonder her father had keeled over within two weeks of retirement. 'Goodbye. Thanks for phoning.'

Would Hannah ever think of her, like she thought of her own mother? 'Hannah!' Bunny yelled, slamming down an A4 pad onto the desk. Hannah appeared suspiciously quickly.

'Granny's been burning you up again.'

'Don't talk about it,' said Bunny. 'Now sit down and look at this. I am at the top of my own tree. I have four professional activities, the TV and public appearances, the school, the books and the catering company. Lottie runs the catering company and Lucinda runs the school, we have eight full-time staff working across both businesses on a flexible shift system, twelve part-time support staff, hopefully sixteen by next week, and we pull in extra when necessary to do the business, when there's a rush on, as there is today. Listening? Now I have an agent for the books and an agent for my TV work, and a press agent who is supposed to be in charge of publicity though you wouldn't know it. Joanna is in charge of my day-to-day sanity, plans my month with me in advance and tells me what I am doing when. All regular staff are on a profit-related bonus scheme which the accountant works out with Robin the book-keeper. And it all gets done somehow, though on a wing and a prayer most of the time. There! That do?'

One of the girls stuck her head through the door. 'Bunny, Studd is here. He says you said you could do a lesson this afternoon.'

'Oh Lord, I'd forgotten. Hannah, could you tell him I can't possibly do it today, best will in the world. I'm going to have to call a halt to these lessons, Hannah, really I am. I just don't have a minute.'

'Now that Christmas is over, you mean.'

'Jennifer will be free for half an hour before the fennel arrives,' Joanna yelled out.

'Good, could you ask her to teach Studd, what? What do you think? I know. Carrot and coriander soup. We can use up the vegetables from yesterday's dinner parties. Soup would be good on a day like this anyway. God, I hate January.'

'You know, Mum, you have put into practice some of the best female management techniques.' Hannah was looking (almost) impressed. 'You have a flat management structure, little demarcation, you bring in freelances when required, and all full-time staff are used efficiently across the business and get a share of your success. It's brilliant.'

Bunny looked at her amazed. 'Is it?'

'Yes, you really know how to get things done.'

'Do I really? Thank you, Hannah. You actually approve of something I am doing. My cup runneth over. Talking about getting things done. You and Studd.'

'What, Mum?'

'Well you are, you know, taking precautions?'

'Mo-*ther*!'

Slipped over the demarcation line there, thought Bunny, marching through the kitchens. She then suddenly realised that Lottie, who was checking out the haggis crêpes for the City Caledonian Society's Burns' supper, wasn't wearing any make-up and had obviously decided to stop being a blonde. She had apparently found God in an evangelical church in Chelsea, as well as a new man. And she looked so serene. Dear me, how unLondon.

Later that afternoon, after the last van had driven off with its consignment of *The Bunny Cooks Company* assistants in blue-and-white striped aprons, all ready to serve at half a dozen functions right across the City, everyone who was left sat around the main classroom kitchen sampling Studd's soup which, in spite of nearly boiling over twice, actually tasted rather good. 'Almost edible.' Lottie was dunking in her wholemeal bread, with a saintly expression. The phone rang in the office and Bunny, groaning because Joanna had already left for her train, went to answer it. All the staff looked whacked, and she knew there was a bottle of claret sitting on top of the filing cabinet.

'Bunny? Jenna here.' The seriously Liverpudlian voice was crisp yet, after years of smoking, enviably gravelly.

'Jenna, what can I do for you?'

'The make-up girls have been telling me that you have actually been teaching your daughter's boyfriend to cook. Is that true?'

'Yes.'

'Well, we think that is really a masterly touch which we know viewers would love to share, so how about it?'

'How about what?'

'Bringing him along!' Jenna sounded full of fake enthusiasm. 'Tomorrow. What's the dish, what is it?'

'Haggis shepherd's pie with a whisky sauce for Burns' night.

'Exactly. Studd can be a young Burns and watch while you cook! We can get wardrobe to do him up with ruffles. What do you think?'

'That it is a bloody awful idea, Jenna.'

'Deadly serious, sweetie. We need a little young blood in the show. Everyone on this week is post-menopausal. Anyway, you owe us that nice warm spot in the bestsellers.'

'Bugger off, Jenna.'

'I'll expect you both then, chuck. Ciao.'

Bunny found the claret and went back into the kitchen. She could actually write the script which her mother would deliver after she had watched the show tomorrow morning. With difficulty, Studd had been carefully kept out of the conversation for the whole of Christmas. The fact that he lived with his single mother in a council flat would have given Marjorie the vapours, herself having been the upwardly mobile product of both. So Hannah and Bunny had an unspoken agreement to keep mum.

Bunny thought Studd would swoop around the room with joy when he heard the news. But he didn't. He went all silent and brooding, which made the girls flutter round him all the more. 'I'll be 'opeless.'

'You don't have to actually cook, you just have to look interested and I'll let you help with the sauce.'

But he just sat there blushing, until Hannah told him to get a grip and stop being a wimp. At which he actually managed a 'Thank you, Mrs H,' which made Bunny blush, because she hadn't wanted him on the show in the first place, but that was life. He was such a passenger, while Hannah was unfortunately turning out to be a chip off the old block; she was attracted to men who needed to be carried. Poor girl.

London Heathrow

He really didn't know how many more of these horrible plastic airport hotels he could stand. They seemed to spring out of the ground around Heathrow like clones of each other, all demanding gold cards and offering ersatz hospitality. Christopher sat on the bed, flicking switches on the television. CNN gave him the latest on some ghastly demonstration in Iraq, and he turned down the sound. When would she phone? He'd have to check out by 9.30 to catch the Washington plane, but he felt so tired, exhausted. He was shattered by yesterday's flight. Nairobi was getting worse and worse and arriving in London two hours late had not helped. Helen was out, and he was so tired of the endless stream of drinks and nibbles he was offered by airlines to distract the boredom; they made him bloated. And why did they always show the same on-board videos? He had almost got to the point of asking for the children's colouring kit. Anything rather than face all those papers in his bulging briefcase.

He put his hand in his pocket and out came the usual shower caps and tiny soaps with which he would shower the kids on his rare visits home. This did not help. 'Will you still be our Daddy?' He could still see Liddy's pale, anxious little face when he had sat her down and tried to explain that he and Mummy would not be living together any more. Theo hadn't seemed to care. Too young to understand, he had zoomed around the room with his new turbo-charged model car, oblivious to the tension. Sarah had gone into pathos-mode, had not worn any make-up. All of which had made him feel such a rotter. He hadn't meant to fall in love. It had hardly been malice aforethought.

How they had packed off the ghastly hell grannies and Bunny and her mob without anyone noticing, he would never know. All professed to having had a super time and had pressed invitations on Sarah to visit as soon as she could. 'It's most important you retain a London frame of reference Sarah, for the children's sake if not for yours.' And Sarah had said, 'Yes Bunny,' as if taking an instruction for the amount of flour she would need for a quiche. They had had just half a day together as a family, before his plane left, but it had been hard. The only thing keeping him going was that at last he had played the game and been honest about his feelings for Maria Antonietta.

God, when would she *ring*? He needed to talk to her. There was a knock on the door. 'Hello, maid service.' A large black woman pulling a huge loaded trolley behind her poked her head through. 'I'm leaving in ten minutes, I'm just waiting for a phone call. Thank you.' The door shut resentfully.

What a great time for his mobile to be on the blink. Christopher shifted on the bed, adjusted his cases and neatly tied on his Executive Club airline labels. Next stop Washington.

He would never understand women. Going away to school at six probably had not helped, but even although he had loved, and had been loved by, three women, four including Mother, he still did not understand them. Women were on an alien planet. They were capable of taking on enormous tasks and then giving up or firing off in a rage if not constantly appreciated. He leafed through the copy of *My Lady* magazine he had picked up in the lobby the previous night. Helen was there on the inside page, shoulder pads akimbo projecting toothsome confidence as editor. Articles were trailed about female orgasm, female circumcision, male inadequacy. *Are you Female or Feminine?* screamed one title. What did that mean? What's the difference? Are you male or masculine? You wouldn't ask that of a man. Neither word inferred any more or less testosterone. It was all a load of tripe.

Or was it? '*The Female Woman is the lone cat who prowls in the night. Tough, sensual and gloriously independent. Females don't keep their men, they entrap them for life,'* he read. '*Think Lucretia Borgia, Catherine the Great, the Duchess of Windsor, Bette Davis. Female women eat gazpacho and radicchio, hot raw and crunchy, drink cocktails.*' Christopher shivered. Helen and Maria Antonietta were Female then. Large-boned, elegant, bossy, assertive and seductive. Who else was Female? Bunny, of course!

'*The Feminine Woman pleases her man by pleasing herself. She's the sort who buys that little black number with cash and then tells him it cost half. A sophisti-Kate, she's Daddy's little girl who dresses up to the nines and stops the traffic. Eats avocados. Drinks sherry and champagne. Think the Princess of Wales, Margaret Thatcher(!) and Marilyn Monroe.*' So. Doreen and Marjorie, God help us, were feminine; their clinging manipulative helplessness concealing steely determination. And Sarah? Definitely. He couldn't help smiling as he thought of her that last night in that pink dress whirling round the floor, and the way she had got old Robert Gordon eating out of her hand. It hadn't cost half a new dress, it had been second-hand, for God's sake. Unbelievable. But she was his one and only feminine woman. Through and through.

When they had first met, and afterwards when they had talked and courted their way through some fine restaurants in the West End, which he had always been allowed to choose, she had remained sweet, if slightly distant. It was what he had found so appealing about her, having been bossed about all his life by Helen and by Mother before that. *He* had asked *her* to marry him, unlike Helen.

He shut the magazine and threw it in the bin. Thinking about Sarah was not helping. He glanced at his watch and paced the grey carpet, looking out through the hotel's triple glazing at the grey skies and the planes which silently took off and landed every twenty seconds. The trouble with divorce was that it was a self-inflicted bereavement, which somehow negated all the years spent together. The fun, the shared failures and the good times. Both children, born in Queen Charlotte's Hospital, had been triumphs of love over common sense and financial prudence and they had wailed and sucked their way into life in Bedford Park.

He couldn't pretend the future was not going to be painful. But he had to move on. He needed to get out of the strait-jacket of the bank and all the stress and family pressures it stood for. He needed a life.

Women! Female or feminine, he would never understand them. When he had told Maria Antonietta that he had finally confessed the truth to Sarah, had she been pleased? No. She had gone berserk, railing at him in broken Italian interspersed with curses, spitting and flashing like a diva singing Tosca. What had allowed him to think she would want to marry or even live with him in Washington? In Foggy Bottom! The way she said it made the place sound like a disease.

They had been in the airport surrounded by heavily armed security guards all hugely enjoying the scene, then she had flounced off to her own plane, declining even a kiss or a backward glance, leaving him to endure the long flight to London.

Stress was now ranged in knots all along the back of his neck. He had left messages in three places that he would be here until 9.30 come hell or chambermaid. Five minutes to go. He picked up the remote control panel. Flicking channels, he took in a children's cartoon, more stuff about a hurricane somewhere, an old James Stewart movie and finally, he supposed she was ubiquitous, there was Bunny grinning furiously while some little turd in a funny eighteenth-century costume was stirring something. The woman standing next to him looked positively aroused. Women!

The chambermaid banged on the door again and, sighing, Christopher picked up his cases. The world was confusing enough without his internal world losing the map. He shut the door behind him, leaving Bunny projecting mutely to the walls.

North London

Bunny was in pink mode! Whenever she felt it necessary to go down fighting, Bunny usually wore pink. And to underline the fact that this was war, she had asked the production staff to place a large vase of cyclamen-pink carnations on the working surface of the studio kitchen. Hopefully the blooms, now luxuriating under the tropical studio lights, would take the viewers' eyes away from Studd.

How could she trust him? Suddenly feeling vulnerable and even more nervous than usual, she paced up and down, checking and rechecking the ingredients and the cutlery. The fact that she was also talking about Robert Burns made her edgy. One never knew whose toes you could tread on with a sacred cow like that. Or was he a sacred bull? He'd certainly put it about a bit, judging from what Joanna had dredged up on the Internet. She couldn't pronounce half the words.

And so to celebrate the bard in all his glory, there stood Studd. Wardrobe had done their best to service Jenna's fantasies at only a few hours' notice. Some bright spark had remembered that Burns would probably not have worn a kilt, while another smart arse had apparently remembered that they had just finished doing *Treasure Island* at the National so, as one of the make-up girls was married to one of the production staff, there had been a nightmare of late-night taxis, resulting in Studd now standing resplendent in a long embroidered waistcoat, breeches and a kerchief. It was a case of Jack Hawkins meets Tam O'Shanter! It only needed Jenna kitted out as Long John Silver and you'd have the whole crew.

Bunny could not, however, deny the effect he was having. Jenna and the weather girl had salivated right through the News, the Business News, three sets of commercials and even Mario doing suggestive thigh exercises with three overweight checkout girls from Rotherham. All only had eyes for Studd, particularly the checkout girls who must have ricked their backs in the effort. And he was only too aware of this, pushing his hands through his black curls and trying to look moody. Little runt. Bunny liked a man with rather more flesh on him.

'OK, Mrs H?' Studd whispered.

'Fine,' she couldn't help hissing, 'now take your elbow out of the butter and on air call me Bunny!'

Three minutes to go. The resident interior decor adviser was babbling about the fun in using cocktail shakers as toothbrush holders (why?) and Jenna was smiling sweetly over her shoulder. Then, suddenly, thirty seconds to go! 'Stand up, Studd, don't slouch, and smile!'

'And now we are going over to Bunny. Many of you know that tonight is Burns' Night, when people all over the world celebrate the life and writings of Scotland's top poet, Robert Burns. Now Bunny is going to tell us how to cook haggis shepherd's pie in whisky sauce. Sounds yummy to me!' While she was speaking, Jenna was walking across the studio to the kitchen. Her eyes had that purposeful gleam of a killer whale on heat, boring into Studd, who was now standing to attention.

'Now let me introduce you to Studd, whom viewers may remember Bunny discussing before Christmas. Studd is Bunny's daughter Hannah's boyfriend and, in a *wonderful* gesture we thought, Bunny offered to give Studd *free* cooking lessons, in return for Studd giving Hannah the green pass to go up to Scotland at Christmas to be with the family!' Jenna was talking to camera two as if to a child of four and a half, which she had long ago decided was the mental age of the average daytime viewer.

'So Studd, how have you found Bunny's cookery school?'

'It's wicked Jenna!' Studd looked at the camera and quite simply oozed charm. 'Bunny's cool. Always lots of booze in her classroom, and nice women in pearls and stuff. Know what I mean? We had a really good time. Bunny's daughter, Hannah, she's a cool lady too.' At this he arched his eyebrows, just to make the point, Bunny decided, that Hannah was the best lay this side of the Shepherd's Bush roundabout.

'Now,' said Bunny interrupting firmly, 'tonight as you say, Jenna, is Burns' Night, so we're going to cook haggis shepherd's pie in whisky sauce. It's a lovely easy way to cook haggis and so simple.

'At all Burns' suppers there is, as you will probably know, the Address to a Haggis.'

Then up on screen came the first two lines. 'Fair fa' your honest sonsie face, Great chieftain o'the puddin-race!'

This, read out by Bunny, probably put the cause of Scottish independence forward by a decade.

'What's sonsie mean then Mrs H, sorry Bunny.' Studd stood hand on hips, grinning at the camera. 'I'll get into trouble if I call her Mrs H.'

'Appetising I think, but perhaps our Scottish viewers will let me know if I have got that wrong.' Bunny couldn't at this moment care less. All she wanted was this hell to end.

'The haggis is mutton mixed with oats and traditionally is put inside a sheep's stomach, though these days it is more often in thick cellophane. You simmer gently for twenty minutes, it is already quite well cooked, and take a sharp knife and cut. Studd would you like to do that?'

So Studd, of course, took the knife and disembowelled the haggis, which spilled streaming all over his thumb, causing him to swear, and then over the rest of the working surface.

'Now you need the tatties, potatoes mashed up with cream and butter, and orange turnip (you may know it as swede) which is the bashed neeps that is traditional with haggis. It is best mashed up like this in a bowl and which you are going to layer into the dish, just like a shepherd's pie. Quantities are on Ceefax page 552. But first of all we are going to make a whisky sauce which Studd, is going to do' (God help us, Bunny thought). 'Then he is going to mix it into the haggis.'

'OK, Mrs H, sorry Bunny. Anyway, you melt butter into the pan, with one tablespoon of lemon and a half teaspoon of salt and one teaspoon of whisky.' Studd liberally sloshed enough whisky into the butter to make several people fail the breath-alyser, and mixed it in. Bunny had one eye on the studio clock while Studd started showing off. He managed to burn the butter, then some of the whisky caught alight. Into the smoke, confusion and the noise of fire alarms and sirens, several men in peaked caps rushed into the studio with extinguishers.

Bunny seized the pan and, with just twenty-five seconds left, rescued the situation by shoving what she could collect up of the haggis into the dish, followed by splodges of neeps and tatties. Whack, on went the cheddar (sod it, she'd forgotten the celeriac) and then she whammed it into the oven. 'So cook at gas mark six for twenty minutes.'

'Well done, *Studd*,' said Jenna, who was trying not to cough in the smoke. 'Now Bunny's bringing out the one the studio staff did earlier, isn't that right Bunny?'

Et tu, Brute?

'You *are* a laugh, Jenna! Well, here we are! Grab forks, stick in and cheers to Robbie Burns!'

Studd, his kerchief now black with smoke, put his arm round her and gave her, to her shocked surprise, a kiss. And two million viewers, who had previously considered haggis disgusting, thought what a lovely boy, and hadn't Bunny misjudged him? They hoped she wasn't a snob, in spite of those terrible clothes, and wouldn't it be nice to have a young man like that going out with their daughter?

Then came the commercial break. 'What the *hell* were you doing? I told you to keep the light *low* for melting butter!' Bunny spat at him.

'I'm sorry, OK? Keep your hair on. What's the problem. It's my first time you know. On telly.'

'It's called professionalism. *Not* one of your best ideas, Jenna.'

'Oh Bunny, I think he did *splendidly*. Positively wicked in fact! What a simply *ghastly* dish to choose.'

'It isn't ghastly, it's delicious when it's done properly. I'm off!'

Bunny stormed out of the studio and out of the building. She didn't see Jenna kiss Studd on the cheek and whisper conspiratorially that he was a natural; his irreverence fitted in beautifully with the channel's new post-modern production values, and not to mind silly old Bunny. And she would just love him to stay until the end so they could have coffee and cakes together. Then he could meet the producer *properly!*

Clapham Common

Bunny always got her best ideas in the bath. Menus, staff appointments, script ideas for the show. They usually came when she was up to her neck in bubbles. Wow! She must have lost weight, her toe was now right up the tap. Delicious. Warm water guzzling over your foot.

The bubbles were now at least seven or even eight inches high, right over her, which prevented her from having to see the result of forty years too much good living; National Health orange juice and sugar sandwiches before she was seven, and under the blanket feasts and secret caches of sherbet lemons during adolescence. And then for the last two decades oodles of canapés, snacked off trays before they hit the clients' tables. She would never eat another filo spinach parcel as long as she lived! (She always said that, then there was always room for a little one.) But as for haggis! *Never* again, however much money they offered her!

'Life's a bitch and then you die,' Bunny announced to her rubber duck bobbing on the foam, who clearly remained unconvinced.

As her yoga instructor had taught her, she closed her tired eyes and tried to think of exciting, distant places, where her mind could relax from the dozen different crises which had plagued her from 7.30 this morning. Usually the place was Monte Carlo; she would instantly picture the Corniche sweeping down past the flaming blue of the Côte d'Azur, and the sparkling jewels of the women gazing in rapture at the chips being thrown on the wheel at the Casino, or those fabulous shops where pictures of the Grimaldi family looked out from silver frames, just to remind you where you were. But as a typical end to a perfectly bloody day, what shot up into Bunny's disobedient subconscious?

Loanside. Freezing, grey, half-dead Loanside where the waves shot up twenty feet into the air over the harbour wall and the wind, bloodyminded, cut your ankles as it fled across the road. Do me a favour! Bunny opened her eyes. And then who shot into view, not lovely Princess Grace, nor the Monte Carlo Marina, no such luck. Morag the woman with the mole to sink a thousand ships, lecturing her about Scottish nationalism and why the Scots would be better off without the English. 'Of course you would, but then so would *we* be without *you*!' she had said to her. Then Morag had smiled. Such a kindly, wide open smile in spite of that dreadful mole on her face, Bunny had almost offered to man the battlements personally.

It is always an odd thing to view Scotland from London within a brief space of time after having viewed London from Scotland. For Scotland, viewed from a £750,000 stucco job off Clapham Common is, to be frank, fairly irrelevant. Another planet – galaxy even. A far-off place where magazine editors send their photographers once a year to shoot the Glorious Twelfth and the Edinburgh Festival, preferably for the same issue; and a place from where one gets ghastly strange Hogmanay shows on telly with whirling women with seventies haircuts, if one has not the good fortune to be going out.

Yet London viewed from Scotland seemed like a parallel economy, a mad sort of virtual merry-go-round where everyone travelled round faster and faster, burning up more and more money and energy. It surely wasn't sustainable? What a clever devil Christopher had been jumping off. Must be that boarding school instinct for self-preservation. Though Sarah sitting in the carriage behind his painted horse, would probably have just gone along in the London groove happily impervious to the pressures for years. Still, stopping the world and getting off seemed to have done her good. Bunny suddenly realised that Scotland was another state! As separate from England as Monte Carlo is to France. More so. This was probably the most political thought Bunny had had for years.

She wriggled and sent more water spurting down her foot. Now back to Monte Carlo. Enough of Arctic winter and don't, whatever you do, think of anything to do with haggis! Think creamy cakes at the Place du Casino restaurant and luscious café au lait at the Hermitage Hotel. And the flat she would have, where it would be, and how she would furnish it and what sort of maid she would have? Would she have the pert, thoroughly discreet little woman who called one madame and had a son living in Paris, or the plump motherly Monegasque who had been midwife to every Grimaldi since Charlemagne's time? Bunny got neither. Christopher and the bloody woman at the airport slid smoothly into view. Canoodling (a deliciously Marjorie word that, very *Carry On* films) at the check-in.

Talking of whom, the only nice thing which happened in a truly horrible day was that the E & A Bank had signed an exclusive contract for *The Bunny Cooks Company* to do all their UK catering. Lots of dainty things on sticks with whacking fat mark-ups. Poor Sarah, did she know that her E & A husband was fooling around? Perhaps she'd be pleased to hear it? Sex had never appeared particularly important to Sarah. Bunny doubted in fact whether either of them had ever recovered from opening a brown paper parcel when they were both off school, thinking it was the free gift they had ordered from *Jackie*, only to find a peephole bra – destined for Marjorie. At the time it had not fitted either of them and they had both decided that when they reached Marjorie's and Doreen's ages – then about thirty-nine and thirty-seven respectively – they would shoot themselves.

When she'd rung up to thank Sarah for Christmas, that Morag woman had answered the phone saying that Sarah had gone up to Edinburgh by train. And would she like a copy of the SNP manifesto, 'so she would understand Scotland's position?' And she had found herself saying, please, like a small girl being offered seconds of strawberry jelly. She would put it among the copies of *Vogue* and *Tatler* in the school coffee area and fox the lot of them. She might even vote Scot Nat in the General Election if anyone stood for Clapham. One never knew. *She* might!

Bunny always enjoyed the unconventional; wasn't she the one who had first thought of putting strawberries into haddock chowder? Sensational! She was so busy laughing that possibly the rubber duck noticed before she did that her toe was really stuck now, right up the bloody tap. Perfect end to perfect day. Quack quack.

CHAPTER TWELVE

Loanside

For two days, after Christopher left, Sarah lay in bed in a state of cumulative shock and exhaustion. The children, confused and tetchy, were fetched and carried by Morag and Eleanor and a succession of kindly L.E.T.S. members working for Lollops. She refused to let them call the doctor. What could he do except knock her out with drugs?

At either end of the day, the children would come back and would head straight for her bed, where they would lie there, clinging to her. There was never anything to see out of the window; it was still dark in the morning and dark from five o'clock in the afternoon. Liddy seemed to grow up several years in a few days. She read to her brother for hours and, in her stiff upper lip, Sarah seemed to see the redoubtable figure of her mother-in-law who had reputedly run the Indian Army single-handed. 'It won't be so different Daddy living in Washington, because we haven't seen him in ages,' Liddy would say with brutal childish logic while Theo just wanted to Mummy to get better and get up.

While the children were at school she slipped in and out of sleep, her dreams peopled by ghosts. They would come into the room and either sit on the bed, or hover in her mind's eye in some indeterminate space or setting where she would ask them questions and get no satisfactory replies. Generally, they would ask her why she had done what she had done? What had been the rationale? Why had she been such a fruitcake? What had she achieved?

Once, Archie appeared. Only now the room he stood in was not her room but some other room furnished as in some picture of a Turkish bordello with tasselled ropes and heavy cushions. He carried a highly lustred pot in each hand and asked her when she was going to start buying some of his work. She replied that she couldn't because she didn't have any money and that she didn't even know how long she could afford to go on living in Carnforth House. He said nothing, simply looked at his heavy watch which hung down over his waistcoat then walked out again, shouting for Isobel. He seemed really rather small, and by the time he had reached the door he was barely taller than the radiator.

Once, David Robertson came. He hovered darkly in the corner and called her a bitch. She screamed at him, and told him not to touch her. And then Zander rushed in and the man disappeared, and Zander asked if she was going to send a telegram to her mother, and she would say that you didn't send telegrams these days, they didn't exist any more, and anyway Doreen was at the hairdresser's. He looked disbelieving and disappeared. Then Christopher tangoed round the bedroom in a high-winged collar, his hair greased back like a Latin gigolo. In his arms was a woman in a flame red flamenco dress. The two danced round and round, and the woman grew taller and taller, like a giantess, until they disappeared out of the room.

Sarah would wake up from these dreams, sweating and fragile. Fearing to fall back asleep, she would get up and pace the floor, looking out of the window at the sea smashing against the rocks. It was a sort of endless annual general meeting which went on in her head for hours, where she was both on the Board and in the audience of shareholders both announcing and criticising the pathetic dividend of her life. Why she had been so unproductive, what changes would have to be made? The telephone, when it rang, remained unanswered.

One night, suddenly wide awake, she put on a coat and sat before the computer thinking she could maybe surf the Internet. It winked at her. Welcome! Find Out About—? RAPE. She punched in the four letters, almost wanting to look behind her in case of discovery. 'Please wait while the site is contacted' flashed up, so she waited breathless, fearing unasked questions from her now-sleeping children. The site was contacted. Instantly a list of a dozen help lines and services with useful books flashed up on screen. Take your pick. There were handbooks on healing and reclaiming innocence, on legal advice, on female rape, male rape, incest, child abuse, domestic violence, and bullying. Just click. So she clicked on a rape helpline in Cornwall, superstitiously as far away from Loanside as she could possibly get. Click.

'Welcome to the Survivors' Page! Two hundred and fifty-two people have visited this site since the beginning of January!' How many damaged people were sitting out there tapping away, just like her? Horrified yet mesmerised, Sarah began to read their stories. J.G., who had been raped every night for six years by her stepfather and grandfather. P.S., who had been raped repeatedly by her ex-husband once when he was drunk in front of their children. T.T., who had been raped while on holiday in Spain. They detailed the physical damage and the consequences to their lives. In the dark, with the wind howling at the windows, Sarah sat wondering what was wrong with her. Why had her life been ruined from just one incident which had happened so many years ago, when these people had suffered a hell two or three times a night for years? She had not been physically injured, no torn skin, broken noses, infections.

Collusion. The word might have been spelt out in large capitals on the screen for all the power with which it suddenly exploded in her brain. Had she colluded with the attack in order to give herself an excuse to shut down and fail? These women called themselves Survivors and had a page to prove it. What was she? A pathetic nervous wreck set to sink? The sort bloody Christopher's bloody figureheads had been taken off for salvage? A collaborator? The night wound it black sad way to morning as Sarah paced up and down. Tarred and feathered.

* * *

On the third day, the doorbell rang. Looking down from the landing window, she could see Zander waiting below, wrapped up in a long yellow scarf, stamping his feet in the cold air. By now there were black circles under her eyes and her hair stood out matted and knotty as if a whole jar of jam had been knocked over her. She dragged a comb through ineffectively and went and opened the door. He seemed shocked at her appearance but for the first time in her life, Sarah couldn't give a damn. She offered him coffee, walked down to the kitchen leaving him to shut the door.

They sat at the table watching the oystercatchers wheeling out over the sea.

'Here are your photographs.' She shoved them across the table, glad to be rid of them.

'Did you enjoy looking at them?'

'Yes,' she lied. 'You must have had a happy childhood.'

He said nothing, but continued to stare out. She could see lines stretching down from the corners of his eyes into his cheeks.

'You're joking, Sarah. I'm afraid it wasn't. All our pictures were posed like that, pretending to play happy families. Classic downward spiral. Your sainted Archie had been bullied by his father who'd lost his job as a weaver and had become an alcoholic. So of course when he started earning big money and had children, he did the same to my father who, not knowing any better, did the same to us. Mother just went along with it and made excuses for him. I left home at sixteen and slept rough in London until I got some help and found I could go to art school on a full grant and then I went into advertising. But it was worse for David; he was more sensitive; he couldn't take all those years being told that he was just a worthless pile of shite.'

Sarah closed her eyes, suddenly thinking of all those Survivors on the Web who had overcome their pain. David had passed on the damage to her. Bastards. 'All men are rapist bastards.' A.B. from Woking had written that on the Survivors' Page. She looked at Zander sitting there drinking his coffee.

Looking very much at home and a survivor in his red knotted kerchief at his throat, brown cords, expensive Italian woollen sweater. A big, attractive man so sure of his ground. Suddenly she wondered whether Morag or Eleanor had told him that Christopher had left her? Not today, thank you; she suddenly remembered the posh voice her mother used to door-to-door salesmen. When he had finished she thanked him for coming and showed him out, but she only relaxed when she saw him walking off down the street. It was when she crept back into bed that she finally realised she had lost Christopher for good.

The next day Sarah opened her eyes, saw that there was a small pink light creeping onto the sea, and then felt she could get up. She had a large mug of tea and was up and dressed before the children. She made the porridge and took them to school herself and told them that today she was to be very busy. Theo went in smiling, for once without hitting out at the other children.

This was Day One of her new sink-or-swim life. She went to the answering machine, which had been flickering for over two days without respite. There were seven messages. From Christopher, Doreen, Bunny, Marjorie, the TV company giving her a schedule date for the programme's transmission, Christopher again, then Zander. She did not call them back. As she tidied up the house she made sure she looked in the mirror regularly throughout the day, something she never normally did. And even if her hair was scraped back and she had not a scrap of make-up on her face, the mirror reassured her that she was human and existed. That she was a Survivor and that the vanished Christopher was an adulterous Bastard though not, to be fair, a rapist bastard. 'But I am a Survivor and Christopher is a Bastard.' She repeated this aloud until eventually the words and syllables became jumbled up and ceased to have meaning and then suddenly she found herself mumbling that she was a bastard and Christopher was a survivor.

She pulled out an Edinburgh directory and made appointments over the next few days with a solicitor, a beautician and a hairdresser, a colour analyst, and Lord Gordon. His secretary sounded surprised but, after coming back, said that Lord Gordon could spare her ten minutes. She also made an appointment for an agency to come and clean the house. She hadn't been a kept wife all these years not to know just how self-affirming spending money can be.

Now, for the earning of it. She spent the day piling up all the possessions she had never liked, which Christopher had bought and would never miss, onto and around the dining room table. Most were antiques or good quality modern pieces. She also added nine bits of jewellery which Christopher had given her over the years, and then rang a valuer from an Edinburgh auction house to come and value them and arrange which sale they could go into. She called a local joiner who took all the voluptuous figureheads down from the wall and carried them, mute and unprotesting, upstairs into the attic. The yacht pictures were stacked, waiting for bubble wrap.

The phone rang three times during the day; she ignored it. It was important not to be distracted. Processing the past, processing all the pieces of information she had overlooked, signals she had missed, mistakes she had made. If she was to be a Survivor then she had to process all the data in her life before she deserved a future. 'Please pick up the phone, Sarah, I need to speak to you.' Christopher's voice sounded tinny in the panelled room.

She went all over the house, from room to room, piling up things she couldn't raise money from, but which cluttered up her life. Out! Books, and clothes and dreary old towels and sheets and blankets and shoes and any number of Todd family things, surplus to immediate requirements, were pushed into twenty-four black bin bags and piled into the car to be spread bounteously among the town's four charity shops. Denuded of several pictures, the upper landing now sounded echoed and thin-walled. But there was a mirror, which reassured her that Sarah Hunter was real.

She dropped off the big bags at the charity shops on the way to picking up the children from school. The ladies in the first shop gasped with gratitude as she staggered in, and then, recognising her in spite of her unkempt appearance, asked if she was all right. 'Fine, just having a sort out.' Sarah found a lipstick in the glove compartment, making herself slightly more colourful for the next shop. Finally, when she had offloaded all bin bags, she went to the florist and bought two bunches of flowers. Normally she went for pale pinks, or restrained purple tulips with a little greenery, but today she bought two huge exuberant in-your-face bunches of lilies, one for herself and one for Morag, and headed for the school gates.

On Day Two, she got up and this time put on make-up and a smart suit. She headed for Edinburgh and spent the morning having a pedicure, a manicure and a full body massage, with all sorts of exciting double-barrelled oils, with a large girl from Potters Bar who had worked on cruise ships for twenty years.

She came out with every blackhead removed and every muscle deknotted. She had a little lunch in Jenners with the other ladies of the shiny bag sorority, and then went to have her colours analysed. 'How painful it is leaving the comfort zone!' said the woman unsympathetically, picking up Sarah's black jacket as if it had lice. 'Never wear black dear, you're a Spring Hourglass.' So Sarah, who had been given little black numbers for years, made a mental note to chuck out all the rest of her clothes she had not already given to Oxfam and hurried out down the street.

Next stop: Mr Fred's, who after an interesting career which had taken in the Gorbals, Watford, Beauchamp Place, and Beverly Hills, as well as a most expensive mid-life crisis, was now waiting to give her a new head. It took three hours to streak and cut and condition her hair into an expensive strawberry blonde, but it revitalised her. Mr Fred pronounced her a wee knock-out. She staggered out in shock at the bill. Ten yards down the street, she paused to look at herself in a shop window and, like God resting in the middle of Creation, saw that it was good. Incredibly good, in fact.

The day ended, and Sarah sent out for a pizza for her children, who wondered why Mummy looked so funny.

Day Three. She woke up and knew that she was still alive, because her hair had a luxurious silkiness and was also hugely glamorous in spite of having been slept on. And before the children woke up, she fished out her colour chart and, holding it in her left hand, ran her right along the clothes in her wardrobe. Soon a generous pile of her clothes on the bed translated into twelve more bin bags by the hall door, which were offloaded on the now familiar charity shop ladies on the way to school. 'Thank you *so* much, Mrs Todd. You *do* look better.' On her return, Sarah looked in her wardrobe and saw just one skirt hung there and a beige jacket which she had bought in Simpsons of Piccadilly ten years before. She put these on and, ignoring the phone ('Please pick up the phone if you're in. I am in Mexico City. Sarah, do pick up the phone we need to talk'), ran for the Edinburgh train.

As her train chundered into Waverley station she took out the list of where to shop in Edinburgh culled from the *Tatler* Bunny had brought her at Christmas, and started with the first shop. And with her swatches of necessary colours for a Spring Hourglass person, a spring in her step and a nice flexible credit card, Sarah started to shop. As any girl knows, it takes at least £5,000 to lay the beginnings of a good wardrobe and Sarah having, in spite of initial timorousness, an eye for design, a good figure, and distinctive colouring, made a start! By two-thirty, as she ran for the train, she had six shiny bags on each arm and a new pair of shoes on her feet. She suddenly thought of Bunny as a teenager, exuberant and embarrassing in black leather boots and red hotpants impersonating Nancy Sinatra while stomping around the room. Bunny had never been able to sing in tune.

The answering machine had been busy.

'*Bleep*. Sarah, it's Bunny. Are you *ever* in? Do ring.'

'*Bleep*. Sarah, it's Mother. This is the third time I've rung and you know how I detest talking into machines. Phone me back as soon as possible. Love to the children.'

'*Bleep*. Sarah, it's Christopher. *For God's sake* please pick up the phone! I thought you'd taken the children to your mother but she tells me you're not there. So call me please. My number is—'

'*Bleep*. Sarah, it's Zander. Just ringing to see if you are feeling better. You looked really pale the other day. I was worried. Call me.'

The *Loanside Mercury* also rang to say that as she was on the telly on Friday night about that Robertson man, could she give a wee interview with a picture?

And then after all the voices had spoken, the lights on the phone went back to a plain green light. Waiting for more calls. But she didn't call them back. She and the children spent the evening admiring her new colour-correct clothes, hanging them up and then making pancakes, shooting them defiantly up to the ceiling, and powdering them with sugar.

Day Four. Sarah got up and dressed carefully. Her hair was still silky and expensive looking and her appearance at the school gate made heads turn, in spite of the wind which reduced everyone to the same dishevelled muddy mess. As she drove back, the wee women from the charity shops waved at her expectantly. Nothing today, sorry.

At 9.30 a.m. the cleaners arrived. They were crisp and pleasant and, if they looked at the dust everywhere and then at Sarah's newly minted self with a certain disapproval, they kept their thoughts to themselves, and started upstairs. At 9.45 the man from the auctioneer's came. He obviously didn't see any dust but accepted coffee and sounded terribly enthusiastic over the motley collection heaped up all over the dining room. He was not an expert on the jewellery or the rare books, or the pictures, but he was sure they would get a good price. His colleagues would value them back at the office. He whipped out an auction diary and together they went through dates of five auctions where they could all be sold.

After lunch the van from the auctioneer's arrived and the possessions were all neatly packaged up, receipted and removed. The cleaning women, who had just reached the ground floor, started hoovering the carpet and polishing the tables where the possessions had been. It was all very satisfactory.

The phone rang only twice. The first was Morag, and the

second from the school saying they had had two calls, from Carshalton and Bogotá, both wondering if the two children were still alive, and could she please ring her mother and husband as both were frantic with worry, and the school was in the middle of an inspection. The children came home and Sarah taught them how to make French toast, which they ate in front of the television. She did not call.

Day Five. Sarah, who was now having to contend with a ridiculous number of wolf whistles from the normally restrained Scots, travelled up to Edinburgh once more and swept into the solicitor's office. The solicitor was kind and motherly and said that most of her female clients arrived thinking that they would receive nothing. But that they could ask for half, even if they didn't get it, and that most judges preferred clean breaks these days. Christopher's pension would be the sticky bit though under Scots law, a percentage could be earmarked. Sarah sat in the red leather chair and said that her husband had promised that she and the children would be well provided for. And the lady solicitor just looked at her.

Her marriage was then laid out for inspection like a dinner service at an auction. What were their ages, their children's ages, their education, careers, salaries, money, (inheritances didn't count in divorce settlements by the way); finally, of course, outstanding debts and assets?

But dreams, hopes, expectations – these were not included in the assets. Sweet and sour tastes of failure and despair came back into her mouth, almost making her choke. She was told that it would be advisable to go for a Separation Agreement even if nothing else happened for the moment. She could also apply for legal advice and assistance if she could not afford legal bills. This would become legal aid if she went to court. The machinery creaked into action. She shook hands with the lady and went back home. The children were out playing with friends and so she sat staring at the fire. Tears didn't fall, because she really couldn't decide which bit of her life hurt most and anyway, excuses for failure become rather thin once one is past thirty-five.

That evening the phone rang several times in the now-echoing house. Unheard.

Edinburgh

After the weekend came Day Six.

The New Town office door, composed of several tons of best establishment mahogany, banged behind her and Sarah stood in the street. A highly charged ten-minute appointment with Lord Gordon had netted her a project. Always useful for a soon-to-be-divorced lady with an ancient, threadbare c.v. and intellectual muscles which had not been flexed in years.

'Do you have a project?' She remembered that word, and how important it was amongst the American bankers' wives she would meet at the bank's parties. These women would never work anywhere if they could help it, yet always gave her their card, and would talk about their projects with huge drive and self-assurance as if at any moment they could assume a top job in a corporation. They would have strangled themselves before they could have said, English style, that they were 'just a housewife actually'. So now she too had a project.

'Loanside could be such a special place,' she had told him. Had it sounded hard sell or just a new-girl with a new broom? 'Archie Milne Robertson is by far the most exciting resident they have had – you can't count Butcher Cumberland exactly a local hot property however many nights he spent watering his army there. So for all the Robertson fans internationally, and nationally, and people interested in ceramics of the period, there could be a real focus where they could see his work, study his life, see where he worked, and stay and spend their money in Loanside. We could get a Robertson Website and market Loanside internationally.

'At the moment, what I am thinking about, purely as a private individual, is just a small start to focus people's ideas. To show how the Robertson heritage might begin to be marketed given the local will, a Lottery grant, Arts Council money and help from the private sector.'

'Now we're getting to it,' he had growled.

'What I would like is a small amount to put on a modest exhibition somewhere in the town, where we could educate the residents about what is right under their noses, and show what might be possible. I could do a short proposal and I am sure it wouldn't need much money. I did a Robertson exhibition a few years ago in St Andrews, and this could perhaps be a catalyst for change in the town.'

'I wouldn't bank on that, my dear. But how much would you want?'

'I'm not sure. I'd have to work it out, but possibly just a few thousand, less than five anyway. You would be the sole sponsor and you could perhaps use it to invite clients from the art world.'

Sarah felt a bit out of her depth here, but then thought to herself that other people would be earning big salaries probably knowing just as little.

'And you would give me a proposal in the next few days, fully costed and with a venue and with a list of exhibits tracked down? And it could be this year, this spring and we could tie it into our two-hundredth anniversary.'

'Yes.'

'Though it's a wee bit late in the day, isn't it?'

'Yes. But then something needs to happen to the place. It's dying on its feet. However many Government and EC grants are pushed into it. The town's civic pride has gone and commuters are just camping.' She had seen that he was listening now, plump fingers pressed together. 'Anyway, I had this idea for the exhibition when we spoke at the ball. I don't know how much longer I'll be in Loanside, but I'm certainly not a camper!'

He had smiled and told her to send him the proposal within a week and that he would discuss it with the relevant board members. And to give his regards to her husband. Time up. The secretary had appeared and in fourteen seconds she was out in George Street. Husband. The word suddenly seemed a piece of borrowed furniture.

On Day Seven Sarah went in to see Eleanor in the museum. She was sitting there pricing goods for the shop. Loanside's Fishing Past looked uninviting as an exhibition in spite of nets draped across the ceiling and the model fisherman at the entrance.

'For goodness' sake, come in and give me some good news. The whole place is dead. Why don't we just shut up in January and February?'

And then Sarah told her of her idea of doing an exhibition showing how lustreware was developed and why Robertson was such a master craftsman and big blown up pictures and explanations, and a small potter's wheel for people to have a go throwing a pot. And lustreware for sale, and so on.'

'Great idea, but we've only three months to go till the end of the financial year and we're broke. Skint.'

'Well the E & A aren't, and they have said if I put in a proposal under £5,000, they will consider pledging money for an exhibition.'

Then Eleanor took the phone off the hook, opened up a packet of lemon puffs and they drafted out the exhibition, an interactive, hands-on, exciting exhibition with talks and maybe even drama students in costume. Could be done on a shoestring with a bit of imagination. Then Eleanor ran up a draft proposal and rang up for appointments for Sarah and her to see the local council and the local tourist board, which could now give a grant to market local tourist events. And it all began to happen. From an idea in her head, it was now a reality and Eleanor, who had been sunk in January apathy only an hour before, now seemed to think it was quite natural that they had a new project, if a little rushed.

'It could be such fun, even done at the last minute. And the TV programme on him on Friday; couldn't be better. We must tell everyone. Sarah, you do look very smart today. Very glamorous, that new hairstyle.'

'Thanks, Eleanor.'

'Now let's start digging up those pots?'

And for the rest of the day they hit the phones. Just occasionally one has days when everyone you ring is in, and is nice to you, and of course would like to do what you want. It usually happens when you are not in a hurry and don't need an answer quickly. But the gods were with them, and the day developed into a glorious detective story.

Sarah rang up Jeremy Lofthouse, who, after he pretended not to know who she was suddenly changed tune when she reminded him that they had met at Zander's private view. He said he knew where to get five Robertson plates. Four were still in the Arts Centre in St Andrews, and he knew that were quite a few knocking around in private collections in London. It would cost a bit for transport and insurance. He would get back to her. He had an idea that some East Lothian packers he knew might like to sponsor the removal and packing. Who would write the exhibition programme notes? It would need to be someone who knew their stuff.

She rang her old department at the university to see whether Donald Gosford was still there. He was. Professor Gosford would be back in the office after lunch they said. This cost her an effort, but Sarah pushed her feelings into the box in her mind, marked 'Pending' and cracked on.

She rang the *Ceramic Review* and the Tate and the Arts Council. Then she began to track down people who knew people who had examples of Robertson's work. How many pots does it take to make an exhibition? In the heat of battle, she did not allow herself to think of the career path she had lost, how she had once had ambitions to follow in Roy Strong's footsteps, to become the youngest female curator ever.

Day Eight was spent on the phone. More pots seemed to turn up every hour, the owners flattered and keen to lend them as temporary exhibits. All this, as Eleanor reminded her, was being done without any sort of money on the table, nor was Sarah even on the museum committee, and so she was co-opted on with a couple of friendly calls to members and a draft proposal was knocked out with a list of current exhibit offers included. Press and PR campaigns would be a necessity. Sarah suddenly thought of Bunny, and how she and the school were never out of the papers.

Sarah called those L.E.T.S. members who had shown her

pots which had been given to their parents and grandparents to pay for groceries and clothes, pots which had paid for carriage repairs and plants. For Archie had scattered his pots everywhere as his own local currency, in order to buy time, to provide food on the table and to keep his house and his wife standing tall. Sarah's luck held. She invited them all to watch the documentary in her home and such was the local curiosity about Carnforth House and its renovation, that almost everyone said they could come. Finally she rang Zander, who promised to be there. Though she was surprised that he had none of his grandfather's work to lend.

Her afternoon was spent wheeling round the local supermarket finding nibbles and wine. All of which meant that by the time the phone rang ten minutes before the programme started, there were over twenty people standing around being frightfully social on a wet January Loanside night, and already having a jolly time. Christopher's tone, however, was not.

'I've called and called all week. I even called your mother and the school. If I'd had no luck this evening, I was going to call the police.'

'Well, I'm here now. Sorry. Do you want to talk to the children?'

'Not at the moment.'

'I'm sorry.'

'Good. Who have you got in the house?'

'Oh a few friends. The programme about Archie Robertson is on tonight.'

'I see. The one you did? Well, get someone to video it, will you? I'd enjoy that.'

'Would you?'

'Of course. So how have you been filling your time?'

'With very little difficulty.'

'Look, Sarah.'

'Yes.'

'I'm sorry about all this. I'm sorry if I have upset you, but in the end it'll all be for the best. You'll be much happier without me drifting in and out.'

'Very Pangloss. If you say so, Christopher. I just hope both of us will be happy. And the children.'

'Yes. Give them my love. One reason I called was that my attorney here says he should know the name and address of your solicitor, so I naturally gave him our solicitor's address. Can't remember the number, though.'

'Well, I'm using another Edinburgh solicitor actually. If you wait a minute I'll give you her number.'

'I see. I had rather thought you would be using ours.'

'Oh no, I don't think so.'

'I see,' Christopher said again. And Sarah, who was by now being called by her friends because the programme was starting, gave him the number. She couldn't think of anything more to say. Getting real was only going to be possible in stages. The doorbell rang and, outside, Zander was standing there in the rain.

'Must go, Christopher, I'll speak to you soon.'

'Who's that?'

'Zander, he's come to see the programme. Must go.'

'I see,' repeated Christopher yet again. 'Goodbye.'

Sarah doubted if he did see, but then myopia seemed to have been the overriding quality in their marriage. Zander was already shaking off his wet coat and hanging it over the banister before taking off his wellington boots on the rug. The theme music of the programme had started and the others called her again. Eleanor stuck her head round the door impatiently. Sarah went in, Zander following behind her. He looked very much at home. But then he was.

Houses are only ever lent to you, she had said to him. How much longer would she be mistress of Carnforth House?

CHAPTER THIRTEEN

London

It was Bunny's fortieth birthday. The nerd who ever said life begins at forty had never had to share an office with a born-again Lottie, who spent the whole morning going round the kitchen singing hymns at the top of her voice. She had also apparently acquired a younger man, no doubt as fresh-faced and upbeat as she now was. It was all very unnerving. Added to this, a bird-brained client organising his mother's birthday bash had just rung up asking for Brown Windsor soup. Ugh! The very name brought back visions of the draughty sixties hotel dining rooms her parents used to take her to, with soggy cabbage and disgusting glass oil and vinegar sets, half-cold food, and that postwar rationing mentality which the British didn't manage to shove off until the end of the seventies. 'Do me a favour,' muttered Bunny who, being Bunny, was soon wondering if one could do a classic consommé and finish it off with Madeira and just call it Brown Windsor.

The office was stacked with cards. Her mother, just to finish her off, had given her an unwearable tan handbag with a copy of the *Z Plan Diet for the Over Forties* and Auntie Doreen had sent her a set of lace doilies and a tube of cream for breaking up cellulite! Sarah, on the other hand, had sent her a linen tablecloth and a book called *Downshift*! which, on the cover, said that twelve per cent of the UK work force last year downshifted to a less stressful lifestyle. Bully for them. She couldn't afford to anyway. Not with her family's spending habits. There was a thirties glass brooch, obviously picked off the back of a Portobello stall from Hannah (at least she'd remembered this time) and Edward had stumped up from his *own* money, as he always emphasised, on the usual small bottle of lavender water.

Forty was getting serious. Almost fifty. Time to reassess. How did women who had been really beautiful cope? Sarah, for instance? Particularly when your bastard of a husband just announces he has met someone else and is buggering off to live in the States. Cold, unfeeling bastard. If Edward ever did that to her she would do such a number on him he would be kneeling broke and desperate before her, begging her to take him back. Trouble was, Sarah would never have the chutzpah to be like that. Somehow the stuffing had been knocked out of her somewhere along the line. She had never been the same after university, and none of the family had bothered to take time to find out why. On impulse Bunny rang her number. The answering machine replied, so she left a message anyway, thanking her for the present.

What an odd sort of relationship cousins were. Close but not too close. People talk about sisters' rivalry, yet because she and Sarah had been extensions of their mothers' egos, they had somehow been pitched together in endless competition.

Yet in the last fifteen years or so, alliances had shifted. Marjorie and Doreen, who had fought each other unceasingly, as their husbands had climbed up the Council ladder into middle management, competing for the best houses, holidays, furniture, jewellery and cars, with their daughters brought in as colluding reinforcements, were now allies against their daughters. Bunny and her weight, her round-shouldered daughter and her long-suffering husband. Poor Sarah, newly abandoned and heading for the gutter.

All this paranoia was exhausting. God, she was tired. Bunny picked up *Downshift!* You too could be a serial downshifter making small changes to your life! Take a day off work, sell off all unnecessary furniture! What would Studd fetch, for starters? 'Any advance on £4.50? How much am I bid for this young man with the chewing gum? What about Monte Carlo? Was that upshifting? Perhaps she could buy a nice scenic cottage near Sarah and spend the day nursing her investments, living on cheese sandwiches and whisky and reading bonkbuster novels.

Bliss. On impulse she redialled Sarah's number. This time she answered.

'It's me, Bunny. I'm calling to say thanks for the present, it's hell being forty and to ask if you're OK, do you need anything? A hit squad for Christopher, for instance?'

She expected Sarah's usual cool reserved tones, but instead she laughed. (Probably because she had no more bloody Hilditch & Key stripey shirts to iron.) Sarah told her she was hoping to organise an exhibition and had approached Christopher's bank for sponsorship. If it went ahead she could certainly use some PR advice if Bunny could spare her some time.

Bunny had never been into pots, unless they were the sort you could put high-margin food inside, but suddenly she was inspired. Why not get out of London for a few days and have some fun? She could come up and help with the launch! She could hear Sarah's hesitation and realised how odd that must sound after all these years, but she plunged on. She would get her press agent to give her some strategic advice and send in the girls to do the catering – perhaps the E & A would pick up the tab if she was doing the other catering for them? Why not? Let's be The Two Musketeers once again. Turn back the clock! This last idea, coming as it did on her fortieth birthday, rather appealed to Bunny.

'Bunny that could be fun. I never thought you would be interested. Anyway, I am going to need more of your advice because I am going to have to start looking for a job now.'

'Good God. I wouldn't recommend it, I am rigid with stress these days. I want to be a kept woman.'

'Says the original Superwoman. As if you don't manage the lot brilliantly. Happy birthday, Bunny.'

Superwoman, Bunny thought. Ha bloody ha.

Loanside

Already mid-February! Crocuses and snowdrops were now pushing through the soil, deceived by the harsh, early spring sunlight, which showed up every cobweb and greasy smear on every window, then flooded into Loanside, exposing the dust and grey of the winter, and the pinched white faces of the children. It was now light in the mornings until nearly five in the afternoon, and there was a more sociable air in the town. People no longer battled by, shoulders hunched, but greeted each other in the street, and talked of the tourist season which if in Loanside, was always a slightly theoretical concept, at least gave a sense of optimism to the local traders.

The Robertson exhibition was now firmly fixed on the local agenda. Sarah wrote a piece in the local paper appealing for Robertson exhibits and talking about her plan that the exhibition could be a catalyst for regeneration of the town. People who had only looked past her before, were excited and wanted to talk. The community council asked her to come and speak (Eleanor went along to hold her hand and talk her through the politics), and the local traders' association asked her what they could do to help keep the visitors happy.

Her new-found celebrity, gained from the Channel 6 television programme, also helped put the exhibition on the map, though it struck Sarah as odd that somehow people never look at you in quite the same way once you have been in their sitting rooms. Videos were passed from neighbour to neighbour, producing comments about how well the town looked in the film and what a lovely man that Archie must have been (but his poor wife!). Also how knowledgeable Mrs Todd was! And so Sarah found herself in the role of local high-flyer, which made her panic at first until Morag told her it was all a piece of piss, wouldn't last and that she must not get big headed.

The absence of Mr Todd seemed to attract little comment, for there were enough women with absentee husbands away working on the oil rigs and in the forces to hide among. Sarah told Morag and Eleanor that they were having a trial separation and that she still hoped to sort things out. She spoke in optimistic tones and she knew she could not fool them, but there was no need to announce to this newly interested world that he had run off with a Snow Queen Lollobrigida and there wasn't, sadly, a snowflake in hell's chance of his return.

It was this lack of hope for the marriage which hurt her, even more than the fact of the other woman's existence. Perhaps she could have been one of those women who turned a blind eye, in the belief that he might one day have come back? But that wouldn't have been right for Christopher. Life had to be played by strict rules; an eternal public school cricket match.

The Archie Milne Robertson Exhibition – Loanside's International Genius took off like a rocket. The proposal to the E & A Bank for £4,500 was for a three-week exhibition at the Loanside Museum, comprising exhibits, brief illustrated histories of the east coast Scottish potteries and of lustreware, Archie's life story with his connections with Loanside. His work in its international context would be positioned in small cells throughout the room made up of eight-foot high illustrated storyboards, all provided by L.E.T.S. members at cost. Target audience: interested educated visitors, East Lothian residents, art students and the art world.

There would also be pottery demonstrations, including the use of the modern lustres (now thankfully relatively inexpensive and available in jars). The iron ark with the remaining animals by local craftsmen would be restored during special afternoon sessions. Children would be able to copy Robertson's favourite motifs of heraldry and flowers in the painting hours in small groups with volunteers (more L.E.T.S. helpers). In short, a Rolls-Royce exhibition with the added value of the community's own commitment to the exhibition's success.

Her proposal just caught the spring meeting of the bank's sponsorship committee. Not only because it was small, relatively cheap and an E & A employee's wife was doing the graft (no doubt they assumed Christopher would keep her wise), but also because the venue belonged to the local authority, with no comeback on insurances or other costs, it meant that within two weeks a cheque for £4,500 was lodged in the brand-new Robertson Exhibition a/c, signatories Sarah Todd, Director for the *Robertson International Genius* exhibition, and Eleanor Mackie, Director of the Loanside Museum.

One of the worst tasks was to stock the museum shop with suitably Robertsonian souvenirs in the time available. Sarah left this to Eleanor to armwrestle her contacts in the crafts trade while she tackled the PR. Morag's younger brother Kevin, a computer whiz at Heriot Watt University, launched a Robertson Website featuring Sarah's original article, pictures of the pots and Robertson, and also a few carefully chosen sights of Loanside with suitable tourist details of where to stay.

Kevin also had the exhibition posted on L.E.T.S. noticeboards world-wide, which resulted in local exchange schemes from Canada to Australia hearing about how Loanside L.E.T.S. was helping to regenerate their community. It seized the *Zeitgeist* when international banking scandals were making the public feel that their lives were being ruled by big business, fat cats and trading blocks; and so even before the pots had been assembled or the programme notes written, the Internet, though almost entirely new to most Loansiders, had spun its magic around the world. Soon the first bookings were being made in the local hotels. Faxes started arriving daily at the museum requesting details from as far away as New York, Vancouver and Perth, Western Australia. Loansiders discovered they were on the map after all.

Then everyone said that they already had a piece of the action, for Archie had been nothing if not lavish in how he had bartered his pots and dishes for food, medicine and clothes for his family. His work had been, in time of desperation, his own private local currency long before Lollops. From the council estate to the manse, out these long forgotten pieces came, some cracked and low grade, others museum quality. All were dusted off and brought up to the museum. Some had been used to keep bills in, others had contained loose change, pot plants, hairpins. A stunning pink and gold lustred vase had propped up the rector's laundry door for the last twenty years.

Best of all, a large full-length portrait of Archie came to light, painted by Robert Noble, East Lothian's famous artist who had attracted artists from all over Scotland to paint the magnificent countryside round his home. He was famous for never having had more than £10 in his bank account, and always traded paintings for goods ands services. Sarah suspected he had introduced Archie to the ways of barter. Although Noble was known for landscapes, this painting was a revelation. Sarah had until now never realised just what a big powerful man Archie must have been. The paint was thick and often scraped back to show the texture of skin or cloth. It showed Archie in his mid-forties standing by a chair, his fingers resting on the back wearing heavy gold rings on each hand. They were large potter's hands, with well-shaped nails. He was dressed in a black morning suit with a high winged colour, and a yellow waistcoat, magnificently embroidered with birds of paradise. A thick gold watch chin glinted as if to underline his material success. Deep-set blue eyes, thick-set eyebrows and thick curly hair swept back from his forehead. Here was the sexy, self-confident gentleman potter. With a wife from a family with enough money to pick up the tab if the going got rough. Sarah and Eleanor were thrilled and put the portrait on the front cover of the catalogue and on the posters.

But of course, raising their heads above the parapet brought the sceptics out to play. A couple of community councillors disliked the world-wide publicity, perceiving it as hype which would end in tears and raise the locals' expectations. Lothian Council, with one eye on how few councillors of the ruling party were actually elected from Loanside, also dragged its feet, until articles started to appear in the Scottish press and Sarah charmed both the leader of the council and the chief executive into co-operation.

The Tourist board, too, initially thought it all very small beer, although they offered a £250 grant for posters. To them, Loanside, stuck in the forgotten corner of East Lothian, was neither noted for its golf like upmarket North Berwick and Gullane, nor famous for its beauty. It was hard to get excited about the putting green or the crumbling harbour. It had never attracted tourists from Edinburgh (unless they were desperate, lost or crazy about oystercatchers). Still, it is a wonderful thing what a quiet word uttered by a bank chairman in someone's ear at the New Club can achieve. Suddenly *Robertson Exhibition* signposts appeared on the A1 and, although with just seven weeks to go they said it was hopelessly late to catch any sort of mailing, they managed a leaflet drop to the Edinburgh hotels.

No one had bargained for Sarah's endless energy, which drove the project forward. These days she ran rather than walked, and drove like the clappers up and down to Edinburgh seeing people who could help. She now had shining eyes and red cheeks. She scooped up her children in her arms and carried them along in the excitement of it all until they almost forgot about their parents' problems. Carnforth House came alive, a powerhouse of ringing phones, and piles of leaflets.

Sarah's PR machine soon began to gather steam. She targeted the women's magazines and fine art press, and the country house periodicals, and the national Scottish and local radio and television. She contacted church women's guilds, the university graduate magazines, trade union newsletters, the library information sheets. Now along her kitchen walls there were long lists of Things To Do, a large planning calendar and hit lists of journalists. 'Local housewife fights to save rural community' was a good angle, as was 'European ceramics colossus rediscovered in Scotland.' The 'David and Goliath' bit struck a chord with the reporters as did (alas) the delicious sleazy quality of Archie's own life. And soon small mentions and articles, as well as requests for interviews, filled Sarah's life. She now gave live interviews on radio, and though she knew she probably sounded *far* too enthusiastic, in the laid-back media world, the fact she was a housewife who had bought Robertson's house and had two young photogenic children helped to spin the magic.

It is in situations like this that you discover who are the deadweights and the passengers, and who are the life-enhancers. One or two locals and shopkeepers, suspicious of an English incomer making waves, made odd remarks in the post office which almost put Sarah off her stroke, but then others came up to her, thanking her for what she was doing for the town.

Her mother and Marjorie, too, found the whole business completely uninspiring once she had made it clear that she would be too busy to give them a little holiday. One day, after trying vainly to enthuse them with her own excitement, Sarah suddenly realised that all her life, whenever she told them what she was doing, they had always responded with what *they* were doing that week, or what *they* had done in *their* lives which was similar and just as exciting. As if everything she did was merely an echo of their own life history.

Sarah wondered if Bunny had tumbled to this and called her to make sure she would be coming to the launch. She needn't have bothered. Bunny was already booked by the E & A to do the catering and would be up two days before to help with anything else Sarah might need. She would bone up on Archie before she came so that she would not be the most ignorant woman in the room. The next day she rang back to say she had actually bought a piece of his work at an antique shop in Kensington Church Street. Pink job with knobbly gold bits and a funny shape. And yes it cost a bloody fortune and no she would not be putting avocado dip in it. Sarah couldn't help thinking that this rediscovery of Bunny was a small miracle.

Another miracle occurred when her old lecturer Donald Gosford rang, agreeing to write the exhibition notes and inviting her to lunch. She hardly felt any pain at all. Zander came down from Leith once or twice a week with ideas for the exhibition, although Eleanor said it was best not to give him too many details in case he tried to take over. Artists' families could be funny, she said, she knew from bitter experience, and the Robertsons were more funny than most.

Jeremy Lofthouse was impressed when he heard Donald Gosford was involved, and if at first his spotty bow tie and pained expression did get up the noses of several of the exhibitors, he did lend many more Robertson pieces. By talking about Sarah's first 'magnificent' Robertson exhibition, he gave others even greater confidence in Sarah's vision. He also found a packer who would donate his services at cost in return for a mention in publicity material.

Then he offered to take the exhibition to Edinburgh when it had finished. But, by then, Sarah was talking about a permanent Loanside Robertson Centre, complete with a working pottery school and exhibition, until he suggested that she might apply for one of the new Lottery grants, though she would then need to hand the bid over to the council to sort out. So she decided to stop talking about that. Instead, to her astonishment, she asked him for a job. To her relief and amazement, he smiled and said to ring him. After he had gone, Sarah hopped about the room, while Eleanor said that there was a brand of Englishman who made all self-respecting Scots foam at the mouth and he was one, to which Sarah replied that she would risk that for a monthly pay packet.

For besides Robertson and pots, money was her chief concern. Christopher hadn't called since that night of the programme. The children had written to him and odd postcards had arrived for them with strange-looking stamps. Letters came from her solicitor to let her know that the Separation Agreement was progressing, but that was all. Christopher had obviously kept the joint account going and was still paying the bills, but when alone in the dark without the comfort of the ringing phone, it was worry about money that kept her awake. She was dependent on him in so many ways and she did not know how much longer she would have before real poverty began to bite.

She bought cheaper food and stopped cooking Bunny's morning recipes, although she still watched her for a minute or two each day on the kitchen TV before she started on the press calls. In spite of Bunny's light-hearted tones whenever they spoke on the phone, Sarah could tell Bunny was not happy. She now had Hannah's boyfriend helping her on the morning show these days and though other viewers would not have guessed, Sarah knew Bunny was hating every minute. On the other hand, Bunny just had so much going for her. You couldn't go into a bookshop without seeing her face on books piled high by the door.

Money was the real challenge. Not for her diving out to buy a Robertson pot in Kensington Church Street. She didn't have a bean of her own. Except the child benefit she had been saving up all these years in a savings plan for the children. That would not amount to very much, just two to three months' expenses if she had to cash it in to keep the house on. Where would they go to live? Go south? Stay here? She could not even begin to decide. So while dashing up and down to Edinburgh, Sarah began to sell as much as she could. She now regretted having been so generous to the charity shops. She sold all her jewellery except for her wedding and engagement rings, to a New Town jeweller for £2,000, and cleared out the cupboards of anything that would bring in a good price. The auctioning of her furniture and pictures brought in another £3,000, a fraction of what had been paid for them, but better than nothing. One Sunday she took a table at a car boot sale and raised another £300. She opened up her own bank account in the name of Sarah Hunter.

Next, she moved the children downstairs to the first floor and let the two top bedrooms to foreign language teachers, who were working for a year at the high school. They were young and, having boyfriends, were almost always out, but they paid up £250 each including bills each month. The first month's rent went straight into her new account too. Sarah found to her surprise that, whereas before she had barely ever remembered to fill in her cheque stubs, and had little idea about what was in their accounts, she was now fascinated by money, asking for weekly statements. But then, for the first time in her life she was hungry and now appreciated just how much worry Christopher had shouldered.

Just seeing how carefully money had to be spent for the exhibition, made her conscious of the waste in her own life. Now she traded more on Lollops, and penny pinched in a way which would have appalled her smart Bedford Park cronies. Finally she was growing up. Of course, as a thirty-eight-year-old woman it would have been a terribly good joke if it hadn't been so pathetic. But then, aren't the best jokes always on a knife edge?

Fife

The mountains in the distance were still covered in snow and small villages dotted along the valleys seemed huddled against the white striped fields. Sarah gazed out of the window of the train at this long-remembered landscape, associating it with other times when she had been coming back for vacations down south, preparing to click back into her new world once again.

She looked down at her newspaper. On page three there were details of a rape case. The victim, who had given evidence against the defendant whom she accused of raping her was pictured, in a smart suit, surrounded by her counsel. The man, Sarah read, had forced his way into her parents' house. He had muffled her screams by shoving the sleeve of his coat inside her mouth. After which he had both raped and buggered her several times, and had hit her about the head viciously with a cricket bat, leaving her bleeding and unconscious. The woman, a twenty-six-year-old sales executive, was a single mother, and her background was gone into in some detail. She had reported the rape to the police and had dropped her right to anonymity in order to encourage other women to come forward and seek justice if they were raped. 'I am not a victim by nature, and I decided when he left me that I was going to fight all the way. He is not going to get away with this.'

This was progress. She was actually reading such a report after years of allowing her eyes to glide over anything on the subject of rape in the papers or turning the sound down if rape came up on the news. A painful memory came back; a younger Sarah sitting in the loo in the students' union looking at the sticker which had been pasted on the sanitary towel disposal unit. *Raped? Phone . . .* But never once, in the confused fog of those days, would it have occurred to her to report the rape, or even seek help. Just saying the very word in her head had been enough to scare her into silence. And as for telling her family or friends or going public! What a lost cause for the feminist movement.

Still, now she was going back to St Andrews to discuss her second exhibition of Robertson's work, and she was able to read this report in the paper. So that was good. Too late for her own justice, but she had his house which she loved. For the moment at least.

She turned the pages, taking in the foreign news, the editorial and the obituaries, then tried to read the personal finance section. It was a foreign language she needed to learn for her new single life. She tried to understand the latest movements of the stock market. What did PEPs or TESSAs mean, let alone yield or price over earnings ratios? She might as well be reading German. But she would have to learn. So she read on with great perseverance about futures and the movement of copper and how the banking and pharmaceutical sectors were rising, until her eyes were drawn once again out into the wild white landscape beyond. An investment strategy, this was apparently what one had to have. Long term, medium term and short term. Flexibility and a mixed bag of investments for future security.

She wondered if the journalists writing this stuff were half as well organised as they appeared to be in print. Did they actually keep their money in old socks, or in the post office? What was an investment anyway? Most people just muddled along, making decisions which seemed all right at the time. Her own investment in marriage made for the long term had turned out to be only medium term after all, and providing half the returns she had expected. For soon Christopher would be living in a flat in Washington, and she and the children would be in some starter home or draughty farm cottage. If she were lucky, Jeremy might give her some sort of job, and the children would be in the afterschool club to be fed and collected by someone else.

Holidays, meals out, new clothes, all would be just good times past, unless provided by their father for them during school holidays – until he had another family by the Italian, of course. Or until they could leave home and make their own money. And then, unless she could soon find hundreds every month for a pension, she would be faced with an old age, making do with soups and eggs, and one bar of the fire. A lousy return on a long-term investment contracted for better or worse. An independent financial adviser would have judged it a very poor decision. Her mother had always said that marrying a divorced man was asking for trouble. Of course she had said that before she had met Christopher and realised that his mother had a title, after which he had merely been unlucky. Odd, how she missed him. If only the clock could be turned back to about five years ago when the distance had started to come between them. Perhaps marriages were like the stock exchange, both ruled by the greed and fear of investors' insecurities?

She picked up a taxi from Leuchars station and, as it drove into the town, took in the new buildings and the restaurants and the pubs which replaced the old familiar ones. The driver dropped her outside the art history department in North Street and, as she got out, the same biting icy wind hit her, followed seconds later by the familiar salty air. She paid the fare and stood looking up at the new arts centre. One of the doors opened and a young woman, obviously a student, came rushing out. She had long hair and her arms were full of files. It might have been Sarah on another plane of time. Any minute, one of her old friends would be calling out to her asking when they would meet up at the Criterion for a drink, except this was now, she noticed, an Irish theme bar. Anyone, looking at her, would have seen a woman in her thirties, hair swept up in a French pleat, wearing a smart beige coat, carrying a sensible briefcase and wearing sensible shoes. The sweet bird of youth had, alas, definitely fallen off its perch.

Professor Donald Gosford was printed on a wooden sign on the door. It looked odd. Was this the man who had once got so outrageously drunk he had performed Zorba's dance on the table? Who had once swum nude in the sea one February for a dare and had derided the University Court in the student newspaper for its lack of democracy? He was now a professor. She smiled as she knocked on the door.

The office was still a mass of books piled high, papers and files. She fully expected him not to remember her even though his lectures on ceramics had been burned into her very soul. But the man who greeted her seemed so pleased to see her. He asked her if it was all right, he had ordered pizza. He was wearing a suit and a knitted tie and his face, though lined, was still handsome and smiling. He moved much more slowly than she remembered and was greying at the temples. He had the tired, distracted air of someone blessed with a much younger wife, two boys under three, and a very large mortgage on a very small house. All of which she soon learned he had, as their lunch progressed. Wife number one, whom she remembered as a postgraduate psychology student, had left with most of the equity six years after Sarah had graduated and was now a professor of American history at Bristol. His manner was still charming, although there was just the hint of middle-aged disillusion. And, for an instant, Sarah was reminded of Christopher and the jokey way for years he had spoken of his 'second' family, the resentment barely concealed.

He made coffee and they talked of Carnforth House and the exhibition and how it had come about and about themselves and their children, and what she would like him to put in the programme notes, his fee and about whom they should invite to the launch party. Outside the wind wheeled and howled in the afternoon gloom and the birds circled, as they always had, in the cold St Andrews light. She told him she felt that at any moment he would begin to discuss one of her essays and ask her about next term's options. He laughed and told her he still had her dissertation somewhere and was soon plunging into a filing cabinet.

'I'd love to see Carnforth House, Sarah. Must be rather wonderful if it hasn't been too badly modernised.'

'You must come over for lunch and see it before the exhibition. There is still the studio and the old iron ark.'

'I'd like that. Are there still the fish motifs carved into the wood panelling? He once wrote about them in a letter to his sister. Said they could be turned to show hidden apertures, useful for keeping the good malt away from his wife's family. He must have thought they were a mealy-mouthed lot.'

'Yes, I can imagine him writing that, but don't forget two generations have lived there since he died. The fish carvings are still there but I haven't found any secret cupboards, just bits of old lustreware stuck in the windowsills and the fireplace.'

'He was a bit of a lad, wasn't he? You can imagine him and Isobel fighting hammer and tongs!'

Sarah said she could and looked at her watch. 'I'm going to have to go soon Donald to catch the school run. Thanks for seeing me; it's been wonderful and you haven't changed at all. I keep wanting to pinch myself I'm back here. I bet all your students now are going on to do MBAs, or PhDs in arts administration. Young people now are terribly focused and serious, much more than I ever was.' Her tone was light, but there was no ignoring the pain.

'Yes they are, but then they have to be, the competition is so much fiercer and they have to shoulder quite a lot of debt to get through the course. Here you are, *The Role of Archie Milne Robertson In The Rediscovery Of Lustreware In European Ceramics*. Beat that! A wonderful piece of work.'

'Thanks to you!' She could see it even had the original large green paper clip she had bought for luck.

'No, don't do yourself down. It was brilliant. I give it to my students if they're interested in the subject, just to show what they have to aim for.'

'Now you *are* joking!'

'Look, Sarah. It's none of my business, but can you tell me why you left us like that? I know it's none of my business, but I never understood why. I even rang you at your home, and your mother told me you were out.'

'She never said.'

'Well she perhaps didn't want to upset you. I know it's ancient history and you've made a good life for yourself. But why did you leave? You had a real future here.'

He was looking at her, half-embarrassed as if presuming to cross the years to an old relationship, but daring to do so just the same. 'I sometimes felt guilty,' he was smiling, 'if the fact that I was desperate to ask you out, had scared you off. I tried not to show it because you needed to concentrate, with your finals, but you were something special, Sarah. Sorry. I'm embarrassing you. I've never forgotten that cape you used to wear, and how it sailed along the road. I could always tell how harsh the wind outside was by the way it swirled around.'

She could still feel the heaviness and texture of the cloak. Tears began to prick the back of her eyes.

'I certainly never knew you felt like that!'

'Well, everyone else did too at the time, but you were so wrapped up in your work. You never even fell asleep during tutorials.'

She laughed, and began to twist over the strap of her leather bag in her fingers.

'Well, it was all a long time ago.'

'Sarah, so what made you give up? I have often thought about you over the years. I suppose at times when my own life has not been great. Typical male fantasy, isn't it? The girl who got away.'

She turned away and looked at the window. On the ledge she could see the newspaper lying, still unread. She opened it up and folded the paper over so that the article on the rape trial was at the top, and showed it to him. He looked at it uncertainly.

'Donald, unlike this girl, I was, still am, a terrible coward. A wimp. I couldn't have done what this girl is doing, standing up in the Old Bailey, speaking openly to the media.'

He was looking at the newspaper, mystified.

'Do you remember the night of the party Jeremy Lofthouse gave? For the end of the exams. You arrived with a girl who had a green hat, do you remember?'

'Dimly.'

'Well that night, at that party, well, I was raped. By one of the guests. On top of everyone's coats. In the bath. Sounds pathetic, stupid, doesn't it? Most people went in to do it voluntarily on the coats in those days. Pre-AIDS. But I had just gone to sort out my contact lenses. I didn't know who it was. Anyway, I know now. He's dead. It's a sad sick joke, really. You see, I now know he was David Milne Robertson, Archie's grandson, believe it or not. He was an accountancy student who must have been up from Edinburgh visiting friends. And I am living in his house! It came up at auction following his suicide. I'm living in the house of the man who raped me, while rushing about organising an exhibition of his grandfather's work. You couldn't make it up!'

She was still twisting the strap of her handbag over and over, noting the tight regular stitching on the leather. He was standing very still and, when she looked up, he was looking at her as if memorising every pore. 'He told me you had said I was a good lay. I don't know if you did. I told him that I had never slept with you, but he didn't believe me. Afterwards I felt so dirty and guilty. I didn't seek help because I didn't know where to go. I was so programmed you see not to make a fuss. I didn't have this girl's bottle either, so I just went away.'

She was now standing there, shaking. The effort of putting the worst event in her life into the English language for the first time was leaving her feeling not just naked but such a bloody fool. And cold. Other women coped with far worse. Why hadn't she?

'Sarah,' she could hear the horror in his voice but couldn't bear to look at him; still she turned the strap of her handbag over and over.

'I am so sorry. I am so sorry,' he was saying.

'It doesn't matter now Donald, he's dead, committed suicide, so it's all ancient history.'

'Actually I do remember meeting him that day. He had come over to the department after looking at your exhibition. He had brought some of his grandfather's pieces he wanted me to buy. He wanted one thousand pounds and I said the department didn't have that sort of money. He obviously needed money. He noticed you in the tutorial room and asked me who you were. Anyway, I said that we would all be going over to Lofthouse's house for an end of year party and did he want to come? *Bastard*. Why didn't you tell someone, Sarah? Couldn't you have gone to the police?'

'You forget what it was like then. The Pill was only just becoming acceptable if you weren't married. And counselling and things like that were still so new. Nowadays, you can get trauma counselling if you're so much as burgled, and at police stations they have rape suites with soft lights and post trauma syndrome counsellors. But it wasn't like that then. People would have said I had led him on, that I'd asked for it. It would have been such a scandal. So I didn't want anyone to know and anyway I didn't even know who he was.' Her voice now came out in small puffs in between sighs and chattering teeth. 'Look, Donald, I'm sorry. Now you know. I have to go. Please don't tell anyone.'

'Sarah, please stay. Sit down and I'll make you some tea. Please.'

But she had already grabbed her papers, shoved them into her briefcase, and stumbled to the door. Then on the landing she suddenly had a flashed picture of the man's solid shoulders outlined in the cheap bathroom light, then felt the unpitying weight of his body on hers and then the robbed hope. Suddenly, she ran blindly down the stairs and out into the darkening street.

Loanside

It was late by the time she arrived back in Loanside, the lights of Fife now at a safe distance across the black waters of the Forth. Shivering, she unlocked the front door. The babysitter had her coat on, ready to leave. 'Fifteen Lollops, that'll do nicely.' Sarah scrawled the cheque and showed her out. Upstairs, the children were in bed sleeping heavily. The beam of the lighthouse picked out their curls and the beauty of their faces in repose. How wonderful it must be to sleep like that! Creeping down the stairs, her fingers felt a knobbly fish on the banisters and she thought back to what Donald had said. She tried to turn it, but it was merely carved wood. But an overwhelming desire for vengeance overcame her. Bastard men! Who ever once said revenge is a dish best eaten cold must have been a cold fish himself.

She switched the heating back on and all the lights and found Christopher's compact disc of *Cavalleria Rusticana*. Perfect revenge music. That was the point of clichés; they worked. She started at the top of the house, where she supposed the two teachers were asleep, and started to work her way down, trying to twist every carved fish she found in the wood of the panelling and stairs. After an hour she had felt 205. All except two were simply carvings. And these two were small knobs which twisted round and opened up small cupboards. Both were empty. They would all have been known about and cleared out long before, by the Robertson boys or Isobel's family. She was being absurd. How could you take revenge on the dead?

Grimly she continued down the stairs into the kitchen, although most of the panelling had long since been replaced with tiles. Nothing. She opened a bottle of red wine and gulped it down, feeling its warmth, then, noticing yet another fish, this time low down the panelling behind the kitchen table, gave it a tweak. It twisted open with a creak and the panelling slid back. Sarah pushed away the table and knelt down. Her fingers felt sawdust and then, suddenly fearing earwigs or other creepy crawlies, she went to get rubber gloves and a torch. As she crouched down, she saw a package. Old recipes for Isobel's lentil soup probably.

The package was wrapped in grimy oilskin and, sitting up at the kitchen table, she carefully unpacked it. Old string broke in her hands before she had even untied the knots and then a small notebook, with a broken spine and yellowing pages, fell onto the tablecloth.

Amazing. The handwriting was Archie's. She had often seen that ink scrawl. He must have cleverly stuck this notebook in here to keep it safe from his wife's hated family and from his creditors. No one would have expected the man of the house to go near the kitchen; they would have been searching in his studio or the upstairs rooms. Copper oxalate, silver sulphide, copper sulphide, silver oxalate, purple of cassius, gold dissolved in aqua regia, all detailed in method and quantity, page after page. The name of each lustre and the recipe produced was written in large, squirly writing, underlined in scrollwork. Green lustres, not the clear lustres of the Pilkington factory, but clear green and gold, and silver, and blue and pink. And so it went on. She kept on searching until she found it. The Red Poppy lustre. There it was, the recipe for the finest red lustre since the sixteenth century, of a fire and clarity which went back to tenth-century Egypt!

Her eye went down the list of ingredients. How had he done the red lustre? Gold dissolved in nitric acid, mixed with Japanese red clay, nothing unusual there, bismuth carbonate, red ochre, mercuric sulphide. Then she saw it. Two tablespoonfuls of blood. Blood! Ridiculous. That *couldn't* be right. An organic material like blood would dissolve immediately at such a high level of heat in the muffle-kiln. Unless he had found a way of keeping the blood intact? No, it had to be symbolic. His blood hadn't been spilt in northern France, so had Archie decorated his work with his own lifesblood in recompense? Weird!

A card fell out onto the table. 'All that lustres is not gold. I have discovered this to my cost, for life has its own strange alchemy. But if you can throw a pot or two, then use these receipts and gold could come your way. If not, be generous and give these pages to those who can. Archie Milne Robertson 4th June 1938.'

Sarah sat holding the card and the notebook in her hand. She could smell his sweat. Now she shivered no longer, nor tasted the bittersweetness of revenge. This was pay-back time.

CHAPTER FOURTEEN

Leith

It was already getting dark by the time Sarah arrived in Leith. Two or three iffy characters were, as usual, hanging around the street corner. It was an area which, however many bistros spread into, still gave her the creeps. Of course they could just be waiting for the bus, but they probably weren't. Here the drug culture was nothing if upfront. Zander had once told her that the dealers always came out in the late afternoon to supply their punters for the evening. She had been horribly shocked. The problem with you, Hunter, is you are too middle-class respectable, she said to herself. Where's your street cred? But then she had never been able to deal with too much gritty urban realism. You could take the girl out of Carshalton, but you couldn't take Carshalton out of the girl. She locked the car carefully and ran up the stairs to the studio. Zander was going to be so pleased.

He was working on a mixed-media collage seven feet square. Iron strips and bits of industrial scrap were neatly arranged along the floor. On the windowsill, the jars of money were still immaculately dusted and ranged in order of size. She had never met anyone who was so obsessively tidy, yet who chose to work with such mucky material.

He seemed to be surprised to see her. He obviously didn't know she had found the notebook, nor that the press had gone mad. She threw him a copy of the previous day's *Scotsman*. 'There, what do you think? I made the front page!'

He stood up and looked at her photograph on the front page

holding up the notebook. 'The Scottish *Daily Mail* have also asked Eleanor and me for an interview. What do you think? And here's today's *Telegraph.*' Sarah felt just for a moment like hopping round the room.

Zander stood upright and held both papers in his hands. He read carefully, then stood looking at her.

'So you've found it. The notebook with all the lustres.'

'I did.'

'Where?'

'You see, it says, underneath the pictures. In a secret cupboard in the kitchen. It was Donald Gosford, my old tutor at St Andrews, who told me that Archie had said in a letter about putting in secret cupboards in the panelling. I twisted one of Archie's carved fish and there it was.'

'With all the lustre recipes?' He sounded as if he could not believe it.

Sarah laughed. She took the *Telegraph* from him. The picture had been taken in the kitchen next to the secret cupboard. It showed her proudly holding up the notebook while underneath ran the words, 'Found: Lost Lustres Recipes of Top Scots Ceramicist (He used his own blood!)'. A ceramics expert from Bute's the Mayfair auctioneers was quoted as saying that this find could be worth in excess of £20,000 at auction.

She told him she had rung Eleanor straightaway. She had gone into raptures and had come round with champagne and her special camera to photograph every page ('just in case'). They had rung him up immediately, but he had been out and they hadn't wanted to leave a message. So then they had rung Jeremy Lofthouse in the middle of a dinner party, who had said that frankly it was one of those rare special events to savour, just like finding an unknown Mozart concerto. A bit over the top, but whatever!

The next day they had taken the book to his museum in Edinburgh, and he had organised his arts buddies on the *Scotsman* to come down to take Sarah's picture. For which she had posed gladly for a bit of publicity for the exhibition, which was now, of course, going to attract much more excitement from the ceramicist fraternity! The recipes in Archie's spidery handwriting could be projected from slides onto the ceiling of the museum. The nationals had then picked up the story the next day and Morag's brother had put news of the find on to the Web. Five offers had already come through from the States to buy it.

'Not that it's for sale, of course!'

'So where is it?' Zander was looking out of the window, drinking from a large glass of wine. Good. She could enjoy a glass of wine now.

'It's in the museum safe. You must come over and see it. Archie left a short note with it. You see, there's a small picture of it under the article. I would have brought it over tonight, but I didn't know if you would be in. You know I've been ringing you all week.'

'I've been away. I'm doing a commission for some people in Telford. Did they say who it belonged to?'

'The book? Well, I found it in my house, so I suppose it belongs to me, but I intend it to be exhibited in the museum. I think the man at Bute's was probably exaggerating about how much it is worth. You know what, Zander, I wish I'd met Archie. I know you said he was difficult, but he must have been quite a character. Have you seen the Robert Noble portrait of him which has been handed in? What a hunk!'

He was silent. The studio was now gloomy in the unconvincing light of a March late afternoon. His black hair stood out against the white powder of the papier-mâché on his overalls. She thought of the mistletoe and how she had begun, slowly, to think of him as a replacement for Christopher in her mind, as the true meaning of being single was beginning to sink in. Archie's grandson. Yet in some deep subterranean way she still felt just as married as ever, with a distant sorry sense of proprietorship, rather like a redundant manager who, however disillusioned, still reads about his old company in the paper.

'I think you're out of order, Sarah. I don't want all this fuss, all this publicity.' His voice was harsh. A different voice from the one she had grown used to. Sarah looked at him astonished.

'What do you mean?'

'This is *my* heritage you're suddenly putting a spotlight on.

Mine, not yours. Even though apparently I have no claim to my own grandfather's book. *Caveat emptor*, don't you know, old bean!'

His mocking Bertie Wooster tones were even harsher.

'OK, the *Telegraph* may blether on about Red Poppy lustres. Don't get me wrong, I'm sure it will bring people into Loanside, but what are the other papers going to write about? You've done your publicity too bloody well. So now it's not Archie, the toast of Vienna, the inspirer of Lucy Rie and modern ceramics. Or even Archie, the luminary of godawful bloody Loanside. No. It's going to be Archie the womaniser, Archie the drunk, the bankrupt, the opium taker. The man who fathered wee bastards all over East Lothian, who died dead drunk owing money. But you're far too high-minded to think like this, I know. Robertson's your property now, isn't he? Just because you did your friggin' degree on him, bought his house and found his recipes.'

'Stop it Zander. Don't be absurd.' She tried to keep her voice steady. He was pacing around. Suddenly he scrunched up the newspapers and threw them onto the table.

'So, what shall we have next? David's suicide with a nice double-page spread in your Scottish *Daily Mail*, with every fact angled for maximum *Schadenfreude*. Or how about my brilliant career, my running away from home, sleeping rough, making money, gambling most of it away? And all this bloody fuss just to satisfy some do-gooding English lady-bountiful. Well, I've had enough. I am withdrawing my support.'

'Zander! Please! I'm sorry. I didn't know you would take it this way. I only wanted a bit of publicity for the exhibition, but I didn't even think the papers would be the least bit interested in me finding an old notebook.'

'You haven't learned anything, have you? You have never left your precious, bloody ivory tower.' He turned his back and, without offering her any, poured himself another glass of wine.

She could only look at him, uncertain. 'But I thought. I thought you wanted to have this exhibition. I thought you agreed it would do Loanside some good.'

'A wee exhibition yes, a few pots and a few more people

thinking well of him. A few L.E.T.S. people lolloping about with their grotty wee chequebooks. Fine. Better than a bloody beetle drive. But we're talking about *my* grandfather and yes, he was a bastard who pretty nearly destroyed my life before I was even bloody born let alone David's, but yes he was my grandfather. Inheriting his talent is the reason I am now able to charge lots of money to financial service companies to adorn their ghastly, soulless headquarters. I am the one with the talent.'

'I never said you hadn't got the talent.'

His eyes now blazed down at her.

'So what do we have now? It's All About Archie, who never paid a bill in his life unless it was in pots. Archie, the waster who needed some tight-arsed minister's family to sort him out. Another no-good bastard artist, who needed respectable people to help him when the chips were down.'

He was shouting now, his face red and blotchy, and she could suddenly see that she had been given only half the script, only seen half the person. She'd misread the signals.

'Zander I'm sorry. This isn't getting us anywhere. I beg your pardon. But I'm going.'

'I really do beg your pardon, but I'm going,' he mimicked in an English accent. Half her brain thought how irritating Scots must find it when the English put on a Scots accent, while the other half told her to back over to the door.

'Oh, what the hell. Look Sarah, don't go.' As she moved to the door, his tone suddenly changed.

'I don't want to stay. Zander, I'm sorry you feel like this, but I'm off.'

'For God's sake, woman, you don't need to go off on your high horse. I'm allowed my opinion.'

'Of course you are. But I've got to go.'

'Oh I'm being dismissed now, am I?' He put down his glass and came towards her. He was smiling and, uncertainly, she smiled back.

'You're far too nice, aren't you Sarah? Too pretty and nice for your own good. All right, I'm going to stop being angry now. Stop being a bit of rough.'

His hand was now touching her cheek. A big hand covered in clay. She shivered and tried to move away, saying that she had to get home to get the children from a friend's.

'I'm only going to give you a kiss, for God's sake. To make up? I bet that tight-arsed English husband of yours, when you had him, never ever gave you a proper kiss.'

So he knew. Christopher had left her and he knew. Who had told him? His hands were round her shoulders. Quite gently. They were standing just where the mistletoe had been. He apparently wasn't angry any longer. He kept saying he was sorry, and to let him kiss her.

Sarah stiffened. His hands now passed down over her body, and he began to kiss her on the cheek, pushing her against the wall as he did so. The knowledge of the huge, overwhelming strength of a man suddenly came back to her. Christopher had all these years been so light, not really there in bed with her at all somehow. He was right. She hadn't known passion. Hadn't wanted to. She had always been frightened of it. She'd hated it if Christopher had ever been even the slightest bit less than gentle. But now she had been let go by Christopher. Sacked. So what was her problem?

She jerked her head and in that instant it felt like one million volts went through her. He stopped and looked at her. She gazed at him, horrified. Then crashed her heel down on his foot. He staggered sideways and, in his surprise, brought down one of the strings holding the huge dangling puppet figure of his brother, which had been dancing and grimacing above them. 'Sarah, for God's sake! What's the matter?'

She broke free, tore open the door and ran out onto the landing. The old, sick unconquerable fear engulfed her. Then came the sound of the falling wire and plaster, and a man swearing. Once again, she flew down stone stairs, and out to the early evening street.

Washington

Someone once said that at the World Bank no one ever picked up a draft report, without picking up a red pencil at the same time.

Whoever it was had obviously suffered. So his own report, from the outgoing (*when* outgoing, for God's sake!) director had been returned, was a sea of red corrections. It had taken him hours to write it, too. Days! All about creating plurality of approach in HIPCs or Heavily Indebted Poor Countries. Or Hopeless Causes, as Christopher and his colleagues secretly called them.

There should also have been another World Bank saying, that when you make executives do all their own typing, they take twice as long to do half the amount of work. But then, in this super-politically correct environment where sharply dressed women ruled, you couldn't even ask an admin. girl to make you a cup of coffee, let alone say, 'Take a letter, Miss Jones.' If you did, you'd be up on a sexual harassment rap, before you could say International Monetary Fund.

Christopher, on this spring-like Washington day, was feeling what his mother would once have called, 'idgy-wadgy', which meant he felt out of sorts and, if not quite yet depressed, then on the irritable side of pissed off. He had flown over 10,000 miles in the past two weeks and was now covered, metaphorically, in red ink. Administered by an old dodo, into whose shoes (please God!) he would surely be stepping by the end of the month? Christopher couldn't wait. His deliciously witty letter of resignation to the E & A still lay like a snake in the memory of his laptop.

This evening, he and Maria Antonietta would go out to dinner with some colleagues. She had calmed down, they had made up in New York at the Plaza and they were now officially 'an item', which made life a lot easier. He was no longer the bashful Englishman. It was common knowledge that his wife and he were divorcing. All very amicable, he would say, super lady. Shorthand for, I am getting on with my life. And sure enough, proof of this progress in life's mortal coil came in the thick brown envelopes from the realtor, with details of flats to rent.

Was this divorce, like his first, almost too amicable? He picked up a letter from Sarah, which had arrived that morning with tiny pictures drawn by the children. No doubt guaranteed to make him feel a heel. Yet he was impressed by the style, and by the fact she now had a computer, and amazingly was online with an e-mail address. (Sarah, who barely knew how to use the microwave!) He was determined to always remain nice about Sarah. He owed her that. He had already pulled Maria Antonietta up, when she had teased him about Sarah going to the ball like a Cinderella in a second-hand dress. What a bitch her sister must be for telling her! He had to have a bit of loyalty. And some days, his past seemed more real than his present life with Maria Antonietta and the flickering terminal. With both he was supposedly fighting world poverty like some conquering superhero. But then again he would soon be in control of two per cent of the World Bank's current $19bn budget, which would do wonders for his future.

It then suddenly struck him as ironic that a man who spent his working life telling the third world countries that they had to break down the barriers between sectors, should prefer his private life to function in such carefully sealed compartments.

A cutting from the *Daily Telegraph* fell out of the letter. Sarah, waving some sort of notebook she had found behind a secret panel, which had belonged to that mad potter who had once owned the house. An extraordinary find, it said. £20,000! Another surprise to see she was currently organising an exhibition of his work. Was Loanside ready for such excitement? Almost certainly not. Maybe the notebook would be another asset to throw into negotiations? He hoped everything would stay as friendly when the lawyers started working out a deal about the house and his pension, come to that. He'd better reply nicely before the going got tough.

He looked at his watch. 12.45. Time for lunch. Everyone else could just e-mail him and download unreadable guff for the next hour. He dialled Maria Antonietta's number. A disembodied voice told him that Contessa Guicciardini was away from her desk right now. Christopher stood up, stretched and patted his stomach. Not bad for a man of forty-eight. You are as young as the woman you feel. A thirty-five-year-old firecracker, in his case. '*Allora ragazzi mangiamo la pasta!*' he announced, rather proud of his rolling r's in an otherwise flat Italian accent. Then, ruefully, he patted his stomach once more. Better have a bagel, old boy.

Clapham

It was hardly fair. Her first free weekday morning for years and the sun had to shine so harshly that every streak and splash of bird lime on the windows showed up in glorious detail. Such is life. This sun wasn't friendly; it was the sort of fascist sunshine which made people top themselves if their businesses were going under and made sensible women rush out for face lifts and colonic irrigation. And yet, because the trees had hardly any leaves yet to mask the noise, there was also the winter accompaniment of the unremitting grind of brakes as the traffic mashed its way around Clapham Common.

In spite of this, Bunny was intent on making herself as happy as a person could after a seriously bloody few days. For this purpose she placed a thick linen cloth on the table for her breakfast. She never subscribed to her mother's terrible attitude of keeping everything 'for best', presumably until the day when you finally popped your clogs, and someone else would have to do the laundering. No, today she would have the works. The freshly squeezed orange juice, the whole pot of real coffee and the fattening croissants – two! – plus confiture de God knows how many calories and *real* butter. None of your dieters' axle grease for her this morning. This was put onto the cloth in fancy dishes with fancy cutlery. Then Bunny sat down to look at the post and ignored the newspaper.

The house was silent. Bliss. Bunny sitting here like lady muck at 9 a.m. on an ordinary Wednesday in a silent house was not unconnected to the series of small volcanoes which had rocked her life in the past few weeks. First, Hannah had left home to 'shack up' (delightful expression) with Studd. This decision had led to more tears than Bunny had thought possible. Hannah had been determined, and Bunny had finally realised that she had lost the little girl she had never really had time to get to know. She had given in to a sort of mourning, then had ordered half a van full of General Trading Company household goods which had been delivered to their new Kennington flat. Hannah was now seventeen and had just left college and landed a job as a teagirl at a Wardour Street voice-over studio. Her business studies A Level was apparently a waste of time. Bunny now began to appreciate her mother's horror when she had flunked her own school exams. But of course Marjorie had not raised a murmur of protest when Bunny had told her about Hannah. In fact, she said what an eligible young man Studd was and in the most sought-after employment. To be blunt, Bunny's.

For one morning Rhoda, her agent, had faxed informing her that her contract with the *Good Morning With Jenna* was not being renewed and that due to his huge and growing popularity, Studd would be replacing her. Studd! The contents of this fax were repeated with varying degrees of accuracy in the newspapers over the next few days as Studd was discovered and taken to the nation's bosom. He appeared on talk shows and was seen at the new Bond première with Hannah in black leather. People said Bunny was getting a bit past it, and could now move over to a nice game show, if she were lucky, or a daytime chat show, or she could open a restaurant. Because she had always been large and not pretty, she was somehow being treated like a fifty-five-year-old as opposed to someone only just forty. But then, she was just so bloody tired. All the time.

Was she upset? About Hannah, distraught. She had always hoped there might be a time when they could get to know each other. After the next busy patch, after the next series or book, or contract had been completed. Wrong. As for the show, she loathed Jenna just as much as the early morning starts. It would be fun watching Studd instruct two million experienced housewives how to boil an egg – rock hard – and how to make soggy spaghetti while rippling his muscles and grating parmesan suggestively. He had, at least, the grace to thank Bunny for the job and 'the gear for the flat' in a grimy postcard with a panda on the front. Couldn't spell, she noticed.

On this spring morning, the other occupants of the house

were also out. Juanita, clever girl, had one day overheard their neighbour, Sir Geoffrey Askew, remarking to his housekeeper through the open window that there would be lots of surprises in store at Channel 6, and please could he have another dippy egg? Correctly interpreting this as a potential takeover, Juanita had invested several years' salary in double quick time before the US bid, and now had taken herself off for three weeks' holiday in the Seychelles on the profits. Edward had also left for the Cheltenham National Hunt Festival for all three days. One of his favourites, Lucky Bunny, was racing in the 2.30. She warned him it would probably romp home last, but she had kissed him and waved him off.

The phone was silent. Sign of a career hitting the skids. There were usually twenty messages each day when she returned, and Bunny hoped that Lucinda was holding the fort at the office.

The office. To complete a total *et tu, Brute?* of a month, yesterday Lottie had handed in her notice. She had found God, she said, and was striking out to work as a cook with a charity for the homeless in the East End. Her new man would also be giving up university for a year to join her. Super. Though Bunny could not help noting that she was planning to charge a thoroughly ungodly commercial rent for her Chiswick house.

After Bunny had come down off the ceiling with the shock, she had managed to talk Lottie into a two-month leave of absence by dangling an extremely large carrot. A partnership. For Lottie and Lucinda with a twenty per cent stake each. Lucinda, being Lucinda, cracked open the Bolly while Lottie said she would pray about it. As she poured the hot coffee, Bunny said a quick prayer to God to persuade Him to show Lottie that her true vocation in life was with Bunny Halifax. Then started on the second croissant.

Then, during all this upheaval, Sarah had stunned the family by appearing on the front page of the *Telegraph* looking drop-dead gorgeous, waving a notebook with some old formulas for glazes she had found in a secret kitchen cupboard. This was apparently worth £20,000! The Loanside exhibition had suddenly become sexy, rather like Hay-on-Wye and the Buxton Festival. She'd met two people in the City asking each other if they were going to 'the Robertson show', in the same tone they would normally talk about Glyndebourne.

Bunny had found herself saying that Sarah actually was *her* cousin (rather than the other way around). The clients had been terribly impressed, as if Bunny could not possibly be related to someone so beautiful and intelligent. Bit miffing. But then *Bunny Cooks* would be doing the catering and she would be helping out beforehand, so there was an odd sort of reflected glory. She wondered if Christopher had seen Sarah on the front page, and whether one could *get* filo pastry up in Loanside?

Bunny finished picking the crumbs off the plate and picked up the post. There were six begging letters from charities – most a huge con, as five were enjoying big bucks, service providers to the government these days; one local conservation area newsletter and yet more credit cards offering over £75,000 each on a super double platinum Flaunt It Card. The more debt you had, it seemed, the more you were offered. Which probably explained why Bunny's credit rating was now assuming six-tier wedding cake proportions. Another if-you-fall-under-a-bus missive from a friendly life assurance company, a very thick bank statement which clearly would need two glasses of claret to even open, and then some junk mail from Exeter addressed to something Halifax. Either B or E, hard to tell, not that either of them knew anyone in Exeter.

She was about to throw it out, but opened it anyway and saw it was from Sands Bank. Frightfully posh, but clearly just a come-on; neither had an account there. Poor Edward kept the rump of his money in the building society. The Halifax, needless to say. Edward liked to be tidy.

Dear Mr Halifax,
Due to our merger with the Bedford & Buckingham Bank plc, we are now handling our private banking activities at our new Exeter headquarters. As you requested, here is an updated

statement of your account. Should you have any queries, please don't hesitate to call.

Isn't it ridiculous what a time it takes to read long numbers with lots of noughts on the end? £628,000. Six hundred and twenty eight thousand pounds. Must be a mistake, Bunny thought. Another Mr E. Halifax. She would ring up and tell them. Or ask Edward.

What a joke.

Ask Edward.

She sat there and in the next few minutes digested the truth and the reason why she would not be asking Edward. It took a little while longer for her to tease out all the different strands of what it meant. Betrayal is so bitter to the taste. It took more time for Bunny to work out that Edward would not have expected her to be here today. He or Juanita always took in the post. She was either out at work or having a lie-in at the weekend. That he had never intended her to know, however bothered and upset she was about money. This was clearly *his* bank and *his* money. Where had he got it from? Racing? Inheritance? Who knows? The harsh rays of the sun were now in her eyes. As she got up to lower the blinds, Bunny found she could barely stand.

What did one really know of a person, however long you were married to them? Poor Sarah had only just discovered Christopher had obviously had a secret life. Cold-hearted bastard. Edward, in contrast, because his apparent hopelessness had been upfront, had been so easy to live with. Always so pleasant to her, as long as he was given his freedom to do exactly as he liked. And how she had justified him to the world. Especially her mother. 'When is Edward going to find another job? He's only forty-three, in his prime. I can't understand with all his private education how he can just sit around doing nothing but watch television.' Her mother would repeat this *ad nauseam* while watching *Neighbours*.

Bunny had never complained about the cheap perfume he gave her for presents, nor of being the family breadwinner. She had bought the house with its monster mortgage because

Edward had said that they had a certain style to maintain. She had worked right through Hannah's young life and had missed it. All the birthday parties she had cooked and organised for other people over the years and yet the nanny had always done her own daughter's. So Hannah had grown up, unnoticed under the endless trays of food, and then had obviously given up. Bunny was the workaholic in the family, you see, the driven one with the talent and the energy; this had been the conventional wisdom. Edward had told her so.

But the real truth was that she had never been good-looking and cooking had helped her find herself a husband. Way to a man's heart. He was her distinguished, almost attractive, husband who ventured into candlewick loo-seat land to marry her in spite of his family's disapproval. So she had worked that much harder in order to hang on to him, to give him the life he had been accustomed to. To keep him and make the marriage worth his while.

What a mug. Bunny could feel the sides of her mouth turning down as she sipped her coffee. She was after all no different from those dopey women she had interviewed as cooking assistants when she had come back from Scotland. Their husbands had traded them in. How pathetic she had thought them. She would never be betrayed like that, she had thought. Then she thought of Sarah. All that hidden intelligence burning away and yet she had obviously not known about Christopher.

Bunny sat for an hour quite still. Practical details shifted in her mind like the angry cars changing gear outside. Dreams bit the dust. Monte Carlo went down first. What a joke. Might as well read that book on downshifting. In a few weeks, the back-tax demands for Jenna's show would come in and, if the next TV series were not to happen, all her books would be remaindered before you could say coriander. She would have to return to stuffing vine leaves for executives in City banks, praying the school bookings kept up while just working for the taxman. It was all the constant, unending worry and responsibility of it all that got her down. And for what?

Anger slowly seeped through Bunny, a cold thin poisonous consommé of fury.

Still the letter lay on the table. She had choices, but what were they? She could seal up the envelope and carry on working as if nothing had happened. She could have a scene with Edward and demand to know why he had hidden all this money all these years. She could photocopy it and then quietly take it to lawyers, who would screw him into the ground. She knew a firm of real English pirates. She could poison him with a nice curry when he came home flushed with triumph from the races. She pictured herself in tears before the judge, acknowledging to m' lud that she had no idea cardamom was fatal when mixed with arsenic and sell her story to the *Mirror* for thousands. She could stay married or she could become single. Whatever she did, there were now 628,000 reasons to change her life.

Suddenly a shaft of a smile hit Bunny's face, every bit as decisive as the sunlight which now cut through the London fumes outside. Slowly, she sealed up the envelope, so that it looked unopened, and then did what she always did when she had a plan. She got out her notebook and made a list.

Washington

Christopher was sitting in the large greeting area outside the Chief's office. He may have been dressed in Savile Row's finest, with just a suggestion of New York chic, but inside he was still the gangly boy hanging round his housemaster's office waiting to hear if he had been made a prefect. Then, it had meant control of the tuck shop, a fag to sort our your room every day, a striking red blazer and trips downtown every Saturday afternoon for hamburgers and a Coca-Cola.

The feelings of anticipation were still the same, but the rewards a little different. Confirmation this afternoon of his position as Department Chief of the Cross-Sectoral Cooperation Department would mean a great package. The children's education would be paid for. Liddy could come to Princeton or Yale when she was ready. Other men bought big family houses in Maryland or Virginia, but for him, it was to be the new duplex which he had just signed for. Nice distance from the bank's offices and the Kennedy Center and the best restaurants. Plenty of gossiping with the White House boys and girls. The Pope was supposed to be coming next year, and Maria Antonietta had promised to introduce him. Her uncle was a cardinal.

The Executive Assistant, having offered him regulation decaf, then announced that the gentlemen were ready to see him and ushered him into the conference room. As he stood at the door, he just remembered in time not to rub his shoes on the back of his trousers.

Afterwards, thinking about it, he realised that he had always rather prided himself on his ability with World Bank kremlinology. After surviving in a conservative bastion like the E & A for years, coded office politics had come naturally. And yet that afternoon, this skill had eluded him. He saw that the decision for everyone to reapply for their own jobs had given rise to huge staff insecurities and that in the subsequent downsizing, an assistant director on secondment from a third tier Scottish bank wasn't exactly on the fast track, but he knew he had not been given a piece of the code. Why had they told him unofficially that the position was his, he had asked? The men on the panel had smiled and said that, effective though he had proved, it was his lack of languages that had kept him out of the frame. Even Christopher, they said, had to acknowledge that tenth-grade French was just not enough in the global village. They had been looking for at least three languages spoken at fluent, if not native, level.

He said he understood and managed to walk out of the room in a straight line. Just about.

London

It was already eight o'clock in the evening when Edward came back to the house. He had made £10,750 in the past three days and was smiling as the taxi drew up outside. No lights were on, and Bunny's car was not in the drive, which meant she was still out. He paid the driver, picked up his cases and walked to the front door. No one answered the bell so, fumbling the keys, he unlocked the door and went in.

Bunny *was* in fact at home. But home for Bunny was now a three-bedroom mansion flat on Prince of Wales Drive in Battersea, convenient for the bus to Sloane Square, walks in Battersea Park, and just a few minutes' drive from her daughter's flat and the school – traffic permitting. Not too far, in fact, from where her ancestors used to knock together bits of furniture in their shop in Clapham Junction. This flat may even have been lived in originally by one of their customers. What a nice tidy thought.

Bunny poured herself a drink and put her feet up, trying to imagine what Edward would do and think when he arrived home, flush with cash. It had been interesting having a chat with the bookie round the corner and seeing a completely different picture from her apparently directionless husband. They had been rueful in their praise for the eye Edward had for talent in the paddock and were obviously relieved that theirs was only one of several firms Edward patronised. 'What a nose he's got for a winner, Mrs. H,' they said. Bless his little cotton socks.

Now the great thing about catering, as any careers adviser will tell you, is that it teaches you to organise. And Bunny, after twenty years of feeding thousands across London, could handle logistics like a Russian general. Her plans had been carefully evaluated and brilliantly implemented and now her new life rose like a soufflé.

First, she had rung the school to say she would be out of action for three days and to cancel all appointments. She could hear Joanna choking with horror on the other end, but then Lottie and Lucinda would now have to start earning their partnerships. Then she had gone round to have coffee with her neighbour, dear Sir Geoffrey, now many millions richer having sold Channel 6 to those nice Americans. He had agreed on the spot to buy the house. *Her* house. Thank God she had the sense to buy it in her name. He had written a note to this effect, giving her a cheque for five per cent, and had rung his solicitors to start proceedings. 'Could probably exchange contracts in a week, Bunny darling.' Though it would take a few days to send off for the deeds and get a redemption figure out to the building society, Bunny's £400,000 mortgage would soon be paid off and history.

Next she had rung a client, one of London's most select rental agencies. Yes, a delightful unfurnished let had just come on the books. Prince of Wales Drive, six months renewable. That would do nicely.

Then Bunny had rung Harrods removal service, who were as usual charming and efficient and had sent in the packers. They had taken down all the billowing curtains, the Venetian lanterns and the huge mirrors and had sent them round to Battersea. The installation with the Battersea dogs had taken two hours to take down and now seemed terribly appropriate, given her new address. The joiners said it would be up and twinkling in a day. All her possessions were driven off to her new home while any furniture surplus to requirements was sent to Bute's the auctioneers. Soon the house had the echoing strangeness of a dismantled life and Bunny realised just how brave Sarah had been moving her life to Scotland.

Packing took a day and half and on the morning of the third day Bunny, after a night staying in a nearby hotel, let herself back into the house and went up into Edward's rooms.

It had been months since she had been into his part of the house, which consisted of his bedroom, dressing room and study. Their lives had been so busy, charging forward on separate tracks, that she had never been in them unless he had been there. She stood there, taking in the four-poster bed and the heavy mahogany furniture. The large swivel dressing-table mirror, the collection of silver brushes on his dressing table. These were not rooms, more like an colony, where he had lived, feeding off her. She stood there, her hands on her hips. She remembered how she had stomped down the street impersonating Nancy Sinatra, singing something about boots walking over people. It had been the one and only time Carshalton high street had ever seen her in red hotpants. How hysterical she and Sarah had been, getting tipsy on too much cider on a bench. Little tinkers. 'Well Edward, you upper-class trilby-hatted bastard, you ain't seen nothin' yet.'

The girls from the cleaning agency arrived promptly and then soon, snaking their way along the road, came a fleet of taxis from the firm who for years had ferried canapés for her throughout London. The men all knew her and were pleased to be invited in for coffee and cakes. Bunny explained that they would be heading north of the river with a cab each full of goodies bound for a different charity shop. 'Build up not your treasure on earth, boys,' Bunny said and the men laughed.

And so it came to pass that Edward's magnificent collection of Herbert Johnson hats, his cherished ancient tweeds, his cashmere coats with the brown velvet collars worn for winter meetings, his Tattersall check shirts, cavalry twills and every pair of Gucci loafers he possessed, found themselves on their way to the Imperial Cancer shop in Chiswick High Road. His collection of Japanese prints headed for Cancer Relief on Ealing Broadway, while his entire collection of *Private Eye* back issues, *Winnie the Pooh* first editions, and Edwardian binoculars, landed on the Hampstead branch of Oxfam. The Wagner collection, consisting of 500 CDs gave Bunny particular pleasure to part with. She had always loathed those bloody women with horns coming out of their heads. Off it went in a taxi to the Ebury Street Red Cross shop. Goodbyeee to you too, Brunhilde.

As for all Edward's files, including his bookies' statements and tax bills, these were taken down in evidence and put into another cab and sent round to a firm of solicitors in Kensington High Street for whom Bunny had supplied a client dinner only the previous month. They were specialists in high-profile divorce cases and the partner Bunny had chosen was lean, mean and, until he had sampled her girls' cooking, obviously had not sat down to a square meal in months. All this delicious paperwork would be red meat to him. Just wait till he got his teeth into Edward.

It was really a wonderfully executed deconstruction. By lunchtime Edward's bedroom, dressing room and study echoed to the sound of the Clapham Common traffic. By 3 p.m. the phones, electricity and gas had been cut off, by which time Bunny had moved into her new flat and very cosy it was too.

She had taken Sarah's book to heart and had decided that the time had come for some smart urban downshifting for the new millennium.

Yet so strong remained Marjorie's fifties conditioning, Bunny found she really could not allow her man to go hungry. So, after she had organised her new housekeeper, Bunny popped into the school and had baked just the sort of chocolate cake she knew Edward really liked. Sticky and black, with big chunks of chocolate inside. She then took it back to Clapham and left it on a plate with a knife and a napkin on the drawing-room floorboards. On the cake she had written in white icing. 'Welcome Home Edward.' with an arrow to show just where to cut. Dear Edward had never been the domesticated sort. She had also left a torch by the front door. She had always told her girls that it was an eye for detail which marked out a real professional.

Once Edward had run right through the house with the torch and had found not so much as a curtain rail, he came back into what had once been the drawing room. He saw the cake and, being hungry and still in shock, started to cut it. It was fresh, still warm and smelt delicious. Crumbs fell onto the bare floorboards. His knife finally cut through a polythene packet which had been placed in the centre layer. This he found contained a letter from Sands bank informing him of the balance in his account, a letter from a Kensington solicitor informing him that the house had been sold and that he should vacate by the following day and that locksmiths would arrive at 9 a.m. to change the locks. And then, written on an invoice from *The Bunny Cooks School*, there was a short note. 'Dear Edward, Please buy yourself a life. Only this time use your own money. Love Bunny.' Edward stared at the letters in his hand for a moment, then he shrugged and started eating. On the second slice he choked on Bunny's wedding ring. But then, of course, it was always likely that he would. For, as Marjorie had always said, Bunny had such very large fingers.

CHAPTER FIFTEEN

Loanside

Only forty-eight hours to go before D-Day! Loanside's museum had undergone a complete metamorphosis. The town's seaside past had been swept into the storeroom, including the grainy pictures of fishermen and their nets and the brown photographs of the high street and now the main hall had upturned lights and whitewashed walls. One could have been in a gallery in New York or Mayfair, except for the call of the gulls and the oystercatchers outside and the continuous crash of the waves on the shore 100 yards away.

Bunny swept into Loanside in a large hire car to join in the fun. She chatted up journalists, answered the phone and played with Liddy and Theo. She persuaded them that sleepovers were cool and that they would be missing out if they did not stay with their friends. With E & A footing the catering bill, she planned an international buffet fit for Loanside's new superstar. Sarah, she said, not Archie. Though the pots were OK.

To everyone's astonishment, Loanside began to change. The Internet magic had worked. Americans, Canadians and Austrians began to arrive. They filled the shops, hotels and restaurants and spilled on to the high street, which now had flags and bunting strung across from one end to the other, punctuated with banners: WELCOME TO ARCHIE'S TOWN! Already the Traders' Association estimated that £50,000 had been pumped into the local economy.

After years of presiding over dust and empty rooms, Eleanor had a new gleam in her eye as she rushed about with her clipboard.

She and Bunny hit it off immediately and made last-minute exciting changes to the show. Now, when the visitors came down the steps into the main hall, they would be met with Archie's portrait and huge blown-up photographs and text introducing his work and life and restoring him to his rightful place in twentieth-century decorative art. The ark had pride of place in the children's area and the lustre recipes were reproduced on huge screens. At last, his was no longer just the name of the grotty sixties wing of the Loanside primary school.

In the excitement, it seemed to Sarah that Bunny had changed, although she was working so hard she could have been mistaken. She seemed less noisy yet more alive somehow. She said she had a lot to tell Sarah; that Hannah had left home and that she herself had moved and was intending to concentrate on building up the school and the catering business, and possibly doing some writing. She did not mention Edward, but there was now a singleness about her which seemed somehow to suit her. Sarah did not like to ask her more than she wanted to tell.

The night before the launch, Hannah rang as they were just about to start dinner. Bunny spoke to her for a long time in the hall and, when she came back in, there were tears in her eyes. Hannah and Studd had invited her for Sunday lunch. Sarah poured her a large glass of red wine. 'Do you think it is ever too late to start again?' It was the first time in years she had ever asked her advice. And Sarah said that no, it was never too late to make a new beginning. And hoped she was right.

It is strange how public perceptions shift. For weeks now in Loanside, everyone seemed to think that it was a foregone conclusion that there would be a permanent Robertson Centre, with a small school teaching ceramics and lustreware on the patch of wasteland behind the museum. No one could believe that such a simple idea had not been done before. Sarah had been to meetings where her ideas, so off-the-wall to many when she had started, were slowly being taken over by other people with titles and decision-making powers. There was now talk of EC finance from the Economic Regeneration Fund to promote arts tourism. Sarah had let them take over, for her sense of self was now elsewhere.

She had fought so many dragons in the past few weeks, and somehow survived. She had now finally woken up and could see possibilities for the rest of her life. In May, she would be starting work for Jeremy as a trainee curator, under the Women Returning to Work Scheme the Government's local enterprise company ran for women who had been at home bringing up children. Twopence halfpenny salary and a million pounds' worth of high-octane self-esteem. She couldn't wait.

But she had not yet replied to the solicitor who had informed her that the Separation Agreement would be through any day, nor had she rung her mother, whose crocodile tears over her divorce had taken up much of their last, one-sided conversation. What a life poor Sarah and the children would have on bread and scrape!

There had been arrows which did breach the high walls she had been building all round her life. There had been several silent phone calls. She had known instantly that it was Zander. She had said his name and then had felt the sick taste of fear in her mouth, as well as regret for losing a friend. She had spoken his name, but he had said nothing. She had changed her lock and put chains on all the doors, she now used the answering machine to monitor her calls. She told Eleanor about Zander's disapproval of the exhibition. Eleanor had shrugged and said mood swings were a Robertson speciality and that three generations of Robertson family dysfunction were not her problem. And Sarah had wished privately that were true.

There had been silence from Christopher. It was as if he had ceased to exist. The children seemed to have become wholly hers. Only the pictures of yachts and black seas, now neatly stacked against the wall awaiting instruction for shipment, reminded her of the man whom she had loved and had once thought she had known.

By 11 a.m. on the day of the launch, Sarah had given three interviews for local radio, two for the Scottish evening news on both TV channels and one for the local cable station. The museum was now a hubbub of bodies, not the paying public, but the sponsors and the council representatives and still more journalists. While Sarah manned the press desk, Eleanor was instructing her ladies for the shop. Ceramicists throughout East Lothian – thankfully there were still plenty – had spent the last month turning out Robertson-style pieces. Next to this, at Sarah's insistence, there was an information table about Loanside L.E.T.S., for half the exhibits had come through the Scheme. Down the middle of the room were the long, white-clothed tables set up for the evening buffet.

By midday Bunny had left to pick Lottie up at the airport, but *The Bunny Cooks Company* were already out in force; three well-bred girls with gleaming pearly teeth and turned-up collars had commandeered the tiny museum kitchen and were now calmly mastering the eccentric oven.

All of East Lothian life was expected: well-kent local councillors, Enterprise Board dignitaries, the gentry and tourist board honchos, as well as E & A's leading Scottish and even some London clients, Arts Council big shots, and the great and the good from the museum and gallery worlds bussed in by an increasingly excited Jeremy Lofthouse, who rang to see how his cutting-edge show was making out. 'His'. What a cheek. Eleanor fumed.

By two o'clock, Sarah had spoken to all the media and Eleanor told her to go home and be back by 7 p.m. Sarah found her coat and walked out to the entrance of the exhibition. *Edinburgh & Aberdeen Bank are proud to sponsor this unique exhibition* was up there in two-inch letters beside a magnificent *vaso di pompa*, an ornate vase three feet high, lustred in pink and gold with that hallmark flashy glamour which had always so intrigued her. Sarah stood for a moment, looking longingly at it and, as Eleanor was nowhere to be seen, she caressed the cold, beautiful surface. What wouldn't she give to own this?

Above her, the Archie in full evening dress looked down mockingly.

'Don't touch the exhibits, please!' Bunny's voice boomed just behind her and Sarah jumped. She was coming in the main door, flanked by two assistants. 'You've met Lottie *Todd* before, haven't you, my soon-to-be partner once she has returned from saving souls. And this is Rupert, Lottie's brand new husband, whom you *may* know!'

Bunny burst out laughing at Sarah's shocked expression on

seeing her stepson, last seen in Kew with Helen and his twin sister all those months ago. He seemed to have grown even taller and was standing shyly, holding hands with Lottie, whom she had also last seen in Chiswick High Road, though wearing considerably more make-up.

'You're married! Does, does your . . . does Christopher know?'

'Of course not. They only got married yesterday. Fourth time lucky for Lottie. Very sly of them not to tell anyone. Apparently they are relying on you to back them up when he does. And Helen!'

'Can't wait,' Sarah said.

Lottie and Rupert asked where the kitchen was and, still holding hands, went into the main hall. 'Bunny! Christopher will go completely ape, you know that. As for Helen! Rupert has only just started at King's. He must be ten, even twelve years younger. Anyway, what are they going to live on?'

'Sarah, I think perhaps your Surrey upbringing is showing a little here. Marrying a younger man is "in". Anyway, there is absolutely nothing wrong in marrying a younger man who is nice to you and, to put it bluntly, doesn't spend all your money like Edward or run off with other women like you-know-who. I think Lottie might just have landed on her feet. Rupert is transferring to Imperial College to be nearer Lottie, who is to be my new partner. Once she and Rupert come back in a couple of months from helping the poverty-stricken in the East End.

'What! Rupert in the East End? I've never met anyone with more fussy or expensive tastes. I spent years trying to stretch the housekeeping cooking for him.'

'Well, he and Lottie have been Born Again! Which presumably means you can get by on loaves and fishes. Anyway, Lottie assures me that when Rupert follows Christopher into the City after his degree, he will bring Christ to commerce, and make enough to look after her and the baby in style.'

'Baby!'

'They did the test this morning, just to finish me off. Still, if our expansion plans for the business work out, we're going to have a crêche built in the school car park. I can't really see her putting on nappies. Nor your stepson come to that. But miracles can happen Granny!'

'Ex-stepson. And ex-granny come to that.'

'There you are, you see. Every cloud has lustred lining!'

'Very droll, Beverly Anne!'

'Oh, won't it be fun having a baby to cuddle? Perhaps Hannah and Studd will do the decent thing and make a granny of *me*. I might make quite a good one. It is so much harder doing the motherly bit to your own child.'

'Well, if you're talking about miracles, I think with the mothers we've had, it *is* one that we have turned out even vaguely normal.'

Sheer relief came into Bunny's eyes and very slowly she bent down and kissed her cousin on the cheek.

It was nearly after three when Sarah walked back along the high street. Several people greeted her and stopped for a chat. Most would be coming tomorrow for the first day of the exhibition. 'Whoever thought we could get so excited about some old pots?' said Morag's mother, who had rushed across the road to greet her. 'I'm going to Marbella when I've sold mine!'

The day was still surprisingly warm and sunny, with those incomparable vivid Scottish colours, where sea vied with sky for blueness, and the golf links matched the deep green of the distant Fife hills. Sarah knew that she had come to really love Scotland. She did not belong, but she felt at home. Good enough for a new life.

She could hear the phone ringing as she went up the path. She raced into the house and snatched the phone off the hook. 'Why don't you just grow up?'

'Sarah? Is that you? It's Donald Gosford.'

'Oh, I'm sorry, Donald. I've been having a nuisance caller.'

'You must sort that out. Don't let it carry on. But look, I know you'll be busy, but the thing is, I need to tell you something. Before tonight.'

'Go on.'

'You see, I've been thinking. I've remembered something.

About that night at the party. The man who came to sell me the pots was, I think, called Robertson and was a relation, but he wasn't an accountant, and his name wasn't David either. I remember he said he worked for an Edinburgh agency, something to do with graphics or advertising. His name was Ally or Andy?'

'I see.'

'So I think that man, well, he must have been someone else.'

'Yes I see. Thank you, Donald.'

'Are you sure you're all right, Sarah? I want you to enjoy tonight and be the belle of the ball, without any bad memories. You deserve it. The man who hurt you couldn't have been the one you thought.'

'Thank you, Donald.'

'It's not too late, Sarah. You know, to work in the field.'

'No. I'll see you later.'

He rang off. Sarah poured herself a small brandy and sat on the stairs, watching shafts of sunlight pick up the dust floating in the panelled hall. The man was in advertising. Ally. Alex. Alexander.

Zander.

Sounds came back to her. Rod Stewart singing, '*Da ya think I'm sexy.*' She was back in St Andrews in the dark of the party. She had danced with him for half an hour or so. She hadn't seen his face clearly, but he had moved well, unusual for those days, and had been great fun to dance with. Their bodies had moved well together to the music. Then her contact lenses had somehow become all greased up in the heat and she had gone out to find the bathroom, bumping into Bunny, who had laughed at her groping about.

'Just tell me your secret, will you, how you can be as blind as a bat and still find a man with a nice tight bum.'

'I bet you don't say bum, Bunny, in that posh cookery school of yours.'

'No, we say be-haned and rarly fun!'

They must both have had a bit too much to drink, for they had doubled up with laughter. Then she had found the bathroom and was standing at the sink, when the door had been flung back and he had been there in the semi-darkness, shouting at her for laughing at him. She had told him he was being ridiculous, which made him even angrier. He'd found, he thought, the woman he'd been looking for, for years. He'd wanted her all evening. He didn't (slap) like (slap) being humiliated. Then he started tearing her clothes off, ignoring her protests, dodging her teeth and fists. Then he had pushed vigorously into her body. She had been too amazed to cry out. Then all she remembered were his shoulders heaving up and down, and thinking that she did not even know his name.

How well she had blanked it out. It was the only way she had been able to cope. She could just imagine pitying articles about women like her in Helen's magazine. *Just Who Are The Date Rape Wimps?* with an information box titled *Fight Back*, telling you how to get legal aid.

Yet what tape must have been running in his head that night, for him to think she was humiliating him by having a joke with her cousin? Who had put it there? And why had it said 'David' on the back of the photograph? It was as if the person who had taken the photograph could not have cared enough to distinguish which brother was which. If only Bunny had saved her.

Exhausted, she fell asleep where she was on the stairs, and awoke half an hour later to the doorbell ringing. Bunny obviously was back to change. She opened the door. Zander stood there. She tried to slam it shut, but his foot was already on the door frame. 'Look, Sarah, don't be like this. I just want to talk to you. I don't want a scene.'

'Zander, please go away.'

'Look, I wanted to say I'm sorry about the other day. Please, Sarah, I just want to talk to you.'

'Go away. It's OK about the other night, but I have so much to do before tonight and I don't want you here.'

'For God's sake, the whole of Scotland knows the launch is tonight. Sarah, calm down. I just want to talk to you.'

He stood in the hall and she was rooted to the spot, white and trembling. Normal social behaviour seemed to desert her; she was so frightened.

'What is the matter? You look as if you've seen a ghost.'

'I am. I have. You see, Zander, I know who you are.'

'I should think so. Of course you know who I am. I've never

met anyone so obsessed with my family before. In fact, when I read that article I realised you know more about Archie than I do.'

'No, nothing to do with him. It's *you*. I have finally realised who *you* are.'

She was now shaking from head to foot and tears were flooding down her face so fast she could hardly see him. He was once again the indistinct threatening figure of her nightmares.

He was concerned and came up to put his arm round her, but she froze and jumped away from him.

'St Andrews.' She could only gasp rather than speak. 'Don't you remember I met you at the party?'

'Sarah, come on, calm down. It's years since I've been to St Andrews. Tight-arsed, boring place.'

'I met you at a party.' Her teeth were now gritted. '1979. You had come to flog some pots to the fine art department because of the Robertson exhibition there. You went to a party that night. And you met me, and we danced and then, and then.'

She had to stop. He was looking at her, concerned, as if not really listening, and slowly the meaning of what she had said arrived into his eyes. They looked at each other. Horror and fear reflected in both.

Her breath was now coming out as fast as a marathon runner's. 'You raped me. In the bathroom.'

'You've been drinking brandy. There's the glass. I can smell it.'

It was the sudden small smile around his lips that did it. She smashed the glass against the wall, lunged at him, the glass going for his face. 'You raped me there in the bath. You bloody bastard! You evil bastard.' Twenty years' festering hatred broke through the nice girl act she had so carefully maintained. Before her, too, was that other betraying bastard, Christopher. Zander grabbed her arms and locked them in an embrace of savagery and passion. He dashed the glass from her hand and, holding her face in both hands, crashed her against the hall wall.

'No, you haven't changed at all. You're still a stuck-up, stupid, beautiful bitch. No one laughs at me! No one! What the fuck do you know about anything? I didn't rape you. You bloody well were asking for it!'

He was kissing her spitting mouth and together they were

now on the carpet rolling, fighting, the blood from his cut face running over her hair. She was kicking, twisting and screaming as he pulled her long hair back so that her mouth met his lips. Dimly she could hear footsteps. Crack! Zander was hit over the head and before he knew what was happening he found himself being dragged out of the house and booted down the path. Bunny, an avenging valkyrie with a rolling pin in her hand, was shouting as she kicked him, 'Lay one finger on my cousin again, you bastard shitbag and I'll have your balls for croûtons!'

Absurdly, Sarah found herself hoping that there would be no neighbours in the street to hear. Before she passed out.

When she came round she was lying on her bed and Bunny was bathing her forehead with lavender water.

'Bunny.'

'No, don't try to talk. Look, here you are. Water, and some Rescue Remedy. Don't try to talk. And don't worry about anything. Eleanor knows you will be late. I didn't say why, though.'

Bunny's hands were gentle and soon, though she still trembled, Sarah could sit up and take a cup of tea.

'I wish you'd told me, Sarah. Instead of just leaving like that.'

'What do you mean, Bunny?'

'St Andrews. That night you were, you know, attacked. If only you'd said. I could have helped. I'd have backed you up. Why didn't you trust me?'

'I couldn't. I was so ashamed. I thought if I did, you would tell Marjorie who would then tell Doreen and it would be such grist, you know.'

'Oh, Sarah. Their endless stupid one-upmanship. As if I would have *ever* told them.'

'But it would have come out. As it is, no one ever knew. Not Mother or anyone.'

'Yes, but Sarah you left all you really loved behind and just gave up. I never liked cookery, I only ever did it to make money, but you really were happy with your work. Wouldn't it have been better to have faced it?'

'I'm such a coward, Bunny. Not like you. Oh, what if you hadn't come back? Just now!'

'Now don't cry, because I did. At least you weren't fighting in a swimming pool. Then you would have had to save *me*! Lucky I had a rolling pin in my handbag. Edward always said I as a ballbreaker. There, you're smiling. You're looking better already.'

'You're talking about Edward in the past tense.'

'Yes. I've left him. Finally. It was about money in my case, rather than sex. Edward now has a sore throat and is not enjoying his reality check. He is now apparently sending nasty letters via my solicitors but, as I've chosen a firm of Rottweilers, he'll have a job on his hands. Actually, I think you could do with a Rottweiler, Sarah. Drink up.'

'Do you think he will come back?'

'Edward? No. I'm feeling ten years younger. I wouldn't have that parasite if he came back flambéd in cognac. Oh, you mean this man? No. Wouldn't think so. Not after the mess you made of his face. But I'll see Eleanor about posting security on the door tonight. But Sarah, listen, tomorrow you must go to the police. I don't know what the law is up here, but I'll back you up. We'll get the best lawyers. I've got plenty of dosh now I've flogged that bloody house.'

'Oh, Bunny.'

'Now don't cry. I recognised him immediately. Oh, Sarah what is it with us and men?'

Later, Bunny helped Sarah bathe and sat her in a chair while she put on her make-up and dressed her in her new pale green dress with its short bolero jacket.

'This is a wonderful colour for you, Sarah. You know you don't look a day over thirty. If I didn't love you, I'd hate you. Now, don't start crying again. I'm not going to talk any more. Tonight you're going to be the hostess with the mostest and tomorrow I'm not going. I'm staying till we sort everything out. Lottie can cope with loverboy. Do them both good. Now, look at yourself. Who's a stunner?'

Bunny went upstairs to get ready while Sarah went to make some tea. She could hear the gurgling of the old taps on the top floor filling the bath and Bunny singing. Then the doorbell rang. Sarah jumped. A key rattled in the lock and then a hand came through the letterbox. As she opened her mouth to scream, Christopher's voice called through the slit. 'Sarah, are you there? Look, I'm sorry, but could you possibly lend me £10 for the cab? I have not got enough sterling.'

The flap fell back. And then the doorbell rang. She stood there, not knowing what to do. It was like being in the middle of some sick black Feydeau farce, put on by the gods, who were now in the front stalls killing themselves.

Finally she opened the door and stood, looking at her husband. He asked if she would mind if he came in and if she possibly had any money. He would pay her back as soon as he could.

Fumbling and silent, she somehow found money in her handbag, then watched him go out to pay the cab driver; he was still tall and immaculately dressed, his Burberry folded neatly over one arm, his briefcase on the other, but she noticed that he stooped. And there was more grey hair at his temples. When he entered the hall she could see he was shocked by the emptiness of the house, which now echoed, denuded of all figureheads and pictures. She also saw that his eyes were strangely blank.

'Sarah, forgive me, I didn't ring beforehand. I see you are going out. Forgive me, but I wonder if we could have a word?'

'The children aren't here, Christopher, and I have go out soon. It's the launch party for the Robertson Exhibition, you know. Bunny's here. She upstairs getting ready.'

'Yes, I'm sorry. I won't keep you. You look pale, Sarah, are you all right? Could I get you some tea?'

'No, don't worry, I'll do it.' Yet she found she hardly had the energy to stick the kettle on, let alone to charm or please.

She had no idea what she wanted to say; there was no script. Helen's magazine would advise, she knew, vengeful scenes of retribution. Cut the legs off all his trousers, pour his fine wines down the sink. But after this afternoon she had little fury left. She felt pity for him, enough to make any self-respecting women's magazine despair. But then, how much of their relationship had been pretence? He had never really known the real her, nor she him, obviously.

It was the first time he had sat in the back sitting room, which overlooked the garden. As they drank their tea the sun began to fall behind the hills in the distance and the sea crept up over the beach. Haltingly, he told her that the secondment to the World Bank was over. The job of director he believed he had been promised, had gone to someone else – to Maria Antonietta, who had known apparently since Christmas. She now found him inconvenient and an embarrassment. It was all over.

His chin was soft and crumpled, as he sat endlessly flattening out the fabric on his pinstriped trousers. Sarah found it hard that he could barely look at her. What had that woman done to him?

'What will you do now?'

'I am not sure. I very much doubt that there will still be a job for me at the E & A, unless they think it cheaper to keep me on. But they are a clannish lot and I'm certain that they will have been told of my application for the director's job. New blood will already have been brought in to my old department. Anyway, I am forty-eight. It doesn't get easier.'

Sarah remembered her dream of the woman in red dancing around and, as if answering her unspoken thoughts, Christopher said, 'She was clever, exciting, beautiful too, but it was altogether foolish.'

'Deceiving me, you mean?'

He couldn't look at her.

'Do you have any idea how much it hurt both me and the children? I am more angry for the children than for myself. I'm only too aware that I must have been inadequate, too clingy and dependent by half for you. You never asked why that was and I never told you. But the fact was that I did my best to make you happy. And then, having had years hearing of your deep concern for those twins of yours and the perfect Helen, *my* children were just supposed to be ignored and swept away under the carpet. Do you have any idea how *selfish* you are? And would you have really come crawling back if you had landed the director's job and she had *not* chucked you? Am I just to be made a convenience of? Get real, Christopher. You're going to have to do a lot better than that.'

He seemed completely taken aback by her new tone. He gaped at her taking in for the first time her new clothes and hair and sense of purpose. Would he have the courage to stop acting just for once?

'Sarah, you're quite right to be angry. I am not expecting anything at all from you. I don't deserve it. The fact is, I just need somewhere to stay, because I have almost no money. Practically none. I wondered if I could perhaps stay here, in the guest room, for a couple of days while I sort something out on the work front? I'll have to talk to the Gordons, of course, eat humble pie, and then, assuming I'm out of the bank, I'll go back down to London to the headhunters and see if they can fix me up.'

'I don't know. Bunny will probably want to kick your head in for me.'

'I don't blame her. She must be off men. I gather they've split up. I always thought she had known about Edward's second family. Obviously not.'

'His *second* family? That really takes the biscuit! I don't think she does even now! Poor Bunny. You bloody men. You all make me sick.'

'Look. Sarah. About you and me. I don't expect forgiveness. I don't know if there is a future for us. But I just wanted to say now how sorry I am. I've been looking into a black abyss for the last week. All if know is that all my life I have just been mouthing other people's directions in order to be the right sort of person, and do the right thing. And now I'm off the map. I am not good husband material. I'm so very sorry.'

His face crumpled and, not liking her to see his tears, he turned away, clearing his throat and took out a handkerchief. It seemed ridiculous that it was so well ironed and carefully folded. He looked older now, more uncertain, yet kinder too. The arrogance and the waspish tongue seemed to have disappeared.

'May I just ask? Were there others, before her?'

'No. Only you. More fool me not to value what I had at the time?'

'Oh, stop snivelling, Christopher, and grow up.'

There was silence. Perhaps when we stop painting life in black and white, it is in the shades of grey that we find our healing. Could she forgive him now? Did she want to? Wouldn't the betrayal simply regurgitate itself back into their lives in every unguarded moment like a badly cooked meal? You surely couldn't get a recipe much more risky and dangerous than marriage.

Just then, Bunny came downstairs. Her dress was cerise, ankle length and swirling outwards with a border of gold leather. She wore a hat tilted over one eye with matching curled feathers which swooped over to the other side of her head. When she saw Christopher, she stopped dead and looked like a rocket about to bang.

'Well! Good evening, Christopher. I must say you have immaculate timing. Have you come to completely finish Sarah off? We've had a lot to cope with already today. It's Sarah's launch for her exhibition tonight, so if you do anything to spoil it or upset her, I am personally going to turn you into *foie gras*. Do you understand?

'Yes. May I come? Would you both mind?'

Sarah nodded. She half expected him to offer his arm to them like an Edwardian gentleman off to the music hall with his womenfolk, but then she realised that he had stopped acting. He looked directly at her and thanked them both. Bunny gave him five minutes to change into a dinner jacket while they waited for him in the hall.

'Sarah, are you going to take him back?'

'I don't know. I don't even know whether to stay in this house or not.'

'Well, whatever you decide Sarah, take your time. Remember, we don't either of us ever have to *do* anything we don't want to. Christopher! Hurry *up*! We're timing you.'

He was down with five seconds to spare. Bunny then said that Sarah should walk between them because she needed looking after. And so, dressed up to the nines, they walked out of Carnforth House.

Leith

When Zander came into the building, he could hear the sound of the jars of coins crashing onto the floor all the way down on the ground floor. Someone was in his studio. Kids. All he bloody needed! His face, cut across by Sarah's brandy glass, had stopped bleeding but he was still savage with the shock and furious. What were those kids after this time? Money? What a joke. He ran up the four flights two stairs at a time and burst into the studio.

'What the *fuck* are you doing!' Even in the dark he could see his precious mobiles were rolling over on the floor, crushed and dismembered, and the air was thick from the powder from the papier-mâché. And then he saw, too late, that these were not kids.

They were out for kicks, they also outnumbered him. Zander tried to fight them off and get them out of the room, but he was forty-four years old and breathless. He also realised that they were armed with knives. They kicked him in the liver and in the ribs. He fell. Then they kicked in his back and his spleen; the blows and slashes to his crotch were agony; his mouth was filled with blood. Then there came the numb sensation, and for the first time in his life the knowledge that he was being physically overpowered, and that there was nothing he could do to save himself. There came a vivid flash of the young Sarah gazing up at him, wide-eyed and fearful, her face so close to his that he could still feel her warm breath. Oh, God! And then he saw the boot coming straight for his head. I can't believe this is happening, he thought.

'I can't believe this is happening!' Sarah said to Eleanor. She felt as bubbly as the champagne which was now causing the room to sing. No one wanted to leave and now that the speeches were over, dignitaries had stopped being dignitaries and were starting to party. Congratulations poured down over her. What an enormous change this would make to Loanside. How beautiful and exciting Robertson's work was. What a triumph! What a show! Great food!

Sarah stood observing the room, which now swirled before her as conversations locked and interlocked and contacts were made and refreshed. For the first time she was no longer afraid of Zander making an appearance like the Bad Fairy. There were far too many goodies in the room. Morag at the L.E.T.S. table seemed to have signed up half the country, while Lord Gordon as the sponsor stood resplendent in his kilt. He had just asked her if she would like a job working with the E & A corporate art collection, so she now had two professional openings. He was, however, only coolly civil to Christopher. The E & A staff and clients also did not engage him in conversation. There was clearly a price to pay.

Donald Gosford had greeted her earlier in the evening with huge pride and affection, which had ruffled Christopher. He was now deep in conversation with Eleanor. They both suddenly turned and smiled at her. 'Are you OK?' he mouthed. She smiled back and nodded. What might have been.

Christopher was at the other end of the room, talking to Lottie and Rupert. She saw the shock register on his face, clearly on being told that they were now married and that he was soon to be a grandfather. Then he had smiled, that wonderful generous smile which occasionally lit up his face, such as when he had beaten off the other bidders for a figurehead. Like the Cheshire Cat's, his smile had been all she had remembered of him in the last few weeks. How lovingly he had smiled at her when he had toasted her at that dinner party all those months ago. 'To my wife,' he had said. It still hurt.

Bunny was standing over by the buffet. A hit! Her presence this evening had completed a circle in Sarah's own life, but her media glamour had given the occasion an extra *frisson*. She was looking magnificent and exuded such confidence that, though the tabloids may have written her off, she had clearly found herself a new script. She was surrounded by admirers. Most enthusiastic of all was Jeremy Lofthouse, who was gazing at her enraptured. But then, Bunny had always appealed to flamboyant men.

Above the fray, Archie's portrait looked down over the room and at his work which, mounted on stands, now glowed red and green and pink in the light. She'd done it! But perhaps she now had other fish to fry.

Then Christopher came up carrying two glasses. 'This is all marvellous, Sarah. You are so clever. Congratulations.'

'Thank you.'

'I'm proud of you. I rather think you have been wasting your time with me.'

'There's lots we could tell each other about who we really are. If we wanted to.'

'Oh, Sarah. I wish to God we could.'

Sarah closed her eyes, feeling the bubbles rise to the roof of her mouth. She could feel him close to her, could smell that familiar Jermyn Street aftershave. Forgiveness also is expensive, but you have to buy it for yourself first, before you can afford it for other people.

'Coo-ee! Coo-ee!'

Sarah opened her eyes, and there on the other side of the room two familiar figures dressed in matching check coats and Tam O'Shanters stood on the steps, each clutching bunches of carnations wrapped in kitchen foil. Marjorie and Doreen had spotted Bunny and were now announcing to the whole room that they had collected twenty-two coupons from the *Daily Mail* and that they had got half-price train tickets all the way from Carshalton plus two nights at the Loanside Housetrust Hotel. 'We got the last room! Sarah and Bunny said not to come, but we felt we just *had* to support our poor little girls!'

Jeremy Lofthouse was looking at them in morbid fascination, while Bunny's face flared. As they danced down the steps into the room, Sarah took action. 'Perhaps, darling, this *may* be an opportunity to start working your passage back!' she said, and kissed Christopher gently on the cheek. She just caught the beginning of his smile before she pushed him firmly in the small of his back into the path of the advancing sisters.

Across the room, Bunny looked at her and Sarah nodded back. Silently, Bunny seized a bottle of champagne and Sarah took two glasses. And while Marjorie and Doreen were being introduced to Lord Gordon and were saying, 'how *surprised* they were to see Christopher! Of *all* people!' the cousins exited stage right, out through the storeroom and the back door. Once out in the street, they began to laugh. Then they kicked off their shoes, hitched up their skirts and raced towards the beach. By the time their toes hit the sand, the sun had become an orange memory behind the hills and the thick black line of the Firth of Forth lay before them.